LOVE
AND
DEATH
IN
SHANGHAI

Love and Death in Shanghai

This volume first published in England in 2018
© Elizabeth J. Hall
First edition published 2018

Paperback ISBN: 978-1-9997842-7-0
eBook ISBN: 978-1-9997842-8-7

Cover design by Lucy Llewellyn at Head & Heart Book Design

Typesetting by Robert Harries at Head & Heart Book Design

LOVE
AND
DEATH
IN
SHANGHAI

ELIZABETH J. HALL

In memory of my wonderful brother, John Hall, who, during his thirty-three years in the police force, rose from being a cadet to Chief Superintendent of Greater Manchester.

The finest cop of all.

And to my family and friends, near and far.

PROLOGUE

SHANGHAI, NOVEMBER 1947

The woman clung to the rope ladder which flowed down the black hull of the SS Cleveland, headed for San Francisco. Her feet slithered on the oiled rungs. A red high-heeled shoe splashed into the sullen ripples of the Huangpu River, the other dangled from the toes of her left foot. The ladder tilted. She screamed. A sailor swung alongside to help her climb. The woman's left arm hooked round his neck. Her hand pressed a red pillbox hat to her head, a matching handbag looped round the wrist. She clutched the lapels of a sable coat with her right hand. The woman's daughter, rescued, watched from the ship's deck and shivered.

The ship had left the dock in Shanghai an hour earlier when the women were at a party with American soldiers in a hotel on the Bund. They had heard the siren's moan and saw the wheeze of grey smoke from the funnels, as the ship moved along the putrid curve of the river, past the grand buildings, and away from a Shanghai mortified by decadence, gang warfare and Japanese occupation.

The hotel manager had telephoned the ship's captain to say that the fiancée of Colonel Fields, US Pacific War hero, was delayed by traffic but could be ferried out to meet the ship at the lighthouse where the Huangpu River met the Yangtze.

Sailors pulled the woman on board. She looked around, laughed, stroked her coat, and pouted a kiss to a sailor. The ship's captain and bursar arrived to greet them. The engines throbbed.

Captain Summers suggested that passports be checked over a whisky in his cabin and escorted them downstairs, his hand on the woman's elbow as she swayed down the staircase, tilted on the single shoe. They sat in shiny leather chairs opposite the captain's desk. The woman took off her hat, placed it on her lap, and brushed back her hair through her fingers. The bursar, standing next to the captain, consulted the ship's manifest. "Confirm your name, please, Madam."

She sipped the whisky. "Tatiana Shuttleworth, but professional name is Lulu. It's nice and warm in here."

"And your date of birth is 1902?"

"No, that is wrong. I was born in 1907. I am only forty. My daughter, Elizabeth, is twenty."

"Place of birth?"

"Harbin, China. My family is Russian. Daughter born in Shanghai. Father English, but he dead. We British by marriage."

"Reason for travel?"

She looked at a cluster of diamonds and rubies on her left hand. "I am to marry my fiancé, important man, Colonel Fields. He waits for us in San Francisco."

"Last address?"

"101, Weihaiwei Road, Shanghai, but we interned, by the Japanese, because we British, in Yangchow camp for two years."

She opened her bag, pulled out a white handkerchief, trimmed with lace, and patted her eyes.

The bursar looked at the passport photograph, then her face. She reminded him of Marlene Dietrich in that old film about Shanghai Lily. A good looker – bright blue eyes, brown waved hair, prominent cheekbones, and a sly Russian accent. He wondered how her teeth were so good after all she had been through.

She twisted the white handkerchief, dabbed her cheeks, and looked down at the damp red shoe, and the other foot smeared in grease. She pulled her skirt over a hole which crept up the silk stocking over her right knee.

"Terrible, terrible. We lose everything. Only allowed one thing. I take red shoes, Japanese guard say that *two* things, I say he not speak good English. One pair mean two. You understand?"

She laughed, looked at her foot and wriggled the toes.

The daughter looked up and pulled the blanket round her shoulders.

"And I take the dolly auntie in England gave me a long time ago. She is now in my suitcase, but where is that?" She looked down and sobbed.

The captain offered more whisky. "You will get the doll back. Not the shoe, I'm afraid."

He laughed. "Do not be distressed, ladies, you are safe now. We have arranged your cabin. Your suitcases are there. You will, of course, travel first class. Please come for dinner with me when you are settled. My bursar will escort you to your deck."

The woman turned to her daughter, spoke in Russian and stretched out her left hand. The ring sparkled. The captain bent to kiss her fingers.

She paused on deck as the ship bumped into the churn of the Yangtze and the Huangpu. She leaned on the rail, looked across the water and inhaled the stench. The Huangpu had, for years, caught and submerged the consequences of murder, destitution, and chaos. It had swallowed the bodies of humans and animals, garbage, illicit drugs, guns and knives.

She looked back at Shanghai. Evening mist filtered the tiered skyline. She raised a fist and shouted into the breeze: "Ya nikogda ne vozvrashchat'sya – I am never coming back."

1

Sam Shuttleworth sailed into Shanghai from Southampton in September 1924. He swung his long legs out from the bottom bunk, stood, naked, and looked at the girl sprawled on her back, arms above her head.

"Come on, Nurse McArthur, we dock in an hour, and you have to be out. My mates will be back soon. Come on, it cost me a lot to get rid of them for the night"

He looked at her tight nipples, her belly button, and the fuzzy hair bristling round the bump of the fold between her legs. She turned onto her stomach.

"Come back to bed, Sam. There's plenty of time."

He saw the curve of her buttocks and felt an erection stirring.

"No time. I have to get dressed and shaved and you have to get back to your cabin."

He picked up five limp condoms from the floor and wrapped them in a handkerchief. The ship throbbed under his feet. He pulled on his socks and underpants and stepped over to the porthole to see pale light hang over the river.

The girl sat up, head bent under the layer of bunk above, blonde hair covering her shoulders. She yawned, stretched and pulled her knees up to her chest.

"Will you write to me, Sam? Will you visit?"

"'Course I will, if there's any post. But you'll be in Nanjing. It's a long way from Shanghai."

"You've got a lovely body, Sam. All that muscle. And so nice-looking. Do you love me, Sam?"

He looked in the round mirror hung on the cabin wall, and flicked back his dark hair. Girls had always said they liked his big grey eyes. He smiled at the image. He must get his teeth seen to.

"Listen, you're not so bad yourself. It's been fun these last few weeks, but you'll find some nice doctor in Nanjing. Or a missionary. They used to eat missionaries. My teacher in school told me." He laughed. "I have to go on deck, so be out of here in ten minutes. I'll see you up there."

He dressed in a blue shirt and blazer and grey trousers and picked up a heavy raincoat. He flushed the condoms down the toilet in the communal bathroom in the corridor and tucked the handkerchief into his coat pocket. He lathered the soap, shaved, put the razor with the handkerchief and went on deck.

When Sam was ten, he had heard about China from his teacher in Lord Street Primary School in Warren, Lancashire. Miss Hargreaves was a spry Scot with russet curls and oval glasses, engaged to a soldier with the Lancashire Fusiliers. On her desk, held in a curve of brass, Miss Hargreaves kept a globe of the world in pale colours, much of it pink. She called this The Empire. She told the class that she had cousins who were missionaries in Africa and China. Every school day began with prayers for their work in saving the souls of brown and yellow heathen babies. She showed blurred brown pictures of naked children outside mud huts, and said how wonderful it was to bring light to their darkness. The children, in their clogs and sparse clothes, looked at her, uncaring and unknowing.

Sam had turned the globe, traced the outline of countries and drawn his finger along the blue lines of rivers wriggling to the sea.

Miss Hargreaves gave Sam an atlas when he left school and told him not to forget his learning. She gave him the name of a teacher at the local night school. They both knew that he would, like the rest of his class, be in the cotton mills by the time he was fourteen and living with his parents and three other children in a bookless house with two bedrooms, a sitting room, a scullery, and an outside lavatory.

Sam won a book as a prize – *Harold, the Last of the Saxon Kings* – for being the best reader in the class. He covered it with brown paper and drew a picture on the front of Harold, in a horned helmet, a tunic, short skirt, and crossed leggings. He thought Harold a fine name for a great warrior.

When he was sixteen he went to night school for two years to study English and maths and worked in a mill during the day, gathering cotton reels. The supervisor showed him an advert for the Shanghai Police. Good pay, more in a month than his father earned in a year, and good prospects. He applied and was accepted when he was twenty.

Miss Hargreaves wrote to him to say how pleased she was that he could now make a good life, and that she was still Miss Hargreaves as her fiancé had been killed in the war. He was sad about that. She was a nice lady.

He leaned on the ship's rail and thought of the line of the river he had followed in Miss Hargreaves's classroom. It was now the wide, grey Yangtze as it entered the China Sea. The yellow, silted Huangpu, its tributary, came to joust where the two met beneath a lighthouse. The waters hissed, bucked, and tossed spray over the ship.

"How far to Shanghai?" he asked a sailor.

"Only about ten miles now. Stay here and you'll have a good view as we get into 'Shai."

Sam looked down at tugboats which sidled alongside to guide the Bengal into dock. "Is the water always as dirty as this?"

The sailor laughed. "HuangPU by name, HuangPU by reputation. This is a good day. Don't fall in here, mate. Instant typhoid."

The river was streaked with oil smears, the colour of dragonfly wings. Dead fish and wooden crates floated round the hull. The harbour fluttered with the flags of warships and passenger liners. Sam recognised those of Britain, America, Canada, France, Japan, and China. Fishing boats, sampans, and decorated junks pushed across the water. Men with long poles, in tattered calf-length trousers and straw coolie hats, called and sang. Cormorants, like black ghosts, perched on wooden columns, wings stretched out to dry.

"They still use them," said the sailor, "the fishermen make sure the birds are full up, or put a ring round their necks so they don't gobble everything, then make them dive to grab the fish."

Sam leaned on the deck rail. "I've never seen that, even in pictures. I'd rather use a line."

"There's lots here you've never seen before, believe me. You wait."

* * *

Nurse McArthur cried and held him as they left the ship. He detached himself.

"Good luck. I'm sure we'll meet again. Happen I'll come and visit." He was relieved to be off the boat. She was pretty, but had become a bit clingy. He didn't like that. He looked forward to action and good pay.

He thought of his mate, Billy Wigg, who'd got a girl into trouble when he was nineteen and had had to marry her. Billy and his wife had come to say goodbye when Sam left for Shanghai. The baby's face was caked in snot, a dummy in his mouth, as he held out his fat arms to Sam. No thanks.

Two police officers waited for the seven new recruits. An orange sun was veiled by hazy cloud and mist hung over the river. Sam shivered. They walked through a building, vast like a warehouse and smelling of sweat and sacking.

"No formality at customs here," said one of the officers, "anybody can get in and they do. No papers needed. Just sign in and put the date, 14 September 1924. There's a van waiting. Just get your suitcase, the rest will be sent on later."

They pushed through beggars in rags, flower sellers, rickshaw drivers, and women offering good luck trinkets. The van struggled through tangled streets, its horn sounding at every junction, to the red brick training centre at Gordon Road. They were met by Police Commissioner McKuen, and given a mug of tea and a digestive biscuit.

The commissioner, ribbons and medals across his chest, stood to address them in front of a wall map of Shanghai patched in different colours.

"This will be your base for six weeks, then you will be posted to one of the ten stations across the International Settlement. You will then be in charge of a small group of mainly Chinese officers. With hard work, you can rise in the ranks quite quickly. Better pay and all that. The Chinese and Sikhs have their own barracks at Central Station. Here is the sector we cover – the International Settlement."

He drew a circle with his finger around a purple part of the map.

"Here we are. Next to the International Settlement is the French sector, then the Chinese sector, Chaipei or Chinatown. Lawlessness is common; violent crime is common, the gangs are well established and the national political situation is unstable. You will learn more about this as you go along. You will now be introduced to your mentors and shown your rooms. You will report for duty and collect your uniforms tomorrow morning at 8.30am. Good luck."

Sam's mentor, Sergeant Eddie Nicholson from Yorkshire, took him to a narrow room on the second floor of an annexe. There was a bed along one wall, and a sink in the corner, with soap and towel.

"You can get a shower of sorts down the corridor – cold water out of a pipe. You'll share a coolie with the six others; he'll shine your shoes, belts, and buttons and get you food if you need it. Otherwise, there's decent food and drink in the mess room. Good bar. Once you're sorted out, I'll take you out for a bit of fun, even though you are from Lancs. I'll be your mentor for the six weeks you're in training, so just ask me anything. I arrived four years ago and, boy, have I learned fast. Meet you later. Eight at the entrance."

2

Sam and Eddie left Gordon Road and walked into the brisk evening. They wore tweed jackets, flannel trousers, and dimpled, grey felt trilbies. Eddie was the shorter man, thin and knobbly, with a long face and turned up nose. He had to walk fast to keep up with Sam's pace. Cigarettes, bought by Sam on the boat, balanced and bobbed on their lower lips.

"Nice to have a Craven A," said Eddie, "there are thousands of cigarette brands here from Woodbines to The Rat. God, some of them are nasty."

"Where are you from?"

"Barnsley, and proud of it; joined at twenty-five to get away from coal mining and earn some money. Got promoted to sergeant last year. I have a girl back home, and we'll get married on my long leave in two years. She'll like it here. We can rent a place, have a servant. More money. How about you?"

"From Warren, a little town near Manchester. I was twenty-two on 10 September. We had a bit of a party on the boat just before we docked. I wanted a bit of adventure and travel and to get away from weaving sheds."

"Well, they might tell you the job's mainly routine, but you'll get adventures. It can be bloody dangerous. You have to learn to watch yourself."

A rickshaw swerved across the road and drew up.

Eddie patted a wheel. "Posh one, this. Nicely painted and with cushions. He'll want to charge more because we're foreigners. I'll halve the price he asks and offer two coppers. You'll learn."

The rickshaw driver refused and pulled away, then came back to accept. Eddie and Sam sat back on the cushions as they crossed Xinzha Road, into Bubbling Well Road and along to Zhejiang Road. A Sikh policeman in a red turban directed traffic.

Eddie pointed. "Do you know what the Chinese call them? Red Heads because of the turban. They can get very rough with those batons. The Chinese don't like it and we get complaints. Usually from interfering do-gooders."

Trams, cars, bikes, rickshaws, and motorcycles rushed and dodged, seemingly with no lanes, although Eddie assured Sam that traffic in Shanghai, even in the French Concession, moved on the left-hand side of the road. There were, unexpectedly, Sam thought, traffic lights. He wondered what his family would have thought of him being driven in a rickshaw through a big city. He rolled back his shoulders.

"Amazing, isn't it?" said Eddie, "First place in China to have lights. But this isn't really China. It's Shanghai. Lots of wealthy Europeans and Americans – you only have to look at the cars."

They passed small courtyards and alleyways. Chinese wearing tunics, trousers, and round hats sold spices, rice, animals, fruit, and vegetables; flies clung to raw joints of meat; washing hung from windows.

"You have to learn about those places, lad; ordinary Chinese live there, but lots of villains, too. You'll visit a couple of alleys as part of the training."

"I can't wait to get started. It's a bit different from where I come from. Exciting."

Eddie laughed.

They came to the junction where roads met in a swirl of dust, noise, hooting, and skidding. The smart racecourse terraces and the clubhouse were just in front of them.

"That's for the toffs," said Eddie, "Full of gents in top hats and ladies in silk frocks and fancy hairdos. Mainly white, of course, although there are one or two wealthy Chinese; and listen, the Chinks will bet on anything – number of beans in a pot, ants crawling up a post. And they don't like to lose face as they call it – and that can mean trouble."

Sam looked along Nanking Road towards the temples and long department stores, windows glinting. He had never seen such big shops. Eddie paid the driver.

"Fancy stuff. You can buy anything here from diamonds to a dishcloth. It's a bit different from where we come from. Still, you takes your choice. We're earning a lot more money than we would back home. The police is tough, but you get a nice life out of it. You'll get a bigger room and your own coolie when you're done with the training. Loads of bars and girls, sport for free, hunting and shooting. Not like being in a factory or down a coal mine, eh?"

He asked for another Craven A. "Good promotion chances. Work hard and learn the lingo. I'm no good at languages so I probably won't get much further than sergeant. Top ranks are usually reserved for the posh boys. Anyway, here we go. Plenty of time for shops, but where we're going is something else."

Sam thought about promotion. He looked forward to learning languages and to working hard. Miss Hargreaves always said he was clever, and he had won a prize. He wondered where that book was now. In some dusty cupboard in Warren. He hoped his ma hadn't thrown it away.

They walked through the entrance of a square building under the tower.

"Here we are, lad, The Great World. Don't get lost. Keep your money inside your jacket. You've never seen anything like this place. And watch the women on every floor. You might get dragged somewhere you don't want to be."

Sam looked around. He was in a great hall. The crowds jostled him, and Eddie grabbed his arm. A woman offered a bouquet of carnations; an old man offered to take him to the second floor to buy birds; another wanted him to see the acrobats and magicians. He was given a token to play the slot machines and offered a free turn at roulette. He shouted to Eddie. "What is this place?"

"OK. It's run by a Chinese chap called Huang Chujiu, who owns chemists' shops and all sorts of other things – tobacco factories for one. He made lots of cash from inventing a potion that was supposed to improve the brain; then he sold two other amusement arcades and built this."

Sam stared at the stalls, the Chinese signs, the shouting for custom and the people bowing and offering lucky charms. "What goes on here?"

"I tell you, they'll take wax out of your ears, cut your hair, shave you, pull your teeth, polish your shoes, and massage you. Don't get undressed. You never know what might happen to your cock – on sale in the market tomorrow. And watch your bum, too. We'll go and get some grub on the second floor. You'll have to get used to chopsticks. Not good for ice cream."

After eating, they went up to the roof garden and looked out over the city. Eddie swung his arm. "That's the tallest building. Sassoon House. Part of it's the Cathay Hotel." He pointed to his left. "See that bloody great building? That's the Hong Kong and Shanghai Bank, guarded by two enormous bronze lions, which are supposed to roar when a virgin walks past. They never have. Over there is the British Consulate. See the Sikh guards? Then the Shanghai Club – not for the likes of us."

He pointed out across the Soochow Creek. "That area's called Hongchew. That building over there shaped like a liner is the Astor Hotel and that's the Russian Consulate with iron bars all round it, and guards. Very nasty, too. See those square blue patches. Those are swimming pools in the French Concession and you can see some nice parks and gardens."

"I didn't expect it to be as fancy."

"Only part of it is. Jew boys building hotels, fancy houses, and parks. Hardoon, Sassoon everywhere. Look, that green over there's a cricket club."

"I didn't know the Chinese played cricket."

"Don't be daft. Not the Chinese. Only the high class English. Now, as a Yorkshireman, I'm a dab hand at turning my arm, but they wouldn't look at me."

"I've watched a bit of cricket. My dad likes it. Why's a spin ball called a Chinaman if they don't play cricket?"

"It's a googly bowled by a right hander. Oh never mind, I'll explain later."

Eddie slapped his back. "Some very upper crust people in Shanghai. You might meet some. Pots of money about, and lots of poor buggers who die in the streets. You'll certainly meet them. Illness, poverty, murder, the lot. And in the streets just round here, the ladies of the night. Brothels galore. Nearly all tied up with gangsters. Lot of trouble. You'll meet that, too. By the way, the Chinese aren't allowed to use the parks and gardens. Except if they're looking after children. No dogs, either. The high-ups say the Chinese have their own spaces."

"That doesn't seem right. I thought this place was just on loan."

"Forget all that. The old Shanghai hands have made this home, and aren't going to let it go. Too cushy a life."

He pointed out the shacks along the Soochow Creek and the Huangpu River.

"Shocking down there – full of rats, filth, disease. Poor sods can't earn enough to eat. It's called Chinatown. Daft, isn't it. You can't go chasing criminals down there, or in the French area. Not part of our policing territory. Another problem. You'll learn all about that."

They walked down one floor and were engulfed in noise from jugglers, acrobats, brightly coloured birds in cages, magicians, stallholders, and girls with slits up their skirts touting for business.

Sam bought a fan to send home to his mother. He imagined her face when she saw it. She would be tickled pink.

"What are all these doors round the walls?"

"Guess."

Sam shook his head.

"That's where people chuck themselves out when they've lost all their money gambling. Not a nice end, is it?"

Sam refused herbal medicines, incense, masks, games of cards, and Mahjong. He turned and saw, chalked on a board outside a tent:

MADAME BO CHINESE FORTUNES
VERY GOOD VERY CHEAP

"I've never had my fortune told," he said.

"OK pal," said Eddie. "I think you're safe. She's probably a hundred years old, talking a load of rubbish; might be a man; might be blind; most fortune tellers are. Ask him or her how much to start with. I'll go and look at the monkeys and the stuffed whale and meet you here in half an hour. Whatever you do, don't accept any opium or anything to eat. Someone'll have told you that opium is a real problem and big business. I can't tell you how many policemen have been kicked out of the force for getting involved."

Sam pushed back a red silk curtain printed with a gold dragon.

Madame Bo, tiny and bent, crouched on the concrete floor of the booth, a Chinese zodiac at her feet. She wore her hair in a pigtail, topped by a round, embroidered hat, and a long black tunic over wide black trousers. Her feet, in slippers, seemed to be only a few inches long. She blinked at him, eyes deep within wrinkles.

A red and green parrot with a thick black beak gripped a thin metal perch which swung above her. It looked at him through one, round, unblinking eye.

"His name Ping. He speak English. You say English word."

"Hello," said Sam.

"Foreign fuck devil." The parrot shrieked, squawked and shook its body. Tiny feathers flushed out from the tail.

Madame Bo laughed. "He like you. He give me from sea captain. He good boy. Now we do fortune."

Sam saw twelve tiny jade animals, in a round frame, set out in numerical order between the spokes of a red and black spinning wheel; a metal finger pointed to the first sign, the rat. "How much?"

"What you want give. I very wise. I give you good telling." She looked at the circle of zodiac animals and, set beside them, small statues of the same animals in dark wood.

"You nice looking English. You choose two animal."

Sam chose a tiger and a dragon.

"Give me date of birth,"

"Tenth of September 1902."

Madame Bo spun the finger of the wheel and waited until it stopped. She consulted a large brown book, and scratched at charts hanging behind her.

"You brave and passionate. Also have temper, can be too daring and jealous. You look for true love. Need lot of love. Have nice family. You good to people and job."

She peered at his eyes and mouth.

"You be very successful. Soon you meet beautiful lady from another country. Watch out for other tigers in signs. They love, but they fight with claws. Lady bring you happy and sad. Your big love will be daughter. Shanghai good for you now. Later much danger and war. That all I can say."

She lowered her head. Sam put ten cents on the table next to the ring of animals. She stood and bowed. "Thank you and goodbye."

The parrot glared and scratched. "Foreign fuck devil." He spat towards Sam.

Eddie was waiting for him. "Well?"

"I'm going to meet a beautiful lady from another country. I don't believe in all that rubbish, but you never know."

"Plenty of women around. The high-ups don't like us going with Chinese – problems with VD amongst other things. There are some nice English girls, daughters of bankers and diplomats. Parents want them to marry the posh boys in business. Big, handsome fellow like you might be lucky." He winked. "The Russians are good lookers, but after a passport or money, or both. They're stateless you see, since the revolution. Ended up penniless in north China, next to Russia. Real gold diggers but, boy, are they sexy."

"Who's *your* girl?"

Eddie took a photograph from his pocket. Sam saw a plump girl, with ringlets and a round face, breasts pushing at a cotton dress, "Jean. She works in a woollen mill. She's got nice blue eyes. Never done it with her, that can wait. Doesn't stop me having a bit of fun out here. I'll show you some good places another time."

He grabbed Sam's arm. "Let's find a bar and have a whisky, there's a nice one in the next street."

They sat at the bar. Hostesses offered tickets. "Nice dance and champanska?"

Eddie waved them away. "What happens is you buy tickets from the girls, then you get as many dances as you've paid for, and a glass of something that tastes like piss. Probably watered down ginger beer. Better lookers elsewhere in the bigger places." He yawned. "Let's go."

Eddie went to his small room off Nanking Road and Sam back to barracks. There was a letter from his sisters, his mother and Billy Wigg. His sisters had been left a little house, next street to Dad's, by Ma's great cousin who had died. Ma missed him. Billy Wigg's baby had whooping cough. Poor sod, should have taken more care with girls, like *he* did, except once down by the canal, but it was OK. He wrote to his mother telling her about his journey. She would be pleased to know that he had arrived safely and was settling in. He paused and saw her, plump in the armchair, legs bursting with varicose veins, and his father dripping ash from his pipe onto his overalls. His eyes prickled.

3

Sam and the other recruits finished training. He went to the armoury to be allocated his weapons – a baton, a slim dagger, a bulletproof vest and a .45 Colt automatic with a lanyard loop. Each gun had a walnut grip and was marked Shanghai Municipal Police, with a registration number underneath.

"These get stolen if an officer gets killed. Let's hope it doesn't happen to you," said the officer in charge. "There's also a trade in thieving, so watch out."

Sam stroked the blade of the dagger and remembered practising with one to stab through sacks hanging from a bar. It gave him a sense of power which scared him at first. He wondered what it would feel like to use it on a body. He held the gun by the handle. It felt heavy. His own, he thought. He was a good shot and reckoned that he could protect himself and kill a few villains. He would write to Billy Wigg and tell him how proud he was to be a real police officer and have weapons. Billy had started a decorating business in Warren. It sounded a bit dull after the training in Shanghai.

Assistant Commissioner White addressed the recruits in the large meeting room. He stood, hands behind his back, legs apart, and asked them to sit.

"You will graduate next week and then be on duty. You have done well. I would particularly like to congratulate Constables Shuttleworth and Webb who have received top marks in all the examinations."

The men clapped, Sam looked at his feet.

"As you know, we have an emergency situation at the moment. There is intense fighting in the Chinese sector. The Volunteer Corps and extra naval troops have been called in. Thousands of refugees are coming into the International Settlement. This sort of thing is not unusual. Our job is to keep order in the Settlement, whatever is going on outside. Last year, there were many hundreds of murders and over a thousand armed robberies. This is what you are up against. What you have been trained to deal with. Now it gets real."

Sam nudged Brian Smith and raised his eyebrows.

The assistant commissioner took a deep breath, coughed and looked at the ceiling. "Now, a word about women. You can smile, and I know your mentors and other officers will have talked about this. You are young men; as you know, you can't marry, as part of your contract, for six years, until after your first leave. It is understood that you will want female company. There are nice English girls about – nurses, typists, secretaries, and so on, mainly spoken for. The church social clubs are a good place to find company. Plenty of churches, all religions. Some lads go with Chinese or Japanese girls. One or two have married them. That won't do your career any good, though it might be useful for learning Chinese."

The men laughed.

"If you go out with a White Russian, just make sure she isn't connected to any criminal gangs. It is not advised to use the brothels. If you do, be very careful – some are owned by the gangs. Do not use opium, get drunk, or get into trouble. If you do, your career will be very short. Understand?"

The men nodded. "Yes, sir."

He stared at each man in turn.

"You will each have a small platoon of five Chinese policeman in your charge. They are mainly good men and work hard, but watch that they don't get sucked into any illegal bribery work. They are brave, and don't like to lose face. This has its downside. They sometimes get themselves killed just because they feel they always have to stand their ground. Mortality rates amongst them are high, sometimes six or more a day. We are proud of this Force and hope you are, too. Good luck." The men stood and saluted as the assistant commissioner left.

"I need a beer after that," said Sam, "I've said I'll meet Eddie my mentor. Let's all go to the bar."

Eddie sat at the bar and ordered pints of bitter. "I'll treat you."

"Who are all these gang leaders?" asked Brian.

Eddie laughed.

"You're not likely to meet them. Far too grand. Here goes… there's Huang Jinrong, police officer in the French Concession, thanks to daddy's influence. They call him 'Pock marked Huang' for obvious reasons. Du Yuesheng, 'Big-Eared Du' in charge of opium scams. Has a team of bodyguards – one used to be a chauffeur at the American Consulate. Guess what they call him? – 'Stars and Stripes'. Then there is Chang Tsung-chang, the 'Shantung Monster', six foot seven, mother a witch, father a trumpet player – executes people who get in his way."

Sam swallowed his beer. "I wouldn't like to meet any of them. Who's in control?"

Eddie finished his pint. "Nobody. Bloke called Sun Yat-sen is trying to unite the country, but only really has any power in the South. South against North. Warlords fighting each other. Loads of kidnappings."

"Are we likely to be kidnapped?" asked Sam's mate, Brian.

Eddie laughed. "You're not important enough. Listen, big case last year. Bandits derailed the Blue Express between here and Peking. They took hostages to a cave. One was an American heiress who hid her jewels under a stone and they were recovered after the bandits were caught. Are any of you American heiresses? Well then… Who's buying me another drink? Sam, we're on duty at ten. Brothels and drugs here we come. Have a rest and get changed."

* * *

Sam wrote to Billy Wigg and sent him a photograph of himself graduating – tall and proud in the blue serge uniform and peaked cap with the SMP badge, hand on the holster of his gun. He thought Billy would be jealous. The only weapon he had seen Billy use was a fishing line when they went up to the reservoir to catch trout. And what would his ma think about him being able to speak Shanghainese? Some of the others never mastered it.

4

Night patrol started at ten that night. Sam and Eddie stood at the door of the Station in heavy topcoats with holsters strapped across their chests and bulletproof vests underneath.

Eddie introduced two Chinese constables. "Come on, lads. This is Ho and this is Chang. Always have Chinese on duty with you. Couldn't manage without them." The men smiled and bowed.

"Talk some of the lingo to them, Sam." Sam said a few words in Shanghainese. Ho and Chang clapped. Eddie patted him on the back.

"How come you're so good at it?"

"I used to do a bit of amateur dramatics at our local church society. I could always do different accents. It made people laugh."

A chill breeze stirred the stiff branches of sycamore trees, made dead leaves scurry and flicked scraps of litter. The pavements gleamed under street lights, bicycles, with no lights, dodged along the streets where smells of cooking wafted from doorways and windows. Sam sniffed the scents of mist and food. He was longing to get going.

Eddie stopped outside a pawnshop. "OK. We're going to start near Nanking Road and visit an old alleyway, famous for prostitution, then a drug den. We might see some gambling, but they usually get wind of us first and scarper. By early morning, when the night soil men come out to collect the shit, you'll probably have seen some horrible sights, so be prepared. We'll get snacks from stalls and have breakfast when we get back about six in the morning."

They approached Gongxing Alley. The guard sat on a stool under a canopy.

"Every alley has a guard," said Eddie. Make friends with them. Evening Mr Hǎo. Any problems?"

"No, all quiet, sir."

"Just showing a new man around. Here's some cigarettes."

The guard bowed his head, then spoke to the Chinese constables. They laughed. "I understood most of that," said Sam, "some husband and wife problem."

"Clever bugger," said Eddie. "Get to know the alley guards. They'll tell you a lot."

He led them down the row of houses and into another alley. Red lanterns and long advertising placards swung from metal posts. "All the alleys have names. Like Avenue of Prosperity or Virtue or Strength. Always watch your back down here. You never know."

Sam looked round. "What are they selling?"

"Here's another pawnshop, a barber, a tailor, a grocery, a hot water store (not for baths of course – for tea), a wine shop – don't touch it, a Chinese medicine chemist, a rice store. Anything you want. Some of the whores have their name on a lantern outside the house where they work. That right, Ho?"

Ho pointed to a white lantern with red writing. "That name say Fifi."

They went down an alley which branched off the main street. Food stalls were open and they were offered sesame cakes, fruit, and tea. Chang pointed to a decorated stone carving of curled leaves above wooden doors. "Very old, very pretty. This alley called Many Pleasures."

Dogs scuttled, sniffed and tore at bones in the gutters; beggars looked at them from half-closed eyes, hands outstretched. Ho and Chang pushed them to one side.

"They won't bother us. Just don't get too close," said Eddie, "The smell and the lice will get to you. Now we move on. Let's go and visit Madam Tsu."

They pushed through a door. Sam had difficulty seeing through cigarette and cigar smoke. He choked on the smell.

"Always look behind the door when you visit one of these places," said Chang.

Four men crouched round a game of Mahjong. The tiles were shuffled away. One of the players bowed and offered cigarettes. "No play for money." Eddie laughed and asked for Madam Tsu. She came down the staircase, smiled and bowed, "Good evening, sergeant. Business very good, very clean."

She wore a long red gown and black high-heeled sandals, her hair piled in bunches and held with tortoiseshell combs, her eyes black with mascara. She waved a sweet smelling cigarette in a long holder.

"We have to inspect," said Eddie, "In case of gambling." He winked at Sam. "Do you have your licence, Madam?"

Madam Tsu handed him a piece of paper which Eddie glanced at and returned.

They went upstairs into a dim room with a sickly smell of incense and perfume. The carpets, embossed with black roses on green velvet, were stained and scuffed. Thick, red velvet curtains draped across a window. A row of girls, seated on a red couch, dressed in gauze trousers and flimsy bodices filed their nails or combed their hair. Sam noticed the black mascara, the red lips and the heavy powder. He looked at doors leading off from the room.

"Don't ask," said Eddie.

Sam put his hand on the gun. "What are we supposed to do?"

"We won't interrupt," Eddie replied, "funny business this. See, it's legal. Brothels have been registered since 1920 but were supposed to close by now. All to do with the Moral Welfare League. God, what a pain in the arse they are. This one is only small and, so far as we know, not connected to a gang. The old doll pockets the money. Seems to keep it clean."

"What about opium?"

"Now opium's another matter. There's a known den just along here. Not usually a problem in there. Sleepy old addicts mainly, but somebody supplies them. We'll go up the back way. Keep your hand on your gun and let the Chinese lads do the talking."

They climbed the stairs of a three-storey house. Eddie banged on the door, shouted, "Police" and pushed into the dark room. Ho and Chang, guns drawn, looked behind the door and pulled aside the thick curtains, drawn over a single window. There was a clatter outside. Sam coughed as he inhaled the curls of sweet smoke. Two beds were pushed against the wall. On one, two bodies sprawled, eyes open, gazing at the ceiling. Two men in dirty rags sat on the other, swaying as they sucked on long pipes. On a table were pots containing wooden tweezers, sticks, and small piles of a substance resembling tobacco.

Eddie sniffed the equipment. "We'll just report this and the vice squad will come back to make arrests. The dealer probably escaped through the window. In the nastier places, there's sometimes a shoot-out. Two of our Chinese lads were killed last week. It's a bad business. About half the Chinese cops are on protection money for opium smuggling. This stuff is small beer, but there's big trade for big money. It's the buggers who run it who are the problem, not these poor sods."

They ran down the stairs and Eddie handed round cigarettes.

"Now, listen it's about two o'clock. Let's grab some tea and sesame cake from a stall, and wander up Nanking Road into another alley. If you need a piss, do it against a wall," he said.

They walked up Nanking Road. Half-clothed men, and some children, lay in the gutters, limbs tangled. Their faces were squashed into the filth, or turned upwards, staring. Eddie poked one with his foot.

"Are they dead?" asked Sam.

"Most will be," replied Eddie, "from starvation or opium or murder. When it gets cold, they just freeze to death. Christ, here's one in an American sailor's uniform."

Chang bent down to feel the neck pulse. Sam saw blood on the man's white tunic and a hole in the material. His shoes, hat, and belt were missing.

"Shot and robbed." said Eddie, "We'll have to get this one picked up by the ambulance and do a report for the American Consulate. What a fool if he went about on his own. Probably got into a fight about a woman or opium. Not a lot to do about the rest. They'll be swept off the streets and put into carts by our Chinese cops tomorrow. No telling where *they're* from."

Rats scuttled about amongst the bodies, and Sam saw a face chewed and gashed, flesh hanging from the lips and eyes. He vomited.

Eddie kicked the body to one side. "Don't worry. That happens to most people. You'll get used to it. There's worse. I'll show you down this street."

Sam wiped his mouth on his sleeve and Chang offered him tea with whisky from a flask. Eddie banged the side of a building with his hand. "In this wall are drawers where people put babies, dead or left to die, by people who can't afford them or because they are girls." He pulled one open.

Sam lowered his head. "I can't look."

"You'll have to one day, and report it. But there's fuck all anybody can do," said Eddie. "There are two in here. Stone cold. Just left naked in this night weather. Come on, let's get more tea."

"There is Chinese saying," said Chang, "Heaven is high and the Emperor is far away. It mean no one watching and nobody care."

Sam wiped his mouth on his sleeve again. "That's a bit bloody depressing."

Eddie smiled. "But true."

As the dark began to soften, they walked down an alley and met two men carrying buckets and emptying them into carts. Eddie stopped and waved to them. "Most people don't have toilets or anything," he said. "They piss and shit in these wooden buckets, called night stools, then put them outside the houses. They're collected by these night soil men before light. The carts full of shit get wheeled to the dock, mixed with water, and sold to farmers who come to the night soil dock north of here and pick it up for fertiliser."

The night soil collectors called out as they moved from house to house. Birds began to mutter, cocks screeched, and dawn slid into the sky.

"Let's get back to the Station for breakfast," said Eddie, "I just fancy bacon and eggs. What's up with you, Sam?"

"I don't think I can eat anything." Ho and Chang laughed.

"You must, then get a good sleep," said Eddie, "you deserve a treat. Tell you what, tonight, I'll take you to a little private place where there are some clean, decent girls. Come prepared and smart. It's too long since you had a good fuck. Let's just go and report the dead Yank and the opium place."

Sam slept until two in the afternoon and went to the canteen for pork and dumplings. After lunch, he practised at the shooting range and went to the gym to pummel a punchbag and lift weights.

At six, he had a cold shower, shaved in warm water prepared by the coolie, dressed in a laundered shirt, jacket, and corduroy trousers, put six condoms in a pocket with his wallet and smoked two cigarettes whilst he waited for Eddie in the Station lobby.

"The house we're visiting is off Thibet Road, in an alley called Endless Pleasure," said Eddie. "Good name, eh? The top floor is run by a French woman, Madame Claudette. The girls are French and Chinese, with a few White Russians. You can take your pick. The Chinese do a very nice massage called Shiatsu which really gets you going, the French are a bit toffee nosed and the Russians always want more pay. It will cost you two dollars and you might want to give the girl a bit extra. Don't be nervous."

Bright paintings of fruit and a tapestry, embroidered with ladies in long flowing dresses, hung on the wall at the entrance. Sam looked at the chairs and a low table in pale walnut on a carpet of green and red wool. He smelled sweet smoke curling from incense sticks. His cock swelled.

Madame Claudette was tall, with thick make-up and heavy green eyeshadow. She wore a robe embroidered with flowers and herons. Her dark hair was tucked under a pale blue turban held by a brooch of tiger eye. Fingers tipped with red varnished nails held a long, jewelled holder with a pink cigarette. "Please gentlemen take off shoes and give me coats."

She passed the coats to a girl. "Monsieur Nicholson I know likes Pearl. For you, Monsieur, I recommend Jasmine. Very nice Chinese girl. Nice and slow."

They paid their two dollars.

"I'll see you here in an hour," said Eddie. "Madame Claudette will give you a cup of tea with whisky if you're out first." He winked.

Sam went into a low-lit room with a bed at one side. Jasmine closed the door. She was tiny, with loose, thick, black hair, green eyeshadow over brown oval eyes and thin pencilled brows. The blue silk gown, opened to show the cleavage between her small breasts. She smiled, "Take off clothes."

His fingers trembled and he had difficulty unfastening buttons. He felt his cock harden.

He pulled at his shirt and trousers and stood in underpants, bulging with the erection. Jasmine slipped off the gown and approached him. Her breasts were small and firm, the nipples protruded from their dark surround, her slim hips furrowed down to black pubic hair. She put her hands on his shoulders and leaned against him. He held her waist and came, gasping and squirming.

He looked down at the stain in his pants and wanted to run away. "Sorry, sorry. You see, I haven't …"

She smiled. "Now you take off pants, wash and I give you massage."

He rolled up his sticky underpants, put them with his trousers and went into a small side room with a basin, to wash his genitals. Jasmine led him to the bed. She began to press his head with her fingers, finding points around his scalp and ears, then neck and shoulders, spine, buttocks, legs, and feet.

"Points on foot speak to body," she said. "This point stomach, this lung, this heart, this … she giggled and turned him over. His cock swelled again. The end of his shaft tingled. She moved down his body, pushing her fingers into points on his chest. She stroked his erection and moved down his legs to his toes, and up his body to the groin. He wanted to come, but focused on the ceiling and held back. She took a condom from a table, slid it over the erection, and then stroked his balls.

She took the shaft in her fingers, squatted above him then lowered herself onto him, opening his lips with her tongue and fluttering it inside his mouth. She moved slowly. He held her thighs. He gasped as they moved together. As he approached orgasm she moved faster. He came and felt the splatter of sperm in the condom. She rolled from underneath him, peeled it off and wrapped it in paper.

"That nice?" she asked.

"Very, I want to kiss you."

She washed her hands and handed him rose-scented soap and a towel. Sam dressed. She opened his mouth with her tongue. "You visit again?"

"Oh, yes. I'll ask for double time next. Here's an extra fifty cents. Thank you."

Eddie was waiting outside sipping a glass of whisky and smoking. "You look a bit stunned. Now we leave a dollar with Madame Claudette. She is very careful about the girls – they get health checks and are well looked after. A bit extra helps. How was it?"

"It were grand. I'll be back. Soon."

He gulped down a cup of black tea and lit a cigarette.

In his room at Gordon Road, he poured a glass of whisky, took his underpants from his pocket, washed them in carbolic soap and hung them over the chair to dry.

5

The new recruits were allocated to one of the ten police stations round the International Settlement. Sam went to Yangtzepoo Road near the creek. Mills and warehouses stretched past the Station; the tall tower of the Shanghai waterworks loomed above, reminding him of the mill chimneys in Warren.

He reported to Sub-Inspector Davidson from Manchester at 8am on 5 November 1924. It was bonfire night, Sam realised. As children, he and his mates used to collect great piles of wood and stack them into a pointed heap with Guy Fawkes, made of sticks and rags, on top. They threw paraffin on the bonfire and off it went in a great, tangled blaze. There were always a few fireworks – bangers, rockets, and sparklers – and treacle toffee, made by one of the mams. It stuck your teeth together and burned your throat when you swallowed.

He wondered what his family were doing in Warren now – seven hours ahead in time. They would be at work, perhaps on a tea break. They would miss him as they celebrated bonfire night.

He coughed, and knocked on Davidson's door. Davidson held out his hand. "Welcome. Nice to have another Lancastrian. I'll show you to your room, then introduce you to the Station. Your trunk will come along later. You will share a coolie, Wang, with Denis Gee in the next room. He's on duty at the moment. Wang'll see to your needs –

polishing shoes, buttons, and badges, washing, ironing, and so on. He'll get you food if you're late in. He'll even cut your hair. When you've been in the service for a couple of years, or if you get promoted, you'll be able to afford something outside the Station, if you want."

Sam looked round. The room was a small oblong with a planked floor, a narrow bed, a wardrobe, a small wooden table with one drawer, a sink with a small square mirror above it, and a rail for hanging clothes. The small, one bar electric heater was off and he shivered. There was a shower cubicle down the corridor.

Davidson walked him round the Station, a two-storey building with offices on the top floor and an open space downstairs where other constables, Chinese, Indian, and British, typed reports, answered the phone, and filed case notes. In the basement was a small gym with a vaulting horse, weights, mats, wall bars, and a punchbag, and a billiards table in the room next door. The bar and dining room were in a narrow annexe.

"This is your new colleague, Sam Shuttleworth," Sergeant Davidson announced to the men in the main office, "we'll soon show him the ropes." Sam raised his arm as they waved.

They checked Sam's papers with a clerk and went into Davidson's office.

"This is a funny old place. Here's a map of the area. Near the Huangpu, of course, so can be a bit smelly and watch out for the mozzies in summer. Plenty of river trouble – smuggling and what have you. The trouble spots are marked with red circles, but there could be trouble anywhere, especially now. Mainly it's the usual thing: petty theft, lost property – not much handed in – disputes over money, boats, women, opium selling, fights, traffic arrests. The Sikhs sometimes get overenthusiastic about arresting people for crossing roads at the wrong place; not that there are wrong places, they sometimes make it up for something to do. There's the more dangerous stuff, and we've had a few incidents in the past few weeks – armed robbery down Wayside and a kidnapping of a wealthy Chinese businessman from his office on Lay Street."

"What happened?"

"He ran a furniture store. Well, that's his story. Rumour has it he was head of a gang and kidnapped by rivals. He was returned for a bloody great ransom. Beaten up something terrible, though."

"Who will I be working with?"

"Five Chinese. No corruption, so far as I know. All excellent shots. It would be good if you could say a few words to them when you meet. They speak English, well, sort of, but try to slip in a bit of Shanghaiese if you can. You'll go on patrol together today, then you'll work out how to split up your duties. The Chinese lads will walk you round the area later."

Sam looked at the sergeant's desk. There were files, pens and pencils and two photographs. Davidson picked them up. "That's my mum and dad and that's my girl back in Manchester. Home next year to get wed."

Sam smiled. "Pretty."

Davidson wiped the photographs with his cuff, and put them back on his desk. He tapped Sam on the arm. "Listen, I know this is a funny request, but I see from your joining notes that you were in a dramatic society in England. The commissioner has sent a message round to see if we can find a bloke to be in a play with a group of Brits here. I don't know what his connection is, but he's very keen to find somebody who has to be tall and handsome."

They both laughed.

"I don't mind having a go," said Sam, "what do I have to do?"

"Turn up at the Palace Hotel, just off the Bund, at seven on Thursday. Dress casual but quite smart and ask for Annabelle Dyson. I don't know any more. Come on, let's go and meet your lads."

The Chinese constables stood and saluted as they entered. Sam pulled his shoulders back and tried to look stern but friendly. Davidson asked the men to sit. "This is Constable Shuttleworth. He is looking forward to working with you. He graduated top of his class and speaks Shanghaiese quite well but is still learning."

"Good morning men," said Sam, in Shanghaiese, then switched to English. "I know we will get on well. I am one for hard work and discipline. I'm sure you are used to that. Let me assure you that I will never ask you to do anything that I wouldn't do myself. We will stick together and be a good team. Tell me your names."

The men stared at him and introduced themselves; they were all small and thin, in uniforms that looked oversized. Sam noticed that one of them looked nervous. His eyes wandered round the room; he cracked his knuckles and jiggled his legs.

"Confucius saying that leaders should be willing to do what they ask of others," said another.

Sam smiled. "I know a bit about Confucius. A great man."

They walked the streets and alleyways, chatting to policemen on duty at the barricades and sandbags, and asking alley guards and shopkeepers about any problems. They went through the Sincere department store and met the manager who reported some pilfering of ladies' underwear and tobacco.

They did a night shift on Wednesday and arrested three Chinese for gambling and two Russians for being drunk. The Chinese were taken to the Station gaol to wait for a court hearing. The Russians were collected by the police from the French concession.

"Now they go to Chinese court," said one of the officers. "They live in French Concession, but Russians have no state, so Chinese law deal with them."

When they reported back to the Station, Sam was handed five letters, forwarded from Gordon Road.

One was from his mother. She wrote once a week, the flimsy paper covered in her sprawled, looping letters, with capitals in the wrong places. She spoke of her health (she didn't like to trouble the doctor), the weather (it had turned cold), his sisters (Ivy was courting, Bertha now ran eight looms at the cotton factory), his brothers (Derek was out of work, Jimmy was naughty), his father (he had joined the Paperworkers' Union, and it wouldn't do him any good). Billy Wigg was doing well with his painting and decorating. There was another baby on the way.

Auntie Nellie, who lived ten miles away in a mining village, wrote to say that Joey had fallen out of his cage and died because the poor thing couldn't fly. She was going to get another. Her false teeth were giving her trouble again. There had been a pit accident with five men killed.

There were three letters from girls he had courted in Warren. Doris had found someone else as he was so far away and she hadn't heard anything from him. Thank God for that. Barbara was moving to Wales to go into service. Nancy missed him and thought she might come out to China. Fat chance.

6

On Thursday, Sam finished duty at five in the afternoon, showered, shaved, and changed into grey trousers, black shoes, a blue shirt, and a grey sweater, knitted for him by his sister Bertha. He wondered if he should wear a tie, decided not, but changed his shirt to a white one with a starched collar. He splashed on some Yardley lavender aftershave, bought from a market stall, and smoothed his hair with oil. He cleaned his teeth and smiled at himself in the mirror.

As he left, Denis Gee was going to his room next door. Sam punched his arm. "Evening, Denis. Had a good day?"

Denis took the cigarette out of his mouth and stamped on it. "Christ you smell like a bloody brothel. Is that where you're going? And no, since you ask, terrible day. Shot at, pissed on, and big argument with a stallholder. We know it's not carrots he's selling. I'm off for a few beers and early night. Have a good time."

Sam took a rickshaw to within fifty yards of the Palace Hotel, then walked. Cars were lined up outside – Bentleys, Packards, Fords. He walked past them, breathing deeply, neck stiff, head straight and high. The Chinese doorman, dressed in shiny top hat, red coat, and black trousers bowed.

"Good evening, sir."

"Mr Shuttleworth for Miss Dyson."

The doorkeeper lowered his head again. "The bell boy will escort you to the Belvedere room."

An Indian boy in a turban and a blue suit with shiny buttons approached, balancing a brass message tray across his palm. He led Sam to the lift, which he called an elevator and opened the springy, criss-crossed steel bars. The interior was as big as Sam's room back at the barracks and lined with velvet. The boy pressed the button for the fourth floor. Sam looked at the pictures on the walls, one the outside of the hotel, one flowers, one trees, grass, rocks, and a pool with fish.

"That Yu Yuan garden," said the boy, "Very beautiful."

"Thanks. I've read about it. I'll visit soon." He pointed to the flower picture. "I know what that is, it's a chrysanthemum. I had to learn to spell it at school." He named the letters and laughed.

The boy looked puzzled. "This one magnolia. Flower of Shanghai."

They walked down a corridor on the fourth floor and the boy knocked on a red door with a brass plate, marked Belvedere room. Sam smoothed his hair and adjusted his jacket. "Entrez," someone called. The boy opened the door, announced, "Mr Shuttleworth," lowered his head and left.

The room was filled with pipe and cigarette clouds, mixed with the smell of whisky, coffee and perfume.

"Hello, there," said a man with a small pointed beard, long grey hair, a smoking jacket, and narrow velvet trousers, "You must be the new recruit. I'm Jeremy, the producer. We're the Belvedere players, called after this room where we rehearse."

Sam held out his hand, Jeremy clasped and held it. "We do a play once a year at the British Consulate, or the club, or in one of the small theatres. All very jolly. This year we're at the Consulate, doing a play called *Maria Marten and the Murder in the Red Barn*. Heard of it?"

Sam shook his head. Jeremy tapped the script. "It's a Victorian melodrama based on a true incident in Suffolk. We desperately need someone to play the villain, William Corder. Dear Gordon, who was playing him originally, has had to go back to England – got a very nasty disease."

41

Sam looked round, bewildered. He had no idea what a Victorian melodrama was. They just did plays at St Barnabas's Dramatic Society in Warren. The other players stared at him through a haze of smoke. Jeremy waved his hand towards them. "Here are the others: Annabelle, who is playing Maria; Jeff who plays Tim Bobbin, the simpleton; Beth who plays the gypsy. Donald is Pharos Lee, the copper; Babs is Maria's mother; and Hugh is Johnny Badger, in love with Maria."

Sam was confused by all the names, "What's the play about?"

"The story is that William Corder, the squire's son, seduces Maria and she has a baby; he kills them both and gets found out when her ghost comes back. Great fun. It starts with a maypole dance and a gypsy lament."

Sam stared at Annabelle. She blew smoke towards him. Jeremy wafted it away. "Now, let's try you out at reading. Of course, you'd have a long, twirly moustache in the part. Let's see how you get on. If you're no good or don't like it, no hard feelings; we'll keep looking for our villain, but there's not much time. OK, Annabelle we'll do the scene where you and Corder meet and he pretends to be ill. Sam you start off reading. Remember, you're a villain."

Sam took the script, glanced at it and tried to stop his hands shaking. He took a deep breath.

This way lies the cottage of the pretty maiden who has occupied my thoughts so much of late. She is coy yet shall be mine for I have set my heart on possessing her. But I know not how to proceed about the business.

"Very good," said Jeremy, "now move on to after the gypsy's told him Maria is going to the fair. He pretends to be ill. Annabelle."

What ails you sir, are you feeling ill?

'Tis nothing — just a little giddiness. The day is uncommonly hot. I'll just sit here under the shade of this tree and I'll soon recover, never fear.

I'll fetch you water from the cottage. I'll be but a minute (runs into cottage)

Better and better. My plan succeeds most excellently. By now, the other bumpkins will be at the fair and I shall have the maiden to myself. Ha! Ha!

The players applauded. "You'll do," said Jeremy.

"Marvellous!" said Annabelle, "that northern twang really gives the part a new dimension."

Sam stared at her and took out a cigarette. She took off the cloak she wore as Maria. He saw fair skin, a few freckles over the nose, a mouth bright with red lipstick and blonde wavy hair which stroked her neck. Her breasts pushed out a pink sweater of soft, thin wool tucked into brown, belted slacks. She wore black, high heeled sandals and smoked a pink cigarette.

Jeremy tapped on the script. "OK. Now Sam, this is a big part; can you learn it by Christmas? The play's on Boxing Night."

Sam nodded, and looked sideways at Annabelle. Jeremy talked them through the next section over sandwiches and drinks. Sam sipped a beer. Jeremy clapped and called out: "Let's now look at the section after the baby's born and is ill. Tim says 'give it the knob of the kitchen poker to suck' etc., etc. Maria is forgiven by her father... *When laughingly with outspread arms you ran towards me and I trembled lest your feet should fail etc., etc.* Corder poisons the baby, so move on to Act Two, Scene Four where he kills Maria in the red barn. Off you go."

* * *

"That's wonderful," said Jeremy at ten o'clock. "Sam, you and Annabelle work marvellously together. There's a real dynamic between you. Thank Christ for that. Now, try to learn the first Act by next week. Word perfect, please."

Sam thought he would struggle with some of the language, but would get by. Annabelle picked up her handbag and walked over to him. "I'll give you a lift back, I have a car and driver outside."

"I was going to grab a rickshaw. But thanks. Yes."

The chauffeur, a Sikh in a white turban and red jacket, opened the door of the Buick and helped her in, hand on her elbow. Sam climbed alongside. They sat back in the soft leather seats and the driver took his place at the front, behind a glass screen.

Annabelle smoothed her slacks. "My apartment, Bashir."

The interior smelled of polish, tobacco and perfume. Sam took out a packet of Capstan, Annabelle opened a silver case half full of oval Sobranies – pink, purple, and gold, held by a flat, red elastic band. They offered each other cigarettes. She took a Capstan; Sam lit it for her with his lighter; she coughed and laughed. "That's a man's fag, for sure. Nice though."

"What's that you smoke?"

"Sobranies. Russian fags. Easy and cheap to get here. So, Sam, what do you think of our little group?"

"Hard to say. I don't know them well enough. Who's Jeremy? Is he your boyfriend?"

She laughed. "Jeremy? He's a pansy, couldn't you tell. He'd fancy you before me; has a sweet Chinese boyfriend from Manchuria. It's illegal, of course, so they're very discreet, but anything goes in Shanghai so long as you're not caught. Don't go repeating that. Even then, it's usually OK if you have money."

"Where do you live?"

"I have an apartment on Avenue Pétain, the French sector, obviously. All the nicest buildings are there. Daddy rents it for me. He and Mummy have a bloody great mansion on Bubbling Well Road, near the park, but I need my independence. My sister lives with the P.'s and I have a brother in England. By the way, Daddy plays bridge with your commissioner, what's his name, and the families see each other at parties and such. Mummy hosts parties all the time – whist, bridge, and even Mahjong – just to pretend they're in China. We sent an SOS asking the commissioner if he could find someone to play Corder when dear Gordon, as Jeremy calls him, got ill. That's why you're here, I'm glad to say. Where do you live?"

"In barracks at the station in Yangztepoo Road. I've only been here for six weeks and haven't found my feet yet."

"What's the accent?"

"Lancashire. Warren, near Manchester. Mill town – where I worked from fourteen, went to night school, applied for the police here and here I am. Wanted a bit of travel and adventure."

"How come you can act?"

"There was a church amateur dramatics group and I enjoyed it. It made a nice change."

"And what do you do for fun, in the police?"

"Not much time for that yet, especially with the emergency. I like sport and go to the gym a bit. I used to do a lot of fishing. I've been told there's good hunting and fishing in spring along the creek so I suppose I'll do that later."

"Ever played tennis?"

"No, but I always fancied it. The only place to play where I come from was part of the golf club and you had to be a member."

"There are some courts at the cricket club here. I play there. I'm bloody good. I play in the first team. I'm a marvellous coach. I'll teach you in the summer. I'm sure you've got a bloody good arm." She squeezed his biceps. They took last puffs on the cigarettes and put out the butts in the ashtrays on the back of the seats. Annabelle put her hand on Sam's thigh and stroked it. She turned her head towards him, opened her mouth and kissed him, thrusting her tongue to touch his palette which she rubbed with the tip. She put her arms round his shoulders and stroked his neck. A shiver ran down his spine and between his legs. He felt the tingle of an erection. He held her waist.

She pulled away, looked at him, and kissed his nose. "Fancy popping into my place for a nightcap?"

He wondered what came next. He shuffled away from her. His hands shook as he fumbled for his cigarettes, dropped them on the floor and bent to pick them up. His face was hot, his erection pushed against his trousers. "I can't, I'm on duty at four in the morning."

"Shame. Don't be nervous. When are you free? They do give you time off, I suppose?"

"I have the weekend off this week."

"OK. Tell you what, meet me at my flat on Saturday at about 2pm. It's number 15, in the Sauvigny Apartments. I'll show you the building now. Ring the bell and I'll be ready. I'll show you some of Shanghai; we'll have a drink and then come back to my place for dinner. My maid's a great cook and she'll leave us something before she goes. Here's my phone number."

He took a mauve card. "All right. I'll be there. We could practise our parts for the play."

She laughed. "There'll be more interesting things to do."

They drove down an avenue of tall, bare trees, past two churches, and arrived at the Sauvigny building.

Annabelle pointed down the street. "Look at this. Do you know, these are plane trees, imported from France? Trust the bloody French. Mind you, it does look lovely in spring and summer."

She leaned over and kissed Sam again; she flicked her tongue inside his mouth and placed her hand on his crotch. "Nice."

The driver opened her door and held out his arm. Sam tried to flatten his erection with his right hand.

She turned to the driver. "Bashir, take the gentleman to his lodging. Sam don't forget your copy of Maria."

He lit another cigarette, gave the driver the address, but asked him to stop before they reached Yangtzepoo Road so that he could walk to the Station. His legs trembled.

7

"Where can I get a really nice suit?" Sam asked Denis Gee.

"Depends how much you want to pay and how much time you've got."

"I need to get it by Saturday."

"OK. The cheapest way would be to get one made by a tailor down Huanjung Street, but you're too late for that. They're fast but not that fast. You'll have to go to one of the department stores on Nanking Road. Try Wing On or Sincere. Not the cheapest but a decent selection. Who're you trying to impress?"

"Nobody you know."

He bought a brown and black tweed jacket, black trousers and three white cotton shirts to go with the tie his sister had given him last Christmas. He added a brown overcoat, and a new brown felt trilby with a shiny blue feather tucked in the band. He had used all the previous month's salary.

The assistant at Wing On parcelled everything up in brown paper and wished him good luck. He inspected the cameras on the second floor, looked down the eyepieces and examined the shutters, but decided to learn more about photography before he bought one, and do some overtime to afford a good model.

On Saturday morning he put on khaki shorts and a sweater and went to the gym. It was unheated so he began with skipping. He looked at his legs. The suntan from being at sea had long faded, but his muscles were taut and firm. He posed, bending his arms at the elbow and tightening his biceps. Then he crouched and tensed his thigh muscles. He asked another constable who was peering through the shutter of a camera to take a photograph of him with a barbell above his head.

"I've just bought this thing," said the constable. "I've no idea if that will come out, but I'll let you have it, if it's OK. Good muscles."

Sam wished there was a mirror to pose in front of. He laughed, went back to his room and turned on the heater.

He asked his coolie Wang to bring him a pork sandwich and a pickle for lunch. He cleaned his teeth, showered, and sprinkled his body with talcum powder, Lavender Garden, to go with the aftershave. He slid on his trousers and one of the shirts from Sincere and knotted his tie. He shrugged into the tweed jacket, decided not to fasten it and looked at himself in the small mirror over the table. He stood on the table to examine himself from the waist downwards.

"Right, old son. You are looking good. They always called you a ladies' man. Now's your chance."

He folded six condoms, in their paper packs, into an inside jacket pocket, just in case. His cock moved. He put on the overcoat and hat and tucked the guidebook to Shanghai under his arm. He wished he hadn't eaten pickles, cleaned his teeth again and spat into the bowl.

He took a rickshaw to the intersection of the Rue Lafayette and the Avenue Pétain then walked. The leaves were beginning to curl into autumn; he smelled the musty damp and trailed his hand on the mottled bark of the plane trees.

The Sauvigny apartment building was four storeys high and made of rough stone with curved balconies in green ironwork and windows with small, squared panes. He went into the entrance hall, and stepped onto a thick grey carpet. He smiled. A bit different from Warren.

There were plants on a central table, one an aspidistra like Auntie Nellie had, but much bigger. He went to the desk and asked the concierge to ring for Miss Dyson.

Annabelle came out of the lift. He could smell her perfume from ten feet away. She was dressed in a heavy green, belted coat and matching hat pulled down over one ear. Her blonde waves tumbled around the brim. She wore short black boots and black gloves. She smiled and he wondered if she always wore that bright red lipstick to show how white her teeth were.

"You look very smart. You don't really need a tie but it's nice."

He stretched his hand towards her. "I like that scent you wear. I might get some to send to my sister."

"You'll have to order from Paris, then. It's Chanel number 5. I have it shipped over. Glad you like it. Let's get going."

They left the block of flats. Sam asked if she wanted a taxi.

She shook her head. "Let's go by rickshaw. I travel around in cars too much. We'll see more anyway."

Sam hailed a smart rickshaw with padded seats and asked her where they were going.

He instructed the driver, in Shanghaiese, to go to the West Gate of the Old City. The driver complained that it was a long way. "I'll double your fare."

Annabelle put her hand on his wrist. "Very impressive. I can hardly understand a word. They say that people who can act are good at learning languages, but I'm not."

"It's not all that difficult. You just have to keep at it. Anyway, I have to speak it for the job. You don't get promoted without it."

She leaned on his arm as she climbed out of the rickshaw and led him along a street of brown buildings, then down an alley with lanterns and stalls which sold antiques, fried food, and nuts. A monkey leapt from stall to stall, a peanut in its bony claw, eyes blinking and darting.

She pushed her body into the bend of his arm and they opened the plan of the old town. He breathed in her perfume again.

She pointed to the middle pages of the book. "Here we are and we're going into this big square where you can buy anything from birds to beans and nice dumplings, then there's the Yu Garden and the

Jingshan Temple, home of the town god who's supposed to protect people. Not doing a very good job."

"How do we get there?"

"Along here. Let's first go into the teahouse in the middle of the lake and get a snack on the second floor. Your hands are freezing. Let me hold one and put the other in your pocket." They walked across the zigzag bridge of nine turnings.

"I've seen pictures of this," said Sam.

"This pavilion is supposed to be the one shown on the willow pattern plates. Do you know the story?"

Sam shook his head. He looked at the tilted spurs of roof, the tiers of columns and the bright red of the walls, carved with grey filigree. They went to the second floor and ordered green tea and a sesame cake.

Annabelle offered him a cigarette. "The story of the willow pattern is about a rich mandarin with a beautiful daughter who fell in love with one of her father's clerks. It has a sad ending. The clerk was banned by her father, they ran off over the bridge but the father had them killed and they were turned into doves, like you see on the plates."

"That's sad. Is it an old Chinese story?"

She laughed and shook her head. "I think it was made up in England after they copied blue and white pottery from China years ago."

He lit the cigarette and sucked in the smoke. "Nice cigarettes, but not manly. I couldn't smoke these with the boys."

They paid and walked back over the bridge.

"Why did you join the police, Sam?" she asked.

"Better pay, good prospects, education, adventure."

"What does your family do?" she asked.

"They work in cotton mills. Nothing special. I have a little brother who's only seven. He'll be at school until he's fourteen. Like I was," he said.

"Is that all? My brother didn't finish at Oxford until he was about twenty-four. Kept failing exams," she said.

"Aye, well, that's different. When did you come to Shanghai?"

"Two years ago. Daddy transferred from London to make even more money. I miss London," she said.

"What do you do all day?" he asked.

"Shop, meet friends for tea, read – mainly magazines from England – play tennis, swim, get my hair cut and my face done. Come on, let's go to the other side of the lake."

"The building over there is the Pavilion of Rolling Up the Rain Curtain."

"That's a funny name."

"And now look at the marvellous rockery. Over here is the little Pavilion for Viewing Frolicking Fish. Look at all the goldfish and carp."

"I wouldn't mind fishing in there," said Sam.

She laughed. "That wouldn't be fair, would it? Along this corridor is the Chamber for Enjoying Ten Thousand Flowers with carvings of plums, orchids, bamboos, and chrysanthemum and, in front, a four hundred year old Gingko tree."

"I'll bet you can't spell chrysanthemum," said Sam.

"CRYSANTHAMUM."

He laughed. "Two mistakes. I had to learn how to spell it at school, so I know."

"You know a lot, don't you?" she said.

"Not as much as you know about Shanghai and probably a lot of other things. You're a good guide. I didn't want to leave school. I had a good teacher. I went to night school after, though."

"Well, you've made up for it. I learned nothing at school."

"What was your school like?"

"Posh place where they tried to teach us French and sewing. Me, sewing? Can you imagine?" She pretended to prick her finger and laughed.

"Then finishing school in London where we were supposed to learn how to host dinners, hold a tea cup and a wine glass, and talk nicely to people. God, it was awful."

"What did you do when you left?"

"Bugger all. I wanted to be a nurse. Out of the question. The parents wanted me married as soon as possible. I wanted sex, not marriage, so I travelled – France, Italy, Switzerland, then came here. Lovers in every country."

He imagined her naked on a bed, mouth open and head to one side. He felt his cock move.

"Then bloody Shanghai. You know what they call this place? Paris of the East. Well, it's full of people out for a good time, apart from the Chinese, unless they're rich. The Brits, Americans, French have a ball. Russians mainly whores and gangsters. Good-looking soldiers from all over the place. I think my sister's having an affair with an American marine, even though she's engaged to a Brit. Terrible, boring man, a banker made of cardboard."

"How do you know she's having an affair?"

"The way she looks at marines in cafés. Bulging cocks in tight trousers."

She put her arm through his and leaned against him. "Here's my favourite thing, the Jade Peak. They say it has ninety holes for water to cascade through. It was found in a river and brought here."

"I haven't got a camera yet but I'd like to take a snap of you in front of that."

She took his hand and kissed his cheek. "I think it's time for a cocktail," she said, "I know, let's go to The Paris. We can use Daddy's account there."

Sam waved down a rickshaw, spoke to the driver and shook his head twice. The driver nodded.

"I told him it was too much and I'd find someone else, so he halved the price."

She kissed his cheek.

They pulled up outside a building with blue lights and a miniature illuminated Eiffel Tower, a French flag perched on the summit, in the window. Inside were small tables, covered with red and white oilcloths, ironwork chairs, red velour settees in corners and, above them, dim lamps of coloured glass.

A European waiter in a black suit and bow tie showed them to a corner table.

Annabelle sat, crossed her legs, and lit a cigarette. "The vodka's good here – Russian influence. Let's ask what he recommends."

"We have our special cocktail, the Black Dog, le Chien Noir; it is one part vodka, one rum, one coffee liqueur, topped and shaken with black coffee, ice and cream. I make it special. I am Russian."

Sam nodded and watched the waiter mix and shake the liquids in a long, metal container – black, clear and brown – then plop in the cream and ice. He served it in two tall glasses.

Sam swallowed a quarter of the glass, and ran his tongue over his lips. "I've never tasted anything like it." His throat burned and his head throbbed. It was nothing like the pints of pale ale he drank in Warren.

Annabelle placed her hand on his thigh. "So, I've told you a bit about my sex life, what about yours?"

He shrugged, blushed and finished his drink. "Not as exciting. A few girls in Warren, one on the boat and one here."

"I can guess where that was. Any good?"

"Some of it. I know what to do, you know."

"I've embarrassed you. Let's have another drink. I'm sure you're very good at what you do."

The waiter refilled their glasses. Sam wanted to have Annabelle in bed, responding to his feeling her breasts and entering her. He sipped the drink and felt his cock push against his trousers. He realised that his tongue and lips slurred his speech.

"What about in Shai – lovers, I mean. What about Chinese men? They say they have small, what my dad would call courting tackle."

Annabelle fell onto his shoulder, laughing. "I've never heard that before. Only two Chinese lovers. One was a poet. Divine – tall, thin face, round glasses, long, slender fingers. I have a snap of him somewhere. Not bad courting tackle."

She spluttered into her glass. "The other was a diplomat, a lot older than me, and not such good tackle. A bit worn out."

She took his hand. "Let's go. I'll just put this on Daddy's account."

They breathed in the cold air, clung to each other, kissing, swayed back to Annabelle's flat, and took the lift to the fourth floor.

Sam took off his coat. "Why is it so warm?"

"Central heating. It's a new building. Thank God. You'll see why in the winter. Bloody freezing and damp."

He looked round. The main room had two soft velvet armchairs, a low settee, a dark table, and green velvet curtains.

She pointed to a door. "The bathroom's in there. I'll get you a drink, then use it. Dinner is set out in the dining room next door to the bedroom. Gin? Vodka? Whisky?"

"Whisky, please."

Sam sipped his drink until she came out of the bathroom. "Your turn."

The bathroom had a humid smell of pine and roses. He touched the white bath and basin, and looked at the shelf of cosmetics, bath lotions, and perfumes. He had never seen anything so luxurious. He recalled the outside toilet in Warren, with newspaper cut up to wipe yourself. The ones in barracks were not much better and smelled of piss.

When he came out, Annabelle was lying across the settee, a green silk calf-length dress pulled up to her knees. The fabric swathed round her neck and was pulled into the waist with a black leather belt. She was smoking a mauve Sobranie in a matching lacquer cigarette holder.

"Come and sit down here, I've poured us some champagne. Taste it."

He drank it like a glass of beer, the bubbles spinning down his throat. She poured more, put out the cigarette and placed her arms on his shoulders. He pulled her towards him and tasted the smoke and lipstick as they kissed.

She pushed her breasts against his chest. "Let's go into the bedroom. We'll take the champagne with us."

She took off the dress and he saw the silk underslip and stockings, held up by suspenders. He wanted to stroke her long, smooth legs, her small waist, and the mound of her abdomen. She removed the slip.

Her nipples, dark and wrinkled, stood out from her breasts. He took off his jacket, shirt, vest, trousers, and socks, and stood in underpants, his erection hard and thick.

She smiled. "No problems there, then."

She pulled down his underpants and he stepped out of them. She stood back, looked at him, touched his shaft and took off her stockings, slip, bodice, and knickers. He gripped her round the waist, feeling her belly with his cock. "Shall I put a sheath on?"

"No need. I'm perfectly clean, and a girl here knows how to protect herself. I've never had any problems."

They fell on the bed. She guided his erection into her and they both came, gasping and trembling, then separated and lay on their backs. He felt semen ooze onto his thigh and dribble onto the white sheet. He wondered what to do about it. Sex without a sheath was a bit messier but better feeling. Oh, boy!

She put her hand across his chest. "That was a bit sudden, but nice. Which positions do you like best?"

"What do you mean?"

"I'll show you. Let me come on top this time." She straddled his thighs and grasped his cock, teasing the foreskin over the glans. "Stroke my tits. Rub the nipples. That's nice."

She placed his shaft against her belly and, pushing up and down on her knees, rubbed him. She lowered herself onto him. The penetration was deep, and Sam shuddered. She moved slowly at first, then more quickly, threw back her head and fell forwards as they came.

She sat back and eased herself off him. "Here's a cloth."

He wiped the end of his cock, screwed up the cloth, and put it on the bedside table. "That was good. Let's do it again."

She played with his nipples. "How is it that you've got so little hair on your chest, but such a lot round your courting tackle and on your legs?"

"Don't know, must be coming from a cold climate."

"What was the girl on the ship like?"

"Nice, but not as nice as that. She was a nurse, going to work with missionaries."

"God help her, but he won't. Poor sods. Terrible places they work and they pick up awful diseases. Women and children die, and they convert about two people in ten years."

She reached for her cigarettes, put one in her mouth and one in Sam's and lit them.

"There's a big centre here. Mummy gives them old clothing. By the way, do you know they call man on top the missionary position? God knows why. I once fucked a missionary here. Terrible experience. His mind wasn't on it at all."

Sam laughed. "I can't smoke this fag. Too sweet. I'll get mine."

"And the girl in Shanghai?"

They lay on the bed smoking.

"That was just business."

She laughed. "Stub out your fag in this ashtray. "

They finished the champagne, taking it in turns to drink from the bottle.

She wiped her lips. "Listen, women here will tell you all sorts of things about the Shanghai clinch, the China, squeeze or the Geisha grip. It's all rubbish, in my view. It's the position that counts."

"How many positions do you know?"

"Dozens. We can try them all."

"How come you know all this?"

"Lots from a very experienced Italian who was supposed to be teaching me grammar in Venice; and you can get every sort of sex book here, and magazines full of naughty stuff. Very naughty. I'll tell you what I like. I love my breasts being squeezed round the nipples, and my clitoris stroked."

"What's that?"

"Let me show you. Put your finger on this little fleshy bump peeping out between these folds, and gently rub it. That's lovely."

He stroked her breasts and felt them tighten. He sucked the right nipple, the moved to the left. She moaned, put her tongue in his right ear, and flicked the inside. She stroked his upper body, then between his balls and buttocks. "Let's do the dog." She crouched on all fours. "Now come in from behind." He put his hands on her thighs and thrust inside her, moving from his hips. He came first.

She gasped, "Keep going," and fell forwards onto her arms. They rolled onto their sides, and slept, entwined, for an hour.

She woke first. "Are you hungry? It's nearly midnight."

"Starving, and I need a drink of water."

"I'll open some wine, too. Good French stuff. Here's a dressing gown and I'll put my knickers on. The maid has left chicken in a creamy sauce, noodles and vegetables, cheese and biscuits."

"I've never met anyone like you. I like it when you talk about sex. Even better when you do it. And you're posh."

"Can't help that. Posh doesn't matter a lot sometimes." She giggled. "I have to say, a policeman, particularly one so handsome and well built, with those sexy eyes, makes a change."

They ate at the table, then sat on the settee, drinking red wine with the cheese. The dressing gown flapped round Sam's wrists. He rolled up the sleeves and looked at a teak cabinet. "Who are all these photographs?"

She picked out three. "This is my parents and my sister, Davina, in front of our house."

He saw a tall man in a boater, blazer and flannels, a plump woman in a big hat and long skirt and a young woman who looked like Annabelle, but shorter. They stood on a trim lawn, by a Magnolia tree. "And this one is my brother up at Oxford."

The brother was handsome, with a black moustache and wearing a striped blazer and flannels. "He looks a bit like I imagine William Corder in the play."

She laughed. "Does bugger all except gamble."

"What does your sister do?"

"Fuck all. Gets bored. Has affairs, plays cards. Goes to parties and dinners with the terrible Clement." The third photograph was a man of about forty, standing with a gun under his arm and a dog at his side. In the background was a grand, stone building with columns at the entrance. "This is the man who wants to marry me and my parents want me to marry *him*. Lord Bostridge of Filton. He came out here on some diplomatic mission – Daddy met him at a dinner. Here he is in front of his mansion in North Yorkshire. Pots of money. In the House of Lords since his father died four years ago. We're supposed to be getting engaged. What do you think?"

"Do *you* want to marry *him*?"

"Don't know. Only met him a few times, once out here a few months ago, a couple of times in England. Nearly twice my age. Never married. Wants a son, of course. Maybe he's a queer boy. He kissed me on the cheek when we last parted. He writes to me every week about his shooting and going to drinks or parties and what he does in the House of Lords. Sounds ghastly. I'm supposed to be going to England next year to see if it works out. Have some more wine."

They went back into the bedroom. "Lick me down there."

He crouched over her and tasted a mixture of salt and sweetness. She came immediately, pushed her nails into his shoulders, then crouched between his thighs, put his cock in her mouth and licked and sucked the end.

He felt the spurt of sperm. She spat into a handkerchief. "Some people never try that. What do you think?"

"It's all right but I like coming into you best."

"Sit on this chair," she said, "and I'll crouch on your thighs. You can kiss my breasts whilst you're in." She rubbed against him, raised herself, paused, and slid onto his shaft. He sucked her nipples and held her buttocks as she moved on him. As she came, she flung her arms round him. He arched and fell back in the chair. They walked naked into the dining room and ate cakes, with a sweet wine.

Sam felt his eyes closing. "I'm starving, and I've never eaten with no clothes on."

"It's all that exercise. Let's get some sleep, and then we'll have breakfast. The maid has the day off. What time do you have to go?"

"I'm on duty at four this afternoon and I need to get ready. They think I'm in barracks, but my mate and the coolie will make up some story."

They slept until nine when she brought him a glass of orange juice. "Freshly squeezed, to build up your strength."

Her hair was combed and she wore a black, silk dressing gown, embroidered with chrysanthemums.

"There's that flower again," he laughed.

He stood up. "Nice and big again," she said, "let me curl round you whilst we stand."

She ran her forefinger round the tip of his cock. He stroked her breasts, thighs, and clitoris.

He lifted her to grasp his waist with her legs; she put her arms round his neck and he entered.

They both moved quickly then kissed as she lowered herself.

They wiped themselves. "You're bloody strong," she said. "I'll bet you could do any position. Let's have breakfast first."

He put on the dressing gown and followed her into the dining room, his hand between her legs.

She wriggled. "Stop it. That's for later."

She fried eggs and ham. "Do you like your job?"

"Yes. There are some good lads. It's a bit boring at times, but hard work now, with this emergency."

"Every day in the papers there are reports of crimes – murders and shootings and kidnappings. There's stuff hushed up in the police, too, I bet. There's fighting outside Shanghai all the time, and sometimes it comes into the city. My Chinese poet always said that, according to one of their leaders, Sun Yat somebody, foreigners were just guests here and that we were all dancing to destruction because the Japs had their eyes on taking over."

"That's why we're here. To control crime in the Settlement."

She laughed. "Don't be so serious. My poet thought we should all be out. He was very intense. He said he would be in trouble with either the nationalists or the Japanese one day. I think he's gone to Canada. Daddy worries about us. I don't know how long he'll stay, although he's making a fortune. Mummy is scared. She daren't go out except sometimes in the car to one of her fancy shops or a hotel for tea."

"I know about the troubles, but you can't go around worrying all the time. The police and army are well trained and well armed. It's just that the gangsters are so determined."

She leaned over the table and pulled back his dressing gown. "You have a fantastic body. All muscle. Let's try the wheelbarrow."

"What the hell's that?"

"I crouch on my hands with my back to you. You lift me and hold my thighs whilst I wrap my legs round your waist. The rest is easy. Provided you're nice and stiff, like you are."

When they had finished, he lowered her. "But I can't see your face doing that one," he said, "I like watching you."

"I know, but it takes longer because there's more effort in keeping the position. My arms get tired though. Let's not bother with that one again."

He had a bath in a sweet smelling lotion which bubbled around his body. He watched his cock float, limp, amongst the suds, stepped out of the bath, sprinkled talcum under his arms and between his legs and dressed.

"God you smell like a pansy. Don't let any blokes near you. See you at rehearsal next Thursday. When are you next off duty?"

"Friday night and Saturday morning. Unless things get worse."

He walked back to the Station and went into the canteen for tiffin of roast beef and potatoes and roly-poly pudding. Two officers joined him.

"You look a bit rough," said one.

"And what's that sweet smell?" asked the other. "Where've *you* been?"

"Out for a walk. I need to change. On duty in six hours."

He gave his shirt and underwear to Wang to take to the laundry, lay on the bed, and slept. He dreamed about Annabelle, head thrown back, straddling him. He woke with an erection. What a girl. Where else would you find this? Better than by the canal or in the woods in Warren.

8

Sam and Eddie met for a drink at the Carlton café in November. Sam ordered whisky. "God, it's cold and damp. Reminds me of home."

"Me too. I can't wait to get back next spring. Jean is saving up for the wedding. How are you getting on? Been to see Jasmine recently?"

"No. Involved with somebody else. Met her at the dramatic club. I'm in a play. Sergeant Davidson landed me with it."

"Is she a looker?"

"I'll say."

"When's the play? Can I come?"

"You wouldn't want to. They call it Victorian melodrama."

"What the hell's that? How's work?"

"I'm OK. Good Chinese lads to work with. Some rough stuff. Mate of mine injured last week. Not serious, but he's off duty for a while. How about you?"

"Some tricky stuff coming up. We think we've found an opium scam. Fighting in the Chinese sector – you know that area, Chaipei, I pointed out to you. Refugees coming into the Settlements again. Look at all these barricades. Four of our Chinese lads killed last week. They don't ever want to lose face, like I said."

"I know. I've seen funeral processions."

"You'll see more. I have to go. I'll pay. Let's get together before

Christmas. Don't forget to send Christmas cards and stuff early, and do it from the main post office, otherwise they'll take years."

Sam sent cards, bought at a shop on Foochow Road and made of parchment, with pictures of reindeer, chimneys, Father Christmas and "Gretings from China" printed along the top edge. He pushed in an extra "e" with thick pencil into "Greetings" and thought they would do. He sent Chinese embroidered gowns to his mother and sisters. There was nothing in the market that would fit his mother, but she would enjoy showing the material to neighbours. He found a curved pipe in ceramic for his father, a wallet for Derek and a Chinese puppet for Jimmy – a coolie with moving arms and legs and a nodding head. He sent a tablecloth to Billy and Maureen Wigg and a wooden duck for baby Eric.

A knitted pullover and socks arrived from England with a note from his mother, saying, "We miss you, Sam. It won't be the same." Jimmy had made a card with a drawing of the family under paper chains, and a spiky fir tree decorated with coloured balls.

Sam closed his eyes tightly and put the card to his lips. He imagined them having Christmas lunch then playing cards. His ma would have her annual port and lemon, his father two glasses of whisky, his brothers beer, and his sisters shandy. Auntie Nellie would visit, would say that drink didn't agree with her, and then have several glasses of gin and orange.

* * *

The dress rehearsal for *Maria Marten* was held in St Ignatius Church Hall on 23 December in preparation for the performance in the British Consulate on Boxing Day. Coolies brought the costumes in hampers from Jeremy's apartment. Snow blew in gusts, and frost crisped the insides of windows. The hall echoed as the players stamped on bare planks and flapped their arms. Sam helped to unload the hampers.

Annabelle arrived wearing a fur coat and matching hat. "Bloody hell. I don't feel like taking anything off in here."

"Look, darling," said Jeremy, "I've ordered some heaters and it will get warmer. Women in the room on the left, men on the right. Let's get on with it."

Sam, as William Corder, wore a suit in green tweed with lines of brown. It was too large, but very fine, he thought – waistcoat, jacket with leather buttons, tight trousers, leather boots, and a shooting hat. Just like an English toff. He carried a pipe and had a long, stiff moustache attached to his upper lip which tickled. He posed and pushed out his chest. "I want to sneeze with this tickling my nose. I suppose I'll get used to it."

Annabelle leaned against him "My God, I could really fancy you in that. You look like an advert from *The Gentleman*."

He put his fingers to his lips. "Shh."

Annabelle, as Maria, wore a simple, long dress of cotton, a cardigan, and a bonnet. The men wore smocks and baggy trousers in rough cloth, the women blouses and billowing skirts. Sam borrowed a policeman's uniform for Donald who played Constable Pharos Lee.

"Not quite a country bobby's outfit," said Donald, "and a bit big. What do they feed you chaps on?"

"It will have to do," said Jeremy, "roll up the cuffs and hitch the trousers. Now you all know what you're doing. The stage at the Consulate will be lower than this. In fact it's just a high step up, but you'll be fine. Now, Sam, you are supposed to get booed, OK. You are a murderer and seducer, so be as nasty as you can, like you were in rehearsal. The louder they boo, the better you will have done."

"Who exactly is coming to this?" asked Donald.

"The Consul has invited some senior staff, a couple of wealthy Chinese, including the Jung brothers, Mr Sassoon, but I think he's abroad, business people, army and navy high-ups. About fifty in all. I don't know what the Chinese will make of Victorian melodrama. You are all invited to stay on for a dinner afterwards. Loads of food and booze."

"Are your mum and dad coming?" Sam asked Annabelle.

"They always come, not to see me, you understand, but to do the social mix business."

"I'm not used to this sort of thing. Never been to a fancy dinner. Do I have to stay?"

"You'll be fine. My sister will fancy you, but she'll be with the cardboard man. No marines in sight. The actors will have a separate table, so you don't have to dress up. Don't be scared of all the knives and forks, just work inwards. I'll have to sit with the parents, probably next to the ghastly Clement. If anyone talks to you, just smile and ask them about themselves. They can talk about that forever. Then say a pleasure to meet you, or some such rubbish. Anyway, they'll be too busy showing off. They'll all be in their finery, Sir this and Lady that."

* * *

Jeremy clapped his hands. "A straight run-though. We don't have a violin for the gypsy lament, so just do your best. Go."

"Fantastic," he said after the first Act. Annabelle opened the second with Maria in the Marten's kitchen:

I wonder if William will call today. How miserable I feel. I cannot tell why it should be so but I have an appalling premonition of some impending tragedy. My nights are sleepless and I think constantly of my poor child in heaven...

Sam entered: *Curse the girl...*

A boom and the sound of gunshots came from outside.

"Bloody hell," shouted Jeremy, "Get under the chairs."

Sam ran for the door and looked down the street. A barricade had been knocked over and he smelled petrol. Smoke rose from the pavement in dark clouds. Three Chinese police constables stood holding guns. A European sergeant inspected the jagged holes in the sandbags.

Sam ran towards him. "I'm a policeman. What's happening?"

"Are you kidding, mate? I don't recognise you. Anyway it's OK. Three bastards tried to jump over the barricade and let off a bomb –

only small, thank God. Two ran off into an alley. One's shot dead, lying over there. Don't bloody touch anything. We'll call in reinforcements. Get back to your church service, whoever you are."

Sam breathed slowly and went back into the church. "Nothing to worry about, everything under control."

"Did you have to do that," Annabelle yelled, "you're not even armed, for Christ's sake."

"Annabelle," said Jeremy, "remember you're on church premises."

Annabelle took Sam's hand and squeezed it. "I want to kiss you," she whispered.

Sam dropped her hand and went to find his script. "Let's carry on. It just shows how careful you have to be. But we're experienced at that sort of thing."

They finished the play. Jeremy waved his hands. "OK. That was excellent. Time for food. I've ordered some to be delivered in ten minutes. Now you know where to turn up on Boxing Day. Get there in plenty of time, and don't drink too much of the champagne they'll offer."

* * *

On Christmas Eve, Central Station held a party and invited those officers not on duty from around the International Settlement. The room had been decorated with tinsel and balloons. Fifty men arrived, all on standby, and ready to replace others on duty for Christmas Day. They pulled crackers and ate beef with Yorkshire pudding, and Christmas cake, and sang carols round a Christmas tree. The Chinese knew "Silent Night" and "Good King Wenceslas," and sang loudly.

"I am Buddhist," said Gāo, "but I like to sing English hymns. Good breathing practice. In February, we celebrate Chinese New Year. I explain it to you, sergeant."

Just before midnight, Sam left. He walked to Holy Trinity Cathedral on Jiujiang Road, near the Huangpu Garden – barred to the Chinese.

Annabelle said there was always a midnight carol service which she and her family usually attended, but this year they were at the Shanghai

Club for dinner. He walked though streets blocked at intersections by barricades and was stopped twice. He showed his pass and said he would pray for them all.

The red bulk of the cathedral loomed in the dark under the pale of a sickle moon. He found the door under a high arch. The foundation stone, inserted in the wall to one side, said 1866. The interior was vaulted, with a high altar and a carved wooden pulpit with brightly painted nativity figures on the floor underneath. He had read that the cathedral was designed by a British architect, and was the oldest church in China.

The service had started and he heard "Hark! The Herald Angels Sing," with choir and organ. He took a place in a pew at the back. The cathedral was almost full, just like in England he thought. People who never usually went to church liked to sing carols on Christmas Eve. He smelled the melting wax of candles and soft incense.

He had not been in a church since leaving home. This was much grander than St Barnabas in Warren. He thought about how life had changed. No regrets except that he would like to see his family once in a while. So far away.

He knew that his mother and sisters and brothers would go to St Barnabas in about ten hours time. His mother would put on her old, baggy coat and her hat with the paste diamond brooch. She would pray for him and cry. Then she would be up at dawn to start preparing Christmas lunch. They would have a "right good do" as his father always said; then he would shuffle and deal the cards for rummy, saying "No cheating." Auntie Nellie would hold the cards between her teeth so that no one could see. Billy Wigg would be with his family. The baby would be getting big now.

This congregation was mainly European with one or two Chinese, perhaps converts of the striving missionaries. He picked up a hymn book, and joined in "The First Noel." The vicar spoke about working for peace in these troubled times and prayed for our mother countries and our families wherever they were. The service ended with "O Come, All Ye Faithful." The vicar walked to the door, followed by the verger carrying a cross and the choir in white robes. He waited to greet the congregation.

Sam wished the people in his pew a Merry Christmas, shook hands with the vicar and left to find a rickshaw to take him back to barracks. His eyes pricked and he blew his nose into a vast handkerchief, lit a cigarette, offered the driver one, then gave him the pack. "Merry Christmas," the driver said in English. Sam gave him an extra tip.

He went to his room, sat on the bed, head on his folded arms, then had a strong whisky. He slept until six, put on his uniform, checked his gun, had breakfast and went to meet his constables at the duty desk.

"Merry Christmas," they said and gave him a little jade statue of a Buddha, and a picture of a crane and a turtle. "So you live long. These good luck signs."

"I'll treasure them. Here are some English cigarettes and a bottle of whisky for you."

They dealt with minor incidents – a shopkeeper's complaint about a neighbour's noise that put off customers, a theft in a clothing store, and a fight over some chickens.

The stores were decorated with bells, Christmas trees, and garlands, and the streets hung with tinsel and lanterns. He remembered that Warren Tower would have a light on its top, and the little houses below would be warm and bright with home-made decorations of twigs and pine cones and some glitter bought in Woolworths.

He led the patrol back to the Station at 6pm and had supper of rice and lamb, and a slice of fruit cake with icing, then went to the bar. The King's speech would be on at about five the next morning, Shanghai time. He knew that his family would sit round and listen as they always did. He wondered what the King would say about Britain struggling with poverty and unemployment, before ending with "God bless you all."

He went to bed after five whiskies and wondered what future there could be with a posh girl like Annabelle. Not marriage, for sure. She wasn't the girl the old fortune teller had predicted. He would just enjoy life. Good money, good job, plenty of women. The only thing missing was his family.

* * *

Sam and his officers were on duty the morning of Boxing Day, but off for the afternoon. He went for a lunch of noodles and chicken at the Station, read his lines in *Maria Marten* again, and thought he had better, to look smart, take a taxi to the British Consulate on the Bund.

"Only official cars allowed in, sir," said the driver.

Sam got out and paid him at the iron gates, which were guarded by two Sikhs carrying rifles. He showed his temporary pass, given to all the actors, and walked along the central path between lawns and shrubs. He watched his breath, white in the cold, as he ran through his lines silently. Bare willow trees and glossy firs grew round the white building, with square windows, chimneys, and a pillared entrance. A Packard with broad curved mudguards and a Union Jack on the bonnet was parked in front of the door. He was early, but a Chinese waiter in evening dress holding out a tray of drinks greeted him.

"Champagne, sir? My colleague will take you to the players' dressing rooms. Sam took a glass and was led by another waiter along passages lined with red silk chairs, and settees in green and gold, until they reached a large room set out with smaller chairs and a raised dais at one end. "This where you do the play." They went through a side door to another passage with rooms off.

"Here you are, sir. This is where the men will change, this for the ladies."

Sam gulped down his champagne and looked at the costumes laid out on chairs. He changed into his William Corder suit and looked at himself in the mirror. The others arrived, put on their costumes and make-up and admired each other.

Jeremy had told them never to say good luck to your fellow players; it was "Break a leg."

"Why?" asked Jeff.

Jeremy sniffed. "An old tradition in many cultures."

"Does that include Chinese?" asked Donald, wallowing in his police uniform.

"Don't be daft," said Sam, "and turn the cuffs up."

"Here we go," said Jeremy at 6.30pm. "The Consul is going to pop in and say hello. We'll go into the women's room for that. Much nicer smell. Then we're on."

Mr Sydney Barton, the Consul, came in wearing evening dress with a dark sash over his right shoulder, a red cummerbund, and medals. "I am happy to welcome you again," he said, "there is a very good audience tonight. Mr Sassoon is, unfortunately, abroad, but everyone else is here. I look forward to your play and to hosting the dinner afterwards. Do come and join us for a while. Well done. Don't be nervous."

The play began with the maypole dance and the gypsy lament. The audience talked, clapped and a woman sitting at the front whispered, "How sweet."

Sam went on for his first scene with the gypsy. In front of him ladies sat in furs, tiaras, and flowing silk dresses, the men either in uniform or evening dress. He took a deep breath and began:

What have we here? By her dress I take her to be a common gypsy. They bring no pleasant memories to me, for once one of their dark-eyed beauties was partner of my journey to London. Psha! She is dead...

The audience clapped and cheered at the end of each scene. Some fell asleep but woke up for the applause. At the interval, when the audience went for a champagne reception, Jeremy came round to the dressing room.

"Bloody good. They love it. Annabelle, darling, remember don't go over the top in the last scenes. Sam, you're great. Just watch for Act Three, Scene Five where Corder confesses the murder to her father. Be as sentimental as you like."

Sam knelt to deliver the speech:

Mr Marten, your words have touched my heart. I will confess to you what I have denied to my judge… Just now as I slept I thought she came to me, not as I saw her in death at my feet but in all her radiant beauty…

A woman in the audience called: "Serve him right."

Sam spoke the last words: "*When murder stains a soul with fearful dye, then blood for blood is nature's dreadful cry.*"

A bell, borrowed from the fire station, was rung backstage. The audience stood and cheered and shouted "Bravo." The players bowed and left the stage to return one by one. Sam was booed and hissed. He stood stiffly, put his right hand across his chest and bowed. Jeremy kissed everyone, hugged Sam, and squeezed his biceps.

"I think we'll do *Lady Audley's Secret* next year. Photograph now, everybody."

Sam would send the photograph to Warren. Happen it would get in the local paper. He knew he had done well, and would now do other things with the group. It made a change from being on duty. And there was Annabelle.

In the reception room, Annabelle kissed her parents and her sister and introduced them to Sam. "Our new star."

"Well done, old boy," said her father.

"Very interesting," said her mother.

"Do you have much experience?" asked her sister, and winked.

He looked away. Clement, the cardboard man, held out his limp hand.

"What regiment are you?" asked a plump man in a tight suit.

"I'm a sergeant in the police."

"Good show. Bloody dangerous I'd have thought. I suppose somebody has to do it.

The Chinese don't count of course"

They proceeded to the dining room. Sam looked at the long table with its white cloth and champagne bottles sealed with crinkled foil and wire standing in buckets of ice. Tall vases of lilies and carnations flounced in the middle of the table. Rows of five knives and five forks of different sizes, and four glasses were on each side of the place settings, with a spoon and small fork across the top. Napkins were tucked in gold rings with the engraved crest of the Consulate. Sam could not understand why they needed so much cutlery and there were no crackers like they would have in Warren.

The players had a rectangular table, with a cream cloth, in the corner of the room. A bottle of white wine and a bottle of red were at either end of the table.

For the guests there was soup, pâté, fish, turkey, stuffing, roast potatoes, sprouts, and carrots followed by cheese and ending with a Christmas pudding, flaming in brandy sauce. A different wine was served with each course followed by port. The players had turkey, gravy, stuffing, and pudding.

Annabelle sent a note: "*After the meal, and the Consul's toast thank you speech, you will be invited to go to the small room for drinks. The lady guests will go to a parlour and the men to a smoking room for more port and cigars. I will leave at this point and wait for you outside. We'll take the car to my place and send it back here. Daddy and Mummy will be ages.*"

Sam crumpled the note, said he had to be on duty, waved goodnight, and left the table. Jeremy squeezed his wrist. "Lovely to have you. I'll be in touch about the next play. Take your costume with you and bring it to the hotel tomorrow for cleaning."

Annabelle gave instructions to the driver to drop them at the Sauvigny Apartments and return to the Consulate. She put her hand on Sam's chest. "Come on, let's do it in our Maria and Corder outfits."

They kissed in the lift, and ran along the corridor to her flat. They took off their clothes, but couldn't wait to put on the Corder and Maria outfits.

Sam left for the Station at three in the morning and was wakened at nine by Wang who brought tea and crispy rolls.

* * *

71

At the end of December, a blanketing snowstorm covered Shanghai. Branches fell from trees under the weight and traffic slowed between masses of white heaps.

Sam wrote to his mother on New Year's Day to thank her for the pullover and socks. He said he had bought a camera with some overtime bonus and that he had a girlfriend who was a nice homely lass from Surrey. That might stop her asking in every letter if he had found anyone nice yet, but she would want photographs. No chance.

The police officers built a snowman in the yard of the Station. They put a police cap on its head and hung a small Buddha round the neck. "Happy New Year, Happy 1925," they shouted and threw snowballs at each other.

9

Eddie Nicholson was killed in a bank raid on the Bund on the afternoon of 1 February. Sam was on duty with two Chinese constables when the news came through.

Sam sat on the step outside a shop and closed his eyes; they throbbed behind his lids. He stood and told the constables what had happened. "We are very sorry, sir. A good man."

Sam finished duty and went back to Yangtzepoo Station to ask Sergeant Davidson how Eddie was killed. "Shot in the head outside the Russian bank after killing four bandits. Two Chinese officers killed, too. It's happening more and more."

"Now what? He was my mentor and friend. Great bloke."

He imagined Eddie, bleeding from the head, stretched out dead in the snow. They had last met two days ago. Eddie was boasting about beating a Chinese constable at Mahjong.

"I know. You'd better sit down, Sam. You look pale. Take off your hat and have a brandy. We organise the funeral, with full honours. A Miss Hurst is named as next of kin. His parents are dead, apparently. There is also a brother, I believe. Miss Hurst will receive a telegram. Remember filling in those forms when we join up? Next of kin. Religion. That's so they know what to do if you're unlucky."

Poor, plump Jean, Sam thought, getting a telegram to learn that Eddie's been killed and would be buried a long way from Barnsley.

"I would like to write to Miss Hurst to tell her what a good bloke he was and I'd like to go to the funeral, if possible. When will he be buried?"

"You can go. You can be an escort. I'm told he was a Methodist, so they'll ask the pastor from the Mission to do the ceremony. He'll be buried in Bubbling Well Cemetery on Friday morning. The Chinese cops will have Buddhist ceremonies. The families and temples organise it and the police fund pays. It gets lower by the day."

* * *

Sam drove his motorbike alongside Eddie's hearse, protected by a heavy top coat and knee-length leather boots, breath clouds in the stinging air. Frost bristled on the bare branches of sycamore trees along Bubbling Well Road and a crow slurried a patch of snow from a branch.

Eddie's cedarwood coffin with brass handles was covered in the red, green, and white Shanghai Municipal Council flag, his cap placed on top, the badge flashing in the sharp sun. On the roof of the hearse a wreath of glossy tulips from the SMP glowed purple and green. Flowers from colleagues, the Municipal Council, the Police Forces from the French Concession, and the Chinese Sector were piled alongside.

Sam thought it a pity they couldn't have found white roses instead of tulips for a Yorkshire lad and wondered if Jean had received the telegram yet. He sent her a note with the newspaper cutting from the *Shanghai Post and Mercury*. Maybe it would make her feel better. He could not believe that this had happened. Once it had sunk in, he might feel better he supposed. But when would that be? He could not imagine Eddie not being there to talk to.

The procession moved slowly along Bubbling Well Road under a low, grey sky. They passed shops and two nightclubs, then houses, solid and columned with tall windows glinting in the brittle sun. Coolies in thin coats and soft felt hats were dragging dry leaves across the frosted grass; they stopped to watch the procession, leaning on wide wooden rakes. Sam wondered if one of these driveways and gardens was where Annabelle's parents lived.

Eddie had told him that Bubbling Well Road was named after a well near the temple Jing'An, meaning "tranquil repose". Eddie had liked the name and said it was supposed to be lucky to dip your hand in the water, even though it smelled of gas. You could make a wish, which he had on the anniversary of his engagement to Jean. He didn't say what he had wished for.

The Minister, in a plain black gown, greeted the cortège and led them into the graveyard chapel. More flowers had been placed in front of the pulpit. Sam noticed that there was a wreath from Madame Claudette. The chapel was packed with men in uniform from all branches of the force. The deputy commissioner paid tribute to Eddie and the inspector from Gordon Road read a passage from St John's Gospel.

The Minister stood. "This is a sad day. Another good man has been gunned down in the violence which is now so common. He will not be forgotten. We think of, and mourn with, his family and friends in England, and in particular, his fiancée. Let us sing Psalm 23, 'The Lord is My Shepherd'." After the hymn, the mourners droned "Our Father, which art in heaven…"

Sam raised his head slowly and opened his eyes. He stood, stiff and straight, holding back tears. He wondered if Eddie had felt anything when he was shot, if he had thought anything. How terrible to be buried such a long way from home.

Eddie was lowered into a plot at the northern side of the cemetery. Sam noticed black granite gravestones, some new, of policemen who had died. The brown stalks of withered flowers, drooped, forlorn, in the snow. Dandelion leaves pushed through the turf in jagged rosettes and sparrows hopped and pecked at the frozen ground. As he bowed his head, Sam wondered if every country had sparrows and dandelions.

* * *

Annabelle returned from Hong Kong the day after Eddie's funeral. Sam called on her at the apartment after night duty. She opened the door wearing a pink silk dressing gown.

"Do you like this? I had three made in Hong Kong. I've bought you two silk shirts and a bottle of Chanel for your mother."

He stared past her. She closed the door. "What's the matter? You look pale. Have you missed me?"

He told her about Eddie. She sat, and pulled the gown around her. "Bloody hell, that's awful. Why don't you give up that crazy job? Daddy would take you on."

"What? As a security guard like a Russian? That's just as dangerous."

"You wouldn't have to do that. They would train you as a buyer."

He took off his coat. "It's not for me."

She poured two tumblers of whisky and pulled him into the bedroom. She took off her gown and began to undress him.

He pushed her away. "I just want to lie on the bed. Come next to me."

She put on the gown again, poured two whiskies and lit cigarettes. "I'm really sorry, you know. Perhaps a bit of action might help."

She began to open his flies and put her tongue in his ear.

He leaned away and sat up. "I'm not in the mood. I can't."

"Then why did you come here?"

"I wanted a bit of sympathy. I'm angry. He was a good man. I'd better not see you until I've calmed down."

She shrugged and gave him his coat. "You know where I am."

He left the flat and walked along the Avenue Pétain and into a small square in front of the Protestant church. In the flowerbeds, snowdrops peered at the ground, and shoots of crocus tipped with snow, pushed through the hard earth. Magnolia and camellia shrubs were in bud and he smelled the sweet blooms of tiny flowers springing from the bare branches of a tall shrub. He went into the chill of the church, sat in a pale wooden pew and looked at the blue ceiling painted with stars and thought about Eddie. They wouldn't go fishing or hunting together in the spring. They wouldn't have a laugh over a beer. Eddie wouldn't get his leave to marry Jean.

He left the church, found a bar, drank four beers and a whisky, smoked six cigarettes, then took a rickshaw to his room. He slept for eight hours. Wang woke him with strong tea at nine in the morning.

* * *

A week later Sam met Annabelle in Jimmy's Bar. She came in and kissed him on the cheek. "Still upset? I haven't seen you for a week."

"Sorry about the other night. I'm still upset. And I've been busy, trying to take my mind off things."

"Listen, these things happen. You know they do. China's in a terrible mess and it all seems to end up here. People are poor, people get killed. Just have a good time while you can."

"I do know, but I've never lost a close friend before. But I have missed you. Let's go back to your place soon. But let's eat first. I haven't eaten all day."

"Listen, I've been invited to a party at Ciro's – you know, the fancy nightclub – in a couple of weeks to celebrate Washington's Birthday. I want you to come with me. You'll need a dinner jacket and so on. It will do you good. It's very chic. On Bubbling Well Road, down from where Mummy and Daddy live. It's owned by Sassoon – that rich Jew boy. You'll see. Good dancing. Sexy Russian hostesses, so watch it. Some of my friends go there a lot."

"Ciro's is posh. What will I wear?

"We'll have to get you evening dress – not usually required but this is a special occasion."

"One of those penguin suits? They cost a fortune!"

"You've had a bad time. You deserve a treat. We'll get you one on Daddy's account at Marcel's in the Avenue Joffre. Daddy won't even notice. You should have one anyway. Some of the smarter clubs like formal wear."

"It doesn't seem fair to use your dad's account, although I'd like to go to posh places, now I know about the knives and forks. What would they think in Warren? Me, all dressed up."

"You'll look wonderful. Let's go back now. I can't wait to get those clothes off you."

"I'll stay the night."

* * *

Sam was measured for an evening suit and dress shirt by Marcel himself. It would be ready for fitting in three days.

He admired himself in the long mirror, turned, pulled the jacket close and looked at the back view. He thought his bum and thighs looked good in this.

He turned to Annabelle. "What do you think?"

She raised her eyes to the lights and sighed. "Marvellous. You'll be a big success."

"And I'll wear the cufflinks my dad gave me. What are you going to wear?"

"Something fantastic, with feathers. Low cut. I want the other women to look dull."

"They will." He smiled.

Sam finished duty at 5pm, went to the gym where he lifted weights and hit a punchbag for twenty minutes, slept for two hours, and dressed to meet Annabelle. He unwrapped the evening suit from its tissue paper. He stroked the material of the shirt, shook out the jacket and trousers and wondered if he would remember how to handle the bow tie. He hummed and dressed slowly, then looked in the small mirror to smear oil on his hair and part it on the left side. He struggled with the bow tie and sighed when he thought it looked right. He shaved, felt his face and wondered if he was putting on weight – he must watch the after-duty beers and the cakes, and eat fewer dumplings. He tapped the side of his nose and thought he might grow a moustache, like some of the European and American businessmen.

He met Denis Gee, on the stairs. "Where are you off to looking so dapper? Fancy a beer before you go? I've got a couple of hours off, thank God. I could do with a bit of time off. No chance until next week."

"No, thanks. Off to meet a young lady. Won't be late. I'm on early tomorrow. Don't get in the way of anything."

"I'll try not to."

10

Sam took a rickshaw to Annabelle's apartment. She opened the door. "Have a glass of bubbly before Bashir comes to pick us up."

"You look grand, and the perfume smells lovely. I shall be very proud to be with you. Both of us looking such toffs."

"I love the suit. It makes you so distinguished. Hair oil, nice. Nobody would ever guess you were a policeman."

"Or where I came from." He laughed.

They drove along Bubbling Well Road. Sam looked round. "I came up here to Eddie's funeral. I remember passing all these big houses and gardens. It was colder then; the trees were all stiff and bare. It's nice to see a few buds. I wondered where your family lives."

"It's further on. Designed by some famous architect, all curved staircases, fireplaces, and stained glass. Wonderful garden with two magnolia trees just outside the front door. You saw them in the picture, remember? Here we are."

Canopies extended into the road outside Ciro's. Swing doors with brass fittings led into the lobby, thickly carpeted in red. On each side of the door stood two tall, surly guards, wearing red jackets, bow ties, and peaked caps with braid and badges.

Annabelle smiled. "Our friendly Russians. I'll take my wrap with me. Let's go in. I'll just give them Daddy's credit number."

The broad, high room was noisy. Chandeliers hung across the centre and reflected in the dark wooden dance floor. A Russian band, The Moscow Knights, played popular songs. Tables were crowded with couples or small groups of men. Dancers swayed to "Remember." Cigarette and cigar smoke swirled into the smell of wine, beer, and whisky.

Hostesses in long slit skirts, with tight fitted waists served drinks and asked men if they wanted to buy dance tickets. Annabelle nudged Sam. "See that. Once the poor sucker has bought a ticket and had his dance, she'll ask him to pay for champanska at his table. She'll bring ginger beer or something, and so it goes on. They're nearly all Russian hostesses, a few American and Chinese."

She looked round through the smoke. "There are David and Ralph, they're fun."

She kissed them on both cheeks. They stood to shake hands with Sam.

"You're the copper who's an actor, aren't you?"

Sam nodded. "You look a bit different tonight, although I must say you did look good in that Corder suit. We know Jeremy quite well. A good chum."

David offered cigarettes and ordered champagne. "The real stuff, this. I've been caught out with the old story before and paid a fortune for ginger beer. But the hostesses here really are something, don't you think?"

Sam nodded. "They're very pretty."

"You're looking wonderful, Annabelle," said Ralph, "new?"

Annabelle stood and twirled to show her blue silk dress with matching bag and shoes. "Hong Kong. Expensive, but worth it. Glad you like it."

Ralph bought two dance tickets and went off with a tall, blonde, brown-eyed hostess, with high cheekbones and a long face. He came back to the table. "Gorgeous woman. These Russians have a hard time. She is supporting her whole family. I slipped her a bit extra and said no to champanska. She asked if she could do anything else for me, but I probably couldn't afford it. A bit low on cash at the moment."

Annabelle put her hand on his cheek. "Watch it. You know what they're after. It's not your body, it's your passport."

Sam offered cigarettes. "Someone told me the Russians are good at suffering."

David threw back his head and blew out smoke. "You can say that again. The stories I've heard about sick children, five sisters, brothers who can't get work, starving mother and father."

Ralph sipped his champagne. "Some of it's probably true."

A singer took the microphone and began "Deep in My Heart". Her long, silver dress shimmered, one long leg extended through the split of the skirt. Silver gloves stretched to the elbows and her hands caressed the microphone. Silver shoes with six inch heels tapped and swivelled.

Annabelle leaned across the table. "You know the secret of that husky voice, don't you? It's a man dressed as a woman."

Ralph looked at the singer. "What, with those legs and tits?"

"Easily done. Razors and padding."

Sam raised his glass. "I don't believe it."

The singer walked round the room, offering her cleavage as a money box. She wore thick eyeshadow, lipstick, and peach-coloured foundation, her hair, blonde and stiff with lacquer, swept back into a French pleat. Sam peered at her face to see if there was any facial stubble.

"What's your name?"

"Susie. Just put the money there, and no touching."

She went back onto the platform and sang "It Had to Be You." She winked, swayed and caressed the microphone.

Annabelle crossed her arms on the table and put her head down. "My God. Give me some more champagne – fast."

Sam and Annabelle danced a foxtrot. He guided her across the room in long strides.

"Where did a poor boy like you learn to dance?"

"Local youth clubs like the Co-op and Saturday nights at King George's Hall in Burnside, next town to where I lived," he replied. "I like dancing, especially with women."

She slapped his hand. "Naughty. Let's get some more champagne."

He held her waist as she swayed back. He looked at her and wondered how he could have been so lucky. It was good to forget, for a while, what was going on down the streets of Shanghai.

"I have to go soon. I'm on duty at six o'clock in the morning."

"Let's have one last dance, then you take the car and send Bashir back. I'll stay. Those two will look after me." Sam leaned back and looked at her.

She smiled. "Nothing to worry about, they fancy each other more than me."

He held her shoulder. "Not again."

"That's right. Maybe it is time you went anyway. That Russian whore over there is giving you the eye."

He looked round and saw a small, slender woman smiling and holding a tray. Her dark hair waved into her neck around jade earrings and a matching necklace. A blue velvet dress draped her figure. The colour matched wide, oval eyes, enhanced by blue eyeshadow. Her face was round, with prominent cheekbones, tinted with soft rouge. She twitched a smile, mouth closed, towards their table, came towards them, and leaned over to talk to David and Ralph.

David bought a dance ticket and held the woman's arm. She raised her elbows and placed one gloved hand on his right shoulder, the other in his left hand. They moved across the floor and came alongside Sam and Annabelle. The woman stared at Sam without blinking. She smiled and, he thought, closed one eye.

David came back to the table. "What a fascinating woman. Such a sad history."

Annabelle shrugged. "They all have. It goes with the fake jewels."

Sam saw the woman approach another table. "What's her name?"

"Lulu, but I don't think that's her real name."

Annabelle raised her eyes. "You bet. Go on, Sam, get your beauty sleep and watch out for all the bad men. See you at the weekend."

He shook hands with David and Ralph. Annabelle kissed him, putting her tongue between his lips. He moved towards the door. The Russian hostess turned to face him as he left. She smiled again.

11

In the middle of March, the chief commissioner of police called an emergency meeting at Central Station to brief officers on military problems outside Shanghai.

"The railway between Shanghai and Nanking has been cut off. Britain has put a ban on arms to China. Questions are being asked in Parliament. American, British, French, and Japanese marines have been landed from gunboats on the Huangpu. I'm afraid we have to cut down all police leave. It's always the same. Trouble ends up on our doorstep and crime increases. Make sure you carry a gun, even off duty."

"It seems daft," Denis Gee said to Sam over a beer, "when cinemas are showing Charlie Chaplin films, newspapers advertising cocoa, corsets and shoes, with four pages of weddings, and a fancy dress party at St Joseph's."

Sam laughed and ordered two whiskies. "And business still good in nightclubs, brothels and bars. Have a fag."

* * *

On 1 April, Sam and his Chinese officers were called out to investigate a call from a diamond store on Nanking Road. They put on bulletproof vests, and prepared their guns for rapid firing.

Sam smiled. He wondered how he could make the men feel calmer. "We call this April Fools' Day in England."

The van stopped at the corner of Nanking Road. The Chinese looked at him, shifted in their seats, straightened their collars and felt their guns. He pulled up his collar. "You play a joke, like saying a dog's following someone. They turn round and there's no dog there. You say April Fool. Or you pretend to be asleep and someone comes to waken you. You snore. They look at you. You open your eyes and say April Fool."

"Why you do that?" asked Jiǎng.

"Just a tradition."

"We have sayings," said Xǔ, "like 'a sharp arrow still needs a strong bow.'"

"Is that Confucius again? Wise bloke."

"Now, listen. No business about losing face. Just be careful."

They jumped out, drew their guns and slid round the corner, looking round.

Beggars and rickshaw coolies stood looking at the gashed window pane of the jewellery store. Thick glass was shattered on the pavement. The constables looked through the window, guns ready. Shelves and display cabinets were scattered and two bodies, streaked with blood, sprawled between. A single earring glistened in a patch of red under the window.

"It's very quiet," said Yuán, "they must still be inside, perhaps opening the safe."

The door was locked. Shěn and Zōu stayed on guard outside and tried to keep onlookers away. Sam and Yuán climbed through the jagged spikes of the window. They climbed over the bodies, one on his front, arms and legs spread, the other on his back, eyes open, glazed, and staring.

"That's Mr Feng," said Xǔ, "he's been robbed before."

The floor was sticky with blood. Bony dogs licked it, and ran their tongues over red whiskers.

Yuán kicked them out of the way. Three men ran from the back of the shop, carrying sacks and firing. Sam shot two of them. They fell, and slid through the blood.

"Watch out for someone hiding in the back," called Sam.

Yuán peered into the dimness behind the counter. "That's all."

They climbed back out of the window. A car drew up with two masked men inside, shooting rapidly. Zōu shot the driver who fell across the wheel. Shěn was hit and fell amongst shards of glass.

"Cover me," Sam yelled. He turned, grabbed Shěn round the shoulder and, still shooting with his left hand, dragged him round the corner to the van. The firing from the car stopped.

Shěn was bleeding from the left thigh. Sam covered him with his coat and put his hand over the wound. Blood crept through his fingers.

"I've called the ambulance, said Zōu, "Is he bad?"

"Yes. I think the bullet went through an artery in his leg. He's unconscious but breathing."

He took off his cap and pressed it on the wound. The blue serge became dark purple.

More police arrived, inspected the interior of the shop and stood guard outside. Shěn was lifted onto a stretcher.

"There's a few bits and pieces of jewellery around," said the officer in charge, "all a bit sticky. I'll wrap them up and put them into bags with the loot and stuff from the cabinets, otherwise there'll be looters. I'll put some guards on here."

An ambulance arrived, followed by a van to collect the bodies. Sam and Yuán went with Shěn in the ambulance to the General Hospital on Soochow Road. Sam placed his hand on Shěn's chest and felt him breathing unevenly. His eyes were closed and his skin tight and pale.

Sam held his hand. "Just breathe deeply. You'll be OK. We're near the hospital."

A doctor examined Shěn on the operating table. "He has at least one bullet lodged in his thigh and has lost a lot of blood. But he'll live. The pulse is strong. He might need a transfusion. We'll give him oxygen, then operate as soon as we can. You can go now. Come back later if you want."

Shĕn opened his eyes and looked at Sam: "April Fool."

Sam patted his arm. "I'll be back later."

Sam handed his report to Sergeant Davidson, who scanned it. "That store's been asking for trouble for a while. He wouldn't pay protection money."

Sam took off his cap and pressed it. Drops of blood fell on the floor.

Davidson handed him a cloth to wipe them. "You did well. You will all be commended for bravery. This will go on your record and will help your promotion chances. Go and have a cup of tea, or something stronger. Then get changed. Take the rest of the day off. I know leave's been cut, but we can manage. And get your uniform cleaned. They're used to dealing with blood. You might need a new cap, though."

"Thank you, sir, I've never been in anything as bad as that. First time I've had to kill."

"You'll get used to it. Forget the tea. Have a strong whisky."

That evening, Sam went back to the hospital with a bunch of chrysanthemums. Shĕn was awake, his leg wrapped in bandages and supported in a sling. "Nice flowers. I think you call them chrysanthemum."

"Yes, and no one can spell it, except me."

"You teach me."

"Yes, but not now."

"He'll be here for a day or two," said the doctor, "we need to keep an eye on him. His wife has been. She wanted to thank you for saving her husband. Are YOU all right? I know this is happening all the time, but just watch out for shock."

"I'll be fine."

"You very brave," said Shĕn "I want you to come to my house to say thank you. We make you special meal with Chinese wine."

"It would be an honour."

"It our tomb sweeping ceremony on 4 April. You know this? We clean graves of ancestors and leave food and flowers. Big holiday for Chinese. I not in grave thanks to you."

Sam went back to the Station. Shěn's wife had left him some cakes to say thank you.

Sam went to change in his room. Wang shuffled in. "You all right, sir?"

"Get me a whisky. Thanks."

The blood had dried and made the serge of his jacket and trousers stiff. His cap felt like cardboard. He struggled to unfasten the badge, then handed it to Wang who shook his head and said, "Badge stuck in blood. I cut off. You lucky head not like this. Very bad men."

"Just see if they can clean the jacket and trousers by tomorrow, or see where the spares are. The boots need a good scrub and I need a shower."

Sam found his team and shared out the cakes. "Well done, everybody. Shěn's OK."

"You know, sir," said Xŭ, "another Confucius saying is 'To have saved one human life is worth more than to build a pagoda with seven storeys.'"

"I like that. I'm going to write it down."

* * *

He went to Annabelle's apartment at midnight. "God," she said, "you look terrible again. Who's dead this time?"

"No one except some robbers" said Sam, "but it could have been worse." He told her about the attempted robbery.

"Bloody hell, that was brave. Have a whisky and better get that smoking gun into the bedroom." She brought him breakfast in bed.

12

Wang brought Sam's uniform back from the cleaners, did the washing and cleaned his shoes.

"Another cap, sir. Old one gone for rubbish. I put badge in new one."

"Thanks, Wang. You look after me very well."

He wouldn't say anything about the troubles in letters home, except perhaps to Billy Wigg, just to show a bit of excitement. He said he was having a good time and had been to a dance which reminded him of King George's Hall.

* * *

He received a reply from Eddie's girl. The handwriting was worse than Ma's. It sloped across the thin paper like a jagged trail of ants.

She thanked him for his letter and for the newspaper cutting and said how proud they all were of Eddie. Killed so near his birthday, too. His brother Pete had said that going to China wouldn't do him any good and he was right. Sam stopped and read the next part of the letter twice. What with Eddie being so far away, she had met another lad and they were planning to get married when they had saved up. Eddie's pension would help and it was what he would have wanted. And, at last, spring was on its way.

That evening, Sam told Annabelle about the letter.

"Let me read it," she said.

"It's back at the Station. Anyway, that wouldn't be right. It's a terrible thing to do, go off with another bloke like that and use Eddie's money to get wed."

"Don't be so shocked. That's life. What else could she do, poor cow, she probably doesn't get much fun."

"If I got killed, would you be off with somebody else straight away?"

"Sam, Sam, it's a way of coping. You have to do something, not get stuck. That's what Joan or whatever she's called, is doing. What do you think *you* would do if *I* got killed or just died?"

"That's different. Anyway, I wouldn't dash off with somebody else straight away."

"Eddie had been away for a long time. She got lonely. She didn't dash off straight away."

"It's not right. I wouldn't just forget somebody like that."

"You sometimes have to. You'll grow lots of layers of skin, Sam. I can see them starting already. What about that girl on the boat?"

"That was just a bit of fun."

* * *

In May, the heat and humidity came in, and, with them, the mosquitoes, flies, and midges.

Sam hung curls of sticky fly paper in his room. Every evening, Wang threw them out, strewn with black bodies. The nights were airless and Sam found the mosquito net oppressive. The small fan in his room only circulated hot air. He itched from heat rash behind his knees, under his arms and in his groin. Trees fluffed into fronds of green. He could smell camphor under his window and purple flowers pushed through the thick clay soil in the gardens.

Shěn came back on duty. He and Sam walked through a park,

clearing beggars. Sam bent down to smell a rose. "I never knew these grew here. Lovely smell."

"Oh yes. Long time here. Many kinds. Also Russian nursery grow."

"Did you give them to your wife for Valentine's Day?" asked Sam.

"No, too expensive, but we do have a day like that, called Qixi, but in seventh month. I give chocolate."

"I gave my girlfriend lilies. Lovely smell."

"You bring your girlfriend to my house, too," said Shěn.

"Maybe. But she's very busy."

* * *

The SMP now wore the summer uniform of khaki shorts, shirts, and caps with knee-length beige socks and brown boots. The Chinese did not wear shorts.

Sam asked why the Chinese did not wear shorts.

"Not like to show legs," said Shěn. "Too thin."

"Your knees can't be any worse than mine. Bit more knobbly happen."

The constables stared at him. Sam thought his own knees looked very white and wondered how soon they would tan. One of his mates, Dave, in Lancashire used to put gravy browning on his face and arms to look like a tan. They had all laughed when it smeared and ran onto his shirt.

Leave restrictions were lifted. On days off, men borrowed rifles and tackle from the police store and took the police barge, *The Catherine*, to hunt and fish on the creeks beyond Soochow. Sam wished he had brought his own rod. Maybe little brother Jimmy was now playing with it. He hoped it wouldn't get ruined.

* * *

Sam, two officers and two coolies packed sausages, pies, and cool beer in boxes of ice, and put them into hampers. Three lurchers were borrowed from the kennels to gather the game.

Partridge, pigeons, teal, and snipe soared from the ground as the coolies beat the undergrowth. Mandarin ducks sailed the lakes and wild pig, hare, and small deer roamed the hills. The officers fired and the dogs galloped to collect the limp bodies, which coolies stored in great sacks.

Creeks flowed with fat fish. They caught pike, trout, salmon, gurney, and a fish the Chinese called sungkiang. They hung them on wooden bars, six at a time, rigid and glistening in the sun. Bernard Swan took a photograph of Sam and the coolies pointing to the fish.

Sam felt a big fish on his line, and threw a spear on the end of a rope.

"Give us a hand afore I get pulled in."

"Christ," said Ian Wright, "It's a bloody paddlefish. That's pretty rare. You only usually find them in the main river. Look at the size of it. It must weigh forty pounds and be ten feet long; and that's not the biggest there is. Get him in."

Sam helped drag in the fish. It twisted and gasped and finally flopped, still, on the bank.

"I'll get this bugger weighed. I never caught anything so big in my life. It makes the trout back home look like tiddlers. I want a snap to send to my mate. He won't believe it."

The coolies clapped. They could sell game to the markets, making a small profit for the officers and a few cents for themselves. The paddlefish would be cut into slices and sold by the pound. Sam would write to Billy Wigg and ask him to check with Ma what she had done with his line and to look after it. They would go fishing when he got his big leave.

He lay on the riverbank, smoking a cigarette after lunch and beer. He looked at the clouds through slitted eyes. They looked just like the ones back home when he used to lie in the fields of buttercups after a walk. He imagined them looking like countries he had learned about from his atlas – Australia, like the head of an Airedale Terrier; Ireland floating in the sea; Italy like a boot. He fell asleep.

13

Sam was invited to eat at Shěn's apartment on the ground floor of a house in an alley near the Station. He bought tulips for Shěn's wife who spoke no English except "thank you" and "nice."

"She from Szechuan," said Shěn, "make spicy food. You like?"

"I do. I like very much"

Two boys of about two and four stared at him.

"They speak little English," said Shěn, "Say hello to nice man."

"Hello, nice weather," said the elder, "what is your name?"

"Very good," said Sam, "I'm Sam. What are your names?"

"Ping and Fai," said the boy.

Sam clapped. "They are very nice boys."

"One day you have sons," said Shěn.

"Or daughters. I wouldn't mind."

Mrs Shěn served the food, bowed, and went into another room with the boys. They ate sunflower seeds, then chicken with chilli and garlic, vegetables steamed and served with cashew nuts and tofu, followed by mandarins and watermelon. Shěn opened a bottle of deep red wine.

"This made from osmanthus flower by cousin in country."

"It's delicious," said Sam, "sweet and strong."

"Today my five years in police," said Shěn. "Maybe get promotion next year."

"You deserve it."

Mrs Shěn and the boys came to say goodbye to him and waved. Sam took out his camera. "I'll take a photograph. You can have it when it's developed. Now all smile."

Shěn's wife looked down, the boys were solemn. Shěn grinned, his arms round their shoulders. "They shy. Never have photograph taken."

Sam poised. "Ready now. Good. See you tomorrow, Shěn," said Sam, "and thank you."

* * *

Annabelle met Sam at the cricket club. "I can't understand you mixing with the Chinese. What's that smell on your breath?"

"It's Chinese wine. Lovely. Listen, I work with the Chinese. Some are very brave, good mates. And they know their place, but plenty of unfair stuff's going on. Shěn wants to be promoted. It'll take him ages. I might get it after two years."

"Get changed. I've borrowed some kit for you. We can get you your own if you're any good."

There were six tennis courts behind the pitch. He put on the white flannels, shirt, and pumps.

He flexed his arms and back and smiled. "Whoever has these doesn't have my shoulder muscles."

Annabelle squeezed his arm. "A bit tight. See what you can do with a racquet. This one should be OK."

She wore a knee-length white dress with a low neckline.

"This is straight from the new tennis fashions at Wimbledon. I played at our club in Surrey and still keep up with the tennis news."

"I used to watch them play tennis at the club in Warren. From behind the netting. I didn't know any members, of course. It was for the toffs. They used to chase me away. There was no one there with such nice legs as you."

"Well, well, a compliment. I'm a jolly good player, too."

She taught Sam how to hold the racquet, head above the wrist, and how to play forehand, backhand, smash, and serve.

"You're a natural. What did I tell you? You just need practice. I'll get you a pass and you can come whenever you like. Anton's the coach. He'll help you. He's very fond of me."

Sam went to the club every day when he was off duty. Within two weeks, he was good enough to partner Annabelle in mixed doubles, and was selected for the men's team. He could hit the ball hard, skim the net, slice, and spin. He liked the feel of the leather handle and the shock when the ball hit the strings. Annabelle watched and clapped. The team won a tournament for local clubs, even beating the American Consulate team. There was a report in *The Shanghai Times* and the *Evening Post and Mercury* with a photograph of the team – eight suntanned young men, smiling and holding a silver cup.

* * *

Sam and Annabelle planned a weekend in a mountain resort near Hangchow, which she had visited with her parents a year ago.

"Nice walks and swimming in the lake, and a lovely cool guest house. We could stay in bed all day."

An incident on 30 May stopped all police leave.

Sergeant Davidson called in his officers. "Sit down. Get more chairs. We are in real trouble. Some silly bugger's killed some Chinese outside Louza Police Station."

Sam wiped his forehead. "What happened? I was trying earlier to clear streets of crowds demonstrating around Louza. They were all yelling 'Kill the foreigners'. It was mad."

Denis Gee waved a handful of leaflets. "Hundreds of these are being given out. I brought some back. All cursing the Europeans."

The sergeant glanced at the large print. "Sam, Denis, get all the men in. The Chinese boys can help tell us what happened."

"Sir," said one of Denis Gee's men, "newspapers say police beat and torture coolies at Hongkew Station. One killed by sub-inspector at Louza."

Davidson sighed. "What happened exactly?"

"Big student disturbance outside Settlement. Commissioner McKuen send message to stop them entering Settlement. Students come into Nanking Road and arrested. They say Chinese worker killed in Japanese mill near Pooto Road. Mill closed and men smash machinery. Japanese beat them. That why trouble. Students march on Louza Station."

"Bloody communists," Davidson shouted. "They're getting everywhere. Bloody rallies supposed to be to commemorate Sun Yat-sen's death. Only stirring up trouble. Pass round the fags, somebody. So, carry on Jiǎng."

"Then, sir, Inspector Everson at Louza say 'Fire' and shot with rifle. Officers, some Sikh, some Chinese, fire and kill four students. Eight die later."

"Fuck. This means big trouble."

Inspectors went round all the stations urging calm. A general strike was declared, and, on 1 June, shops and factories were closed, the Shanghai Municipal Council declared a state of emergency and police were instructed to stay in barracks.

"Well, this is bloody boring," said Denis.

Sam asked Wang to order noodles from the canteen. "I've heard the strike has spread. Docks closed. Chinese refusing to work in any Japanese or Western company."

"And bloody Commissioner McKuen been sent packing. They say he arrived at the Louza trouble straight from the racecourse, dressed in his blazer and panama. Can you believe it?"

"I'd believe anything. Who's replacing him?"

"Somebody called Ivo Medhurst Barrett. Played cricket and rugby for England. Injured in the war. Might be tough."

"He'll need to be."

Davidson ordered his men back on the streets. "There are hundreds of refugees from the Chinese sector, and troublemakers trying to get people to riot. Just don't react to being spat at or cursed. Nobody seems to know what's going on. Nationalists split into different factions. Get out there."

Sam loosened his collar and hitched up his shorts. "Christ, it's bloody hot. I'll never complain about the English weather again."

Denis laughed. "Let's hope you get the bloody chance."

* * *

At the end of August, Annabelle's father was kidnapped outside the Shanghai Club after lunch with Clement. The doorkeeper hid behind a pillar and said, when interviewed by police, "I saw three masked men throw a sack over Sir Neville's head, and tie his hands together behind him. They pushed him onto the back seat of a black Daimler which drove off towards Jessfield Road. Then I ran in to get help."

Sam received a message to phone Annabelle at her apartment.

She sobbed, "Daddy's been kidnapped and taken God knows where. I'm sure they'll kill him. I've been told I can't go out. Mummy is hysterical and not allowed to leave the house. There's an armed guard all along Bubbling Well Road. The bandits have left a phone message saying they want $50,000 dollars."

The phone crackled. Sam shook it. "Don't contact the police directly," said Sam, "they won't kill him if they get the money, but might if they suspect a trap. Just do as they say. Where are you supposed to leave the money?"

"In a bag at the end of the front garden on Thursday. Daddy's company will pay and deliver the money on Wednesday. We have to get rid of the guards outside or the kidnappers will kill him."

She phoned two days later to say that her father had been left outside the house in the gutter. He was tied at the wrists and ankles, with no clothes except his underpants. Four ribs and his nose were broken, and he had deep cuts on the face, back, and legs.

"Clement and my sister say that they are going back to England as soon as they can. Mummy wants to go, too. They will probably leave in the middle of October and I will have to go with them. Come and see me as soon as you can when your terrible duty run finishes."

"I will. It's a bad situation. I don't blame people for leaving. Fifteen police have asked to go home. The married ones with kids are really worried. I should get leave in a week's time and I'll come round. I'm sorry it can't be before. I miss you, but the situation is very bad. Be very careful and don't go out. It will calm down."

"I'll be glad to get out of here – apart from seeing you. I don't know why people stay. I'd better start packing."

He put down the phone. He imagined her packing trunks. It would be a lot less fun without her.

* * *

He visited Annabelle early one morning, after night duty. The leaves of the plane trees were beginning to turn brown and fall. He kicked the leaves and rattled his truncheon along the railings.

Her apartment looked vast without the furniture. Two cedar trunks and four suitcases stood in the middle of the sitting room. The red curtains still draped the windows. The green carpet, imprinted with dents from furniture legs, looked abandoned. She opened the door. Her hair was dark at the roots and hung down to her shoulders. She wore black trousers, a purple sweater, and no make-up. The varnish on her nails was peeling.

"Come in. There's not much left. It's all going to my parents' house tomorrow, and so am I, ready for off next week. Did you get my cards and your birthday message?"

"Yes. One of the doorkeepers from your building brought them when he was off duty. He got through, being Chinese. A European might have had difficulty."

He gave her a bunch of roses which she placed on one of the suitcases.

"I'll put them in the sink, and take them with me tomorrow. What a fucking mess."

He lit two cigarettes and gave her one. "You were wearing trousers when I first met you. You look a lot thinner now."

"I'm not surprised. It seems like ages ago. I must look terrible.

I'm exhausted. I haven't been able to go to the hairdresser or beauty parlour for weeks."

She stroked his cheek. "You look well, though, in the circumstances."

"I've been doing a lot of exercise. Not much else to do when you're off duty. Not that we are very often. Then we're not allowed to leave barracks. No tennis. I've decided to join the British Club when you've gone. One of our inspectors plays there and says they're short of people. The secretary's going to contact me."

"Will you do the play this year?"

"No. I'll work over Christmas and do lots of overtime. Good bonuses."

"Shame. They're doing *Lady Audley's Secret*. Full of wicked women and honest men for a change. It's also called *Death in Lime Tree Walk*. Guess what happens. I'd have made a wonderful Lady Audley and you could have played the virtuous George. Ah, well, that's that."

He held her and rubbed his hand against the sweater from the waist to her shoulders. He put his hands inside the sweater and unhooked the bra to feel her breasts. He lifted the sweater over her head and dropped it to the floor. She took off the trousers and knickers and he stripped.

They kneeled on the carpet, then lay, limbs tangled. She moved onto her back and raised her legs. He entered her, thrust four times and felt her shudder underneath him.

He looked at her face. "It's been a long time."

"Bloody hard floor. Don't get dressed. Let's just talk and then see what happens. There's only one chair and I'm giving it to the French woman downstairs. One of us will have to sit on a trunk."

He found his cigarettes. "I will."

She pointed to a lamp on the floor near a suitcase. "I've saved that for you. It's your birthday present."

He ran his fingers down the brass fluted stem and the dome made up of small pieces of tinted glass, shaped like butterflies. "I've always liked this, and it will remind me of good times."

"It's the real thing, worth a bit. Now, I've got whisky and vodka and some soda. Nothing to eat. The doorman brings stuff in later."

He sat and smoked. "This feels funny, sitting here on a bloody wooden trunk with my bum bare and my bits hanging down. I'll have a small whisky. I'm back on duty at 2pm. I'll just grab a sandwich somewhere. How's your dad?"

She handed him a whisky, poured a large vodka for herself and lit another Sobranie. She sat, looked at the floor, shuffled her feet and stroked her arms. "Not good. A long sea journey will help, I think. Then we'll see. He wants to carry on working for a few more years; he's only just over fifty. I think he'd be a bit lost without it. Mummy just wants out of here. Davina and cardboard Clement will get married in London soon after we arrive. It's all arranged with St George's Church and they've bought a house in Chelsea. He will still be a boring banker. He wasn't very brave when Daddy was kidnapped."

She wiped away tears with her wrist. Sam found his jacket and passed her a large, white handkerchief. "There wasn't a lot he could have done. He was unarmed and so, surprisingly, was the doorkeeper. Perhaps the Shanghai Club thinks it can't be attacked. Silly, because grabbing rich people for ransom is getting to be so common. We never catch anybody. They disappear into Chinatown. They're usually protected by one gang or another."

"I know. Fucking awful country. Fucking awful people. I know you think they have a wonderful civilisation. So what's happened to it? It's not all our fault like they seem to think it is. I'm fed up with this foreign devil stuff."

"They're not all like that. I work with some good Chinese and there are still some who just want the country settled. It's a bad time. They have to reach some agreements and get the gangs sorted out – they're everywhere, even in the police."

"So, why the hell are you staying?"

"Because there's nothing to go back to, and I like it. I know I'm doing a good job here. I'm proud of that. I miss my family sometimes and my ma isn't well, but I'm OK."

"Would you like me to take your family something when I get back? I won't be all that far from Lancashire when I marry his Lordship."

"That's all right. They wouldn't know what to say to you, and you wouldn't know what to say to them. I can send stuff. How is your boyfriend?"

"That's a funny way to describe him. He's old. He wants to be a government minister and says he needs a wife and family to help with his career. Romantic, isn't it? Mummy and Daddy are very keen of course; a Lady for a daughter."

"It might be all right."

"At least I'll have a mansion with servants, money, a flat in London, and a good social life. I can buy nice clothes and perhaps have a lover or two. Do you love me, Sam?"

"I like being with you. I like what we do, so I suppose so."

She laughed. "That's not the same thing. If you're in love, it must be all you think about, at least for a while, and you just want to be with the other person. I know what love isn't. I know that Davina doesn't love the ghastly Clement and that he doesn't love her. They never look at each other. Never touch each other. God knows how they'll ever have kids. Good luck to them."

"Do *you* love *me*?" he said.

"I like you very much, but I've never loved anyone and probably never will. I like sex. My life has been to do with convenience – for me, for my parents, my lovers. Bloody awful, really. Maybe Lord Bostridge will change that. I doubt it. You should see his letters. All about bloody debates in Parliament and who he's met. Ghastly."

Sam stood and stretched. "What have you been doing since the May trouble?"

"Bugger all. First, we were all terrified to go out. Then we had to have Russian bodyguards. God they're boring. I did pull one in for a quick fuck once. Quite manly, but a bit rough and hefty."

Sam leaned forward and stopped her. "What the hell did you do that for? Were there any others?"

"Two others. For God's sake, Sam, I was bored out of my mind. One works at the British Consulate, one is a German architect. He came to look at the flat. Why are you so shocked?"

"I don't want the lamp. Give it to somebody else."

"Jesus, don't get sulky on me. Did you hear what I said earlier? We've got no contract. You were out of action for nearly three months. Or were you? What do you chaps do when you're all trapped together? Don't tell me there's no messing about. Handsome new recruits? Willing coolies. Come on."

He looked at the floor, then began to pull on his clothes.

"I didn't mess about. I relieved myself a few times, but that doesn't count. It's what blokes do."

"Do they indeed? Listen, let's not quarrel. If it's any consolation, nobody's courting tackle was anywhere near as good as yours. Come on, let's try it out again, but let me put a cushion from this chair under my head. The French woman would understand. No dog positions. This floor's too hard."

"I wonder what you'll get up to on the boat?"

They lay together. He stroked and kissed her breasts and her clitoris. She pulled back his foreskin and ran her finger round it, then felt his shaft and balls. She drew her knees up and he eased himself into her slowly and moved gently until she gasped and came when he did.

They rolled over, lit cigarettes, and she poured more vodka.

"Listen, Sam. You're a nice man, even leaving out the courting tackle. You'll meet some girl, fall in love, and have children. You'll be a really good father. Maybe you'll go back to England. Come and see me if you do."

"I won't go back to England except on leave. Shall I come and wave you off?"

"No. Definitely not. I'll be better on my own. Really. I'll send you a card or two from the boat."

"Which one are you on?"

"The *SS Port of Spain*, sailing via India on 13 October.

He went into the bathroom. The toiletries were gone, leaving a smell of lavender and rose.

He dressed and ran his fingers through his hair which pushed against his collar. He picked up the lamp. They embraced again; she waved and blew a kiss as he closed the door.

He walked up the Avenue Pétain, across Rue Lafayette and into Avenue Joffre. He stopped to look at a picture of General Joffre, the old papa, Commander in Chief during the war who glared from a shop window, his thick, white moustache, and braided military cap shielding small, intense eyes.

He passed windows displaying models of hats, shoes, corsets, and underwear. He wondered if this was where Annabelle shopped or if she got everything straight from Paris. Where had it all got her? What a shallow life, but she was good fun. He had a job he liked, a loving family trying hard to make ends meet, but enjoying what they could. His throat throbbed. But he had learned a lot from her, and she was a good laugh. He wondered what he would do. No more fancy parties. He'd miss the sex. Still, plenty more around for a bloke like him. Young, single, popular with the ladies. What the hell. He wished Eddie were here.

Construction work was going on all around – hotels, cabarets no doubt, blocks of flats and banks. He had heard that a dog racing track, the Canidrome, with a nightclub, was going up on the Rue de Sèvres, further south. More trouble. He thought how strange it was to have so much luxury in the midst of all these problems. He shrugged.

He found a little coffee shop which sold cakes and chocolate. It was packed with people, all speaking Russian, gesticulating and smoking. He ordered a cake and bit into it. The cream oozed out. He licked it from his fingers and sipped the thick, sweet coffee and lit a Capstan. The Russians stared at him, and at the lamp.

He took a rickshaw back to Yangtzepoo Road, said hello to Wang and asked to be woken at lunchtime. He placed the lamp on the table near the window. The frail sun shone through the glass and dappled the butterfly wings. He sat on the bed, lit a cigarette, and poured a large glass of whisky.

* * *

Two weeks later, Sam was shot, during an attempted kidnapping on Thibet Road. A bullet in the right shoulder. The impact knocked him against a wall as the bandits fled. He chased them until he fainted, fell, and was taken to hospital. The doctor gave him the bullet. "Only a minor wound but keep your arm in a sling. No messing with guns or anything dangerous for a month. You can do desk work."

"I'll be bored. Do women count as dangerous?"

"Definitely. The most."

* * *

In December, he was hit in the calf, chasing bandits along Yangtzepoo Wharf and had to convalesce until after Christmas. He began to think that his luck was running out, but forgot the injuries as Christmas and New Year approached. He decided to stop drinking and smoking so much and find a girlfriend.

He wrote to his sister. *"We are advised not to post anything: It's because of the strikes here. Nothing to worry about; you'll get this, and other stuff, later."*

He sent a postcard to Billy Wigg: *"No presents yet, old son. I'll send them on. Got injured twice. Don't tell my ma or anybody. May all your troubles be little ones as they say. Ha Ha. Hope you got the present for the new baby. Glad you called him after me. Poor little bugger. Tell him not to be a policeman."*

The Station celebrated the New Year and Shěn's promotion to sergeant.

Sam shook his hand. "Congratulations, you deserve it."

"This year of the tiger, 1926," said Shěn, "your birth sign. Lucky year for you as well as me."

"I hope so. We could all do with a bit of luck."

He went back to Madame Claudette's. She kissed him on the cheek. "Happy New Year. We still miss Mr Nicholson. A nice gentleman and good customer. You must be careful. Jasmine is waiting."

14

A note arrived from Annabelle, posted on 12 February:

"Bloody cold in bloody Yorkshire. I got married to His Lordship on 3rd January. It should have been 1st April. Here's my address – Bostridge Manor, Filton, North Yorkshire. Remember I'm now a Lady. I don't feel like one. Hope you're staying safe and sane.

Kisses from me to you.

* * *

At the end of April, Sam was called in by Sergeant Davidson. "Alan Gibson, inspector at Kashing Road Station, wants to see you tomorrow at 9am."

"What for?"

"You'll find out. Look smart."

After breakfast, Sam brushed his uniform, pressed by Wang the night before, put on his cap and took a rickshaw to Kashing Road. He crossed the Sawgin Creek, with its muddy embankment where women and children were scooping and filtering mud with their hands and putting bits of metal into baskets.

Inspector Gibson and Sam saluted and shook hands.

Gibson stepped back. "Welcome, Sam. I'm Alan. We use first names here. More friendly. The Chinese, of course, use our formal titles. Now, without beating about the bush, as they say, we want to promote you to sergeant."

Sam stiffened, stretched up, pushed out his chest and moved his feet further apart. "You have come to our attention for dealing successfully with several incidents, for your dedication in working overtime, for your language skills and for your ability to get on with the Chinese. That's very important, especially since the strikes and troubles. You are well respected."

"Thank you, sir. Alan."

"We could do with better relations. Not too familiar, of course. I also want to ensure that discipline here improves. We've had a few instances of drunkenness and some disrespect for Chinese officers. I don't want another Louza here."

"I understand. This is an honour. I am proud and grateful."

"They need you at Yangtzepoo for a while, so there will be a short ceremony in my office on 5 September. You'll get your stripe, then you'll move into accommodation here – slightly bigger than where you are now. You will have your own office – not very grand, but adequate. Sergeant Davidson knows, of course, and he will tell the officers at Yangtzepoo this morning. Report here at 8am, 5 September and we'll take it from there. Congratulations."

"Thanks. I look forward to it."

Sam took a rickshaw back to Yangtzepoo and sent a telegram to his ma and dad on the way. They would be very proud. It was a shame that he couldn't see their faces. Sergeant Davidson shook his hand. "Well done. Alan Gibson will be a good bloke to work for. The officers here have prepared a little celebration for tiffin time."

There was a cake and a card from Yangtzepoo Road officers. Sam's constables saluted, and presented him with a picture of a red dragon on parchment for good luck. Wang gave him a set of lacquered chopsticks, bowed and smiled.

".Thanks for everything. I think I can even eat rice pudding with chopsticks now and the dragon will hang on my wall in Kashing Road."

* * *

That evening over a beer with Ian Wright, Denis Gee, and Dan Williams, Sam said, "We're all off duty on Friday night. I want to take you somewhere to celebrate."

Dan thumped the air. "Hooray! Where are we off to?"

"It's a surprise, but look smart and civil, with jacket and tie."

They took a rickshaw from Yangtzepoo at 9pm. Sam instructed the drivers: "Ciro's."

"Isn't that a bit posh?" said Ian.

"We deserve it, and we can all look posh," said Sam. "I made a lot in overtime last month. I'll pay the entrance fees and the first drinks. You do the rest. You'll need a lot of ten cent notes. Gorgeous Russian hostesses, great bands, nice atmosphere. I've got some cigars."

The Russian doorkeeper, in crimson jacket and cap, bowed as they entered. "Welcome."

"Don't they ever smile?" asked Dan, "I wouldn't want to meet *him* in a dark alley. Built, as my old pa would have said, like a brick shithouse."

Sam looked for the doorkeeper who had greeted him and Annabelle.

"Not here," said an attendant, "Gone."

"Blimey," said Ian Wright as he looked round the dance hall, "I've never been anywhere like this."

The words "Kentucky Orchestra" sloped across a large drum in front of the band leader. The saxophone bleated as they played "Rose Marie."

"They're famous," said Denis, "on the radio. Best negro band in China, they say. What happens now?"

Sam looked round and pointed. "You see the hostesses wandering around with trays of drinks? One will come over when we sit down. She'll ask if you want to buy a dance ticket.

You give her about ten cents a ticket and off you go. She'll offer you champagne. It'll be ginger beer, so don't have it. Go for vodka or whisky. It will still cost you, so drink slowly."

"Now we know where *you've* been going," said Ian.

Sam smiled. "Only once. Can't afford this. I was invited to a party." He remembered how Annabelle had looked that night and how he had been so proud in his dinner dress.

Dan spread his arms. "Well lucky you. Was it with that blonde bit? It's lovely and cool in here. Look at these bloody great fans."

Denis sniffed. "Make the most of it. I like the smell too – cigars, perfume, whisky, women. Perfect."

They sat at a round table at the back of the hall, each with a cigar. Three hostesses came to the table to sell dance tickets. Ian, Denis and Dan bought one each and danced to "All Alone". Sam looked around and saw the hostess who had been there when he came with Annabelle. She stared at him, walked across the room and stood by the side of their table.

Sam stood. Her nose was level with his chest. He lowered his head and looked into dark blue eyes, enhanced by mascara and eyeshadow. Her hair was smoother than he remembered, looked longer, and was gathered into a pleat, held with metal pins on the right.

The rest fell around her left shoulder. With her hair back, her face looked broader. The eyebrows formed a thin arch. Her nose was small and slightly flared, her lips a thin smile of purple-red. His skin warmed and his groin tingled.

"Hello, handsome." Her voice was deep, with an accent. She dropped her left shoulder, skimmed her right foot on the ground, lowered her eyes then looked at him again. "You want dance?"

He nodded and held out his arms. The band was playing "It All Depends on You."

With his right hand, he felt her spine under the red silk of the dress. She placed her gloved hand on his right shoulder. He noticed that the black glove had a red ring on the middle finger. He wanted to stroke her back and put his hands into her hair.

"I like your perfume. It smells of roses. Is it from Paris?"

"No, from a little French shop in the Rue Retard."

"What is your name?"

"Lulu. It is really Tatiana, but we all have professional names. And you? Who are you? What do you do?"

"Sam. I am a police sergeant."

"And so young. You must be very brave and very strong."

"Well, I'm not a sergeant until September. I've come with some friends to celebrate."

"You like dancing?"

"I do."

"I remember you last time you here, you with pretty blonde lady. Where is she?"

"She went back to England to get married."

"You sad?"

He shrugged and drew her closer. She moved her left arm from his shoulder and placed it round his neck.

"Where are you from, Lulu?"

"I was born in Harbin, north China, but my family is Russian. We were forced to China – refugees from Reds after Revolution. My family suffer. Me and my sister want to go to university in Vladivostok. Not possible. Now we work in Shanghai."

"What does your sister do?"

"She sometimes dance and sing at Del Monte. She have very good voice. But she have bad chest. Many days sick."

The band ended on a long, muted note from the trombone.

Lulu took away her hand. "I get you drink? Nice champanska?"

"I'd like vodka and I'll buy five more dance tickets."

"That very nice. We spend time together. Get to know each other." She smiled and trailed her hand along his arm as she stepped back.

She spoke in Russian to another hostess and pointed to a small table nearer the band. He sat and watched her move across the room. The silk dress hung from narrow shoulders and small breasts, collarbones arched above the neckline. Her hips swung as she walked, the hem of the dress brushing her calves; her slender legs swivelled, making the material shimmer. The shoes were black with small heels and a bow at the instep.

He lit a cigar when she returned. "What are you having?"

"Only water. I am working."

"So where did your family come from in Russia?"

"My father was famous ship engineer in Vladivostok, then Harbin. My mother died when I was three. I do not remember her." She looked down, sniffed, and coughed. Sam handed her a handkerchief but she shook her head. "Papa travel a lot. My family was rich. My uncle Austrian Count. He married Russian and his father made him leave."

"You mean he disowned him?"

"Yes, yes, that is right word. My English not very good."

"Your English is excellent. You have a lovely accent."

"But Uncle took jewels. He was killed in Mongolia by Russians. Before that, he gave jewels to my father. When we had to leave Russia, Father put them under a tree in our garden. One day, maybe I go back to find them. You like more vodka?"

Sam nodded. His mouth felt hot and cold at the same time and the drink stabbed his throat. He watched her go to the bar. She came back with a larger glass on the tray.

"This one you not pay for, but pretend, because I working."

Sam put his hand on hers. "What does your father do now?"

"He cannot work. Russians find it difficult to work. If young, they work for Chinese or British or Americans like bodyguards."

He stubbed out the cigar and stood. She held out her hand. "I like smell of cigar. Very chic."

They danced again to the slow "Deep in My Heart". She put her head on his shoulder. He bent to rest his cheek on her hair. "Where do you live?"

"In French Quarter. Many Russians live there. They call it 'little Moscow' or 'little Siberia.'"

"I was there a while back, in a little café."

"Siberia very cold. All snow and ice and peasants."

"Do you live on your own?"

"No, with Father. He has small apartment in house in Rue Bourgeat. I have separate apartment above that. Just a small bedroom and space with stove and sink."

"Not with your sister then?"

"No. She married to bad man. He gamble and drink."

"Why doesn't she leave?"

"He nice when she get paid or he win at cards."

They sat, she brought more vodka and he lit another cigar. He looked at her mouth. "How old are you?"

"I never tell that. I will say that Chinese birth sign is water tiger and in horoscope Libra."

"That's October. I'm September. I'm water tiger, too. I once went to an old fortune teller who said…never mind."

He looked at her face through the twisting haze of cigar smoke. "Do you smoke? I have some nice Sobranies here."

"No, I have cough."

"Can I see you home?"

"Not possible. I work until three in morning, then I go home and sleep. You come next Friday? I finish at midnight."

"I'll be here."

He stood and watched her go to the bar. He wanted to look at her, and hold her again, feel her skin, smell her perfume. He thought there must be something in love at first sight.

Sam went back to the table where the others sat with glasses of vodka.

"Aha, Sam," said Dan, "we were watching you. Who is she?"

Sam punched him on the shoulder. "Get away. Why didn't you have better things to do?"

"We did," said Ian, "we danced and drank. Bloody expensive. Very nice, Sam. It's after midnight. I'm on duty at six. Let's go."

Sam looked around to find Lulu. She was dancing near the bar with a fat European. She looked towards him and smiled.

A rickshaw took them back to barracks. Sam looked up. The half moon was clean cut and pale, surrounded by a purple and pink haze. They smelled the rot of the river. An owl hooted.

"You're very quiet, Sam," said Ian. He pushed the others and laughed.

"Shut up. I'm thinking. Go to bed. Look at that moon. I think it's supposed to be lucky."

"Oh, God," said Denis.

Sam sat on his bed and poured a whisky. Annabelle's lamp cast blurred red and blue stripes of light on the wall. He lay back and held his arms tightly across his chest. "A lady from a foreign country." He smiled. "And so lovely. She needs protection, and I can do that. And make her happy."

He woke early and smiled. He hummed "Deep in My Heart" as he shaved and put on his uniform.

He sent her a dozen red roses from the flower shop on Rue Lafayette, with a card saying, "From your admirer. See you Friday."

* * *

He arrived at Ciro's at eleven and sat at the bar, smoking. The Kentucky Orchestra played "Blue Skies." He watched her laughing with a man at the bar. He didn't like that. She was dressed in green – long robe, earrings, nail varnish, and high heeled shoes. Her hair was loose, pinned by a red comb. She walked across the room.

He stood. "Ten dance tickets, please. That should do for a while".

She smiled and took his hand. "I get flowers. You very nice."

"They are to go with your perfume. And red roses are the flowers of the county, the region, where I lived. It's in the north of England."

"Do you have big house?"

"No. It's small but cosy."

"What is cosy?"

"Little but friendly. I have two sisters and two brothers. They all live in the house."

The band moved into "Are You Lonesome Tonight?"

He put his right arm round her waist and held her left hand. "This is a new song. I've heard it on the wireless. It's nice." They danced, her head pressed against his neck. He breathed her perfume and felt the stirring of an erection.

She looked at him and smiled. He squeezed her hand. "I'd like to kiss you."

"Not here. I working. It is not allowed. Perhaps later?"

At midnight, she cashed in her tickets and collected a grey silk wrap, a bag and a wide-brimmed felt hat.

"Tonight good business. Many men buy champanska."

"Where are we going? To your flat?"

"No. Not my flat. Another better flat."

"Whose is it?"

"A very rich Chinese man. He in Hong Kong on business and with wife. I use flat. When he here, I am friend."

Sam tensed. "I see. Let's call a taxi. Do you love him?"

"Don't be silly. It is business arrangement. Andrei will call a taxi."

She placed her hand on the doorkeeper's arm and spoke to him in Russian. The doorkeeper smiled and went outside to call a yellow taxi. Andrei saluted Lulu and instructed the driver, "Twenty-three, Rue de L'Ouest."

They kissed in the taxi and he touched her breasts. She moved his hands away. "Soon there."

They arrived at a four-storey block of flats in red brick, set back in a garden with stone statues of lions and a circular fountain. The entrance hall glistened with fan-shaped mirrors. Tall gladioli stretched from a silver urn on a glossy wooden table in the centre. Rugs with intricacies of Chinese script and dragons lay over the dark, planked floor. Lulu nodded to the concierge and looked at Sam.

"It's the fourth floor, number 45."

"How does this man make his money?"

She shrugged. "I don't know. He say cotton, but may be opium, may be guns, may be anything. Most girls at club have man like this. We don't ask anything."

"You'd better not tell anyone I came here. Remember I'm a policeman."

"All is secret."

The sitting room was three times larger than Annabelle's apartment. The wallpaper was etched with dragons and camellias in gold leaf and a thick, pale carpet made footsteps silent. Ornate brass lamps with parchment shades stood on marble tables which reflected their soft glow. A silver statue of a Chinese warrior brandishing a broad sword glared, fierce and squat on a mahogany stool. Six doors led from the room.

"Three bedroom, bathroom, kitchen, and office. That picture of Mr Lu and wife and children in Hong Kong. Children, all at convent school in Hong Kong. I hang up your jacket. You want drink? Vodka very good. From Russian shop. It called Moskovskaya."

Sam looked at the photograph of a short, plump Chinese man, a slender woman in European dress, but with Chinese features, and three children, all girls, wearing blazers and panama hats.

"Vodka is fine. Are you working later today?"

"No. Day off."

"Me, too."

They sat on the sofa of red and gold brocade. He put down his glass, took hers and placed it on the side table. They kissed. He ran his tongue round the inside of her mouth, then drew back.

"That was marvellous."

"Yes. Nice. OK. You want bathroom?"

They finished their drinks and she showed him the bathroom where he pulled a condom onto his erection.

She was waiting for him, lying naked on cream sheets in a four poster bed. He looked at her erect nipples and long pubic hair. He stroked her breasts and touched her clitoris. She gasped, stroked his chest and felt his hard shaft. He entered, moved slowly, and looked at her; her eyes were closed and she smiled.

He moved her hips to one side, kissed her hair, and moved more quickly. She shuddered, clutched his arms and cried out. He came into the condom. They lay, looking at each other. He thought that was different to any sex he had had before. More satisfying, deeper, more feeling in it. She seemed to enjoy it, too.

She smiled. "That nice. Not business."

He lit a cigarette, removed the condom and flushed it down the lavatory.

He sat on the bed. "How often do you see this Chinaman?"

"About once a month when he in Shanghai. He old. About forty. He good to me. Buy nice things. Then he go to Hong Kong. He have big house, many cars, and servants."

He could never do that for her. But he sensed that she was unhappy and maybe wanted something more. He wanted to see her again – soon.

"What do you do at weekends?"

"Sometimes I work. Tomorrow I meet Sister at coffee house, then we visit Father and cook for him. Maybe visit Aunt, my mother's sister. She have big apartment in Avenue Joffre. She get jewels out of Russia. She call herself Countess."

"Can I come with you?"

"Not this time. Perhaps later. You come back to Ciro's next Friday like this, and Saturday we can visit."

He touched her breasts again. "I'll do that. I'll get leave. Now, I just want you again."

She held his wrist. "I can do Shanghai squeeze and China grip if you like."

He laughed. "It's not that; it's the position that counts."

"How you know all this. What positions?"

"You're not the first, you know; let me show you the dog. You crouch on your hands and knees…"

"I know this. Some call it the cat. You be my Kotchka, my little cat."

"And what do I call you?"

"Lastochka. Nice bird I like."

"What kind of bird?"

"One with long tail in V shape. Bounce like this." She moved her hand up and down.

"Ah, a swallow. My favourite bird, too."

He put on another condom and stroked her belly, his shaft and thighs tight against her buttocks. He reached for her clitoris and entered, holding her hips. He thrusted slowly, then rapidly. On his last push, he arched over her back and put his face between her shoulders.

She panted, then coughed, and moved her head to one side. He stroked her hair.

"Did you like that?"

"Yes, yes. Very nice. But it tiring. Now I must sleep, bath, and dress. You go."

He wrapped the sheet round her and kissed her forehead then her lips.

"Until next week. I'll be there. Look after yourself."

She was already asleep. He dressed, collected his jacket and hat, nodded to the concierge, left the flat, and took a rickshaw to Yangtzepoo Road.

The sun filtered the mist of early morning, promising a hot day. There were sandbags in square formations at the corners of the main roads with police and soldiers smoking and chatting in summer uniform, but with helmets and rifles. He called a rickshaw to take him back to the Station, and gave the driver a large tip.

Wang greeted him outside his room. "You tired, sir? I have tea and cake. I put on fan. When you leave for Kashing?"

"Thanks, Wang. I leave in September."

"I come with you?

"I think you will have to stay here, Wang. You very good coolie. Maybe they make you number one coolie."

"Thank you, sir."

"Lastochka," he whispered as he put on his uniform. This was the woman for him. He wanted her all to himself. Beautiful, interesting, lovely body. What was it the old fortune teller had said? Happy and sad the lady would make him. She would make him very happy. He knew it.

* * *

Sam and Lulu spent the next Friday night in Mr Lo's apartment after Sam called at the American Pharmacy and picked up thirty condoms.

"Buddy," said the server, "how do you expect to get through this lot?"

"They're not all for me."

They woke at ten on Saturday morning and took a rickshaw to 15, Rue Bourgeat, her father's apartment.

"My father called Dmitri, friends call him Dima, small name for Dmitri in Russian. But you must call him Mr Denisov. My real name Tatiana Denisova, means daughter of Denisov. My sister Raisa. She will come later to eat. She have husband name Aliyev. My father not happy in Shanghai. He angry and argue. He often drink too much vodka."

"What, in the morning?"

"He drink at any time. Come."

They went up the stairs. Wafts of cooked cabbage and urine followed them. She opened the door of Flat 2 and pointed to the staircase.

"I live upstairs."

Sam smelled pipe smoke, vodka, and fish. Dmitri Denisov sat in a wide armchair, like a monkey in the corner of a cage, his hair white wisps; a pointed tobacco-stained beard and stiff white eyebrows wobbled as he moved. A mottled blanket covered his knees and shins and spread down to his feet covered in felt slippers printed with black Chinese letters. He sucked at a pipe and squirted tobacco juice through his teeth into an iron, wood-burning stove. He looked up at Sam, pushed his elbows on the arms of the chair and attempted to stand, but fell back.

"Good morning. You are English, I think?"

"Yes, sir. I am happy to meet you."

"I speak English and French and German. I was famous international engineer with money, big house, dacha. Now nothing, nothing."

Lulu interrupted. "A dacha is a house in the country," then spoke to her father in Russian.

He nodded. "Da, da. Tea or vodka?"

"I will get tea."

She went to a teapot, perched on the top of a fluted brass container with handles, and poured two cups.

"This is samovar. Traditional Russian. I get you also little pie, a pirozhka. Papa, it too hot in here."

Sam looked round the room. Her father's chair was covered in an old knitted rug, with frayed edges. A thin woven carpet, showing a towered building, sprawled on the stained floorboards; a table with an embroidered cloth with lace round the edges stood in a corner, and an oil lamp was set on a chest of drawers next to the stove where sticks glowed and hissed, even though the day was warm.

A picture hung on the wall – a face with big staring eyes, looking to heaven, and surrounded by a hat and cape of polished silver.

Sam stared at it. "What is that?"

"Very precious," said Dmitri Denisov, "called icon. The Virgin Mary pray for us. It from Russia. Many destroyed in troubles. We take this one hidden in shirt. No Russian cathedral here. Only small church. People pay for big building in Rue Corneille. But Russians poor. Not enough money for cathedral. No respect for Russians in Shanghai."

Sam loosened his shirt collar. "How long have you lived here?"

Dmitri Denisov looked at him, his forehead crumpled. "Too long." He began to sing "It's a Long way to Tipperary".

"You know? From war." Sam nodded.

Lulu turned a tap on the samovar. "Papa, shh. We here for five years after Harbin." She brought a plate of little pastries and poured black tea into small blue and white cups.

"These pirozhki with rice and egg."

Sam bit into a pie. "It's all delicious."

Dmitri Denisov pointed to a bowl of sugar. "You are policeman? I hope you good policeman. Too much corruption. Everyone hate Russians. Russians only good for soldiers. They like beautiful Russian women but not men."

Sam nodded. "Your women *are* beautiful. You have a beautiful daughter."

"Two beautiful daughters. Raisa will come later. Did you bring newspaper?"

Lulu handed him two newspapers – one in Russian and the English language *China Press*. He glanced at them both and sighed.

"Situation in Shanghai very bad. You see this. Fighting all around. Chinese want representation on Council, want reform of courts. This Chiang Kai-shek, nationalists, very ambitious. Big trouble."

Sam wriggled in his chair. "It is very difficult."

"It *not* difficult. It impossible! Give me another chut chut of vodka. It about power. Everybody want power and money. Nobody learn anything. Look at Trotsky, Lenin, Stalin and Mussolini, even your Prime Ministers." He pointed to a headline in the *China Press*:

MOVE TO MAKE SHANGHAI SPECIAL AREA
STUDENTS DEMAND MORE AUTOMONY

"What students know? Chinese authorities not interested. Banned meetings three weeks ago, now meetings again. Police do nothing."

Lulu spoke to her father in Russian. He slapped the newspaper. "I will NOT be quiet. Look at what happen in Russia. Land taken, people killed, now we live here in poverty."

"It is not poverty, Papa, we are alive and have enough to live on."

He opened the newspaper, "Enough to live on? This is what rich have. Look at these pictures. Look at advertisements for gowns and hats. Who is this Madame Gingeroff inviting ladies of Shanghai to come and see her collection of handbags, fur coats, shoes?"

"Papa, you know I can make dresses nice like ones in newspapers and magazines. I copy patterns and sew." She glanced at Sam. "I have machine in my apartment."

Her father spat a piece of pastry onto his plate. "And look what keeps Shanghai happy – scandal stories from America. Who cares about woman accused of killing husband and choir singer four years ago in New Jersey? Look at society pages of ugly women, ugly babies. What society? There is no society here. Not real."

Sam coughed and finished his tea. Dmitri Denisov glared at him. "Why you smile? No culture here. All cabarets, cinemas, mosquito press with scandal. Only one good thing here – statue of Pushkin. You know Pushkin? No? Greatest poet and writer in world, even more than your Shakespeare. Killed in duel about love – love, pah. Russian people pay for statue in Shanghai – on Route Garnier."

He spoke some words in Russian and looked to the ceiling.

Lulu waved her arms. "Papa, stop. You know we never go back to Russia. Russia is finished. Stop getting so upset. It's bad for your heart."

"My heart fine. I speak to old Gōng downstairs, you know. He tell me what is going on."

"You be careful, Papa. It could be dangerous. Gōng might be communist. I am going to show Sam my room, then I will make you soup."

"Don't be long."

Lulu led Sam up the stairs and opened the door. "I told you he very angry."

Sam stepped inside. "He's amusing. I like him. Very intelligent. He knows a lot. This is a nice place."

She had covered the bed with a bright patchwork quilt and put up curtains to match. Two pictures, lines and daubs of bright green, yellow, and orange glowed from pale walls where the paint was peeling. Perfumes and cosmetics were in rows on a shelf. He looked at the bottles – Patchouli, Verveine, and Vie en Rose.

"You were wearing that rose scent when we met."

"Yes, my favourite. I carry a small bottle with me always."

"It's your birthday soon. I will give you some really lovely expensive perfume from Paris, and take you out somewhere nice, Lastochka, my swallow." He kissed her.

She smiled. "For your new job I will give you collar pin. Was my father's. From Russia. Gold."

Sam saw a sewing machine and a trail of silk on a table in the corner. "My ma has one like that, but she doesn't use it any more. I think one of my sisters sews."

"Very useful for making nice clothes. Silk very cheap here."

He looked at the pictures. They were by the same painter. Thick spirals of bright oil paint swirled into trees and bridges. A man was walking across a bridge, smoking a pipe.

"My aunt, the Countess, gave me pictures."

"You aunt is really a Countess?"

"She say she Countess. You will meet her, Kotchka. Papa say she snob, but she kind."

"Where did she get the pictures?"

"I think my aunt buy them in Paris when she went with first husband. He very rich. He assassinated in Moscow, then she marry another rich man. He left Russia to live in Canada. I think he now dead, too. I must make food for Papa and sister Raisa."

"What will you eat?"

"Russian food. Today I make Shchi, cabbage soup, and Kotlety, like meatballs with onion and fried. After lunch I shop with Raisa and have tea with friends, then work. I meet you Friday, we go to apartment, then come here?"

"Good. I want to kiss you again. Last night was wonderful."

"Yes. Very nice. We kiss a little here, then see Father."

Downstairs, Dmitri Denisov was asleep in the chair. Lulu began to prepare the soup and meat. Sam twisted the knobs on a big old wireless, with a wooden surround. He could only hear crackling and whistling, or fast Russian.

They heard banging on the door. Lulu stopped stirring the soup. "Who that? That not Raisa. She have key." The banging became louder.

Sam opened the door. A woman fell into the room.

Lulu ran towards the body and touched her shoulder. "Raisa!"

Dmitri Denisov woke, prised himself out of his chair and crouched by his daughter. They spoke in Russian. Raisa sobbed. Sam helped them carry her to the chair and asked if she had been in a street accident. Lulu shook her head, pulled up a wooden stool and sat, holding Raisa's hands.

Raisa was plumper than Lulu, the same dark, wavy hair and round face. But the face was streaked with tears over bruises and blood, dried around the mouth. One eye was closed. The women talked quickly, Dmitri Denisov became angry, waved his arms and shouted.

"What is happening?" asked Sam.

Lulu stroked Raisa's arm. "Her husband home drunk this morning. She ask where he been. He hit her with fists and kick her on ground. She fainted. He leave her there, then he come back and she ran out of apartment to come here in rickshaw. This happen before. He very big man with bad temper."

Sam touched the closed eye. "Let me look at her. I know a bit about first aid. Get some warm water with soap and a cloth to wipe her. Can you speak English?" She nodded.

"Where does it hurt?"

"In arm and ankle and face."

He took off her woollen cardigan and saw bruises on the forearm. Her ankle was swollen under stockings with holes and ladders.

She winced when Sam touched it. He looked at Lulu. "You must get her stockings off. I won't look. Tell your father to stop shouting. Do you have some brandy?"

He wiped Raisa's face with the soapy water. Lulu put her sister's feet on a stool and removed the stockings whilst Raisa sipped tea with brandy.

Sam touched her ankle. "This ankle needs attention. She should go to hospital."

"No. No." I not want leave here. He will kill me."

Dmitri Denisov thumped the arms of his chair. "I will kill *him*," he said, "I wish I had gun. Not any more."

"Then she must go and lie down on the bed. Do you know a doctor?"

Raisa shook her head. "No doctor."

They helped Raisa to the bed and covered her with a thick blanket. She shivered and her eyes closed.

Sam turned to Lulu. "How often does this happen?"

"Very often. He lose at cards, get drunk and he beat her."

"And," said Dmitri Denisov, "she not well. She have TB. Most poor Russians have TB, but hers bad. She spit blood."

Lulu patted her chest. "I not have it bad. Just bronchitis, bad in winter. Doctor say not infectious kind. Papa have not bad TB."

Sam tapped his chest. "It's OK. I was vaccinated against just about everything before I came here and I'm very fit. But you should all be eating well and looking after yourselves. Can she stay here?"

"Of course. But Papa afraid of Boris, that her husband. He come and make big noise and bang on doors."

"His name Boris Aliyev," said Dmitri Denisov, "he say he actor, but no work. He do nothing except cards and dogs. He have other women and he beat my daughter."

He began to cry. "I should not have allowed marriage. Russian men now not good men. He not look after her. She pay everything. She try to keep apartment nice, but he drink and break everything."

Sam stood and pulled at his belt. "Where is the apartment?"

"In Yunnan Road."

"I know where that is. It's in the International Settlement. I will pay him a visit. What number?"

"No, no. Be careful. He very dangerous when drunk."

Sam moved to the door. "And so am I when I'm not drunk. He can't do this to a woman."

"Number 21, apartment 3, but you have no gun."

"Yes, I do, but I won't use it. I'm trained in close combat fighting."

* * *

Sam remembered going to Yunnan Road once – to a good curry house. It was near the racecourse. He asked the rickshaw driver to wait and banged on the gate of number 21. A sleepy, European in a dressing gown opened it. He went up to apartment 3. He hit and shook the door. A tall, broad man opened it.

"Are you Boris Aliyev?"

The man swayed. "Who are you?"

"A friend of the Denisovs."

"I don't know Denisovs."

Sam struck him in the face. He staggered back into the small apartment. Vodka and whisky bottles were scattered on the floor. A thin cat wandered across the table, picking at scraps of meat and bread on a plate.

"You no right to do this. I report you."

Sam hit him again and kicked him as he lay across the rug.

"Listen bastard. You are Russian. You have no nationality. Do you want to appear in front of a Chinese court?"

The man held his arms across his face and shook his head. Sam pulled him up by the hair.

"Do you understand me? You will not go to the Denisov house. You will not touch your wife, her sister, or her father. If you do, I will beat you much worse."

The man nodded and sat on the chair, his eyes closed, his nose bleeding. He sniffed and rubbed his sleeve across his mouth. Sam kicked the bottles across the room, threw the cat out and slammed the door behind him. He jumped into a rickshaw and lit a cigarette.

Lulu screamed when she saw him. "You hurt? Blood on shirt."

"No, That's his blood. He scratched me on the neck, but it's nothing. I don't think he'll be a problem again. How is she?"

Lulu kissed him and Dmitri Denisov shook his hand and said "Spasiba. Thank you." Raisa was sitting in bed sipping soup.

Sam sniffed. "That smells good. I'm hungry."

"You fight my husband?"

"I fight your husband. I hope he learns his lesson. I want you to tell me if there is any more trouble. OK?"

She nodded. "Sam, thank you. You good man."

Lulu put her arm round Raisa's shoulder. "Papa, you must look after Raisa. She have my room upstairs in case bad husband come. I will go to stay with Aunt."

"No, no. She stay here. Plenty room. I sleep on sofa. I look after her."

He sipped his vodka, relit his pipe, coughed, pulled the blanket round his shoulders and shouted in Russian.

Lulu put her head on Sam's chest. "You very brave, Kotchka. I very proud. We all very proud. You go now. I see you next week, yes?"

He pulled back his shoulders and stroked her hair. "It was nothing. All in a day's work."

She kissed him on the cheek. He took her hand. "Now listen. I'm going to take you to the Astor for a special treat next month. You can wear a pretty evening dress and French perfume and I'll wear my dinner jacket and bow tie."

He left the building and whistled as he went to find a rickshaw. He thought he had never been so happy and proud of himself. In love. A beautiful woman, a good deed for her family. He would need to do plenty of overtime to afford the Astor. He smiled as the rickshaw drew up alongside him.

15

Sam and five constables sat, smoking and drinking, in the Station bar at Kashing Road, after early morning patrol ended at eleven.

They passed round a photograph which had appeared on the front page of every English language newspaper in Shanghai. It was from the *Illustrated London News*.

THE FIRST GUARDS IN HISTORY ORDERED TO THE FAR EAST: THE 2ND BATTALION COLDSTREAM GUARDS LEAVING LONDON FOR SHANGHAI –THE REGIMENT CROSSING WESTMINSTER BRIDGE ON 29 JANUARY

The bridge was obscured by two hundred unsmiling men marching, not in lines, but as a crowd of cloth caps, the occasional trilby, all in ties, shirts and coats.

They had marched from Wellington Barracks, past the Houses of Parliament and across the bridge to Waterloo station. Members of the public, wives and sweethearts cheered them on.

The band of the Scots Guards, leading the troops, played 'Tipperary' and 'Shanghai.'

"This not good, Sergeant Sam," said Constable Xu, "Chinese not like British soldiers in Shanghai."

"Somebody has to keep order. You know we're stretched, even with the Russians coming into the force."

"Chinese not like Russians, too," said Xu.

"Who DO the fucking Chinese like?" shouted Hector Murray, a new constable from Aberdeen.

Sam jerked up his head. "That's enough, Hector. You've had too much to drink."

"It's disgusting," Hector continued, "at the weekend, I was off duty down the market off Range Road and some dirty yellow bugger pushed me and spat at me. Awful black teeth and a cap pulled over his eyes. Ran off, otherwise I'd have cracked his head, open, I can tell you."

Two other constables clapped and cheered. Sam stood. "I want to see you three men in my office now, and fast. Leave the beers."

Sam sat behind his desk, the others stood, at ease, facing him.

Sam folded his arms. "Now listen, this is for your own safety and for the reputation of the Force. You know there's unrest. It's a complicated situation with all this fighting and people stirring up trouble. Keep your mouths shut and your hands to yourselves whatever the provocation. There've been serious incidents of officers being in big trouble for beating the Chinese. If you want to keep your jobs, behave. If you can't, then resign. Do you understand? I'm watching you. Dismissed."

* * *

It snowed during the night when he was on duty. Sandbags sprinkled with white, squatted, frozen and unmoveable, at street corners. He decided to visit Lulu after lunch, before going back on duty at six. He knew that she always rested in the afternoon to be ready for Ciro's, starting at eight and finishing at three in the morning. He bought a bunch of white carnations from a stall and called a rickshaw.

He went up the stairs past Dmitri Denisov's apartment and knocked on Lulu's door. There was no answer. He opened the door with the key she had given him. There was a teapot and a cup on the table. A plate and cutlery had been washed and placed on the side of the sink. The stove had been lit, but had gone out, leaving a smell of wood ash. The sewing machine was inside its cover, with a set of matryoshka dolls on top. He went into the bedroom. The bed was made, covered with a green, knitted blanket. On it were silk stockings, two pairs of silk knickers, and a camisole to match. A long dress covered in shimmering gold sequins hung on a hanger outside the cupboard where she kept her clothes. It was low cut, with the breast cups padded and shaped. Sam stroked the tiny scales of metal. At the back, three pleats fell into a tail from the waist. He looked at the label and saw "Sophie, Hong Kong". He looked in her jewellery box, which she kept in a drawer. A pearl necklace lay on top of other bright, cheap glass bracelets and beads.

He wondered how she had bought these expensive clothes and jewellery. A chill settled in his chest. He went downstairs. Dmitri opened the door. "Ah, you want vodka? I hear news on radio. Why British soldiers come here? Police not enough? What this Chiang Kai-shek doing? What Japanese doing? Raisa in bedroom. She has temperature."

Raisa, pale with pink cheeks, lay supported by pillows. He gave her the flowers and sat on the edge of the bed. She called to Dmitri Denisov to put them in water.

Sam shivered. "It's not very warm in here. I'll get you some more wood and coal. Have you seen Lulu?"

"I not see her for a two days. She not upstairs? Maybe she at Aunt or with friends."

Sam shook his head. "She always rests in the afternoon."

Raisa looked down and twisted the sheet. "Sam, you know rich Chinese man is back?"

He leapt up. "What do you mean? Is that where she is?"

Raisa leaned back into the pillows, pulled up the blanket and closed her eyes. "Perhaps."

"I'll kill him. How can she be so nice to me and seeing someone else? It's not right. It's humiliating."

"No, you not go there. You talk to Lulu."

"I will. I'll wait for her. You must eat and keep warm. I'll be back."

Dmitri Denisov sang a Russian song, half asleep in the armchair, and waved as Sam left.

He went back upstairs and waited in Lulu's apartment, watching the street from a window. At four, a black Packard pulled up outside the house. The driver opened the door for Lulu. She got out, carrying two bags with sloping black letters, "Madame Giselle" printed on the pink gloss. He heard her come up the stairs and open the door. He stood in front of her, hands on hips. "Where the hell have YOU been?"

"Why you here? You always on duty. You no right to come to my house when I not here."

"You gave me a key. Remember? I came to see you as a nice surprise. I asked where you have been?"

"Shopping. You not own me. I need new clothes for work."

He pointed to the bags. "That is a very expensive shop. Where did you get that kind of money?"

"I earn."

"How?"

"I work hard. You know that."

She sobbed. He pointed to the wardrobe and bed. "Where are all these fancy clothes from?"

"I make."

"The sewing machine is wrapped up. You haven't opened the machine, and nobody could make that gold thing themselves."

"You should not go in lady's bedroom when she not there."

"Where did you get it?"

"I buy."

"It's from Hong Kong. Someone else bought it."

"Why you look at my things?"

"I don't believe anything you say. You've been to see your boyfriend from Hong Kong."

"Only business, Sam. I need nice things some time."

She took a lace handkerchief from her bag and dabbed the tears.

"Stop that. What kind of business? Sex business?"

"You not trust me? That man only friend now."

"What kind of friend?"

"You not have friends, Sam? What about blonde bitch from England? You no visit Russian and Chinese women? Ugly ones go in brothels. Not have nice jobs like me."

"The Englishwoman is not a bitch, and she has gone back home. Other women are not ugly."

"Ah, so you know them? When you last in brothel?"

"A long time ago, before I met you. You are the only woman I want now. I love you."

"Sam, have cup of tea or whisky. Sit down. You give me headache."

He sat on the bed and put his head in his hands. "I've loved you ever since I first saw you. I don't want you to torture me. And I need to trust you."

She poured him a whisky. He drank it quickly and stared at her. She came to him, sat on his knee, stroked his hair, and kissed him. "I take dress back. Kotchka not be jealous. I have time to make love before work. Let's go on bed."

He stood, hesitated, turned and left. He ran down the stairs and slammed the door to the building. Old Gōng appeared at a window. "What happen?"

* * *

The arrival of the Coldstream Guards caused a strike of Chinese workers, shouts of "Down with British Imperialism", and inflammatory leaflets were scattered from windows or distributed in the streets.

Inspector Gibson addressed the officers at Kashing Road Station. Sam stood by his side.

"Men, we are facing a very serious situation. There has been a large increase in crime due to the disturbances and anti-foreign feeling, stirred up mainly by communists. There are, as you know, extra reinforcements from Britain. You will have met some of them."

They nodded.

"As you will know, refugees from the Chinese sector are attempting to enter the International Settlement and the French sector from Chapei. It must be stopped. There are barbed wire coils all round the Settlements. Any questions?"

"Sir," asked a constable. "We've seen the *North China Daily News*. It tells you how to spot a communist. Is it right?"

Gibson smiled. "It's not that simple, but we are here to stop trouble where we can. The Chinese sector is in turmoil. Mayor Sun Chuanfang is nervous. I repeat – people will try to escape and we have to maintain the barricades. Sergeant Shuttleworth will instruct you. He has something to say."

Sam held up a report. "This is what we found just the other day when we went into Chapei. Chuanfang has set up a force of executioners and soldiers to round up students and anyone thought to be a troublemaker, and to execute them in public. I have photographs here to prove it."

The men were silent. He continued, "It's chaos, and very dangerous. He held up a photograph. "The Mayor's men have cut off heads with those big swords and put them on bamboo poles. Some heads get carried through the streets, some they put in birdcages and hang them from telegraph poles. I expect the bodies go into the Huangpu River." And here are more photos – decapitated bodies of women and children lying in the streets with the rats."

Alan Gibson took over. "I don't think I've ever see anything as bad as this. No wonder people are trying to get out, but we can't risk being flooded with Chinese. The Chinese officers understand this and their families have been brought out into the Settlement. I'll take these photos to the commissioner. All non-Chinese living in the Chinese sector should leave. We'll get out a warning, as if they haven't been warned enough."

* * *

Lulu sent a note to Sam at his office. "I very sorry. Not happen again. Please come see me."

He waited for her outside Ciro's the following evening. She took his arm. "Come home with me."

He sat on her bed and looked round the room. The wardrobe door was closed and he wondered if the clothes the Chinese man had bought were in there.

She opened a bottle of vodka and poured two glasses. "Chinese man go back to Hong Kong. No more. And you here."

He held her and undressed her slowly, touching every part of her. She unzipped his fly and caressed his shaft with her fingers. He threw off his clothes, put on a condom and entered her.

* * *

They woke, cramped in the small bed, and went downstairs to have breakfast with Dmitri Denisov and Raisa.

Raisa opened the door. "Not much food. Only tea. I glad to see you. Papa not well. He cough blood."

Dmitri Denisov sat humming in his chair, eyes closed. Sam looked at him and felt his pulse. Lulu went to buy rolls and butter.

"It's the excitement. I tell you what happening. My friend old Gōng, have spies."

Sam released his hand. "Tell me. I've only got a couple of hours. I have to take some stuff across to the French police today. And you need to look after yourselves. We will bring you more food later. The situation out there is dangerous and difficult to control."

Lulu made tea, spread butter on the rolls and went to sit with Raisa. Dmitri Denisov started a new bottle of vodka.

Sam refused a drink. "And you shouldn't be drinking either, especially at nine in the morning. What does Gōng say?"

"You heard of this gangster, Du Yuesheng? Very bad, very rich, much power. He export opium to France. Americans meet Du with French police chief."

"How do you know all this?"

"Gōng know interpreter. Du say he fight communists if he get

132

five thousand guns and allowed to take trucks, men and weapons through International Settlement. Du say communists plot to take over Settlements and fight nationalist troops."

"It's very strange that Du is being allowed across the Settlement. That has never been allowed before."

"Du tell lies to frighten Municipal Council. What I tell you before? All about power. Rich businessmen give money to fight communists. Communists bad for them. Bad for Du. Kuomintang want power, communists want power. Chiang Kai-shek outside Shanghai with soldiers and want power. Will fight communists. You watch."

"We're always watching, but it's difficult to know what to believe. I have to go. I've told Lulu to stay here. I've told her not to leave the apartment, but I know she has to get to work. Make sure she gets reliable taxis."

"I know, I know. Nightclubs still work, of course. Always do. I get Gōng son to take her."

* * *

"What are our informers telling us?" Inspector Gibson asked Sam.

"Apart from wanting more money, they're saying the communist trade unions are taking over the Chinese areas before Chiang's arrival. And we know that communist headquarters have been set up in the Rue Lafayette, organised by somebody called Zhou Enlai, just back from studying in Paris and there's no light, heat or telephones in Chapei."

"The streets look like bloody war zones. Get some photos for the official records. I suppose the press are everywhere."

Sam took photographs of barbed wire and sandbags across the streets of the International Settlement where shops were boarded and traffic blocked. The Coldstream Guards on duty asked him to take photographs of them, in their battle gear with tin hats like basins, and cigarettes hanging from their lips.

"Nowhere like this for women, eh? Russian princesses, Chinese and American tarts. Hot stuff."

Sam focused his camera. "Just make sure you don't take some of the hot stuff back home with you. Your wives and girlfriends might not be happy. What's going on?"

"Directive that refugees from the Chinese sector must be sent back, unless they have good reason to cross the barricades. Your lot are searching adults and allowing only those with current papers into the Settlement."

Sam called in a Chinese Constable to ask for information.

"Sir, this very bad. Children separated from parents and scream. People who try to cross barricades without permission being shot."

"There must be a better way," Sam said to Gibson.

"Orders are orders, and listen, Chiang Kai-shek and his troops have arrived and joined the communists under Zhou Enlai against the Mayor's soldiers in Chapei. They're likely to take control of Shanghai, apart from the International Settlement and the French Concession. More chaos."

Sam called on the Denisovs whilst travelling between the French Concession and the International Settlements to negotiate defence strategies.

Dmitri Denisov jumped from his chair, spilling ash from his pipe across the carpet. "You watch, you watch. Gōng say new nationalist party. Chiang has arrived in Shanghai by gunboat and been welcomed by business bosses."

He spat. "Rich businessmen being kidnapped and murdered. Frightened of communists. Chiang and Du Yuesheng play games – power, power. Chiang need money."

Dmitri Denisov waved a Russian newspaper at Sam: "You see. Stalin order communist party in Shanghai to collaborate with Chiang. Trotsky against this. Russian newspapers say not trust Chiang, and Du a murderer. You watch for trouble."

* * *

Police intelligence recorded that Chiang had ordered troops loyal to the communists to leave Shanghai. On 12 April, in the streets of Chapei, his nationalist soldiers, wearing white armbands, massacred hundreds of Chinese opposing him. The communist trade unions called for a general strike.

"Why this not in newspapers?" Dmitri Denisov shouted at Sam. "How they not see trucks loaded with dead bodies? What police say?"

"It's all very confusing," said Sam.

Dmitri Denisov spat into the stove. "You say confusing when police not want to tell things."

"Well, all our leave is being cancelled from next week. I'll visit Lulu next week and take her out somewhere nice."

"Before somebody else does. She not very patient."

* * *

Two days later, Lulu sent a message to say that her father was very ill and breathless. Sam bought fruit, vegetables, and meat for the family, and tulips for Lulu. Dmitri Denisov was in bed, supported by pillows, his face pale. He waved a newspaper in his thin hands and spat into a bowl on the floor. Sam saw flecks of blood.

"I not agree with communists, but terrible things done by Chiang troops. You know, old Gōng tell me what happen when workers march to Chiang headquarters to ask for peace and calm? Women, children – in rain. A hundred thousand Gōng say. Chiang have soldiers with machine guns down Paoshan Road. Crowd… bang, bang, poof."

He ran the back of his hand across his throat. "Troops kill with bullets and bayonets, pull people out of hiding in houses. You know how many trucks to carry away dead?"

Sam took away the newspaper. "You should be resting. No. I don't know, although I did take photographs of some of the trucks for the records."

"Records, records. That never appear in records. No truth. Like in poor Russia. What your soldiers do?"

"Nothing. They are on standby."

"Then why they here?"

"To protect the Settlements."

Dmitri Denisov spat again and drank a glass of vodka in one gulp. "Do British, French, Americans know that tens of thousands of communists being killed all time? Do you know foreign authorities sending prisoners back to military courts? Chinese businessmen hiding in Hong Kong or kidnapped pay ransom."

Lulu wiped his forehead with a damp cloth. "You must be calm, Papa. Stop this."

"What your policeman have to say?"

Sam adjusted the pillows. "We know all this. We know that Chiang has set up a government in Nanjing. The Chinese will get representation on the Shanghai Municipal Council and parks will be open to the Chinese. Changes are happening. Lulu is right. You must rest. There is nothing you can do."

Dmitri Denisov laughed and coughed. "You know Chiang Kai-shek promote Du Yuesheng to Chief of new Bureau of Opium Suppression. Funny, funny. Du use opium, deal in opium, now look."

Sam left to go on duty. He walked down the stairs, depressed. He had seen those troops and open trucks of dead bodies hanging over the sides. He hadn't bargained for such terrible sights. He had never seen such cruelty. He hoped the folks back home were not getting news of this.

* * *

Sam's mother wrote to say that she knew there was a bit of bother in China. The MP had been round and said that China was talked about in Parliament. He had remembered Sam's photograph in the paper from when he was recruited. It was captioned "Brave Sam off to China". Sam smiled. If only they knew what was going on. He hoped his mother would be able to get out a bit now that spring was coming. He would send a cheerful letter.

16

At the end of April, Sam was assigned to special duties of organising street defences and was on duty for twelve hours every day. He visited Lulu late one afternoon on his way to talk to officers in the French Concession. She leapt at him, kicking and shouting, and threw a bowl at his head.

He threw up his arms. "Stop. What is wrong with you? Speak to me in English."

"I'm going to have a baby."

"Is it…?" he began.

"Is it yours? Of course. You buy bad condoms? You not wear? I very sick. I not want baby."

He tried to grasp her wrists. "You are not to do anything dangerous or illegal. I will look after you. Please calm yourself. Sit."

"What you want me do? I earn money for family. Raisa sick, father no job. They will starve and have no home."

"Stop that. Stop being so dramatic. We will talk and find a way to deal with it." He smiled. "I would like a baby."

She threw a cup. "You will not have to have baby. Like all men. I cannot work, I will get fat. I ill with it."

"We'll think about all this. When did you last eat?"

"Yesterday I have little rice."

"I am going to bring some fruit and noodles. We'll eat and have some tea."

When he returned, Lulu had not moved from the chair. She rocked from side to side and moaned.

He kissed her forehead. "I have been thinking, I will apply for special permission to get married. The commissioner will probably say no, but I'll try. If we can get married, I can get a married man's allowance, plus one for housing and one for the child. Until then, I can do a lot of overtime and perhaps get some bonuses."

She threw herself at him again, biting his hands. "I not want get married. I don't love you. I cannot work if married. I have no money. Chinese man kidnapped or dead."

"I thought you did love me. I thought the Chinaman was finished. Now I am getting angry. Supposing this is *his* baby?"

"I not see Chinaman for long time."

"Listen. I love you, and I think I have helped your family. I want you to love me. Listen. The police have a dangerous life. I get shot at some days."

"What you mean?"

"There are dead bodies in the streets. There are armed robberies all the time. The Chinese want to take over the foreign settlements. If I got killed and we weren't married, you would have nothing. If we are married you will get a British passport, so will the baby. When my leave is due, we can visit England and get treatment for your chest. We may even decide we want to live in England, away from all this trouble. You can't go anywhere without a passport."

He put his hands on her shoulders. Mascara ran down her face, her lipstick was smudged and her nail varnish cracked. He noticed that the nails on her right hand were bitten. He had never seen her like this. He loved her even more. He kissed her cheek and tried to hold her. She pushed him away.

He stroked a wisp of hair which had fallen across her eyes. "I think you should be comfortable and eat whilst you're expecting. Why don't we ask your aunt if she will let you live there until the baby's born?

Then we can get an amah for the baby, we can get a bigger apartment and you could go back to work. I'll talk to your father and explain everything. When is baby due?"

"Beginning November doctor think. I never go back to work. Boss not want mothers. Chinese taxi dancers getting work. They cheaper. I will have baby. We can ask Aunt. She always love me and Raisa. We visit Aunt together."

"That's a good idea. What is she like?"

"She think she very aristocrat, like I say. She speak French. We will take flowers and you must kiss her hand. You wear nice suit and tie. She like men smart."

* * *

The Countess lived in a large second floor apartment on the Avenue Joffre. She opened the door wearing a long, black gown.

"Entrez." She kissed Lulu on both cheeks. "Who is this handsome man? Monsieur, I am the Comtesse de Lausigny-Chabord. You are welcome."

Sam kissed her hand and Lulu presented the flowers. They sat on heavy armchairs covered in velvet. Sam looked down at the teak floor scattered with silk rugs patterned in black and red triangles. Pictures in bright splashes of trees and flowers hung on two walls. A bookcase with thick volumes stood under the window; a glass and dark wood cabinet containing blue and white plates and cups was opposite the stove. Heavy velvet curtains were drawn back into sashes of gold cord.

He breathed in the heavy perfume and stared at the Countess. She had a long nose which rippled into two small bumps from the bridge; her eyes were deep set and blue; her eyebrows thick, dark, and constantly moving; her black hair was pulled into a roll behind her head. Black shoes with small heels peered from under the robe.

"I see you admire my apartment, Monsieur. My niece has explained that I escaped Russia with jewels?"

She held up her necklace. "Like these pearls. You tell no one. I see you look at my face. My nose, a sign of aristocracy. Do you have money, Monsieur?"

"A little. I hope to have more."

"This furniture and pictures all from France. Books are French: Balzac, Flaubert, Moliere… You read French, Monsieur?"

He shook his head. "Mr Denisov says that *Russian* books and art are very good." "Denisov a peasant."

Sam raised his head. "I thought he was an engineer."

"Still a peasant. No culture even when he marry my dear sister. Let me get you tea."

Lulu looked at Sam. "I will explain."

She began to sob again and spoke to the Countess in a mixture of French and Russian.

"Hélas," said the Countess, "then you will marry. I will help pay. Until then, you stay here."

Sam coughed. "There is a problem. We cannot marry until I have been in the police for six years."

"What job you in police?"

"I am a sergeant."

"Then why rules for such important people?"

Sam looked at his feet. "I'm not very important – yet."

Lulu curled up in the chair and pulled at her hair. The Countess patted her shoulder. "Ma chère, tu n'es pas bien. Go and wash and put on make-up. We discuss all problems."

It was agreed that Lulu would live in one of the bedrooms in the Countess's apartment until the baby was born. Sam would ask permission to marry and get his mother to write a letter to plead the case.

Lulu kissed her aunt on both cheeks. "We must tell Papa and Raisa."

Sam bowed as they left. "I will ask her father's permission to marry her. And I will look after her. Thank you."

* * *

Dmitri Denisov greeted them dressed in a ragged silk dressing gown and a fur hat. "I need a new stove and more fuel. Why you look so serious?"

Lulu spoke to him in Russian. He bounced in his chair, sucked his pipe and spat into the charred wood in the stove. He stared at Sam.

"What happen now? Daughter, go get some biscuits from the shop. I need to talk to this policeman."

Sam took off his hat and placed it on the table. "Sir, I want to marry Lulu, I mean Tatiana, but I have to get permission. It might take time."

Dmitri Denisov spluttered and wiped his nose on the sleeve of his cuff. "What about money? What about home and food?"

"I can do overtime. The Countess will help Tatiana."

"Countess? Countess? Countess of what? She is Svetlana Selzenova, from Omsk. She say she read and speak French. She despise Russia. She cannot read even children book in French. So, do you love my daughter? Does she love you? She not healthy for baby; she have bronchitis. Same with my poor wife. Dead at age twenty-nine."

He began to cry. Sam sat with his arms dangling between his knees.

"I love Tatiana. She will love me once we are settled. I can do overtime and earn more money. I will make sure that your family is all right."

Dmitri Denisov looked at Sam, his eyebrows meeting, his nose pink.

"Good luck then. I hope it's not a boy. Boys be soldiers and policemen. Let me tell you, I would not marry my daughter and I would not marry you. She like good life. You in dangerous work. Corrupt work. You torture people to get information. You treat poor Russians badly."

Sam held up his hands. "Stop. I am a hardworking policeman. I don't torture people. It's a bit rough sometimes, but I can earn. I will get promotions."

"All right, all right. I give you permission because of baby. But I have no money to give."

Lulu came in with a bag of biscuits. Sam stood. "Your father has given his permission for us to get married. I will sort everything out. I'll go and see my inspector tomorrow. Are you pleased?"

Lulu sat and sobbed. Dmitri Denisov poured himself a glass of vodka.

* * *

Inspector Gibson banged his hand on the table. "Bloody fool. A White Russian? Almost as bad as a Chinese. You won't get permission to marry, I can tell you. Commissioner Barrett is very strict about all this. Get your mother to write and I'll help you put a case together, but it might take a very long time and get nowhere." He opened a file on his desk. "Meanwhile, there is big trouble out there. Chiang swears he'll get back the foreign Settlements. Usual stuff. You might find yourself working even longer hours."

Sam coughed. "Is there anything else I can do to speed up my case for getting married?"

"Listen, I'm sympathetic, but in the middle of all this, frankly your problems aren't high on my list. Ask to see the commissioner. He might listen on compassionate grounds. I doubt it. There are two of you in this pickle, wanting to marry Russians, but the other idiot's woman isn't bloody pregnant. You might have a chat. Name of Jack Smethers, based at Dixwell Road. Why can't you blokes keep your dicks in your pants?"

Sam wrote to his mother to tell her that his girlfriend was pregnant and asked her to write to the commissioner asking for special permission for them to get married. She should get the vicar to get it typed and the MP to put in a special plea and send the letter through diplomatic channels.

17

Sam knew he would never forget the day, November 7 1927, when his daughter was born at ten in the morning in the French hospital. He was called from duty, and waited in the corridor.

The matron looked at his uniform and frowned. "We cannot have police in here. Not good for mothers and staff."

"I have permission from the Municipal Council." The lie did the trick. He smiled and sat on a cane chair.

He heard Lulu scream and shout out in Russian.

He stood. "Is she all right?"

The matron took out a notebook. "Elle est difficile, votre femme. She not help us." Sam heard someone call what sounded like "Poussez." then a fragile wail.

A nurse opened the door. "Vous avez une fille. A little girl."

He sat down again and sobbed. He wiped away tears with the back of his hand, and brushed them from his trousers.

"C'est normal," said the nurse. "I bring you tea, then you see your daughter. Very pretty."

The baby lay in a wicker crib, wrapped in a white woollen blanket, eyes closed, a bubble of froth on her lower lip. Her blonde hair was tufted in damp streaks over a tiny bruise on the left of her head.

Sam stared at each feature. "Look at her ears. They are so perfect.

Like little shells." The baby wriggled and squealed softly. He stretched his hand towards her. "How is she? What about that bruise?"

"Perfect. The bruise is nothing. From forceps. You can touch her."

He placed his hand on the baby's back and felt the small movements of uneven breathing. He rubbed her spine, unwrapped the blanket and looked at her tiny hands and feet.

"Hello, Elizabeth. I promise you that whatever happens, I will always try to make sure that you have the best of everything."

Lulu lay on the bed in a room next door, arms stretched out at her sides. He kissed her cheek. "Lastochka. Your Kotchka is so proud. You will have a great big bouquet later. I'll come back when I finish duty at two. How are you? You look tired."

"It was horrible. Never again, pass me my eyeshadow and lipstick."

"You might change your mind when you see her. She's beautiful, like her mother. I want to call her Elizabeth, after my mother, and Tatiana after you."

"Elisaveta nice Russian name. A dotchka, a little daughter. We call her that for short name. Dotchka."

"Your father will be pleased."

Lulu turned away to put on the make-up, then lay back on her pillow.

Sam looked towards the room where the baby slept. "Elizabeth. Dotchka. I will come back later. I love you. I love you both. Your aunt is here now."

The Countess brought a silver rattle shaped like a bell, with mother-of-pearl inlay, and flowers for Lulu. The matron spoke to her in rapid French. The Countess said, in Russian, to Lulu, then in English to Sam: "This woman speaks peasant French. I can hardly understand her."

She looked at the baby and shook the rattle over the basket. "I think she has my nose. A real aristocrat."

* * *

Sam changed out of uniform, had lunch and sent twelve red roses to the hospital. Lulu and the baby were asleep when he arrived. He heard Lulu mutter in Russian, then open her eyes.

"I hurt everywhere. Body too fat. Nice roses. Give them to nurse for vase.

Sam kissed her. "Have you fed the baby?"

"I cannot do that. Too painful. She have bottle from nurse. Hungry baby."

He took a breath but said nothing. Women back home, he thought, always breastfed babies. His mother had told him that he was breastfed for six months and was greedy. She said that was what made him so tall. He frowned.

The baby lay, breathing gently, in a crib beside the bed. He touched her fingers and they curled round his finger.

"Look. She knows me already."

Lulu sighed. "Friends must know about baby. You go tell Olga. I sleep now."

She closed her eyes. He kissed her forehead. "I will come again tomorrow."

* * *

Olga ran a massage parlour and hairdressers on Avenue Wagner and lived above the business. On the way, he sent telegrams from the Central Post Office to his mother and to Billy Wigg.

Olga opened the door. He kissed her on both cheeks. "A little girl. Beautiful. Elizabeth Tatiana, Dotchka for short. She's wonderful. So clever. She held my finger."

"I very happy for you, Sam. Come in. take off coat. Let us have some champanska. Husband again at dog track. He never win."

She handed the bottle to Sam. He twisted the cork, the champagne spurted and frothed. He poured two large glasses. Their fingers touched as they toasted the baby.

He sipped and felt the bubbles froth in his mouth. Olga sat on the sofa and crossed her legs.

"And how Lulu? I love Lulu but she not happy pregnant. She too sick and depressed. How she now?"

"I don't know. She says she won't breastfeed the baby and that her figure is ruined. She might be all right when she is out in five days. I will get her an amah for the baby and her aunt has found us an apartment in the same building as hers – nice, big, and rent free because the woman who lives there has gone to Paris and wants someone to look after it. Next year, we'll find somewhere of our own."

"You will be married by then?"

"I don't think so. It will take time to get permission. I've asked my mother to write in case that helps."

He finished his champagne. Olga poured another glass and stroked her skirt. Her thighs shone in silk stockings.

"Are you happy, Sam? You do such a dangerous and difficult job."

"I don't know. I don't know how things will work out. Lulu is confused, I think. She doesn't seem to know what she wants. You're her best friend. You know what she's like."

"I do know. And she have temper."

"She might calm down now that she has a baby. She worries about her father and sister, but she can be cold to me."

"When did you last do sex?"

"Not since just before she knew she was expecting."

"Is there anyone else?"

He shook his head "No time. Too many problems. Too many terrible things happening. I have to live in barracks most of the time in case of emergencies."

She moved over to him, stroked his hair and kissed him on the mouth.

"Come into bedroom."

The champagne beat in his head. He stumbled as he followed her. He took off his trousers and underpants, she her skirt and knickers.

He entered her. She shuddered. He rolled off her and stood up. He had not used a condom.

Olga stretched her arms and covered her thighs with a sheet. "I not have sex either," she said, "stay for a little. No-one will ever know." She reached for him. He put on his trousers.

"I can't do that. I've been foolish. I can't do this with you, I feel guilty with Lulu lying there in hospital. I love her. This won't happen again. I'll get my coat and be off."

He went back to barracks and sat on the bed in his room. He put his head in his hands. "I have a wife and daughter," he mumbled, "I must not behave like that again. Supposing Lulu finds out. It's disgusting. I have a daughter. The old fortune teller said she would be my joy. I know she will. I'll be a good father and a good husband."

He stood, shook himself and went to the bar. "It's a girl. Drinks on me."

18

Sam took a taxi to the hospital; thanked the nurses; helped Lulu to the car; carried Dotchka, wrapped in a white shawl; and placed her on her mother's lap. The Countess met them at her apartment.

"You have a year for apartment 3 on ground floor. Friend have gone to France to see rich lover. You look after, keep clean, no charge. I find amah to look after baby, too. Very good – worked for nice English family gone back home. She wait for you."

Sam held Dotchka, one big hand spread under her bottom, the other supporting her head as they walked downstairs.

The amah smiled and bowed. She had a broad face, hair drawn back from the forehead and wore a long green robe and felt shoes.

"Me take baby and change. What her name?"

"She is Elizabeth," said Sam, "But we call her Dotchka. It's a Russian word for little daughter."

"Very beautiful."

Lulu sat and looked round the apartment. "Nice. I like furniture and carpets. Now very tired. I lie down."

Sam handed Dotchka to the amah who rocked her and hummed.

"I'll get your trunk from upstairs. Your aunt will bring down your jewellery and the rest. It is nice, but we'll have our own place soon. I've been told the apartments on Weiheiwei Road will be ready next year and I'll put our name down on Monday. I've asked Ma write to the commissioner about us getting married. I'm going to talk to another bloke about it. He wants to marry a Russian girl, too."

Lulu sighed. "Who will do shopping and cooking?"

"Mary will do that, too. She lives in the basement here with the other amahs. She'll be on duty all day every day. She'll see to the baby's nappies and clothes. She'll take it all to one of the laundries. They do it for next to nothing."

"What she cost?"

"Only a dollar a week."

"Then why we not have two amahs, one for baby, one for clean, cook, and shop?"

"Why do you need all that? I don't earn a fortune, love."

"I very tired and very ill." Lulu wailed, and swayed in the chair. "What do you spend money on? You work always. Drink? Smoking? Women?"

He slammed his cap down on the table.

"Now, listen. I have to work hard to support you and Dotchka, you know that. That's why I do so much overtime. No fun, like you think. You don't know what you are saying. I'll cut down a bit as I want to spend time with you and the baby."

"Always baby, baby. I need to have life, too."

"I'm going to get Raisa to come and see you. Your friends can come tomorrow. You're tired. You need to eat well and get better. I have to go on duty. I'll get the doctor to call. Is your breathing all right?"

Mary brought the baby from the kitchen where she had bathed her in a big bowl, put on a clean nappy and a pink dress bought by Olga. Sam held his daughter against his chest; her head rested on his shoulder; she drew up her legs like a frog, heels pink and soft. He jiggled her and kissed the top of her head.

Lulu screamed. "Don't do that, she'll be sick."

"They like it. I've watched Ma and my sister with my little brother. They need to be sung and talked to. Like little nursery rhymes." He laughed and looked at the amah. "There's one about Mary. And another about a cat in a well – Ding Dong Bell."

The amah stared at him, took the baby's fingers. "Dotchka like Mary."

Lulu sighed. "I don't know those songs."

He laughed. "Well the songs you know aren't suitable for a baby. You can learn some, otherwise she'll speak Chinese, pidgin or Russian. That's not right. She needs English."

Lulu slapped him across the mouth.

Mary looked away. "Missee too tired. Missee have bath. I take baby, show her look out window."

Sam gripped Lulu's forearm and stared at her. "Don't you ever do that again in front of servants. Do you hear me?"

"You hurting me. Get out."

"I will. Just remember who pays for everything."

Lulu pushed her head into a cushion and covered her ears. Mary prepared a bottle for Dotchka and hovered the teat over the baby's mouth where a drop of milk settled. Dotchka clamped her lips round the rubber and sucked.

Mary tipped the bottle. "I sing, she sleep, put into cot. Nice fat baby."

Lulu sat up. "She not fat."

Sam watched the baby's eyes flicker then close. He put on his coat and cap. "I need to go to barracks to get ready for night duty. Missee's sister will be here soon to help unpack."

That was the first time he had been hit by a woman. Surprising perhaps. It made him angry and depressed. He'd heard of some women being ill after a baby was born, though. One of his officers said his wife had tried to kill herself. He must take good care of Lulu and the baby.

* * *

Sam invited the sergeant who wanted to marry a White Russian to meet him before a briefing meeting at Central Police Station. They shook hands.

"Sam Shuttleworth from Lancs."

"Jack Smethers from South Wales." He spoke softly and fast in an accent Sam had not heard before, but Jack had a firm handgrip and a big smile.

"I know your problem. I think me and Yana will be able to marry soon, but it's difficult. The high-ups don't like it. They want us with nice English girls. Where are they, I ask you? Anyway, my Yana's lovely. I wouldn't want anybody else. Remember, you have to be determined, and they need us. What's your girl called?"

"Lulu. Her real name's Tatiana. We have a baby, too. Dotchka."

"Ah, little daughter. Nice. For Christ's sake, call your girl Tatiana when you apply for anything."

The inspector walked in. Jack looked up. "Anyway, here we go. Sit here. Our Inspector Loughton doesn't usually take long with these briefings. We'll talk more later."

The inspector stood behind his desk, coughed and began, "Our informers tell us that Chiang Kai-shek has resigned. The Chinese are all fighting amongst themselves."

"What's new?" whispered Jack.

"The nationalists can't get anywhere without Chiang and the cash. He knows this and he'll be back. He's getting married in December. I believe it's a big wedding and taking a lot of time to organise." He coughed. "Meanwhile, I want all barricades round the Settlement inspecting and I want each of you to contact one of these informers on this list. Come and tick off your names."

Jack and Sam went to the Station bar. Sam bought two beers and set them on the table.

"My girl's father heard that about Chiang from a Chinese mate. Is it true he's marrying a Methodist?"

"Yes, but a Chinese one. Important family. He's converting. I'll tell you more later, if you're interested. Bloody boring, all this wedding gossip. But there's more going on, of course."

"Tell me."

Jack drank the rest of his beer and called for two more.

"Our old friend Du Yuesheng and his gangsters have made about five million dollars for Chiang through their kidnappings, extortion and sale of Government bonds."

Sam nodded. "I've heard these rumours. And before he resigned, he appointed that bloke the finance minister, brother of the fiancée."

"Right. Soong Mei-ling. All very political. Chiang knows what he's doing."

Sam took out a packet of cigarettes and his lighter. "Cigarette? Capstan? What did you do before you came out here?"

"Went down a mine for a bit. Every bugger did. Awful. Dad, two uncles and a brother killed in accidents. Two grandads dead from lung problems. Shocking. Couldn't wait to get away. Came to Shai end of twenty-three, made sergeant last year and met Yana. We want to go back home year after next, but she needs a passport to travel and can't get one until we marry. Bugger, isn't it? You'd think sergeants would get *some* perks. It's the commissioner. Right bloody stickler for the rules."

Sam leaned back in his chair. "What have you done about getting permission to get wed?"

Jack puffed smoke from his nose. "Tried to get myself noticed by high-ups. Cracked an opium ring on Cheking Road. Lots of bang bang. Two Chinese constables killed. I took a hit in the shoulder, but it got me a commendation and I've been told it will speed up my papers."

Sam laughed. "Sounds a bit of a dangerous way of doing things. When will you get married if it works out?"

"Probably next Feb. I suppose you could say we're engaged but Russians don't do that, do they? They just exchange wedding rings on the right hand. I've got our name down for Weiheiwei Road. I hope you have, too."

Sam nodded. "Where will you get married?"

"We'll just have a small wedding at the Russian church down Paoshan Road and a reception in a Russian café, I suppose. We'll invite you. Got to go now. On duty soon. Let's get together again."

They shook hands.

* * *

The Countess held a champagne party in her apartment to celebrate the baby's birth.

Sam raised his glass. "To wet the baby's head, as we say, let's sing 'Happy Birthday'."

"I sing her song about drunken sailor," said Dmitri Denisov.

The Countess stamped her foot. "Stop. Do not give him more champagne. He too méchant and ignorant."

"And you…," began Dmitri Denisov.

Sam stopped him. "No. This is a nice party. No arguments."

He told them that Chiang Kai-shek was to marry Soong Mei-ling. Dmitri Denisov waved his arms and wiped his mouth.

"That Chiang. What I tell you? All about power. He do any religion for power. He never Christian. He have wife already – sent to America. Big ugly crook Du now buy banks and sell protection. Controls unions. Controls rich."

"Papa, stop shouting," said Lulu, "you wake baby. Behave."

The Countess poured more champagne for Sam and Lulu. "Oui. Taisez-vous. Stop. You talk bad."

The amah carried Dotchka into the room, dressed in a white satin dress with red dots, and bootees, and a matching cap pulled over her ears. She jerked her arms, pursed her lips, and screwed open her eyes. Sam took her and leaned her feet on his chest, supporting her head.

He smiled, twisted his face and put out his tongue.

"I think she's smiling at me."

Raisa shook her head. "They don't smile as early as that. She do caca."

The Countess recoiled. "Mon Dieu, give her back to amah."

"She's fine," said Sam. "I'll sing her a rhyme… 'Little Bo Peep has lost her sheep, and doesn't know…'"

Lulu held up her hand. "She not need to know about sheep, tell us about wedding. Aunt, where this Mei-ling buy clothes?"

"All clothes made by French tailor."

153

Dmitri Denisov refilled his glass and took out his pipe.

The Countess took it from him. "Not in here."

* * *

On 2 December, the Chinese and foreign press carried photographs of Chiang, Mei-ling, the guests, and Whitey's jazz band. Sam brought *The Shanghai Times* to the Countess's apartment where she and Lulu were having tea. He kissed Dotchka who lay on Mary's lap.

Lulu cut out pictures. "Look, over a thousand guests – consuls, diplomats, naval commanders, businessmen, police commissioners, and newspaper big bosses. Everyone important in Shanghai."

Sam and the Countess looked at the photographs. "I see Consuls for France and Russia," said the Countess, "and many other friends. Look at clothes and room. Very fine."

Lulu held the newspaper away from her. "I would like a wedding like that. Many flowers, nice music, people dressed very fine."

"We haven't got permission to get married yet, but I'll get you a ring."

"I not say I marry you."

"Don't be difficult, Lulu. I'm too tired. We can't go back to England unless you and Dotchka get the right papers. Another sergeant is marrying a Russian and going back next year. It's not easy to get permission; you know my ma has written, so stop making a fuss."

She folded her arms. "We have a baby. I am an old mother. No good time since last summer."

"You are still very beautiful. Please try not to be so bad-tempered. We will have a lovely wedding. We will go to England and I will be very proud of you and Dotchka." She sat and twisted the hem of her dress. "There is no fun any more. I am bored and I worry about Raisa and Papa."

"I'll tell you what," said Sam, "we'll have a lovely English Christmas here in our own apartment. I'll take three days leave. We'll invite friends. I'll get a fir tree and crackers. We'll have turkey, stuffing, sprouts, roast potatoes, and Christmas pud with custard. I'll get in a cook – ours at the Station will know somebody."

Lulu looked up. "Yes, yes. We invite Papa, Raisa and also Olga and Sergei."

"Isn't that too many? I was thinking of inviting two more sergeants who are on their own."

"Plenty room. No problem. We do. I plan."

Sam bought a sapphire and diamond ring for Lulu's Christmas present, a fluffy rabbit for Dotchka, perfume for Raisa and the Countess, and tobacco for Dmitri Denisov.

He found a small fir tree at the florist's and decorated it with tinsel, glass balls, and red Chinese baubles for good luck. He held the baby by the tree for her to look at the decorations.

She stretched out a hand which trembled as she blinked at the reflections.

He lowered her so that her toes touched the ground. He bounced her. "You're very clever. Let's look at your toys and take a snap for Grandma in England."

He sent silk slippers to his mother and sisters, shirts for his brothers and a Chinese drawing for his father.

Lulu wrapped the gifts in red tissue paper, and put them with the rabbit under the tree. "What about Olga and Sergei and your friends? I know, we'll get Olga perfume like the other women and some good whisky for the men."

Sam waved his hands. "A real English Christmas. We'll sing carols – Russian and English, and French, too, if that's what your aunt wants."

Lulu clapped. "And then Russian Christmas in January. Another celebration."

"I'm glad you're feeling better, love. We'll have a really good time."

* * *

On Christmas Day cold mist hung from the bare plane trees and settled on the low cypress in the garden. The sergeants, Rob and Ted, arrived first with boxes of chocolates; a toy dog with blue glass eyes and a red, felt tongue; and a big picture of Father Christmas. Raisa and Dmitri Denisov brought champagne and a small wooden cat puppet with moving legs. The Countess gave one of her pictures. Olga and Sergei arrived. She had been crying, he was drunk. They put two matryoshkas under the tree, then kissed Lulu and Sam. Olga held Sam's arm and looked at him. He looked away, took her fur coat and hat and took them into the bedroom. He stroked the collar and smelled her perfume as he placed them on a chair.

They opened the presents. The champagne spurted. Sam filled glasses. Lulu admired her ring, Dotchka poked at the rabbit's eyes. Dmitri Denisov jerked the cat puppet to make it dance and made mewing sounds. Dotchka laughed.

The guests drank to each other, then to friends and families, and sang carols in English and Russian, before sitting down to eat. The cook, Chan, brought in a crisp, browned turkey, surrounded with sausages and stuffing.

"Just like home," said Rob, "here's to all those who can't be here."

They pulled crackers with trinkets and messages on thin, rolled paper, inside them. Dmitri Denisov found a whistle and blew it loudly. Dotchka jerked in Mary's arms and began to cry.

"Papa, stop," said Raisa. "Don't do that. What your fortune ticket say, Sam?"

He unravelled the paper. "A good year for romance." They clapped and cheered.

He poured brandy on the pudding and lit its dome. Blue wavering flames burned hastily and died down. He began to cut into its plump interior, stuffed with raisins and cherries.

"Watch out. We hid sixpenny pieces in here. Whoever gets one will be lucky."

Olga bit into the pudding, took the sixpence from her mouth and held it up. She smiled and raised her glass. "Good luck for me."

Mary carried Dotchka to her bed, then gathered the remains of turkey, vegetables, and pudding to take to the basement. Sergei fell asleep, Rob, Ted, Dmitri Denisov and Lulu began a game of rummy, Raisa went to lie on the bed, and the Countess left for her nap. Olga and Sam cleared the table and put the dishes in the kitchen for Mary to wash.

Olga put her hand on his arm "Come and see me soon, Sam. I am so unhappy."

He clattered a plate. "Shh. I can't. Never again. Don't bring this up here. It's our Christmas party. Keep your voice down. Someone will hear."

"My husband no good. Out all time – dogs, cards, other women…"

"I can't do anything about that. I am with Lulu. You know that."

"Just a little time now and then."

Lulu came into the kitchen to get beers for the men. She looked at Olga then at Sam.

"What happen here?"

Sam stepped towards the sink. "We are clearing things away."

Lulu shouted in Russian and Olga ran out of the kitchen, wailing. Lulu hit Sam on the chest and broke a plate by banging it on the table. Sergei jumped in his chair, the card game stopped, and Raisa rushed out of the bedroom. Dotchka began to cry. Sam picked her up to pat her back as she lay across his shoulder. Mary arrived to feed her.

Sam handed the baby to her. "Make the bottle and take her down to the basement."

"I think we'd better go," said Rob, "it's getting a bit late and I'm on duty early tomorrow."

They kissed Lulu's cheek and shook hands with Sam. Dmitri Denisov smoked his pipe and hummed.

Raisa looked at Lulu and brought her coat and hat from the bedroom. "Papa, leave the cards and come now."

Olga dragged her husband to his feet and picked up her coat.

Lulu closed the door and screamed. "What you talk to Olga about? I see you touch her and look at her."

Sam leaned on the wall. "Nothing, and I didn't touch her. She was upset. Don't spoil a nice day, Lulu."

"You fuck Olga? The truth." Sam looked down and played with a tassel at the corner of the tablecloth.

"Only once…"

"After I sick and tired and have baby?"

"You wouldn't let me near you all through when you were expecting. It's not much better now."

"All you think about is fuck. You never think about me. I take off this ring. I throw it away. I sell it."

He stared at her and shouted, "Don't be so bloody difficult. I'm fed up with this. I work hard. I do my best. I don't know what you do all day. Maybe you have your men friends round."

"Get out," she yelled, "go back to your Station and your job or your Olga. Don't come back."

He put on his coat. "Who pays for everything? Flat, Mary, washing, food, Raisa, your father. Just remember." He walked back to Kashing Road, drank half a bottle of whisky in his room and fell asleep.

* * *

His coolie woke him at eight. His head hurt. His skin prickled. What a terrible end to Christmas Day. He must make it up to Lulu, but she had to change her ways. It wasn't fair.

He dressed, shaved, put on his thick overcoat, lit a cigarette, and walked out of the barracks. Lights glowed in Station offices and he saw men, mainly Chinese, talking, inspecting papers and filing.

He walked through the French Park where a pale sun had eased the frost from the grass and two children kicked a ball. His feet sank into the softening earth. Two blackbirds, yellow-beaked and agile, chased each other across the garden, pausing to pull worms from the ground.

He bought noodles for breakfast from a stall at the edge of the park, then found a shop at a corner of Route Vallon where a Chinese woman sold chrysanthemums. He bought six white and six purple and walked into Avenue Joffre. He opened the door of the apartment.

Mary sat in an armchair feeding Dotchka who sucked the rubber teat, gurgled, and patted the bottle.

"Where Missee?"

"Her sleep."

He sat down. "I'll wait. You can go, Mary, when you've fed and changed the baby. I'll take her."

He sat Dotchka on his knees and chanted, "A farmer goes a trot, trot, trot... " She gazed at him, put her fist in her mouth, blinked, pulled her ear with the fingers of the other hand, stared at him, and sneezed. He patted her back and said, "Oh, dear." Lulu came out of the bedroom. Her dressing gown had slipped from her shoulders. Her eyes were smudged with black and her face powder streaked. She sniffed and sobbed. Sam lay Dotchka on the sofa, put his arms round Lulu and stroked her hair.

"You're under a lot of strain; your nerves must be very bad what with the baby, your father, Raisa, and the new place. I'll try to help more – visit Raisa, get her medicines, that kind of thing."

"I tired all time. I not like you see other women."

He squeezed her shoulder. "I know and I'm sorry, but you have to let me near you. I love you and want us to have a nice time, but you can be so cold. Do you love me?" She nodded. "I'll make some tea. Hold Dotchka. I've brought some flowers. Tonight, we are going for dinner at Delmonte's to discuss Russian Christmas and what happens next year. You can have the wedding you want when we get permission. This afternoon, we'll go to bed whilst Mary looks after Dotchka."

* * *

On 15 April, Jack Smethers and Yana were married in the little Russian church.

"I hope I remember what I'm doing," said Jack, "It's all a bit complicated and my Russian is terrible."

Sam slapped him on the back. "You'll be fine. Just smile."

The reception – vodka, caviar, and a Russian buffet – was held in a café with twelve guests. Sam took photographs.

"Now the bride. You look lovely, Yana." She wore a long white silk dress with a tiara of flowers.

Lulu stroked the skirt. "Nice, very plain."

19

Sam received a letter from his mother to say that Mr Barrett, the nice commissioner, had written to thank her for her letter and said that Sam had done brave work in capturing gangsters. They all felt very proud of him, but hoped it wasn't too dangerous. She thought the picture of Dotchka at Christmas very bonny, and just like him at that age.

* * *

In July, Sam received his letter of permission to marry.

He waved it at Lulu. "We can get married right away. Just a simple wedding like Yana and Jack."

Lulu snatched the letter. "No, no. It take big preparation. You say I have wedding I want. I want cathedral, fine dress, flowers, picture in papers."

"That's for really important people. Where's the money coming from?"

"You always talk money, money. I important. We borrow, I work, Aunt help."

"How will you work? Hairdresser? Cake shop? Secretary like Yana? You have no qualifications, and I'm not having you going back to your old stuff. Talk to Yana. She'll help. You could make your dress. You used to make all your clothes."

Lulu pulled at the curtains. "I not make dress for very special day. I talk to Aunt and Raisa. We plan for next year."

Sam released her hand. "And I pay, is that it? We'll be moving into our own apartment in autumn. Isn't that enough?"

"We plan so not cost much."

"All right, but just be careful about money. You know what I earn. I can make a bit on the side, but I'm not going to do anything that's not right. I love you. I want us to be happy and settle down as a family. I want us to go to England and find a really good doctor for you."

* * *

The assistant commissioner called a meeting of sub-inspectors and sergeants at Central Station.

"More trouble. Chiang Kai-shek has banned prostitution in cities in the north. The whores will flock to Shanghai. We'll have the Moral Welfare League on our backs again, wanting action."

Jack Smethers nudged Sam. "Oh, not again. God, those terrible women, waving bibles."

"Apart from that, sir, what's this about the opium mess I read about in the newspapers?" asked Sergeant Flood.

"Complete shambles. Zhang Zhijang, Chairman of the Opium Suppression Committee – you laugh, I know it's a joke – gets tipped off about a shipment on the Bund. Shanghai police go to arrest people, our Military police try to arrest the Chinese police and the opium gets bundled off to the French Concession."

"Christ," Jack murmured, "that's what you get when a fucking gangster's in charge." Sam poked his arm.

"Do you have anything to say, Smethers?" asked the assistant commissioner.

"No, sir. Except that it seems like we need to talk to the French and the Public Security Bureau. This is not doing our name any good."

"I agree and I'm sending three of you off, Sub-Inspector Dean and Sergeants Shuttleworth and Todd, to talk to them. They're obsessed with communists, of course. Everybody is, and we're expected to take all the blame and keep order."

"Sir," Flood asked again, "I thought the communists had gone underground. What's happening?

"The Special Branch are dealing with it. I know they're accused of torture to get information. And so are the chaps in security. We need to deny it, but we do also need to swap more information with the French. They're still around, these Reds, using ordinary shops as a cover. Bloke called Gu Shunzhang working under Zhou Enlai. Watch out for them. The shopkeepers might squeal given a bit of encouragement. Know what I mean?"

* * *

Raisa was taken to hospital, unconscious. Lulu sat at the bedside and held her hand.

"She need rest and better medicine. TB very bad when summer come."

Sam put his arm round her shoulder. "I'll take over now. Go and get some rest yourself."

Raisa clutched at his sleeve and said Jesus was calling her. "I see white light and arms pull me into it. Green trees, birds, and music."

Sam patted her arm. "Jesus is telling you to get better. You have to be there for our wedding. You will have a beautiful new frock."

She nodded and tried to speak. "Sam, Sam. Lulu good to me. She have new friend. I tell you a secret. American in big bank. She go to apartment. You be careful. I sleep now."

Sam stroked her cheek and put a cool cloth on her forehead. "I think you have a high fever. You don't know what you're saying. Lulu needs you. We all need you. I'll bring some nice fruit and noodles tomorrow. You must keep up your strength. You'll be out of here soon."

* * *

163

Sam was waiting for Lulu when she came home the following afternoon.

"Where have you been today?"

"Why you here, not on duty? I visit Raisa. I talk to Aunt about wedding. She pay for dress for me and Raisa from Monsieur Charles. I talk to Reverend at cathedral. Can marry there next April. Nice time for wedding he say."

"Who is this American?"

She took off her jacket. "What American? I know no American. I see Russian friends for tea – Masha, Galina, Varvara, Katerina – you know all these."

"Who *is* he? I cannot have you going round with other people. There are spies everywhere. People talk."

He went to grab her arm; she pushed him away, turned and walked into the kitchen.

"They not talk about me. You jealous again. If it Raisa say something, she in fever and not know what she say. When she out of hospital next week, will be different. Don't listen to bad talk, Sam. You work too hard."

"I do work hard, and I need some relaxation, but I'm watching you. I will be very angry if there's any funny business."

"No need watch me. I busy to organise wedding. I talk to priest at cathedral."

"How much does the cathedral cost? I suppose there's the organ and choir and all the bloody rest."

Lulu poked his chest. "You not swear about cathedral. It bad luck. I have savings. You know Aunt help. I tell you, you need to relax more."

"We'll talk about this later. Yes, I do need to relax and I've been asked to join the tennis team at the British Club. They know I'm good and two of their good players have gone back to England. I'll be there after duty once a week and then have matches some weekends."

"What about tennis clothes to buy? What about me and Dotchka?"

"I'll see you as much as I can. I'll visit Raisa and your papa. When we have our own apartment later this year, things will be a lot easier. I don't need a new tennis outfit. My old clothes still fit and they'll wash and iron them at the club. I'm off on duty now. Just remember what I said."

* * *

Mrs Henderson, secretary to the British Tennis Club, wrote to Sam to ask him to come for a trial. She had heard of his reputation, and the club would waive fees if he could be useful to them.

He had a game of men's doubles after duty on Thursday with Jim, a banker from Devon, as his partner.

Mrs Henderson clapped. "Well played. Very strong forearm. Come and have a G and T in the clubhouse when you're changed. It's cool in there .You don't need a tie."

"I have to go," said Jim, "need to take the wife and colleagues to the Cathay for dinner. Nice to meet you, Sam. Just leave your flannels and shirt in the changing room. It will be ready laundered for you on Saturday. I think we'll do well in the match – it's against a team from the Consulate. Mrs H will show you the rest of the fixtures list. The other boys are going for a swim."

Mrs Henderson pointed to a leather chair. "And call me Diana. How long have you played?"

Sam sipped his drink. "I learned back in England, then played with a friend at the racecourse. I had coaching from Anton there and played in the team. We won everything but I haven't had time to play for a while. Work is very busy."

"I can imagine. You're in the police, aren't you? A sergeant?"

Sam nodded.

"Do you smoke? I have some fags new from England, Senior Service. Very smooth." She put her cigarette into a holder. Sam tapped his on the table and laughed. "Shakes down the tobacco."

She lit the cigarettes with a silver lighter. "How do you like Shanghai?"

He tossed back his head to blow the smoke away from her. "Getting a bit hot at the moment. I'm not used to heat. I'm from Lancashire."

165

She laughed. "Where do you live now?"

"Mainly barracks at Kashing Road. I'll probably move into an apartment on Weiheiwei in October. We need a place of our own."

She tapped ash into a tray. "We? Are you married?"

"Not exactly. You can't get married before you've done six years in the police. I have a girl. She's Russian, and we have a baby."

She smiled. "Busy boy."

Diana Henderson made him think of Annabelle. Blonde, big blue eyes, lots of lipstick, nice figure, and wafting a cigarette around as she talked.

"What does your husband do?"

"Runs a company that sells silk. At least that's what they say. Travels a lot. In Peking at the moment. Problems with business he says. Bloody communists. Bloody Chinese with all their bribery and kidnappings."

"It's worse than that. Believe me, I know."

She put her hand on his sleeve. "I look forward to hearing more."

Sam finished his drink. She clicked her fingers at the waiter.

"After the match on Saturday, why don't you come for a boat trip with a couple of other chums? Have some food and drink."

He nodded. "That would be very nice. Thank you, Mrs Henderson."

"Diana." She squeezed his hand and watched as he went to call a rickshaw back to Avenue Joffre.

* * *

The Countess was in the apartment with Lulu when Sam arrived. Pictures of wedding dresses from magazines were scattered on the floor.

Sam looked round. "Where's Mary and the baby?"

Lulu lifted her head. "Dotchka asleep. Mary out shopping. She'll be back soon. Sit down. Come and look at plans."

The Countess held up a page. "I think this one. You have such a beautiful figure, it would look wonderful. What do you think, Sam?"

Sam glanced at the magazine. "She does have a good figure – you choose."

He bent to kiss Lulu. She sniffed. "You smell of gin and tobacco. You never drink gin. I thought you play tennis."

"I had one with the boys afterwards. That's what they drink at the British Club."

"I take her to see Monsieur Charles tomorrow," said the Countess, "he need time to make beautiful dress, do fittings. All must be perfect."

Sam picked up a picture and looked at a long dress in silk. "I have to get back to barracks, I'm on early duty tomorrow."

He went into the bedroom, kissed Dotchka on the head, and stood to look at her. She lay on her back, arms stretched above her head, fists clenched. She sucked her lower lip. The nappy bulged into the long cotton nightdress which rose and fell with her breathing. Her bare toes curled towards her face.

"You're the best thing that ever happened."

He kissed Lulu on the cheek and the Countess on the hand. "See you tomorrow at about six. We can all eat here. It's Friday. Ask Mary to get some fish in. I'm playing tennis on Saturday. Big match. Having drinks afterwards, then on night duty."

* * *

Sam and his partner won their two matches in the Saturday fixture and the club team won five to two.

"Great to have you on board," said Jim, "we all go for a drink now with the gallant losers."

Diana Henderson joined them. "You looked like you were enjoying yourself."

Sam slapped the racquet against his thigh. "It's good to be playing again. I just like the grip of the leather and the twang of bashing a ball hard. Good feeling."

She ran her hand across the strings of his racquet. "Very skilled and aggressive. Are you always like that?"

"Depends what I'm doing."

She looked at him and blew smoke to the left of his head. "Meet outside the door of the clubhouse in an hour. We have a car to take us to the dock."

* * *

He looked at the boat, the *Seagull*, three times longer than the police boat and newly painted blue and white. "This is nice."

A Union Jack and another flag with a coat of arms drooped on poles at the front. A canvas veranda stretched over the middle where there were two cabins; at the rear was a planked open area with wicker loungers and sunshades.

Two Chinese sailors in white trousers and shirts, and blue peaked caps, stood on the front deck, pulling ropes.

"This is my husband's company boat; that's their flag. We go out along the creek, then have dinner. The boys have brought a hamper. Dab some of this on to keep the mozzies away."

"When do the others arrive?"

She shook her head. "They couldn't come. Had to go to Hong Kong for a wedding. Just us two. Have a drink. Bob, the white wine, please."

They sat in the wicker chairs, smoking and drinking chilled Chablis, as the boat left the dock and headed upstream before swinging into the creek. The humidity did not decrease with dusk but a breeze fanned the boat as it moved forwards. Bob lit a red lantern. Insects brushed Sam's face and whined in his ears; moths fluttered, then fell to the deck.

The boys set up a dining table and brought pheasant, duck, salmon, and steamed vegetables, followed by apple pie and cheeses with red burgundy.

She lit a cigarette. "I'll tell you my life story, then you tell me yours. Not much to mine actually. Husband, two children, travel all over the place."

He leaned forward, elbows on the table. "How old are your children?"

"Rosie's sixteen, Roland fourteen. Both at boarding school in England. Wouldn't have them out here. How about you? Do you like it?"

"I don't mind. It's not a bad life all considered. Better than where I come from. I'm a lad from Lancashire. It's nice being on a boat. I like fishing. Once caught a whopper when I went out with the boys. Not such a grand boat as this."

"A glass of port, I think, and the box of Sobranies. We'll sit on those loungers again."

The humidity became less dense with the dark. Frogs and cicadas called along the banks.

Ducks came alongside the boat. Diana threw bread for them; they scrambled and fought in the battle for scraps. The water flurried and settled. A hard moon reflected in the river as the boat sliced the surface. The boys pulled over to a mooring.

Sam stubbed out the cigarette. "Where are we? I'm supposed to be back in barracks ready for duty by midnight."

"You won't be. I told your commissioner that you would have to stay for a long meeting at the club. The boys get off here for the night and stay in that little village. You can just see the lights. We stay here. I assume that's all right. Have some more port."

She took his hand. He stepped off the lounger and pulled her up. He put his hand into her hair and opened her mouth with his tongue. His erection was painful.

She pushed her breasts against him. "Let's go downstairs to the cabin. Do you like to smoke before or after?"

"Both."

The fan in the cabin had been switched on and the mosquito nets arranged.

She placed his hand on her thigh. "Undress me. But undress yourself first. You don't need to wear anything. I'm safe."

He threw his clothes onto a chair and took off her necklace. He unzipped her dress and slid it over her hips and knees. She stepped out of it. He ran his hands down the silk underwear and stroked her thighs.

She took off her camisole, stockings, and shoes and they climbed under the mosquito net.

She stroked his back as they kissed, and moved her hand down to his testicles and shaft. He put a finger on her clitoris and touched her breasts.

He entered her and moved slowly. She gasped as he came. They sighed and rolled over. She stretched. "Nice. Get the fags, there's a dear."

He flipped the net. "Dangerous smoking under these things."

She laughed. "What a funny thing to say. Are you nervous? You're not on duty now."

She stroked his chest and belly. "You said you could be skilled and aggressive, show me."

* * *

He arrived back at Kashing Road at eight in the morning.

"Where the hell have you been?" asked the inspector.

"Sir, I had a serious tennis match yesterday and we had to discuss tactics and the next fixture. I believe the Secretary phoned the commissioner."

"Did he? Who's that?"

"Mrs Henderson."

"Somebody might have told me. I know the old boy's keen on tennis and mixing with the toffs, so I suppose I have to overlook it. Get changed. You're on duty in an hour."

* * *

Sam arrived home at four in the afternoon. He wanted to sleep. His mouth was still dry and rough.

Lulu closed a magazine of wedding pictures and handed it to the Countess. "You look very tired, what have you been doing?"

"On duty until nine, then writing reports. We were very busy. A couple of shops broken into, some rough stuff down an alley. Fighting over women."

"Dégoûtant," said the Countess, "one day, you wake up dead; you make sure you not get killed before wedding next April."

Monsieur Charles would make Lulu's dress, Raisa would be Matron of Honour and fitted by a Russian dressmaker. Sam and his Best Man, Jack Smethers, would hire morning dress.

Sam slumped on the sofa, his eyes half closed. "At least the men won't need dressing by Monsieur Charles."

He slept until Mary carried Dotchka in for her feed. She reached for Sam. He took her in his hands. "Say Daddy."

* * *

Dotchka walked on her first birthday in November. She pulled herself up on a chair, bounced on creased, plump legs, and turned to Sam, who was crouched and waiting a few paces away, hands outstretched. She tottered for three steps. He caught her. "Clever girl. Look Mummy. Do it again, Dotchka."

She was a tall, sturdy baby with big blue eyes and fair, straight hair which trailed in wisps over her ears. She said "Dada" and "Mama." Sam complained that other words came out in Russian or pidgin or Chinese.

* * *

Sam's mother crocheted a blanket in squares of bright wool. It arrived with a note.

She said her legs were giving her a bit of bother and she could hardly get her shoes on. Getting upstairs was hard work. She wished she could be there for the wedding and to see the little girl. There was a terrible rail crash up north, Burnside Rovers won the football cup, Dad was very pleased, and she was glad that women now had the vote. About time. Auntie Nellie had been on a march and waved a banner.

And a woman found a snail in her ginger beer in Morecambe and there was going to be a court case.

He smiled about the snail. He was sorry for his mother. She had worked all her life. How different things were over there. He was sad that she would not be at his wedding. She would have loved to see everybody dressed up in their fine clothes. She wouldn't believe Lulu's dress. Most of all, he wished she could see Dotchka, hold her, and spoil her. He would get a good photographer and send lots of prints home.

20

In November, the new apartments at 101 Weihewei Road were ready to be occupied. They were built in a square block with a garden in the centre. Sam collected the keys for Number 5 on the ground floor.

"The first place of my own. Look at these lovely floors. Teak, they say." Lulu stroked the walls. "Need furniture and pictures. Make it look like home. I bring some from Aunt. She have things in store. And we buy."

"Not too expensive."

The apartment had a sitting room twelve feet square, a bedroom, a kitchen, with a gas stove, and a bathroom. Square windows onto the garden gathered the winter sun, warm through the glass.

Lulu touched a cold radiator. "I glad about central heating. We make this cosy."

Sam laughed. "That's what a home should be. I think we'll be very happy here, and you'll have neighbours. Yana and Jack are already in the next block. Let's look outside."

A short passage led to the garden where Chinese workers were planting trees and shrubs. They looked up at a date palm, whose leaves stretched up to the second floor. Sam ran his hand along the rough bark.

"That's been there for a long time," said the American agent, "they built round it. They're putting a few shrubs in now. Too cold for anything else. There'll be more planting in spring."

Soil had been piled into curved beds constructed from layers of flat stones. Sam touched the glossy leaf of a low camellia and pushed earth around some azaleas with the toe of his shoe. An osmanthus was being dug in, its roots splayed like streams. A worker arranged them in the hole, piled in manure and leaned on his foot to compress the soil round the thick tendrils.

Sam asked him when it would flower.

"Next spring."

"This is going to be nice. Birds and bees will come. Maybe there'll be a vegetable patch. Dotchka can play here in the summer. I'll get her a little spade and a bucket."

The servants' quarter, a low, stone building, was on the opposite side of the garden. Lulu looked inside at the small rooms. "Mary will like living here. Need a shop and cook amah now that we can't share with Aunt. You said don't cost much."

"Maybe we can share with someone else. There are other police and wives here, too. We can't afford more help."

The Countess gave them a table and four chairs in cherry wood, a display cabinet, two pictures, a set of crockery, cutlery, and pans. They bought a bed made of rosewood from Tang's in Bubbling Well Road and two rugs from the Golden Dragon Store.

Lulu arranged the sitting room and bedroom. "It must all look same. Dark wood chic. I buy other things later. I shop with Varvara. Avenue Road and Route des Soeurs have nice things."

The Countess patted the cabinet. "It used to have family silver and beautiful Russian plates. Everything lost. But I give you silver dining set for wedding present."

Dmitri Denisov gave them a samovar and tea cups and a bottle of vodka. Raisa made curtains in brown brocade and gave them a red paper lantern. "You know what Chinese say – red for good luck."

* * *

The wedding was arranged for 3 April 1929 in Holy Trinity Cathedral. The Countess invited Sam, Lulu, and Raisa to tea to finalise the details.

"We have Russian and French hymns, as well as English."

Sam shook his head. "That is not possible. It is an Anglican cathedral. It will be an Anglican wedding. It is what Lulu wanted – the cathedral. If you want Russian or French, it will have to be a French or Russian church. I wish it were – this is bloody expensive."

Raisa and Lulu looked into their tea cups. Lulu tossed her head. "Not swear about church. It bad luck. Aunt pay for clothes and reception."

Sam banged the table. "And I pay for choir, organist, flowers, vicar, and every other bloody thing."

"We not get married then."

"I've had enough of this. I'm under a lot of strain at work. I do long hours and all you can do is act like a spoiled child."

Raisa put her hands to her ears. "Please. It too late for all that. It will be lovely day. Much nicer than *my* wedding. You remember, Aunt? That little building down Rue Lafayette, long Russian service; ten people there. Boris drunk. Reception in Russian Café. Pirozhki and vodka. I borrow dress from Tamara."

"That because Boris not let me organise," said the Countess. "Bâtard. I tell you he bad man then. Now you know. Tant pis."

Sam stood. "You finish all this planning. I have a tennis practice, then I'm going for a drink at the Station. Jack's meeting me."

Lulu lay on the sofa, her face in a pillow. She looked up. "I thought you work all time, not drink."

* * *

Sam ordered beer for Jack and himself. "This wedding's going to cost a fortune. Cathedral, fancy frocks, all that."

Jack offered a cigarette. "Why the Anglican cathedral if she's Russian?"

Sam swirled the beer in his glass and watched the froth. "Wants a big do. Photographer, in the newspapers, the lot."

"Put your foot down. Do you want Yana to talk to her?"

Sam shrugged. "Too late. There's her sister, her aunt all planning like mad. When she's got an idea in her head there's no shifting her. At least the old aunt is paying for the reception – very fancy – champagne and all that."

"Where is it?"

"Chez Alice or something. In the Rue Chapsal. Very chic, as the old girl says."

"You don't sound too happy about it."

"I'm just being dragged along, but I do love her and want to marry her, with all her funny ways. She needs looking after. I want to get us back to England as soon as we can. My ma's not so good and she wants to see us and the baby. You're lucky going this summer. I've got to be on my way now. I'm on duty at midnight. Things to do before then."

"Where are you off to?"

"Seeing a lady from the tennis club. Has a nice flat not far away. Husband in Hong Kong. But I'm with *you*, OK?"

Jack smiled. "Still a ladies' man, eh? Maybe you'll settle down when you're married and living together in your own place. We want to come and see the apartment some time when you're settled."

"Fine. See you next week. So long."

* * *

The Countess arranged for photographers and reporters from the English language, French, and Russian press to cover the wedding. Sam and Jack wore wing-collared shirts, silk ties, and morning suits with carnation buttonholes and a white handkerchief in the top pocket. They waited outside the cathedral for the bride to arrive.

Jack brushed a speck from Sam's collar. "You look like a real toff."

"I'm as nervous as hell. I still worry she won't turn up, if everything will be how she wants it, and if the photos will turn out. I want to send some back home."

"It's normal. Everything will be fine. Look, here she is now."

A black Bentley pulled up at the kerb of the shingle courtyard. Dmitri Denisov stepped out wearing a top hat, cravat, and a long black coat over dark grey trousers. He swayed and held onto the door.

"He looks like he's going to a funeral," said Jack Smethers. "I just hope he isn't drunk already."

Sam helped Lulu from the car. "You look very beautiful. Lovely dress. Jack and I have to go in now. I'll see you at the altar."

She bunched up the satin gown, and held it with both hands whilst Raisa took the flowers. "Make sure Papa behaves. Ask Jack to be with him."

* * *

After the reception, Sam and Lulu returned to the apartment and changed out of their wedding clothes. She draped the dress over the settee, the bouquet of stephanotis and pink roses on the lace bodice, the train spread to the floor.

Sam sat and looked round. "This looks grand, love; you've got very good taste. I like the plates on the wall and these blue candlesticks. They go well with the pictures and rugs. It does look warm and cosy. Let's light two candles for us, and I'll have a cigarette. No more bloody barracks except in an emergency."

"You always have emergency. I never know where you are."

He took out his lighter. "That's all going to change, now that I've got you and Dotchka. I want us all to be happy. Are you happy, Lulu? I am. The wedding was grand."

"I very pleased. Lovely dress." She stroked the silk. "Now we have nice two days in Suzhou."

"Yes. It's all fixed. Dotchka will be fine with Mary. Mary can have the little camp bed in Dotchka's room. We'll stay in a little guest house. We'll see the gardens, temples, and pagodas; a chance to relax."

"And see beautiful women."

He looked at the candles and blew out a stream of smoke. "What do you mean?"

"You know they say most beautiful women in China in Suzhou."

He laughed. "I've got the most beautiful woman here. Come here, Lastochka. Your Kotchka wants you."

* * *

"So, how's married life?" asked Jack Smethers in the bar.

"All right," said Sam, "nice having our own place. Baby likes the garden. Chases the ducks, throws bread to the magpies."

"How's Lulu?"

Sam ordered another beer. "Seems OK. I hope Yana will visit soon. I think Lulu must get bored in the day. I've no idea what she does except drink tea with her friends. She visits her sister, of course. Raisa's not well, nor is their father."

"I know. Plenty of Russians in poor health."

"Is Yana still working at the Russian Women's League? Lulu won't have anything to do with that. I've tried to interest her."

"Well, it's only a little part-time job, but she enjoys it. We're hoping to start a family soon. Happen on the boat home. I'll be glad to get out of here for a rest. Things are bubbling up again, you know. Commissioner getting very nervous, apparently. Seen the newspapers recently? All these reports about crime and how we're not doing our job, and what we're costing. Did you see the one about how we're getting pay-offs for helping with kidnappings? Cheeky buggers."

"I know, but we do have to stamp out this corruption in the police. There was that case the other day. Scottish bloke guilty of helping with a kidnapping."

"Well, he got his comeuppance. Pretty serious that when you're in the police. Death sentence too good for him, I say."

"They say it's worse with the French now that we've tried to close down our casinos. All flooded over to the French Quarter. There'll be trouble. Canidrome and the doggies will be OK. You watch."

Jack punched Sam on the arm. "How's the lady with the husband in Hong Kong?"

Sam coughed. "Don't mention that. She's gone to join him. Bit of a relief, really. I'm done with all that."

"How's that bugger old Denisov? Still cursing and gossiping?"

Sam nodded. "He still gets useful bits of info from the old Chinese bloke downstairs. Don't know what's true and what's rumour, though."

"You never do. Finish your beer, and we'll get some food."

* * *

A letter from Annabelle arrived at the Station. Sam looked at the postmark and wondered why she had written.

Filton Hall, Yorkshire   *25th April 1929*

My spies tell me you've got yourself wed. My old friend Deborah spotted a cutting in the newspaper and sent it. Terrible photo. Why do you all look so miserable? Ha ha. She says you have a baby too. You have no idea what it's like here. His Lordship is a complete turd. The house (manor, God help us) is freezing and has been all bloody winter. He won't allow enough fires. I sleep in a coat. Not with him, I have to add. Useless in that department. Wants a son. Fat chance. Not good with the courting tackle, at least not with me. He likes stable boys and God knows what he gets up to in London. I suppose you'll be due leave next year. Six year stint isn't it? Your folks can't be too far away from Yorkshire. How about a little rendezvous when wifey's not about. At least there's a good cellar here. Fifty-year-old whisky. Cheers.

Here's the phone number.

He wrote down the phone number, tore up the letter and put it in the bin. Oh, boy, those days with Annabelle. Long gone. No, he was a serious married man. No fooling about any more. She sounded unhappy. Imagine being in a place like that. Still, she had money. More than he had, and she didn't have an expensive wife.

21

Inspector Gibson handed Sam a telegram when he came on duty the morning of 17 June. Sam tore it open. "It's from my sister. My mother's died."

He sat on the wooden chair facing the inspector's desk, stacked with reports. He looked at his boots and brushed a rim of dust round the right ankle; he flattened the telegram and read it again.

She would have died yesterday evening Shanghai time, whilst he was playing cards in the club. He had slept in barracks due to being on early duty, without knowing she had gone. Tears pricked his eyes; he brushed them with his sleeve.

Gibson coughed. "I'm very sorry. It's hard when this happens, being so far away. My dad died last year. I know. Take a day off to write to your family, do the obituary for your local paper back home, order flowers; all that's important."

"It's all right, I'll do all that later. I'd rather be at work. She was a good woman, my ma. Suffered a lot in the last few years. Did her best for everybody."

"You could have compassionate leave but it's no use to you, the journey being so long. When are you due to go back home?"

"Next March. A long time."

"Of course. I'm sorry. Chin up,. eh?"

Sam nodded. He thought about his last letter to his ma where he had done nothing but complain – about doctor's bills, time spent nursing Lulu and Raisa, about only earning $258 with living costs at $210 and the fare to England $90 one way. What could she have done about all that? He hadn't even said he was looking forward to coming home next March.

He left the inspector's office, put on his cap and roared the motorbike along the crowded streets back to Weiheiwei Road. Dotchka was asleep, Lulu out having tea with friends. Mary was peeling vegetables in the kitchen. "You home early."

"Yes. I've had a telegram. My mother is dead. I have things to do."

Mary stopped work at the sink, faced him and lowered her head. "I very sorry. Mama very important. Very sad. I get you special hot ginger drink."

He sat. "That would be nice. I'll have some whisky in it."

Dotchka woke and murmured in her cot. He went to pick her up and held her against his chest. Her cheeks were hot and red; she dribbled and pulled her ears. He felt her heartbeat, and breathed the smell of her hair and skin. Under his hand, the damp of the nappy leaked through her nightdress.

"I'm sorry you'll never see your granny. She only had a snap of you; she would have played with you and spoiled you."

His tears spilled onto her head. Dotchka pulled away and looked at his face. She had his large, oval eyes, but they were bright blue, like Lulu's. She touched the tears and put her fingers in her mouth. He handed her to Mary who felt the nappy.

"I change her and give milk and biscuit. We go walk in pram. Missee back soon."

He sat in the armchair, sipped the ginger and whisky tea and thought about the obituary he would send to the *Warren News* and the telegram for his family. He would ask Billy Wigg to call round on them.

Lulu came in wearing a new green felt hat. He stood.

"Ma's dead. I'm sorry you will never meet her. She would have loved you like a daughter." Lulu pulled out the hatpin. "I never have mother. Old people get ill and die. I sorry."

He sat and cried. "She wasn't old. Only fifty-three. Hard life."

She put her hand on his shoulder. "What happen to little brother now?"

He blew his nose into a large handkerchief. "Jimmy's only twelve. I expect Bertha and Ivy will look after him. My dad wouldn't be any use; we'll see next year. It'll be strange without Ma. Let's get out of Shanghai for a few days in the summer. Go by the sea. It will be good for you and Dotchka. Get away from warships on the Huangpu, noise everywhere and dust from putting up all these buildings."

"Tonight let us go to cinema, cheer you. New movie called *Old Arizona* at Metropole. With sound. Or go to dance. New band at Russian Club."

"I can't do that. I just want to be on my own, with you and Dotchka. I'll go for a walk now and call at the post office to send telegrams."

She shrugged.

* * *

In October, Jack and Yana Smethers returned from their visit to Cardiff. Sam bought Jack a drink at the Cotton Bar. "How is the old place?"

"Bloody expensive. Here, I bought fags on the boat. The American Depression really hit jobs and money in Wales and north of England, too, I believe. A drink costs a fortune, not like here. General election of course. Won't make any difference. New picture house opened in Newport. Nice to see everybody. Mam and Dad glad to meet Yana. She couldn't get on with the accent but we had a good time. Sorry about your ma, by the way."

"Yes. I'll miss her and her funny letters. I'm sorry Lulu and Dotchka won't meet her."

Sam lowered his head. "Nothing but trouble here. My father-in-law says his old Chinese mate thinks the Japs are planning a takeover. The Chinese still can't decide who's in charge. Same old stuff – robberies, kidnappings, fighting amongst themselves. I got another commendation for arresting some villains in an opium scam. Two constables killed, two injured. Drought in the north, millions dying. Welcome back."

"When are you off to England?"

"Next March. Plenty of planning going on. Buying trunks already. The wife wants to take evening dress and furs and umpteen bally frocks. That's wi'out clothes for me and the babby. I don't need a lot, but Dotchka's fifteen months now and needs all sorts of stuff."

"Furs? You'll get there in April. England's not as cold as that, surely. But you're going on a fancier boat than us, so there might be dancing, I suppose. And they do have women to look after kiddies if you want."

Sam unwrapped a packet of cigarettes. "Any signs of a little one for you yet?"

"No luck so far. Not for want of trying. Two miscarriages. Doctor says Yana is too thin, so we have to try to build her up. She put some weight on in Wales. Mam made her eat good home-made bread and plenty of meat and potatoes."

"She'll be fine. Let's hope she can get some sense into Lulu about what clothes to take."

"Anyway, we'd like you and a few others to come over for Christmas. There'll be a mixture of Welsh and Russians – and one or two English."

Sam laughed. "I might understand the Russian better than the Welsh accent. Thanks. You get the whisky. I'll bring the vodka."

* * *

Sam visited the Countess, after a night shift, on a brisk January day. The bare branches of plane trees outside her windows rustled and snapped and snow flurried into ridges on the pavement. The Countess sipped tea and pinned back her dark hair into tortoiseshell combs. "What the ship like? What date you go? What happen to apartment?"

Sam added sugar to the dark tea. "We are sailing on the *Coromandel* on 7 March. Raisa will have the apartment, with Mary to help whilst we're away. I'll pay her in advance."

The Countess nodded. "I help Raisa sometimes. She not work now. I very worry about her illness. TB get worse. Dmitri Denisov, too."

"I know and we shall worry. Here's the address in Warren and the brochure for the *Coromandel*."

The Countess flicked through pictures of the dining rooms and lounges on the ship.

"Lulu must get rest. All get rest. You too tired. I give you money for English doctor for Lulu bad cough."

"I know. You are very kind. Thank you. I'll repay you. I just want her to get better. I'm worried that bronchitis might turn into TB if she doesn't get treatment. I'd like to take Raisa as well and see what could be done for her, but it's too expensive. I've had to borrow a bit for this trip."

"Raisa too ill now. She cannot get better. All can be done is help her live. You know – same with many Russians, many Chinese." The Countess looked at the floor and stroked a silk cushion. "I will get you money in cash. Not trust banks."

"We are grateful for all you do. I'm taking my camera and we'll show you photographs when we get back."

"That will be nice."

"It seems like donkey's years since I was in England. It'll be grand. Everyone so friendly. No shootings or kidnappings." He laughed. "At least I hope not. They'll all love Lulu and Dotchka. I can't wait to see my family and friends."

* * *

The *Coromandel* breathed out smoke across the harbour on the Bund and pulled away. Passengers crowded the decks to wave. Sam knew that Dmitri Denisov and Raisa were somewhere there, waving and crying. The Shuttleworths had a second class corner cabin with two windows, two bunks, and a small bed fixed to the ground for Dotchka. The steward, who served five cabins, explained the ship's layout.

"Where is first class?" Lulu asked, "Are any famous people on board?"

"That's two decks above," said the steward, "You can only go up there by invitation. On board we've got Lord Carnell, who's been out viewing the water supplies in north China; there's Sir Robert Denton, big businessman; and an American heiress, visiting London to get married I'm told."

Sam raised his eyebrows. "Let's hope we don't sink then. What's the route?"

The steward pointed to a map on the corridor wall: "Hong Kong, Manila, Saigon, Singapore, on through Aden, Port Said, Naples, Marseilles, Gibraltar, and Tilbury docks. Six weeks. You can get off at Singapore, Colombo, and Marseilles. We pick up mail on the way and take on other passengers. Good old girl. Vibrates a bit in heavy weather. Might get a monsoon around Aden. Have you booked an amah for the baby?"

* * *

In Aden, Sam took Dotchka on deck to watch dolphins alongside the boat. He took photographs of her waving at their slippery humps. She clapped and shouted for more. Flying fish whisked across the bows and, in the waterways, flamingos stood tall and lanky, jellyfish glided through the grey shallows, and dragonflies hovered. Then came the monsoon.

Suntanned passengers became pale. Lulu said she was going to die. Only Sam and Dotchka laughed at the rollers and waited for calm.

He telegrammed Billy Wigg to say that they would be at Warren station at 5pm on 21 April and would be tired after a long journey to get there. Tilbury docks, buses, trains to Warren.

Lulu sighed and lay on the bunk. "I so tired. Does your friend have taxi?"

Sam hesitated and picked up Dotchka. "No, but he'll get us home with all this luggage. Remember, I'm going to introduce you as Tatiana, and we're not going to mention illness or anything like that."

21

Billy Wigg waited, standing by a horse and cart outside the railway station, isolated on the slope of a hill. Sam and two porters carried the luggage on a metal cart under a tunnel from the train. Billy clasped Sam's hand and Sam thumped Billy's other arm.

"You're looking well, Sam. Suntanned, handsome as ever, and look at the lovely wife and babby. Never seen anything like it."

"This is Tatiana, my wife, and baby Elizabeth after my ma. We call her Dotchka as a nickname. It means little daughter. Christ, it's good to be back. A bit windy up here on this hill. Pull your coats round you, lasses."

Lulu looked round. "Where taxi?"

"Gee, gee," murmured Dotchka.

The cart was wooden, painted red and green with large red wheels and, on the side a sign, painted in gloss: **W. Wigg and Sons, Painter and Decorator.** Billy opened a gate at the back and piled the trunks and luggage inside and lowered a wooden ladder.

"Up you get, missus. Sam get up first. I'll pass you t'babby and help missus up. There's some sacks to sit on next to t'planks, buckets and brushes. Don't let babby crawl about."

"Wiggins and Sons. A bit early isn't it? It's good you've managed to set yourself up, though."

"Nay. Sounds better, more important, like. My lads are six and four now. How old's yours?"

"Nearly eighteen months"

"Nice, big, bonny lass. My lads'll like playing wi' 'er. Allotment doing well. Tha'll see. Happen tomorrow? All reet missus? Walk on, Elsie."

The cart horse, brown with white specks in her fur, had thick, white legs, tasselled with grey hair round her wide feet.

Sam looked at the horse's broad back. "Elsie? That's a funny name for a horse."

"Named after me auntie what left me a bit o' money and I set misself up. Doing well. Plenty o' work. More than thi' can say about mills."

Dotchka pointed to the horse. "Where gee gee eyes?"

Billy flicked the reins. "Under them black things called blinkers. Does she understand me?"

Lulu sat on a plank, holding her skirt, with one hand on her hat. Sam held Dotchka and pointed out lamp posts and little houses. The cart jolted on the cobbles down Railway Road, and through the back streets to Greenway Street, decorated with ribbons and a banner saying "Welcome Home, Sam."

Bertha and Ivy stood on the doorstep, newly scoured with white chalk on each side. Neighbours were on the pavement and waved as the horse approached. They cheered and ran to the cart.

Billy Wigg looked at Lulu. "See how important he is?" She looked at the steps of the cart and wiped her hands on her dress.

Sam leapt out, put his arms round his two sisters who kissed him and cried. He lifted Dotchka out. She turned her head away from them. Bertha held out her hands.

"Ah, she must be overfaced, little lass. She'll soon get used to us. Here's a dolly we bought at Church bazaar last week. Does she want changing?"

"No, she's just out of nappies and very good about it, except at night."

Dotchka seized the doll, and held it close. The hair, strands of brown wool, made a fringe on the forehead and fell, tangled to the shoulders. Legs of blue and white striped fabric dangled from under a red cotton dress against Dotchka's chest. The stuck on eyes were bright blue, framed with brown felt eyebrows.

"Dolly," said Dotchka.

Billy Wigg lowered the steps and helped Lulu. She leaned on his arm and placed her feet, in soft, black leather shoes with two inch heels, on each board. She stood on the pavement and looked along the street of houses in pale brick, with fronts varnished in brown.

Sam looked at his sisters wearing headscarves and flowered print cotton dresses, with short sleeves to the elbows of their plump, pink arms. "You've dressed up for us, I see."

Bertha took Lulu's hand. "So this Tatiana. Ee, isn't she pretty. Just like her photos. Now, anything you want, love, you've only got to ask. Come in, we've got kettle on. Dad and Derek are at work, Jimmy's still at school, part time."

Ivy peered at her, head lowered.

Sam shook hands with the neighbours and thanked them for their welcome. They stared at Lulu who looked around, pulled her coat to button it and pulled her soft silk dress down from the waist to cover her calves.

"Come in, it's starting to rain," said Ivy, "we've got tea ready. Do you like our little house? We'll go to Dad's tomorrow."

In the front parlour, Sam noticed the new blue carpet, still with a label at one corner, a pink, velveteen settee, two chairs to match, and a varnished china cabinet. On shelves inside were blue and white cups and saucers and, on top, two stuffed birds covered in glass domes.

"Birdie," said Dotchka.

Ivy clapped. "Clever girl, does she know that rhyme about two little dicky birds sitting on a wall?"

"You can teach her."

The sisters took out the cups and saucers from the cabinet and handed round sandwiches on a large plate.

Sam looked round. "This is very nice, looks right posh. I'm glad Ma's cousin Sally left it to thee. It's good to be back, apart from this rain." He turned to Lulu. "Listen love, it rains here a lot."

Ivy laughed and nodded. "This is tongue, that's sandwich spread, that's cheese and homemade chutney. Help yourselves. I'll just mek a brew."

Lulu sat on the deep settee and pulled at her skirt. She saw a ladder creep up her left leg and crossed her knees. Bertha asked her if she wanted to use the lavatory. Lulu shook her head.

Ivy poured tea. "Now, Sam, you and your little family will have this house whilst you're here. Nowt grand, no wireless or 'owt, but there's two little bedrooms, all ready, t'sitting room next door wi' table and chairs, fire if tha' wants, but it'll get warm, kitchen, toilet out back. Does little lass want to go?" Sam shook his head. "She'll tell us or start wriggling."

Lulu sipped the thick tea with milk and sugar. "Very nice."

Bertha spoke loudly. "Can you understand us, love?" Lulu nodded.

"I'll get us fish and chips tonight, Sam, when Jimmy and Dad get here. Derek's off wi' some lass; he'll sithee tomorrow."

Jimmy came in, thin wrists sticking out of his shirt sleeves, the bones of his knees jutting above his long grey socks, his short trousers hanging loose. He stared through locks of wavy russet hair which tumbled over brown eyes. Sam thumped him on the shoulder. "Grand lad for thirteen. We'll do some fishing. It's great to be back."

"Give yer new sister-in-law a kiss, Jimmy," said Bertha. The boy stared at Lulu and Dotchka and ran out of the room into the kitchen.

"He's very shy and still upset about Ma. Can't get over it. Mind you, neither can we. Here's Dad."

The front door swung open and Sam the elder arrived in blue overalls, a jacket shiny with grease, and clogs. He held Sam round the waist and then, on tiptoe, ruffled his hair. Tears smeared his cheeks.

He turned to Lulu. "Tatiana, is it? And Elizabeth after our lass. Welcome to Warren. Tha'll nod find a better place where'ere tha're from."

He lifted Dotchka from the floor and bounced her. She looked at her mother and began to scream. "What's up, lass? Ar't starvin'?"

He filled his pipe, pushed the tobacco down into the bowl with his thumb, then lit it. The match flared, he puffed, and thick smoke billowed across the room. Dotchka screamed again.

Jimmy was sent to pick up the fish and chips from the corner shop. He returned with three warm packs, wrapped in newspaper. They were tipped onto large white plates, although Sam said he wanted his in the newspaper like they always had, and with a pint mug of tea. Ivy held out her hand for the change, and counted it.

Bertha looked towards Lulu. "Salt and vinegar, love? And have some more tea, Tatiana." Lulu stirred the tea. "No thank you. I have bread."

"Doesn't she talk lovely," said Ivy, "you couldn't tell she were foreign."

Sam sat Dotchka on his lap and fed her fish and batter. She took a chip and squeezed it until white potato squirmed out.

They had tinned peaches and evaporated milk for pudding. Jimmy did not speak, but looked from under his hair at Sam, Lulu, and Dotchka.

Bertha cleared plates. "It's not much, but we'll get you sorted out tomorrow and do a shop when you know what you want. There's tea, bread and butter, and cornflakes i' t' kitchen. Put lid on to keep flies off. Does t'babby like chucky eggs?"

Sam stood. "Thanks, everybody. Dad, we'll have a drink tomorrow. We're a bit worn out now. It's lovely to be home."

Sam put Dotchka into the little bed upstairs, went down to the sitting room and opened a bottle of whisky.

Lulu sobbed. "Why you bring me here? It cold in April. Toilet outside. Only night pot, like Chinese. Food bad."

"Listen, love, you're tired. It was a long journey. You'll feel better tomorrow. We'll go shopping. We'll meet people, we'll have nice walks, we'll go dancing, to the cinema. Bertha and Ivy will look after Dotchka evenings or weekends. They're putting on a show for you. Try to be nice."

"I not understand what people say. What language does father speak? Why your brother say nothing? He dumb?"

"You'll get used to it. Even I don't understand Dad sometimes. Jimmy has always been shy and you're a beautiful woman. Let's just unpack a bit tonight. We'll all go to the lavatory outside before we go to bed, then let Dotchka use the po – what fancy people call chamber pots. We heat water for baths. They usually have them once a week here. The tub's hanging in the kitchen, or there's a public bath and swimming pool not far away. It's not what you're used to, but we're here."

She wiped her face with a handkerchief and sat back in the chair. Sam opened a white envelope. "There's a letter here from the specialist in Manchester. You have an appointment about your chest next week. Not far away, so think about that as well."

* * *

They heard clattering on the pavement at seven the following morning.

"That's, clogs, like shoes but with metal strips on the soles," said Sam, "people are going to work in the mills. And listen, the birds are singing – that means the rain will stop. I'll see to Dotchka, we'll have breakfast, wash, get dressed in warm clothes, go for a walk, and take bread for the ducks. Bertha has borrowed a pram for Dotchka."

The pram was deep and low slung, with a spoked hood that collapsed in creases, and big wheels. Dotchka, strapped in with reins, held onto the sides, sat up, looked round and bounced on her bottom. Lulu wiped the paintwork with a damp cloth. They walked down the hill to the main road. Smoke pumped from mill chimneys; acrid soot tinged the air, and filtered the cool sunlight. Women cleaning and chalking the steps of their houses stopped, waved, and said hello.

"The town's shaped like a fish," said Sam, "a long bone for its spine, that's the main road, then bones coming off it, that's these streets. When I was a lad we played a game where you couldn't step on a nick – that's what we call the cracks – between the flagstones. If you did, it was bad luck."

Lulu stepped on every nick. "I not believe in superstition."

At the bottom of the hill, they turned right towards Sunnyside Wood, passing a sweet shop with jars of humbugs, aniseed balls, and pear drops in the window. Sam bought a mixed quarter pound which they sucked, and some chocolate drops for Dotchka.

"Look, a horsey pulling a cart. That's a rag and bone man. He collects bits and pieces people don't want and sells them; any metal bits are melted down to make other things."

The man flicked the horse with his whip and waved. "Well, ah never. Sam Shuttleworth. Tha' were at school wi' me. Tha' went to China."

"Ernie Sharples. Tha' allus said tha'd work wi' thi' dad when tha' left. Ta da now. See thi' again."

Lulu held the handle of the pram and looked down. "Why you talk like that?

"Because I'm home."

Sam pushed open the wide gate leading into the wood. "Let her walk now. I'll carry her if she gets tired. Are you all right i' them shoes, love?"

Dotchka ran ahead to chase a blackbird on the path. The pram wheels bumped along the gravel. Bluebells and buttercups spread along the side of a stream as it bounced and swished over rocks. A willow tree dipped into the water, green tips spreading across the surface.

They came to a waterfall which dropped from a flat pond into a pool. "That's where I used to catch tiddlers when I was a lad. Look at the ducks on the pond, Dotchka. Quack quack." He flapped his arms. Dotchka did the same. He gave her torn bread to throw to the ducks, who struggled out of the water and clustered round the pram. Further along the path were crested peacocks dragging their tails. Sam stamped and they flared out their feathers. Dotchka laughed and clapped.

Sam lifted Dotchka back into the pram. "Now we'll call in at the mill to ask Bertha what we should buy for dinner. That means lunchtime here. They have the main meal at about 1pm, between shifts, then a lighter meal in the evening; that's called tea."

Lulu adjusted her shoe. "This very confused for me. I not know when to eat."

Tattersall Street mill was up a narrow cobbled street with gas lamps on tall poles. The flagstones were stained by dogs and cats who peed and shat on lamp post bases then quivered their tails and scratched up the dust.

"Doggie," said Dotchka.

"Don't touch," Lulu called. "This bad as Shanghai."

Sam pushed one away. "Bit better fed, though."

They left the pram against the factory wall. Sam went into the weaving shed whilst Lulu and Dotchka waited outside. Women carrying cloth and shuttles stared. Two men sat in a side room drawing threads with long metal pins and hooking them onto the looms. They stopped work and watched Lulu standing outside the office, clutching Dotchka's hand.

Sam approached the foreman. "I've come to have a word wi' Bertha."

The foreman peered at him. "Tha're Sam, back fro' China, aren't ti'? Thi' sister's i' theer." Sam held out his hand. "Aye, I am, I am. Good to si' thi'. I'll go in."

The heavy door opened onto the crash of looms, and shuttles darting between threads. The women spoke in sign language, mouthing and waving. Clogs tapped the flagstones as they moved between looms. A damp, warm smell of raw fabric wafted from the bobbins and machinery.

Bertha, covered in dabs of cotton and grease, came out to talk. Her hair was drawn back into a net, partly covered by a headscarf; she wore a pinny with three big pockets over a cotton frock. In the top pocket, stretched over her bosom, was a pair of scissors and a metal hook. She picked up Dotchka and kissed her cheek. "Eee, tha' do look bonny today. Did t'child sleep well? Daddy says you've fed t'ducks. I'll see thi' in a few hours. Don't forget we're at Dad's."

Sam took Lulu's hand and sat Dotchka on his forearm. "We'll pick up some meat and potato pies and tomatoes for lunch from the market hall. It's only a ten minute walk. Ivy has cooked a hotpot for tea and we'll go round to Dad's at about five."

The market spread round a square where trams clattered, turned, and went back to Burnside, five miles away. Stalls sold fish, meat, and groceries, washing pegs, clothes lines, cakes, and warm breads. Lulu looked at a stall with women's dresses, blouses, and underwear.

She picked up a large brassiere. Sam looked away. "They call it flesh coloured."

"I buy better in Shanghai."

He pointed up the hill. "Look. That's the Victoria Tower. I once won a run up to the top from the woods. I got a medal. Just up from here is the library where I first read about China, then along from there is the railway station where we were yesterday."

Lulu looked away. "I want to forget it. And it begin to rain again."

"I have an umbrella. Now, we'll go and have a nap after lunch, then go round to Dad's house for tea. It's only a couple of streets away. You'll meet brother Derek, another silent bugger, only older than Jimmy."

* * *

22

Sam looked round the cramped sitting room in his father's house. Lulu sat in a wide armchair covered in a tartan rug, which had burn marks and tobacco stains. Jimmy stared at them. Ivy and Bertha clattered pans and cutlery in the kitchen.

He touched a pair of his mother's glasses, open on the mantelpiece above the coal fire, and bit his lower lip. "Nothing's changed."

His father wiped his eyes and blew his nose into an oil stained red handkerchief. "Nowt'll ever change as long as Ah'm 'ere. I wish thi' mam were and all. There'll allus be summat missing."

Derek arrived in blue overalls and muttered, "Grand to see thi." He sat down in an armchair and took off his clogs. "Ah'll need a bath toneet. Off courting."

Sam introduced Lulu. "We'll be leaving after tea, nobody'll see thi when tha gets i'tub."

Derek scowled. "Wher's mi tea? Is yon hotpot done?"

"What is hotpot?" asked Lulu.

Bertha stirred the earthenware pot. "Best end of lamb neck, potatoes, carrots, onion all stewed up together with a bit of salt and pepper. I put a bit of tripe, that's cow's stomach, in to thicken it."

They sat round the square wooden table, covered with a cloth, embroidered in the corners. Sam's father fingered it. "Thi mother med this."

Sam nodded. Lulu nibbled a piece of meat. Dotchka held a curved bone, chewed off the meat, then sucked it, and spooned up the vegetables and gravy.

Sam helped her with the spoon. "A real Lancastrian."

Jimmy spooned up the gravy. "What does she eat in China?"

Sam punched his arm. "Oh, you *can* talk, then. She has noodles and rice and chicken, that sort of thing, and sometimes a pickle. Not as good as Ma used to make."

Dotchka waved the spoon. "More," and pushed her fingers in the potato.

"There's a boxing match tomorrow at t'Temperance Hall," said Sam's father, "Who wants to goa?"

"Me, me," said Jimmy.

"Tha're too little. Derek? Sam?" They nodded.

"It's not for women," said Ivy, "though one or two do go. Tell you what, Sam, why don't you tek Lulu to t' th'Anchor i't snug toneet. Women's allowed thear. We'll look after t'child."

"The Anchor is the pub, like a bar, at the end of the street," said Sam, "let's go. We'll tek Dad n'all. You'll like it."

* * *

"What I wear to this pub? I need to change."

Sam's father looked at her dress. "Nay, nay, tha're grand as thi' are."

Sam took her arm. "We'll get Dotchka settled, and Tatiana can wear what she wants. Come round in about an hour, Ivy, and we'll be ready for off."

Lulu wore a green and white spotted silk dress with a loose belt, black high heels, and a green beret. Sam guided her through the swinging door of the snug, one hand under her elbow. They met a hum of talk, interrupted by the occasional laugh or shout. Glasses clinked and tapped, smoke curled from cigarettes. Men, and a few women, with half pints, sat on stools round square wooden tables. The gas lights popped. All noise stopped as Sam, his father and Lulu walked in.

Sam's father was a regular. "Remember this bugger? Back fra' China for a bit. Watch out." The drinkers jumped up to shake Sam's hand. Two of the women kissed him on the cheek. "Sorry about yer ma, Sam, a good woman."

"Well, this is a time for a celebration," said one of the men. "Who's this then, Sam? A China doll?" He laughed, others joined in.

Sam smiled at Lulu. "Folks, I want you to meet my wife, Tatiana. We met in Shanghai, but she's Russian. She'll have a whisky and so will I."

The men stared. One of the women said, "Tek no notice, love, they're all ignorant. I'm having a port and lemon. Have a sip, see if you like it. Can I feel your frock? It's lovely."

They talked about the next day's boxing match between a man from Oswaldtwistle and one from Corsdale, a southpaw. "That's somebody who's left handed," Sam explained to Lulu.

They wondered who would captain Warren cricket team that summer – the best batsman had turned professional and was tipped to play for Lancashire. They boasted about poaching pheasant and rabbits, using ferrets which they tucked down their trousers to hide them from gamekeepers.

"My dog and ferret's champions," shouted a man called Seth, "catch owt."

"Shut thi' face, Seth. Tha just likes summat down thi' pants."

"Stop that," said Sam's father. "Ladies present."

"Come on, Sam," a woman shouted, "tha' used to 'ave a lovely voice. Give us that pome about woman and childer."

Sam laughed. "Happen I've forgotten it in Shanghai, but I'll have a go."

He stood, put down his drink, took a breath and began:

"Come whoam to thi' childer and me,
Ah've just mended t'fire wi a cob,"

He finished the last verse:

"Ah've no gradely comfort my lass,
Except wi'yon childer and me."

Everyone, including the barman, cheered and stamped. Two women wiped their eyes with the backs of their hands. The bartender pulled a pint. "Ee, Sam, tha can still do thi' stuff. Have a pint o' mild."

Sam turned to Lulu. "Do you want to sing a Russian song? What about that nice Russian one about the butterfly?" said Sam. "I can start it 'babachka machat...'"

"I want to go, I'm very tired."

"She's had a long day and a long journey. I'll get her back home. See you all soon. We'll have some good times. I'll call in tomorrow, Dad. Ta da."

He held Lulu's coat. She stretched her arms into it. "Who that woman kiss you?"

"An old friend. We worked together at the paper mill. She's called Maggie. And she's married to the man who was singing."

"I not like smell. Dirty pipes, beer, and dogs. I not understand songs."

* * *

Sam woke early. "There's a lot to do before we get you to that doctor. We'll see Auntie Nellie, today. We need to catch a bus around ten. I'd best take an umbrella, too."

Auntie Nellie's house in Camburn still smelled of camphor, lavender, budgie, and bird seed. She had lit a coal fire which belched smoke into the sitting room.

"I must get that seen to, but it's hard with so many men laid off."

Sam bent down and pushed coals around the grate. "I'll have a look at it, but we don't really need a fire. It might be raining but it's not cold."

Nellie flapped a duster. "Makes it more cosy. That's a nice rag doll."

Dotchka held Dolly and made her dance.

Auntie Nellie set out ham and tongue sandwiches, scones with home-made raspberry jam, pickled onions, and a jelly trifle. They drank orange pekoe tea with milk and sugar, served in pink and white teacups with saucers and plates to match. Dotchka sat on a black leather pouffe and watched the budgie.

Auntie Nellie gave her an oat biscuit. "Isn't she lovely? Looks a bit like her granny, poor soul. Now then, love, have some more tea. There's not much but we can't complain."

Dotchka stretched her hand, full of crumbs, to the budgie. It flapped, rang the little bell in the cage, then pecked the mirror. Nellie laughed. She spoke slowly and twisted her lips to exaggerate each syllable. "His name is Rudolph, after a film star."

"Auntie. She speaks English and she's not daft."

"Oh... I just thought. I had two budgies before that but their feathers fell off and they died."

Dotchka nodded and chewed her biscuit. Sam pointed to the aspidistra on its wooden stand. "Look at this plant. It's from China, like us. Auntie Nellie told me that a long time ago."

And there was one in the lobby of Annabelle's apartment block. He had her phone number in his wallet somewhere.

Nellie held out a plate. "Have another sandwich, Tatiana love. I do like your frock. Did you make it? Sam's a very lucky man. I hope he looks after you. Do you like China? I always thought he'd make something of himself. That teacher said so, too. What was her name? Gave you an atlas. Went back to Aberdeen. Married a preacher. Has twins now, I believe."

"Miss Hargreaves. Used to play 'D'ye Ken John Peel' on t' piano, and sing 'Linden Lea.' Her bum stuck out."

"Now then, Sam Shuttleworth. Not in front of ladies and children. Do ye remember old Bill two doors down? Well, he's dead. I made this trifle fresh this morning. Real cream. You look as if you need building up a bit."

"Let me explain to Tatiana what trifle is, Auntie. It's made in layers of sponge cake with a bit of sherry sometimes."

His aunt nodded. "Jelly, custard, tinned fruit, and topped with whipped cream when you can get it."

Lulu dipped in a spoon and put the trifle to her lips. "I like, I get Mary to make."

"Who's Mary?"

"It's our maid," said Sam, "she looks after Dotchka and cooks."

"You must be making a tidy bit, Sam Shuttleworth, to have servants."

Sam patted his pocket. "More than I would here."

Dotchka picked out the raisins from the scones, and poked her fingers through the jam, which spread round her lips and cheeks. Dolly sat on her lap.

Lulu took away the scone. "Don't do that. It not nice."

"Dolly want some."

"I'll just get a dishcloth to wipe her down. Now you come again before you go back and I'll come over to see you all in two weeks. I haven't seen the family for a while. Have you got a bad cough, love? Are you enjoying yourself?"

Lulu nodded.

Sam lifted Dotchka from the pouffe. "We're seeing a doctor in Manchester next week."

* * *

Dotchka woke at 4am. Sam took off her wet nappy and left it in a bucket to soak, put on her knickers, and took her downstairs. He found some big marbles in a drawer and rolled them between the chair legs. The coloured stripes in the glass whirled and then settled. She laughed and clapped, "More." He made her doll kick the marbles along the floor and talk to Dotchka.

"Pretty girl like marbles. Pretty girl sleepy?"

Sam lay on the settee, a cushion under his head, held her across his chest and sang, "Hush a bye baby…"

Lulu found them both asleep when she came down at eight.

"I make breakfast," she said, "Nice eggs and toast and tea in big mug like you have. Dotchka have milk."

"Come here and give us a kiss." She leaned over, kissed his cheek, ruffled Dotchka's hair, and put her head against the baby's forehead.

Sam pulled back the curtains. "It's a nice day. I thought we'd go to that little park with swings in Whitehall Gardens then visit my ma's grave. I'll get some flowers to take."

"I very tired today. I rest. Maybe go for little walk and buy magazine and food, then have sleep. I make dinner tonight. We celebrate. Get wine."

He laughed. "You won't find wine. Get some bottles of beer, or we could try my dad's carrot whisky."

"Whisky not made of carrots. Carrots for eating."

"My dad makes elderflower wine and potato wine. Tastes nothing like wine. Don't touch it. Bloody strong. He drinks too much of it since Ma died, Bertha says. Would you like her to make you a cardigan? She'd like it if you said yes."

"I will. I ask for grey wool. You take pram. I get you food to take in case Dotchka hungry."

"And crusts for the ducks and pigeons."

He strapped Dotchka into reins which held her in the pram, but Dotchka wanted to walk down the street. She poked at every crack between the flags, stroked every lamp post, and pointed to the dog turds and stains left by piss.

"Don't touch caca," said Sam.

She said something in Russian, then something in pidgin. Sam lifted her.

"Speak English in England. Come on, we'll get you in the pram along the main road. It's a long walk to the park."

Mrs Ainsworth from two doors down was bringing back a basket of shopping. "Where thi' off to Sam? Right bonny lass. Is t'wife not wi' thi?"

"She's resting. I'm off to Ma's grave and giving t'babby a swing i't' park."

Mrs Ainsworth offered Dotchka a piece of scone. "That's a good walk. Tha could tek tram up to t'cemetery. Lovely day. They've got some nice daffs i t'market."

"Thanks. I'll walk. Pushing this thing a couple of miles uphill'll give me a bit of exercise."

"Ta da, then."

"Say bye, bye, Dotchka,"

"Funny name. Foreign is it? Well, it teks all sorts."

"Bye, bye," said Dotchka.

Sam strapped Dotchka back in the pram, and walked along the pavement by the main road. He pointed out horses, shops, trams. Dotchka clapped and waved. They stopped to talk to people who recognised him and asked about China and his family. An elderly cousin gave her a small bag of pear drops. Sam took the bag and put it in his pocket. He bought a bunch of daffodils at the market, and a biscuit for Dotchka, then set off up the hill, stooping to push the heavy pram.

He lifted Dotchka onto the path and swung open the iron gates of the cemetery. "Come and help Daddy, Dotchka. I'm out of breath."

Bertha had said that Ma's plot was ten yards from the gate, on the left. There would be a little blue vase on the grave, but no headstone. He held Dotchka's reins tightly as she skipped along the gravel. She picked dandelions, their heads now white globes.

Sam picked one. "Dandelion clocks," and blew. "Here you are – one o'clock, two o'clock." Seeds floated in a puff of white stalks and Dotchka tried to catch them.

He looked at headstones in granite – black, grey and mottled red, crested with stone angels or bunches of leaves. These were the old Warren families – the Fieldings, the Wadsworths, the Hindles, lined up in death. Inscriptions in gold read: **Fell asleep 24 June 1922... At rest... Peace at last.** Here the stone of a child, aged two, not far off the same age as Dotchka: **Our angel has gone, the pain never will. All our love, Mummy and Daddy.** Primroses had been planted in the earth on the grave and a wooden doll leaned, spindly, against the stone. Dotchka reached out for it.

Sam picked up Dotchka and kissed her. "No, you can't have that. Look after Dolly. She looks sad."

Further along was a grave for two brothers, killed in the war: **In memory of our dear sons, Edward, aged 20, and Cuthbert, aged 24, died for their country in 1917. They shall not grow old.**

He found his mother's grave with its blue vase. He looked down, saw grass creeping across its mound and wished that he had brought a trowel. He knelt down on the damp and held Dotchka across her waist, lowering his head. "When I get some money, I'll put a headstone here, Dotchka. It'll be in white marble with black letters and it will have a nice poem on it. Maybe you'll write it. And listen, this grave is where *I* want to be buried when my time comes. I'll write that down."

He removed the old, crumpled flowers from the vase, shook them, put them to one side, and replaced them with the daffodils. "Your granny is in here. She's watching over you. She was called Elizabeth, too. You never met her, but she loved you. Wave bye, bye, Granny. Come on, let's go to the swings and then to Auntie Bertha's. She'll be home for lunch soon."

He stood, stared at the grave and flowers, saluted, and put his daughter back in the pram.

"I've picked up some fish and chips," he said to Bertha, "and a dab for Dotchka. I thought you might be hungry and not have a lot of time. I've put some daffs on Ma's grave. Listen, I'm not thinking of going just yet, but I want to be buried there, too. I've told Dotchka and I'll write it down and give it to thee."

"Nay, Sam, I want to be buried wi' Ma, too. Plenty o'room. Let's see who meks it first. Salt and vinegar?"

Lulu came down from the bedroom. "You have telegram from China."

He tore it open and stood staring into space. "I've been promoted to inspector. We'll have to cut our visit here a bit short."

Bertha gasped. "That's good news Sam but not so nice about the visit."

Lulu kissed his cheek. "How short?"

* * *

The Warren News came to interview Sam and to take photographs. Lulu had her hair washed and waved by a hairdresser in Burnside, then brushed it out and curled it herself with metal tongs. She tied Dotchka's fine wisps into two bunches on top of her head.

"It's only *The Warren News*," said Sam, "go easy on the lipstick."

There was half a page in the 1 May edition about the Shanghai hero, his promotion and his beautiful wife of Russian extraction.

"Lovely photos," said Bertha. "Look at little las wi' her doll and lovely hairdo. Shame tha're not i' uniform, Sam. Tha'll have all t'neighbours wanting to talk to thi.'"

Lulu peered at the print. "What this about Russian extraction? I Russian. I send paper to Raisa and Papa and cross out that 'extraction'."

Sam laughed. "You're British now, love. That's why it says 'extraction', but do what you want. Remember, we're off to Manchester tomorrow to see this consultant chap. Very good reputation old Doc Ferrers back at barracks says. We need to be off early and get train tickets. Bertha will take Dotchka to play at Billy's house wi' his lads."

* * *

From Manchester Victoria Station, they took a taxi to the Royal Free Hospital in Oxford Road, passing bulky buildings and statues – the museum, the town hall, shops, hotels, Queen Victoria again.

"Very smart, nice shops here," said Lulu, "I come back here. This queen everywhere in England?"

"Oh, yes. Very important lady. Now, let's get you right first. The consultant will know what's best."

Mr Simmons was tall, slightly stooped with grey hair, and glasses with a thick brown frame. He did not wear a white coat, but a grey suit, a blue shirt, and a tie with small shields on it. His office, in the private wing of the hospital, was large with windows overlooking the street.

On the walls were photographs and paintings of hills and lakes, labelled Ullswater, Keswick, and Windermere.

He rose from behind his desk to shake hands with Sam and Lulu.

"The Lake District," he said, "we have a house there. Most picturesque. Do you know it? Please sit down. Now, Mrs Shuttleworth, I have received your case notes. I don't think we are too late to do something about your illness, although chronic bronchitis, as you know, is very difficult and we don't want it developing into anything worse, do we? We have developed some new treatments here and there is now better medicine. Let me first examine you. I'll get my nurse in. Mr Shuttleworth, could I ask you to leave us for about ten minutes.

Sam was called back into the office; the nurse left and turned to smile at him. Mr Simmons tapped his pen on the desk and made notes in a file.

"Do sit down. This is what we should do in your case. I strongly recommend sea air, rest, wholesome food, gentle exercise, and daily doses of pills to attack the bronchitis. Left untreated it would, of course, get worse, especially in China where I hear that TB is so rampant. I run a small, private clinic in St Anne's, near Blackpool. I can get you in there for six weeks. It is by the sea and the staff are excellent. I want you to go there in the next few days to meet the doctors and nurses. Your husband and daughter can visit at weekends. When you leave the clinic, you must continue to take the pills every day for another year."

Sam stared at him. "How much will it cost? How do I pay?"

"My office will bill you every week. This visit will be included. The clinic will discuss fees with you. About £150 for the whole treatment, I would think, then the medicine to take back with you."

They left the hospital and took a bus back to the station. Sam sat, his arms folded. "Where am I going to find that kind of money? It's more than my dad earns in two years. I'll have to get your aunt to send more. Does your father have anything?"

"He have a little but need it to live. I thought your family have money. You take out loan?" Sam looked out of the window. "I might have to. Now we've come this far, we have to get you better. And we'll be back in Shanghai sooner than I thought. I'll get that sorted out whilst you're away."

Lulu packed a trunk and a suitcase to go to St Anne's. Bertha kissed her. "We'll miss thi' love. I'll get on wi' a cardigan for thi'. Thee get thi'sen better. Nasty thing, bronchitis. Ivy and me'll help wi' Dotchka, Sam. We can tek a bit o'time off between us."

* * *

The clinic was a long, one-storey building by the beach at St Anne's. The receptionist checked Lulu into her room, painted white with pictures of trees and birds on the wall, and overlooking the sands. A wardrobe stood along one side and a dressing table across from the bed on the other. There was a toilet and bath along the corridor.

Lulu patted the bed and opened the wardrobe. "Room very small, but clean, very nice. I put photos and make-up on dressing table."

The doctor greeted them. Sam thought he looked too young and too good-looking to be a doctor, but he wore a white gown with a stethoscope round his neck and carried a sheaf of notes.

"I am Dr Marsden. I will be looking after you. We have very high success rates here, Mr Shuttleworth. Your wife is in good hands. You can visit whenever you like. Try to give us a little notice, that's all. I'll take her off for examination now. I'll let you say your goodbyes."

Sam took Lulu's hands. "See you on Saturday, love. I hope you're not lonely. I'll miss you. Let's have a kiss."

* * *

Billy Wigg wanted to go fishing like they used to. "Wife's mother's over, they'll want to natter. Come over for breakfast, see t'lads and t'missus, then we'll pack some lunch, beer and fags. It'll do thi' good."

"Right, my tackle's still here i'one piece. That bugger Jimmy hasn't dared touch it."

They climbed the hill above the woods in a misty, warm drizzle, then followed the stream to the reservoir. Mayflowers and daisies sprinkled the banks; meadows of buttercups glowed and rippled in the breeze.

Sam spotted a flash of green and blue. "Look, a kingfisher. Never seen one o' them i'Shanghai. Beautiful."

The bird disappeared into the blossom of a hawthorn tree. A squabble of blackbirds pecked round its roots.

Sam lifted his head to smell the perfume. "Good day for fishing. A bit like Shanghai sometimes. Damp. Boy, I've caught some big 'uns in t'rivers over yon. Things you never heard of here."

"Like what? This reservoir's supposed to have some big buggers i' t'middle. My mate, Dave, pulled in a three foot catfish last week. Remember we used to pull in trout or tickle their bellies till they gave in."

Sam stretched out his arms. "I'm talking fifteen footers, like summat called paddlefish. You can't just catch 'em wi' a line. You needs nets and spears and two people. There's sturgeon too. Let's see what we can do."

They went through the wooden gate to the banks of the reservoir and unpacked rods, lines, bait, and baskets and nestled the sandwiches, wrapped in newspaper, with the bottles of beer, in long grass under a tree.

"There's only us here," said Billy. "Good. Keep it quiet."

They put maggots as bait on the hooks, cast off, and sat on the slope of the bank, waiting. Billy flicked his line and looked at Sam. "Lovely missus. You've pulled in a looker, Sam. How did you find her?"

"She worked in a posh nightclub. There are lots o' Russian women hostesses i' them places. Smashers. I'll tell you a secret. Tatiana calls herself Lulu i' China. Suits her work better. Course, she doesn't work now."

"What are t'women like?"

Sam let out more line. "Depends what you can afford. Plenty looking for American or British blokes for passports. One or two police have Chinese girlfriends, but it's not looked on kindly."

"Do you like married life?"

"That's a daft question. It's different. I don't spend a lot of time at home because of police rotas – night work, emergencies, problems."

"Is she a good wife?"

Sam laughed. "You're in a funny mood today. I'll tell you one thing – she's the only woman who can make my cock perk up just by looking at her."

Billy laughed. "But that's not all there is to being wed, is it? 'Specially when you've got kiddies."

"It's still bloody important to me. I remember the first time I met her. I went into a spin. Still do. She's had a hard life, though. Russians do. Refugees after they had to leave Russia after t'Revolution. Bad business."

"So, does she have family?"

"Father and sister. Aunt wi' a few pennies. Ma dead. They're not in good health. A lot of pneumonia and TB. Tatiana has her chest problems. That's why she's at this bloody expensive clinic in St Anne's."

"What's up wi' her?"

Sam inhaled deeply on his cigarette and breathed out smoke. "Bad bronchitis. Could lead to TB – lots of it i'China."

"Some here, too, i' winter. Bad chests. One o' my lads were proper bad last year." Billy reached for the sandwiches. "Must cost a packet, that treatment."

"It does, but the aunt's offered to pay. I'll look after her and our little one. Marriage? I love them both, that's all I can say, and I've never loved anybody else, probably never will."

"Tha' used to be such a one for t'women."

"Still am a bit, but nothing in it. Not really. Hey, my line's twitching." He grinned. "Summat big. I'll pull him in."

"That Maggie fancies thi', tha' knows. Not working out wi' th'husband. Bit of a roving eye, she 'as."

"Maybe I'll have to call in on her."

Drizzle changed to heavy rain. Swifts darted low across the water and swooped into crowds of midges and mist spread over the reservoir.

"Bloody weather," said Sam. "Nothing new, there. Let's get back. Three each. Not bad. Nice trout supper."

"Sunday tomorrow. I work on th'allotment. Come round. Bring t'family. Have a picnic. I'll give thi' some veg."

* * *

Lulu sent postcards from St Anne's. One to Sam with a picture of a donkey on the beach, one of Blackpool Tower to his sisters, and one to Dotchka – a woman with arms and legs like balloons, bottom in the air covered in red knickers, and a thin man, Adam's apple prominent, with a caption over his head, "Yer cheeks are blooming today, missus." Jimmy thought it funny. Sam said it wasn't suitable for anybody under twenty-one and tore it into pieces.

* * *

Two weeks after Lulu entered the clinic, Sam phoned Annabelle from a phone booth by the Market Hall. He put in his pennies and pushed button A.

"Filton Hall. Lady Bostridge speaking.

"Happy birthday. I know it's a bit early."

"Jesus Christ. Bloody Sam Shuttleworth. What have you been up to in boring old Lancs?"

"This and that. Visiting. Fishing."

"How's the tackle?"

"Don't be naughty. In good shape."

"How's wifey and baby?"

"Wifey in a clinic in St Anne's for six weeks, having an expensive cure for bronchitis. Daughter being spoiled and loving it. Misses her ma a bit but she's happy. How about you?"

"Very unhappy. You've no idea. Can we meet? I can get to Manchester. I'll spend a few days at the Midland Hotel, right in the centre. How about coming up next week?"

"I can come for the day next Tuesday. My sisters are having the baby. I'll get a train about eleven."

"Right, we can have lunch and then amuse ourselves."

"I'll have to be back by seven or so."

* * *

They met in the marble reception area of the Midland. Annabelle put her arms round his waist and leaned against his chest. "You look well, Sam. Don't look too closely at me."

"You still wear the same perfume. It takes me back a bit. You still look grand. A bit thinner. Still smart. Hair longer. It suits you. Nice clothes as usual. So what's going on?"

"Nothing. That's the problem. I'm stranded in bloody North Yorkshire in this freezing mansion surrounded by fields, sheep, cows, and horses. No visitors. Davina came up once on her own – she's now got two brats and the awful Clement is some big banker. Likely to get a knighthood. They live in Chelsea – that's a fancy part of London in case you didn't know. She ran back to London after two days. Don't blame the poor cow."

"Is your hubby in London all the time, then?"

"No, but it's worse when he's here. Tries to get his hand up my skirt all the time, then can't do anything about it. Disappears to the horses – and grooms, no doubt. He bought me a dog to keep me company. Sweet little thing, a dachshund, but frightened of everything. Won't go out unless he's carried. Bloody dog tries to get up my skirt as well."

She took out a lace handkerchief and dabbed her eyes. Sam squeezed her hand.

"As I told you, hubby wants a son to carry on the line. God, you should see their portraits. Ugly, fat, pompous. I go down to London for receptions sometimes – he says it's good for his image. To hell with that. All these bloody ancient lords try to rub themselves against me. God, it's awful. I should have stayed in Shanghai. How about you, Sam, are you happy?"

He laughed. "Everybody keeps asking me that. Shanghai is a mess. Work is hard and can be dangerous. No idea what will happen."

"How about wedded bliss?"

"Not exactly that. She's temperamental, but beautiful. I fell in love with her first time I met her. I saw her first at Ciro's that time we went, then met properly later. Likes the good life and doesn't get it. Hates Warren. Not enough going on. Wet and bleak. I love being back. My ma died last year and everybody misses her. It was a bit of a shock."

"Sorry to hear that. How's the bedroom life?"

"Not a lot of it. I work hard. She can be cold. Has a temper. She sees other people, I'm sure."

"And you?"

"Listen, I love her, and I'd like a settled life, but it won't happen. I have to work long hours and overtime. I've had a few flings myself."

"You surprise me."

She took his hand, pressed his fingers, and rubbed his nails.

"I've ordered lunch with a good wine. Let's have champagne first. Which train do you need to get back?"

"Well, I can be a bit late."

"Let's not linger over lunch, then I'll show you my room. Lovely view." She winked.

They kissed in the lift. He pushed her against the wall, moved his tongue into her mouth, and stroked her breasts."

They undressed and she stroked his erection. He moaned and entered her. She moved quickly, gasping. He thrust deeper. She cried out and gripped his neck. They held each other. He licked her nipples.

She lay on her back. "As good as before. Tackle still in good shape I see. Lovely. I needed that."

"So did I. I pick Tatiana up next week then we're off two weeks later. Why don't you come back to Shanghai?"

"I can't. Parents both ill. What would I do? Same as before? No fun with all that going on there – we do get a bit of news about it. Have to stick it out, I'm afraid. Maybe something will turn up. Look after yourself, Sam. It's raining again. Bloody weather. Once more, for old time's sake?"

23

The following weekend, Sam left Dotchka with his sisters, took a train to Blackpool, then a tram to the clinic to give Lulu a nice surprise. The smell of disinfectant invaded him as he opened the door. He saw equipment to strengthen breathing stored on shelves in the corridor outside reception – bags of sand for placing on the chest, dumbbells, chest expanders, and pulleys. Patients sat in the garden and on the beach, wrapped in blankets. He saw them breathing in deeply, holding their breath, then gently releasing it.

He tapped on the window of the reception. "My wife leaves in a week, I've come to settle some bills. You're new here. What's your name?"

She looked at him then down at her files. "Miss Nightingale. Shirley."

He smiled. "That's a good name for a nurse. Nice blouse." She gathered the papers and tapped the edges on the desk to straighten them. "I'm not a nurse. I do administration. What can I do for you?"

"I've come to see my wife, Tatiana Shuttleworth. Unexpected visit, and I want to check the account. How is she?"

"Just a moment, I'll get one of the nurses and I'll find your file."

A nurse appeared. "I'm afraid Mrs Shuttleworth is out," she said. "We weren't expecting you until the day before she leaves next week."

"Out? How can she be out? Where is she?" He lit a cigarette.

"No smoking in here – very strict rule. She is with Dr Marsden. I think they went to pick up some medicines for her to take away."

He stubbed out the cigarette on the floor, bent to pick it up and place it in a bin. "I'll wait. It's eleven o'clock now. What time will they be back?"

"Perhaps after lunch. You might want to wait outside. It's a nice day. We can give you a sandwich to eat on the beach, and a jug of tea, if you like."

He took off his jacket and sat on the warm sand, eating a beef sandwich, and drinking tea from a thick pot mug. Children flew kites and played with beach balls, and screamed when the ball went into the sea to be rescued by a parent. Families had brought buckets and spades, and rugs to sit on. A father, trousers rolled up, constructed a complicated sand castle with turrets, and a handkerchief for a flag. Women held their skirts when the breeze lifted them. Sam took off his shoes and socks and walked into the cool, shallow water and watched his reflection in the ripples. Flecks of broken seaweed ran over his feet and stuck to his ankles. He scraped them off and threw them onto the beach then lay down to dry, wriggled his toes, and slept.

He woke at two and found Lulu standing over him. Her shadow blocked the sun from his face.

"What you do here?"

He moved onto his knees and stood to face her. "I've come to see you and pay bills. Where have you been? You're supposed to be ill."

She brushed back a strand of hair. "You know I much better. Treatment very good. Room nice. Radio with dance music."

He put his hand on her shoulder. "They said you'd gone with a doctor to get more medicine."

She laughed. "We get medicine and go dance at Tower Ballroom in Blackpool for treat to celebrate."

He dropped his hand and clenched his fists. "Dancing? Celebrate?

What the hell am I paying for? Not for you to go bloody dancing. Who is this doctor? Does he do this with all his patients?"

"Oh, no. He very good to me. You met him. He always ask about you and Dotchka."

Sam kicked the sand. "I'm paying a fortune for this. Doctors aren't supposed to get familiar with patients."

"What mean familiar? Why you think bad for me?" She picked up a handful of sand and threw it in Sam's face.

He brushed it away, leaving smears down his cheeks. "Now I know you feel guilty. You always get bad-tempered when you're in the wrong. You're behaving badly again. It's bad enough you being so rude with my family and so snobbish about being here. Now this."

"I not guilty. Just want get better."

He shook her by the shoulders. "What the hell's going on? Are you having an affair with him?"

She pushed him away. "He want marry me. He very nice."

"You are a married woman with a child. What does he think about that? Maybe he's married, too. Your daughter misses you. She cries when she goes to bed. What do you think you're doing? How do you think this makes me feel? You keep making me jealous. It's torture."

Lulu sobbed into a handkerchief. "Just a little fun. It so boring here."

"I'm going to find this bloody doctor. Where is he? I'll kill him." She wiped her eyes. "He gone home. He not back for two days."

"I'm not coming back here except to collect you. I'm going to complain to that bloke in Manchester. The boss. Does he know what goes on here? I'll pick you up the day after tomorrow. Get your trunks packed, and your dancing clothes. That's it. You're leaving early. Tell that to your lover boy. Discharged. And when we sail for Shanghai, we're having separate cabins. I don't care what it costs. Then *I* can have a bit of fun. And I've got papers to read for the new job. Just try to be nice to people until we go. And say thank you sometimes."

A nurse came down the sands. "Mrs Shuttleworth must not be

215

overexcited. Let me take her back into the clinic. It's time for her medicine."

They sailed for Shanghai on the *SS Tokyo* on 27 June. Sam wrote to the consultant in

Manchester, but received no reply.

24

Sam took a single cabin, noisy, cramped, and reeking of oil, on the lower deck near the engine rooms. Lulu and Dotchka shared the larger cabin. He lay on the hard, narrow bed to read police briefings, newspapers, thrillers, and cowboy stories, went to the gym and flirted with the maids, or with an English girl from Birmingham who was going to Hong Kong to join her fiancé.

The afternoon of 20 July 1930 was hot and humid as the *SS Tokyo* approached the misty skyline of Manila. He sat in a deckchair, hidden behind a square metal pillar, as sporadic gusts blew across the deck and coiled the smoke from his cigarette. He and Lulu had not spoken since she left the clinic, except about practicalities, like buying medicine or preparing for the journey. At meal times they communicated through Dotchka, or sat in silence.

His family had been puzzled but said nothing. Lulu said thank you for the cardigan and placed it at the bottom of a trunk.

From behind the pillar he watched Lulu, holding Dotchka by the hand, step onto the deck from the stairs; her skirt flapped round her legs and she held on to a blue beret over strands of hair which blew across her face. Dotchka tottered as the ship tilted, her right hand pressed Dolly against her shoulder, the brown, wool hair trailing. She and Lulu wore matching dresses in blue and green stripes, made, he knew, in Blackpool. The amah, in a long black robe walked behind. Lulu lifted Dotchka, kissed her cheek, passed her to the amah, waved bye bye and took the stairs to the deck above. The amah led Dotchka across the deck to a small play area where there was a rocking horse and a slide. Sam watched her gallop and slither, shouting in Russian.

He decided to write a letter:

My dear Lulu,

I am not very good at writing except police reports, ha, ha. I am sorry that there is this cold distance between us when we were once happy and talked lovingly as Kotchka and Lastochka. It seems a long time ago. We have a little girl and should be more friendly for her sake. I am a man with a man's needs. You are the only woman I will ever really love, but you sometimes make me jealous and unhappy.

I know that you did not like England except the clinic, but we won't talk about that. I will not ask you to go back again, but I think Dotchka should keep in touch with the family. You know how they loved her. I know from papers I have been sent that things are difficult in China. My new job will pay better. I am very proud to have done so well. I hope that you are proud too. Believe me, it is hard work, but it is what I do. I want us to have dinner on our own one evening soon to talk about what we can do. I am very unhappy with things as they are.

from Sam

He folded the note and put it under her cabin door. After lunch, Lulu lifted her hand and placed it on his arm.

"Seven o'clock tonight. In the restaurant."

* * *

As she approached the table for dinner, he stood, stubbed out his cigarette, wiped his chin with a napkin, and pulled out a chair for her.

Three pale candle flames reflected in her face as she reached across to be kissed on the cheek. Her face was lightly tanned under cream coloured make-up, her hair newly crimped into tight waves and clipped back at the forehead, her eyes lined with black, and framed with blue eyeshadow, her brows shaped and pencilled.

He pushed in the chair. She sat and placed a small handbag in front of her.

"You look lovely. Did you buy that dress when you were at the clinic?"

She nodded. "And you wear smart suit and tie father give you, and his collar studs. What in papers you get about new job. You now important – I know they send things to boat."

He ordered champagne and iced cucumber soup. They touched glasses.

"It says what my new duties will be. I will work with detectives and link between the International Settlement, the French Police, and the Chinese Public Security Bureau. Things are very difficult between them."

She sipped the soup from her spoon. "This delicious. What happen?"

"Same old stuff about looking for communists, torturing communists, Chinese trying to get out of Chapei; your father still calls it Chinatown. There's a big refugee problem. I'll try and make sure we can sometimes go dancing or to the pictures."

"It very boring if I not work. I want nice life in Shanghai. Tea dances, coffee parties, interesting people. I not stay home and knit."

He smiled. "I know. Shall we have the chicken and some white wine, then chocolate mousse?"

"That very nice."

"But I don't want you going round flirting with all these men. You don't know who they are and what they might be connected to."

She finished her champagne. "But you flirt with other women. In Warren, they say you always ladies' man."

"I might have been one time, but now I have you and Dotchka."

"But you never there, Sam. What you want?"

He ordered a second bottle of wine. "A place where I can relax and feel comfortable. I want to play with Dotchka and make love to you."

"All possible, but I do what I want, you do what you want. You sleep in barracks if late or early duty. No jealous, no say bad things about friends."

They finished the wine. He looked down at the table, crumpled his serviette, lit a blue cigarette and stared at her through the smoke. She dabbed tears with a small handkerchief. He reached over the table, put a hand over hers, and rubbed the wedding ring with his thumb.

"All right. I want things to work out. I want a marriage. I want to be with you and Dotchka. You are very beautiful. Please come back to my cabin. The amah doesn't expect you back before ten. My place is not comfortable and the bed's very small but let's try again. I have been so miserable."

He signed the bill and took her arm.

* * *

The humidity and dust of August in Shanghai stifled them as they walked down the gangplank and onto the harbour, noisy with the clattering of rickshaws and shouts of coolies unloading crates and lifting massive wooden containers. Sam called a taxi, and the driver loaded the suitcases and trunks into the boot. Dotchka held Dolly. "Home, home. Dolly like."

Sam smiled and bounced her on his knee. "Yes, we'll see Raisa and Mary; they can play with Dolly."

Raisa, thinner, and coughing between sentences, waited for them in the apartment where two fans whirred and spun, displacing the hot air and wafting the curtains. She picked up Dotchka, and kissed Sam and Lulu. "I well. Mary good amah. She cook nice things. Papa drink a lot of bad vodka and be ill. We have tea, you tell about England, then I go back to him. I buy little cakes for you and cream and bonbons for you, little Dotchka. I very glad you back and Lulu better. Look more heavy."

Mary made tea then swung Dotchka in the air, and sang a Chinese song. "I take her for little walk in garden, see birds. Too hot, but she need walk. Back soon."

Sam nodded. "Don't forget her hat and some bread for the birdies." He hugged Raisa.

"Thank you. The apartment looks very nice."

Raisa smiled. "I clean and make new curtains. How journey? And England?"

Sam walked round the room, touching the furniture, the silk cushions, and the vases. "Good journeys. Fresh air. I wish you had been with us. England was busy and Lulu went to a good clinic. She is much better."

Lulu sat in an armchair, opened a fan painted with flowers bought on the ship and gave one to Raisa. The sisters talked in Russian and Sam knew Lulu was describing Warren. They laughed and flipped the fans.

Sam sat in the armchair. "And how is your health, Raisa?"

Raisa stopped flicking the fan. "Thank you. Nice. Aunt buy medicine for me. It do good. She want see you soon."

"I go see her tomorrow," said Lulu, "Sam work then. Today we see Papa."

Raisa nodded. "He miss you and Dotchka. He not want to die when you away. He no eat well or sleep well or look after self. I move back there now; be better for him. Husband ask for money. I say no money. He no work and have another woman."

Lulu held her as she sobbed. Sam touched her elbow. "Don't let him come near you. You're better off without him. Let me know if there's trouble."

He went into the garden to find Dotchka and Mary. Sparrows pecked at the bread Dotchka had thrown. She stamped her feet and watched them flutter and hop, then ran to Sam and threw her arms round his legs. He put his hands on her shoulders and looked round. The garden was lush and florid with limp banana plants, a bright purple bougainvillea, tall orange lilies, and the date palm. He breathed in. "It's grown, like Dotchka."

Sam and Lulu left Dotchka with Mary and took Raisa, with her suitcase, in a taxi to see Dmitri Denisov. He sat in the old chair, coughing, and smoking a curved, wrinkled pipe, like a miniature saxophone, his shirt splattered with stains, the collar greasy. Sam went to shake his hand and felt the wrinkled flesh and twisted bones.

"We brought back some tobacco for you. This is the one my dad smokes. He says it's a special twist."

"Spasiba. I hope not too strong. You tell about England. Lulu look well. You look well, Sam. Fatter."

Sam patted his stomach and laughed. "That won't last long now I'm back."

Lulu spoke to her father in Russian. He stood up, waved his arms, then fell back into the chair.

She looked at Sam. "I tell him he look ill and weak and dirty. Bad colour. Not shave. Everything in apartment horrible. He say old Gōng look after him."

Sam shook his head. "He needs a new fan and some air in here. It smells. I'll get one and I'll talk to Raisa."

Dmitri Denisov pulled himself up on the arms of the chair. "I very fine. Card from England say you now sub-inspector. What you do? Where Dotchka?"

Sam pulled up a chair next to him. "Dotchka's at home with Mary. I report for duty tomorrow. I'll be based at Wayside Road and be in charge of liaison with the Public Security Bureau and the French Police. It seems that a lot of crime is happening because they don't talk to each other."

Dmitri Denisov spluttered. "A lot of crime happening because of French Police. Corrupt all. Officers deal in opium, sell to France. I find out more. Gōng tell me. I sleep now. Bring Dotchka next time."

"You can't believe all Gōng or the newspapers say. Go and lie down. I'll help Raisa unpack, then I'll go to the market and buy food for the week. But keep it cool and cover it in this hot weather. Lulu's off to see the Countess."

Lulu kissed her father and stroked his arm. "Papa you too thin. I see you again tomorrow."

Sam helped Dmitri Denisov to his bed. "Tell the Countess I'll call in tomorrow after duty. Don't forget to take her the French perfume we bought on the ship."

* * *

The police dressed in the summer uniform of beige shorts, long socks, shirt, and cap. Sam admired his tanned knees and strapped a holster round his chest. He took a rickshaw to the end of Broadway East and walked to his new posting at Wayside Station, the largest building in sight. The heat and humidity made him sweat – dark patches appeared under his arms and across the waist. His groin itched and his hair was wet under his cap. He wiped his face with a handkerchief and thought of the cool in England.

The Station was a block up from the Huangpu River and its wharves with a Jewish cinema on the corner. He saw shops – a milliner's, and, near the Station, the Mascot club which advertised "entertainment and dancing" with a German band, cold food, and cakes.

Inspector Kenny, a bulky Irishman with spiky ginger hair, a brisk moustache, and red cheeks, shook his hand. "Welcome to Wayside. And congratulations. Sit down. Everybody just calls me Kenny. God it's hot. Roll on October. How was Lancashire?"

Sam sat in a wicker chair. "Cooler than this. A bit of rain. Very nice. Relaxing. I suppose there won't be much relaxation here?"

The inspector laughed. "You bet. I'll show you round later. Your office is on the first floor. The block you can see through this window is where some of the Chinese and Sikh lads in the SMP live. Now, you'll have read your brief."

"I have, but I suppose things might have moved on."

"They have, and this won't surprise you, our two main problems have got worse – opium dealing and Chiang's obsession about hunting down communists."

"Ah, yes, I remember that mess a while back where we were accused of getting in the way of the military when they were protecting an opium racket. Didn't all the stuff end up in the French Concession?"

"It's all making gang crime worse, of course. Look at these newspaper headlines. I've started keeping a bulletin board downstairs – newspaper cuttings, just to keep an eye and let the men see what bloody journalists are up to and how they lie. Look at this."

Sam read about unsolved crimes, SMP costs, and inefficiencies.

Kenny took the cuttings back. "You see. As usual, it's all our fault. Nothing about the bloody warlords and bloody Chiang and all the in-fighting."

"So, I'll be working with all sides to try to get some agreements about action on crime – is that it?"

"Just about. I'll give you names to start on. First will be one Etienne Fiori, captain in the French Police and a pal of our old gangster friend, Du Yuesheng. You'll meet Fiori next week. Slippery character. He'll either end up with a bullet in his back, or living in style on the French Riviera."

"Can't wait. Now, what about the communists?"

"As I said, Chiang wants to root them out. So what we usually do, of course, is hand over the communists we catch, to them. Now, I know they'll be tortured and killed. Everybody does, but what can we do? Nasty business. Some of our lads get a bit overenthusiastic and some are taking bribes, for sure. You'll be trying to sort out some of that, too."

Sam nodded. "What about the Chinese force?"

"Some very good Chinese officers are useful for intelligence. One of the problems, as I say, is that nobody talks to anybody else. You'll be one of three officers trying to crack that."

"What's the reporting system?"

"I'll talk to you about that. Let's find your office and have a look round. I'll introduce you to the others. You'll have a little Chinese girl to help with the typing. Very bonny. Cigarette?"

* * *

Sam called on the Countess the following day. Her maid let him into the apartment but the Countess did not rise from the armchair as he entered. He leaned to kissed her hand and saw the prominent blue veins spattered with freckles and brown patches. As she tried to rise, he noticed that she was thinner, wheezing and leaning on a stick.

She pointed to a chair. "You look well, suntanned, handsome. You want tea, or you prefer white wine?"

"Tea's fine, Countess. You are as elegant as ever. I've brought you a few photos of England. The others are being developed. I've mainly come to see how you are but also I can give back some of the money I owe you. A bonus payment was waiting for me. I've just got a new job."

"Ah yes, sub-inspector. Very good. And thank you for perfume. I wear now to cheer me. I been a little ill." She held her head to one side and stroked her neck, inviting him to smell the perfume.

He bent down. "Lovely. Coty perfume. Carnation. It suits your personality."

He looked round the room whilst the Countess hobbled out to check on the tea. He saw pale patches and empty hooks on the walls where three pictures had hung. Two armchairs were also missing.

She returned, followed by the maid who carried in an English teapot, decorated with ladies in hats and crinolines, with cups and saucers to match. Sam refused milk.

"You look for pictures? I sell, and a little furniture. No longer need. I buy this tea set to celebrate your travel. You only pay me little money, pay more when you get new salary. What you do in new job?"

"Thank you. That is very kind. I'll give you half now, and the rest in a couple of months. The job's not clear yet. Some liaison work between the French and International Settlements and the Chinese Police. What have you been doing?"

"The usual, meeting friends, reading. If you work with French, I know Captain Fiori very well. He sometimes come for dinner. Very chic, very handsome. He know everyone. Sometimes bring Chinese friend with him. Very big name."

Sam nodded and smiled.

The Countess poured more tea. "Now, I want talk about Lulu. She look well and say she have very good treatment and get new drugs. That good, but she seem not very happy. I ask her. She say she not like England. Very big smoke and wet. Nothing to do except at clinic. She like very much clinic. Why you smile? She say you and Dotchka have good time."

"It was difficult for her with the Lancashire accent and ways. Dotchka learned to speak like that. Wait 'til you hear her. She'll want to show you the doll my sisters gave her. She carries it round all the time. They're not sophisticated. There's not much money. No fancy life. They did their best. This tea is very nice. Perfumed."

"Verveine. I have to talk open. I know Lulu. I never think she made to be wife and mother. You must not be surprised by anything."

Sam put down his cup and stared at a picture. "I'm not. I love her and want her to be happy. I love Dotchka and want the best for her. I've said I'll try to be around more."

"You know that may not be possible with new job, and maybe she not want you round more. She like social life. Must let her have it."

"But she's my wife."

"I know, I know. Listen. I have to go to Hong Kong for little surgery on heart. Not serious, but very good specialist there. I go for tests there in November, then he plan to operate soon after. I very like if Lulu and Dotchka and your amah come with me. That be very good for me. We stay at my cousin's house. Very fine. By sea. What you think? I pay, of course."

"So long as it's not for too long, I think that's a very good idea. I didn't know you were ill. It would make a nice change in the middle of winter. Something to look forward to. I think Lulu would like it. I can keep an eye on Raisa and Dmitri Denisov. Let's talk some more.

I'm sorry, but I have to go and meet a friend now, but I'll see you soon." He kissed her on both cheeks, which were soft, and thick with perfumed powder.

* * *

Jack Smethers was in the bar, smoking and sipping a beer, still in uniform. They shook hands, and punched shoulders. "Good to see you," said Jack. "I got promoted at the same time as you. More work, I suppose. How was England? Did Lulu and Dotchka like it? Is she better?"

Sam nodded. "I'll tell you more later. Let's talk about work."

"I've ordered us champagne. Double celebration. Triple, one for your birthday, two for our promotions."

"What will you be doing?"

Jack sneezed as he sniffed the bubbles. "I'm going to be working with the Sikhs. Developing new traffic control training. How about you?"

Sam offered a cigarette. "Working across the Chinese and French forces to improve communication."

"Well, we bloody need it. Du Yuesheng's up to his tricks. Just negotiated a deal between the French Council and the French Tramways and Electric Light Companies. You know they were on strike?"

Sam smiled, rolled the bubbles round his mouth, sucked in the smoke and blew it out through his nostrils.

"Anyway, the strikes are over. So he now controls the Tramway Company and he's got agreement for five Chinese to sit on the Chinese Ratepayers Association. Clever sod."

"I know. I suppose the last thing Du wants is the communists in charge; he'd lose the lot – probably have to dig his own grave. It's going to be a problem dealing with those buggers in the French Concession."

"Keep your voice down. Bloody French Police, riddled with gangsters, then there's the Chinese Police. It's getting worse. Bribes, bang bang, and so on. It gets worse. Good luck to you."

They touched glasses again. Sam looked at his glass, and swirled the liquid round so that more bubbles frothed. "I don't know if they'll ever talk to each other. Too suspicious, too much at stake. Well, we'll see. Now, how are you, and Yana?"

"Yana's not good. We've been together for six years and no sign of bairns. The doc thinks she has some tube blocked. They're going to operate, but say they don't hold out much hope. She's very upset. So am I."

Jack tipped his champagne glass, drank in a gulp, belched, and laughed. "Well, they do call it bubbly."

Sam touched Jack's wrist. "I'm sorry to hear that news. Happen you can adopt. Or try treatment somewhere else? I don't know what I'd do without Dotchka. Sorry."

Jack shook his head and poured more champagne. "How *is* Lulu?"

Sam crossed his legs and pulled up his socks. "A lot better. I've got some photos somewhere. She still has to take medicine, but seems to be well. She didn't like England, though, except at the clinic by the sea – posh and expensive, of course. Dotchka got really spoiled by my sisters and loved it all. I hope she'll be all right back here. I've bought some goldfish and some little birds – finches and canaries to amuse her. They flap around and twitter in the cages, the birds that is, and the fish float around the tank. She likes tapping the glass to make them go faster and flip their tails."

Jack stared at the bottle and poured two more glasses. "Sounds like a good idea. What did *you* get up to?"

"Went to pubs, boxing matches, cricket, took Dotchka to the swimming pool in Warren – good big one – she can do doggy paddle now. Little flirtation with an old friend." He winked.

Jack pushed his cigarette into the ashtray. "Now, why doesn't that surprise me? Christ, this humidity is still terrible. Must go. Roll on October. Happen see you both for a drink and a dance at the weekend? I've got a day off."

25

At the beginning of October, Sam received a commendation and a pay rise for arresting the three leaders of an opium ring which operated from an office on the wharves.

"Well done," said Inspector Kenny. "That's a great breakthrough."

"Thanks. I'm celebrating tonight – taking the wife out dining and dancing at the Baltimore. The Babskys are playing. They're one of her favourite bands and she's off to HK with her aunt soon. The old girl's ill and going for treatment. I'm off to pick up my suit from the cleaner's before I go home."

He left his office early and went to collect his evening suit and shirt from the cleaners. Once home, he went to talk to the canaries and finches. "Has anyone fed the birds and the fish?" He poked his forefinger through the grid of the big wire cage and the birds came to peck the hard skin at the end of his finger. Dotchka watched him and said, "Pretty boy, pretty boy. Mary feed birds. Birds happy."

He laughed. "Yes, they look happy. So do the fish. So does Dolly. Now don't you put your fingers in the cage. They might bite."

"At least fish quiet," said Lulu. "You know, I see something in newspaper today about blonde bitch you come with to Ciro's."

Sam looked away from the cage and towards Lulu. "Why? Is she back in Shanghai? She's not a bitch."

"No, not now, and not back in Shanghai, bad luck for you. She dead."

He snatched *The Shanghai Times* from the table.

"That's not possible."

October 15th, 1930

LADY ANNABELLE BOSTRIDGE SUICIDE

Lady Bostridge, wife of Lord Bostridge of Filton in Yorkshire, England was found hanged two days ago in a stable at the family mansion. A groom discovered the body in the early hours of the morning. Foul play is not suspected. Lady Bostridge was four months pregnant. She lived in Shanghai between 1923 and 1926. She was the younger daughter of the well-known Shanghai businessman, Sir Neville Dyson and Lady Dyson, residents of Bubbling Well Road. Her parents and sister, Lady Davina Sinclair, wife of the banker Sir Clement Sinclair, survive her.

Lord Bostridge, a Conservative Peer said, "This is dreadful news. I have lost not only my lovely wife, but also a son and heir."

A family funeral will take place later this week.

Sam sat down. It must have been *his* baby. He thought of their time in Manchester. She was so lively with him, so passionate. But not happy. She killed herself two weeks ago. She was buried by now. Christ.

"It's not fair. Just not possible, not possible."

"Why you pale? You not see her for so long time. How she do such a thing when she expecting baby? Come, get ready to go out. Mary do special supper for Dotchka. I hope evening jacket still fit. You get fatter."

"I can't go. Sorry, I have a bad headache. Too much stress at work. I need some aspirin and some whisky."

Lulu screamed. "It always same. Work, work. No fun. I go to Aunt's to plan visit."

Sam lit a cigarette, sat and poured himself a large glass. "Go then. I'll talk to Mary and Dotchka."

He read the newspaper article again. He wondered if he had had anything to do with her committing suicide. They had had a nice time, but her life was a mess. A baby, too. He hoped she would have had a decent burial. Perhaps there was a family church. He picked up Dotchka and Dolly, held them tightly and sang "Bo Peep."

* * *

The Countess received a telegram to say that she would have the tests on her heart on 15 November. She ordered first class tickets for herself, Lulu, Dotchka, and Mary on the 5 November ferry. "Give time to settle in. Cousin very much want company, too."

Sam took them to the passenger wharf and gave Lulu a bunch of red roses, and posies of primroses to the Countess and Dotchka who held them for Dolly to sniff. "Don't cry, Dotchka. You'll soon be back.

"I hope this bloody boat doesn't sink with all these trunks. Thank God Mary's only got one suitcase. Write to me, and be good. I'm off to a meeting in the French HQ. Top secret." He put his forefinger to his lips.

"My love to Inspector Fiori," said the Countess.

He waved to the ferry as it left, and rubbed his eyes on his sleeve.

* * *

Inspector Kenny called Sam into his office the day after Lulu, Dotchka, and Mary left for Hong Kong with the Countess. Sam said he would write and draw pictures.

The inspector held out a file. Sam opened it. "What's all this about?"

"Very serious. The French Chief's going to brief you fully. We need all the police departments – French, Chinese, and us, detectives, special force, volunteers – working together to crack a spy ring. Come on, we've got a meeting with him in twenty minutes at his HQ."

The French Chief entered, took off his hat and placed it on the table in front of him. He spoke in French, then English, helped by an interpreter:

"We have arrested a group of communists who have talked of a bureau in Shanghai. We have agreed to work across the Settlements in small teams to hunt it down. We believe they were responsible for the attempt to assassinate Chiang Kai-shek last December. I will coordinate this personally, with meetings at 8am daily."

Sam was placed in charge of a team with two French and two Chinese colleagues. On 5 April, they arrested a communist agent and uncovered papers from Moscow in a file labelled "Shanghai Cell."

"Good work," said Etienne Fiori at the daily briefing, "Once we decode the documents, and we have experts working on it urgently, we'll know a lot more. A man called Noulens has been arrested, but won't talk."

* * *

Sam called on Dmitri Denisov and Raisa after a day of meetings. Dmitri Denisov sucked his pipe, wheezed, and coughed. Sam helped him to sit and brought tea. Raisa served soup and pirozhki stuffed with lamb.

Dmitri Denisov nibbled the pastry. "Weather get colder. You hear from my daughter and Dotchka?"

"I had a letter yesterday. I brought it. Look, Dotchka has drawn a picture of their house." They looked at a big square building with four windows and a door, and, in the garden, round-headed trees, and flowers with spiky leaves.

Sam folded the paper. "She draws well, doesn't she? And she's written 'My house and garden.' They seem well, and have found friends.

They might come back just before Christmas if all goes well. Lulu will phone me at work."

Raisa looked thin and pale. Sam took the plate from her. "I miss them, but I hear the Countess's operation went well and she is now resting. You both look a lot better, too."

Dmitri Denisov waved the pipe at Sam. Strands of tobacco spilled, glowing, from the bowl. He stamped on them. "And you? I read newspapers. Police think they very clever closing bookshops, arresting students. They little people. Big people more clever. I know you catch Monsieur Noulens, but he will not be found guilty."

"He might. I have to go now. I have an evening conference. We are hoping to make more arrests, but I can't say any more."

"Courts corrupt. Everywhere corrupt."

"Be careful," said Raisa, "I know it dangerous for police. Come and see us soon. I make you nice food. No need to be lonely in apartment."

He kissed her cheek. "I'm hardly there. Too busy."

Dmitri Denisov sucked his pipe and spat brown liquid into a bowl.

* * *

At the end of November, Sam and Jack Smethers met for a drink in the bar at Wayside Station.

"What are all these rumours about cops being involved in a spy ring?" asked Jack.

"Can't tell you yet. Names have been found. Not ours, I'm glad to say, but expect questions because we're married to Russians – I've had some already. How's Yana?"

"Still trying for babies. New treatment. Lulu still in Hong Kong?"

"Yes, trouble with the aunt's operation. They can't travel yet. Happen not until after Christmas. That would be terrible, but Lulu wants to stay with her until she's better. Dotchka loves it, she says. I miss them. The apartment feels empty. Not that I'm there much. Listen, I'm on duty soon and have to phone a little mam'selle first." He winked. "Let's meet at the weekend.

26

Lulu telephoned to say that the Countess had improved but they could not be home for Christmas as her aunt was not well enough to travel.

"I'm fed up with this. Why all these delays? I miss you and Dotchka. Can I talk to her?"

"No, she out with friends."

"Where are you?"

"In hotel. Aunt resting."

"Who are you with?"

"Friends. We do shopping."

They returned to Shanghai at the end of February when snow still remained in hard patches on the pavements.

They stepped off the boat, luggage following them, carried by two porters.

Sam swung Dotchka in the air, and kissed Lulu and the Countess. "You all look so well." He lifted his daughter so that their eyes were level. "I like your hair in plaits and how you've grown. Did Dolly have a good holiday?"

She nodded, put her arms round his neck, and placed her cheek against his. He held her round the waist and pressed her against his chest. He put his arm round Lulu, kissing her hair and neck. "I've missed you. Let's go home. You've got twice as much luggage as when you went. Are you better, Countess?"

Thick make-up covered the pale tint of the Countess's cheeks, and raised blue veins ran like rivulets down her hands and arms. "Much better. Heart have operation. I live to be a hundred. Trunks here. Get into taxi. How Monsieur Fiori? How my apartment? Raisa? Dmitri Denisov?"

"All fine. Your maid is waiting with fans on, and some nice food. We'll take you home first. Raisa and Lulu will visit tomorrow. God, yet more trunks – clothes, I suppose. We'll get these sent on to our apartment."

The Countess leaned on Sam's arm, and Lulu held her waist to support her as she struggled up the step of the taxi. Lulu sat next to her and Dotchka climbed onto Sam's lap. She played with the collar of his shirt, sniffed the cloth of his jacket, and murmured, "I love you, Daddy."

He breathed into her hair. "I have missed you both so much. Now, I've got three days off and we'll do nice things – tea with cakes at Madame Blanche, cinema for the new Mickey Mouse, go to the park. A family again. Hooray. I'll just make sure the Countess is all right and we'll go straight home."

* * *

He wanted to carry Lulu over the threshold of the apartment but she wriggled out of his arms.

"You hurt your back."

"I'm taking you out tonight. We're going somewhere really nice. All booked. A secret. I want to bath Dotchka and read to her before I get changed. Then you and I can stay in bed tomorrow. Morning off. I've been very busy but I've had two commendations and a pay rise."

"Sam. I sorry. I very tired and have headache. I go to bed. Hong Kong very tiring for me. You tell me about new job another day."

He reached for her. "I want to tell you now. I want to celebrate. I want to make love."

"I too tired. Hong Kong not holiday. Hot weather. Aunt very sick. Dotchka also ill."

He banged on the table. "Why the hell didn't you tell me? I've had four bloody postcards and a letter, that's all, and one of those was from the Countess. You could have phoned me at the Station."

"Stop shouting. Mary and Dotchka hear. I not want to worry you. You so busy. Now, I need rest."

"This is a great homecoming. Are you my wife or not? You've been away for four months and you don't want to talk to me even. What did you get up to in Hong Kong?"

"I not one of your criminals. Stop accusing."

"What did you get up to, I said? I know what you're like."

She stepped across the room, her arm raised, but he caught her wrist. "Well, I'm off back to fucking barracks then, or maybe I'll take someone else out dancing."

"You see. You accuse me then want other woman. Go or I scream."

"I'll see to Dotchka because I promised, then I'll tell Mary I'm on duty. I'll be back to talk to you some more. You and the Countess."

He threw her suitcase across the bed, kicked the trunks and called Dotchka and Mary. "Get her bath ready, Mary, and give Missee some soup – she's not well." He played a clapping game with Dotchka, bathed her, put her to bed, slammed the door on his way out, leapt onto his motorbike, and left for barracks.

He went to the gym where he thumped a punchbag until his knuckles were scuffed and sore, lifted weights, skipped, and shadow boxed. Another sub-inspector arrived and watched. "Hold on, you'll knock the stuffing out of that thing. Are you OK? I thought you were off duty for a few days."

"Working off some energy, then going for a drink. I'll be in tomorrow. Come and join me in the bar. Let's have a fucking party."

He went to bed at two in the morning, helped into his room by the duty coolie, and slept until nine, had breakfast of bacon and eggs, and decided to visit the Countess.

* * *

She lay on a chaise longue, her thin body draped in a black silk robe, and red velvet slippers pushed over swollen feet, mottled red and purple. Her cheeks were pale blue, the lips darker. Wisps of hair fell from under a tortoiseshell comb and her eyes, despite the heavy mascara, were dull, sunk in dark sockets, her hands like claws which moved slowly to reach for a glass of juice, set on the table by the maid.

Sam gave her a bunch of roses. "How are you after the journey? Do you need anything?"

"Thank you. I sleep well last night. These first roses I have for long time. No I need rest. You want tea? I call maid."

"No, thank you. I need to talk to you, and I am sorry to have to ask you this, but what went on in Hong Kong? I need to know about Lulu."

The Countess drew her hand across her forehead. "Sam, I very tired. I not know everything, and it not my business, but I know what you want. Lulu meet this man, a rich American, business in oil, at tea dance."

She sipped the juice, spilling a little, paused, breathed deeply and looked at Sam.

"He say he love her and want to marry. She live with him weekends in Hong Kong. Mary and Dotchka stay with cousin."

Sam stood up and punched his fist into his hand. "I knew there was something. She won't even talk to me and no wonder she hardly ever wrote. How could she leave our daughter like that? Fuck. Sorry. Is this how Russian women behave?"

"Listen, Sam, Russian women learn to, how you say, 'pereshivat', 'survivre'."

He frowned "Ah, survive. You can say that again."

"Don't be angry. She and Raisa have no mother, father no job after Russia. Russian men no men any more. They lose hope. Women on

237

own do what they can to support family. And they live fantasy. What else can do?"

She shrugged and placed the juice glass on the table. Sam asked if he could pour himself a whisky. She nodded. He went to the cabinet, unscrewed a bottle of scotch and filled half a tumbler. "Someone once told me that Russians are good at suffering. What's the point of that?"

"Russians not good at suffering. They do not understand it, only say words and look sad, except when drunk. In China, Russians have no home, not their country, their language. They look for security but not possible, so look for it in money, gambling, drink, love, nice clothes. Not make happy, not give security, but always they look and need."

"I have a good job. I can look after a wife and child."

She shook her head. "Not that kind of need. Russians have lost identity."

"You mean like on papers or passports?"

She smiled and tasted the juice. "You a policeman so that how you think. It more than papers, and Russians not even have that. Identity about soul, about belong, about own culture. That why they make own streets, business and clubs here, but not same. Not happy except in small pieces. They think they can take on identity of someone richer, more powerful. I know, I know. It only, what you say, substitute. Not real."

"I can give security and identity. Lulu and Dotchka have British passports. They are British."

"Sam, Sam, it what you feel. If you feel nothing, you try to fill space. *You* have country, family there, belong somewhere, also married to job. You have ambition. I tell you before, Lulu need more. And she like her freedom."

"We'll go back to England. I'll get a job there."

"You know she hate England. She tell me. Little houses, bad smells, bad food. Not understand language. She never go back. She say England poor and, I tell you before, too wet."

"What the hell does she think it's like in Russia?"

"But she not go back to Russia either. She want, you know, money, love, admiration. She think that make identity, make secure – that take place of suffering."

"I love her, but she doesn't seem to understand that I do a difficult job. I have a lot of problems at the moment – some officers having to take leave because of family problems, not enough men, spy rings, crime, and God knows what else."

"I know, and she love you in strange way, but you not always give what she want. She cannot understand your work. It not interest her. She do not liked to feel owned. I very sorry. You nice man."

"I am a very angry man. I give her what I can. I try not to get jealous and angry. I've tried being around more. She doesn't like that either. And I do try to be nice to her. Look at that bloody wedding. How much does she think I earn? I do overtime. I sell little stories and photos to newspapers. I'll never be rich because I'm not going to get involved in any funny business. I'll get promotions."

"Sam, Shanghai difficult place. False outside. Rotten on inside. You go back to England, Find nice girl. Marry. Have more children. You very good father."

"I'll take Dotchka back with me. Get her a good school. Make her a lady."

"Lulu will not permit that. She very determined."

"I'm determined, too, and she's selfish. But I'm not going to just accept this."

"You protest, you get angry, make things worse."

He banged his empty glass down on the small table. "So, what happens next?"

The Countess leaned back. "Rich man come to Shanghai next week. He want Lulu live with him and divorce."

Sam poured another whisky and stared out of the window at the plane trees, drooping in the heat. His hand shook and the whisky leapt up, splashing his cuff.

"I won't divorce. We've only been married three years."

"Ah, I never married that long even. Things move and change.

You come and see me, Sam. I very ill now. Operation help but not get better. Bad heart still. Not long."

"Of course I will come and see you. You have been very kind to us."

He kissed her cheek and smelled stale perfume and bad breath. He finished the whisky in one swallow and went back to barracks to write to Lulu.

* * *

The Countess died a week later, leaving debts which the value of her furniture and pictures scarcely covered. She was buried in the French cemetery amidst great carved family mausoleums and pitted stone crosses. Dmitri Denisov had insisted that the epitaph, on the simple granite block, be written in Russian:

In loving memory of Svetlana, Comtesse de Lausigny-Chabord, born Moscow, 1856, died Shanghai, 1931.
Beloved aunt and sister-in law. Rest in Peace.

Sam, Lulu, Raisa, and Dmitri Denisov stood round the grave. Sam pulled down his trilby to cover his eyes and looked at Lulu from under the brim. She stood, dressed in black, on the arm of a tall man, his dark hair parted on the left and greased back in strands. He wore a pale linen suit, silk shirt, and striped tie; he held a panama hat in his hands as he bowed his head for prayers. He patted Lulu's hand and glanced, several times, at a gold watch on his left wrist. Lulu looked down and dabbed her eyes.

Sam stood opposite, the grave between them. Raisa and Dmitri Denisov were at the head, gazing at the pale wooden coffin. Raisa wore a wide brimmed, black hat and cried, scraping away the tears. Dmitri Denisov blew into a large handkerchief smeared with ash and riddled with burn marks. Sam looked round and saw, standing on a path beyond the small gathering, a man who looked like Etienne Fiori and, next to him, a small Chinese man in a long white robe and a skullcap.

Long yellow teeth protruded over his lower lip. The pair left before the ceremony finished.

After the final prayer, Sam strode round the grave to confront Lulu. "Did you get my letter? Have you shown it to your boyfriend?"

She gripped the man's arm and looked away. Sam turned to face him. "She is my wife, you know. You have no right to try to part us. I believe there's something about that in the marriage lines."

"Listen, Bud…" the man began, but Lulu took away her hand from his arm and poked Sam in the chest. "This not Gus's fault. It your fault. You come here, to the funeral of dear aunt, jealous and angry. You not speak to me again. You go back to barracks and stay. I tear up letter. I love Gus and want be with him. I want divorce."

Sam stepped closer to her, but Raisa pulled his arm. "Please, please, I will talk to her. This not right place or time to discuss these things."

Sam pointed his forefinger at Lulu and the American and shouted, "This is not the end of the matter. I'll see that it isn't."

"Calm down, Bud, can't you see you're upsetting people."

"I should punch you in the face, and maybe I will one day."

27

Sam worked without a break for six weeks, until the end of April.

"Listen, old chap," said Inspector Kenny, "you have to take time off. You're involved in dangerous work, you mustn't be exhausted, and there's big stuff coming up. We need you. You might make mistakes if you're as tired as this."

"I'm fine. I'm keeping fit. I won't make mistakes."

"You will if this carries on. I'm going to get Smethers to talk to you. I've got an assignment that I want you to do, so get some rest. I know you've got trouble at home, but work won't cure that."

"Maybe not, but it keeps me going."

* * *

Jack and Sam met at the Bar du Sud. "What's up?" said Jack, "you look terrible – too much whisky and women? Kenny says you're working too hard, living and sleeping in barracks, and he needs you for something big."

Sam lit a cigarette and ordered two whiskies. "Not much else to do but work. It takes away the thinking. Bloody Lulu's come back from Hong Kong in love with this Yank and won't have anything to do with me."

"Christ. I thought something must have happened. She's only seen Yana once since she got back but I thought it might be to do with the old aunt's illness. I'm very sorry. What are you going to do?"

"Work, work, work. There's plenty to do. I'll have a rest in September. Go to the seaside. Get my cock in action again."

"That's better. More like the old Sam. There's worse tragedies. Think of all those poor buggers up north, drowned in the Yangtze flood. Think of…"

"I know, I know. But I can't help being mad."

Jack patted Sam's arm. "Listen, I'm buying you a good meal, then get some sleep and go and see Lulu tomorrow. She might have changed her mind."

"She won't and it's torture. I used to think I was good with women. Not this one."

Jack smiled. "Russians can be difficult."

"The old aunt said before she died something about them having lost their identity and being insecure. Is Yana like that?"

"Sometimes. But she's not Lulu."

* * *

The following evening, Sam drank two double whiskies in a bar on Weihewei Road, then let himself into the apartment. Lulu was preparing to go out; she sat at her dressing table, pushed a long hatpin into a black, felt cloche and looked at Sam in the mirror.

"What you want? I say I not want to see you."

He clenched his fists and stood close behind her. "I won't give you a divorce. I know all about this man and about Hong Kong. The Countess told me before she died. You're married to me. We have a daughter."

Lulu adjusted her hat. "This not marriage. Have daughter, that all."

"How dare you say that? I love you, I look after you. I take you to England to get better. I offer to do nice things with you. You refuse. You are in *my* apartment."

"Stop shouting. I need to go to dance. I love somebody else. He want to be with me."

Sam could not speak. A darkness crept into him. He took a breath.

"What about Dotchka? I'll take her away."

"That not allowed. I know. Gus have good lawyer."

"It's allowed if you can't look after her, and spend all your time dancing and flirting. How does *that* look?"

"I can look after her. You cannot. Too busy chasing gangsters, drinking, women."

"We'll see about that. I'll be back. Just think very carefully, Lulu. You don't *think*, do you? You just *do* things. It's not fair. Come on, please let's go out somewhere nice."

He reached out to touch her shoulder. She pulled out the hatpin and jabbed his hand in the flesh around his thumb. "Get out."

He pulled away, shook his arm, and wiped away the spot of blood with his finger, turned, strode out of the bedroom, slammed the door, kicked it, and crashed through the outer door. He hid behind a wall across the courtyard, and waited for her to leave. She closed the door of the apartment, strode across the courtyard, black high heels clicking on the flagstones, and took a taxi at the corner of the road.

He shouted after it, "Just you see, bitch. I'll have a good time in summer."

He sat on a grass verge and wept. He wondered how to get revenge and what would happen to Dotchka.

* * *

Sam was not able to take time off in summer. There were bombs on the Shanghai to Peking railway and accusations in the press of police being unaware of mass assassinations by the communists.

"Just look at these headlines. Bloody hell," said Inspector Kenny to Sam. "But we do have a lead. A big fish, Gu Shunzhang, has defected. Police in Nanking suspect his family has been murdered in Shanghai. They're sending him down here tomorrow under heavy guard. Meet him and find out what it's all about. There's an informer, too. He knows all about it. Take as many men as you want."

Sam and six officers went with Gu and the informer to a house just off Gaston Road. The informer, pointed to an area of disturbed grass, "This is where your family are buried."

The police sent for spades and called for help. A crowd gathered, some climbing trees to watch.

Sam looked down as the spades unearthed three bodies. The heads were missing. The smell was intense. Four people in the crowd fainted.

"Get everybody who isn't working out of here," shouted Sam. "That's an order."

"This is my wife and parents," said Gu and fell to the ground.

Sam picked him up and brushed him down. "Get this man into a car and to hospital."

"His little son still alive and in own village. I tell him."

The bodies were carried away in a van and the area ringed with ropes and sandbags.

Sam went back to the office to file his report. He dragged himself to the Station, leaned across his desk, head on arms, and fell asleep.

* * *

He visited the Denisov apartment for a meal between shifts. Raisa served noodles with meatballs, and Dmitri Denisov poured a tumbler of whisky.

"You look very bad," said Raisa, "I see your picture in papers helping dig up bodies. When you last sleep and eat?"

"I didn't sleep at all last night, and not much for weeks. This tastes good."

"Have more. Eat all."

Sam forked the noodles. "I've seen some terrible sights, but nothing as bad as that. The smell, the smell. I almost fainted myself. All those bodies."

"I not surprised," said Dmitri Denisov, "revenge is a terrible thing.

Communists will punish those who turn. Zhou Enlai very fierce with defectors. I hear your commissioner give press conference. He not understand this mentality I think."

"Who does? It's just savage."

Dmitri Denisov shrugged. "How my daughter and Dotchka? I not see for long time."

Sam put down his plate, cupped his eyes in his hands and slumped in the chair. "I don't know. I haven't been home for a month. We had a big fight about some bloody American." His shoulders shook and Raisa rubbed his back. Dmitri Denisov poured more vodka.

"You remember I tell you I would not marry my daughter and I would not marry you? So now you see."

"Papa, stop," said Raisa, "Sam too tired. He need sleep. I know about this American. I not trust him, but she say she in love."

"Ha, what the hell does that mean? I don't think she knows what love means. I won't agree to divorce."

Raisa held his head in her hands and stared at him. "Women think they know about love. I did once. Look for security."

Sam pulled away. "I've heard that before. I just think it's selfish. I can't stay. I need to get back on duty. There's a lot on. I'll see you when it's a bit quieter."

Dmitri Denisov took his pipe out of his mouth and waved it at Sam, scattering ash on the floor. "I tell you one other thing. Chiang and his nationalists looking in wrong place. Police job to keep order, not investigate communists. Moscow four thousand miles away, Japan very close. How many Japanese now in Shanghai? How many in Chinese sector? And that right next to French and International Sectors."

"I know, but the Japs didn't bury those bodies."

"Listen, I tell you before. This about power. Why you think everyone say Japanese put bombs on railway? To blame Chinese for starting trouble. Chinese weak; no one in charge. I hope I not live to see results."

Raisa held his hand. "Papa, you must not say bad things. Sit down. Relax. Be careful, Sam. I talk to Lulu. You come to us for Christmas. Only a month away."

"Thanks, but I should be able to spend it in my own apartment with my own wife and daughter – Christmas tree, nice party. Get a bit of peace for a while. He leaned back on a cushion and closed his eyes.

Raisa put her hand on his shoulder. "Sam, that not possible. I arrange you see Dotchka some days. Lulu accuse you of bad things. She not want you to see her."

He stood and thumped the chair. "I'll get my own back."

28

At the end of January 1932, police inspectors called emergency meetings at all SMP stations. Inspector Kenny addressed the men at Wayside.

"The Japanese are fed up with the Chinese sniping at them and boycotting their goods. The Japanese naval commander is spoiling for a fight and has told the Brits on the Shanghai Defence Committee he will go into action on 29 January. As of 4pm on 28 January the International Settlement will be under martial law. If you have families, tell them to get provisions and stay indoors."

Sam signed out of the Station, grabbed his motorcycle, and dashed to the Weiheiwei Road apartment. Snow spattered from the sides of the wheels, and the engine growled as he turned corners. He parked at the corner of the garden. Trees and shrubs shone with frost and ice. A neighbour had thrown out crusts for the birds, and huge crows were chasing away sparrows. Sam opened the door and Dotchka ran to him, "Daddy, Daddy." He swung her up to his shoulder and she put her hands on his cheeks, murmuring to him in Russian.

Sam put her down. "Daddy's here, but Daddy has to go to work. He'll be back soon."

Mary took Dotchka's hand and led her into the kitchen. "Dotchka help Mary make soup. Very cold weather."

Sam sat in an armchair and looked at Lulu. "Now listen, whatever trouble there is between us, I must protect you and Dotchka. It was cruel what you did at Christmas. I missed you both. I will bring rice and tins of food and vegetables. I'll see that Raisa and your papa are looked after. You must all stay inside. There is going to be trouble. The Japanese are going to attack Chapei."

"You just make excuse to come here. You never see Dotchka."

"You know why. You won't let me. You and all your scenes. Do you have any idea of what's going on out there? No. Do you have any idea of what I have to deal with? No. It's all dances, cinema, magazines, scandal. You don't care."

"Stop shouting. It all you can do. Everyone say no problem in Settlements, I say just trouble in Chinese part. That their problem. I have to go to hairdresser."

She turned her back on him and went to find her coat.

Sam stood and clenched his fists. "You are not going out. Where's that bloody American? I tell you, no divorce. You've behaved badly. Anyway, it's all officers on duty. I have to go into the Chinese sector to take photographs and record what goes on. It's dangerous. Whatever happens, I want you to look after Dotchka, and if the worst happens then you have to get out to Hong Kong. You have friends there, I believe."

She threw a vase at him and spat in his face. Mary ran from the kitchen and picked up the pieces of blue ceramic.

Lulu stared at him, fists on hips. "Get out. You make drama out of nothing."

"The Chinese sector is very close. There will be refugees. Thousands. We shall be putting up barriers soon. There will be shooting and deaths. Is that nothing?"

"So what you want we to do?"

"I could get you to England, but you won't go, so too bad. Just look after Dotchka. I want to talk to you about her, but not now. I'll be back in an hour with food. Do not leave the building."

* * *

Photographs of sandbags and coils of barbed wire round the International Settlement appeared in the world's press. SMP officers, armed with rifles and pistols, were wrapped against the cold and stared into the cameras. The chief commissioner announced that the Japanese had banned public meetings in Chapei and ordered Chinese troops out. One platoon had refused to leave and was guarding the North Station. The commissioner despatched three sub-inspectors, with Chinese Policemen, to investigate.

Sam and two Chinese Sergeants, Rén and Yán, crossed the bridge into the Chinese sector and hid in a house near North Station, rented by Rén's aunt.

Sam turned up the collar of his coat. "God, it's cold. Those soldiers must be having a hard time. Poor sods. No heat, short of food."

"Very brave," said Yán, "defending station against orders of Chiang. You know Chinese not like to lose face. They will fight for ever."

"Ah, yes, I keep coming across that. Not always sensible, but I know how it is."

They heard the tumult of Japanese warplanes, flying low over Chapei, then the whine of bombs and explosions. Smoke and flames rose above North Station.

Sam waved to the officers. "Right. Let's see what's happening. Get your helmets and bulletproofs on. I'll just load up the camera. Then we'll make for the Station."

Trucks and sandbags formed a circle. The men jumped over buckled railway lines strewn with bodies and eased through buildings on fire. Wooden posts stood smouldering and charred. Twelve soldiers held guns, their helmets gashed and uniform ragged.

Sam held out canteens of water. "Why don't you just leave here? It's hopeless."

"No, sir, we never leave. What we are doing is right."

The soldiers gasped as they drank, spilling water down their chins. Sam looked round.

Two naked babies sat on a bombed platform under a burning beam. They howled, bereft, at the smoke and fire. A soldier put a blanket round them.

"Grab this baby and wrap it up," Sam said to Rén, "I'll take the other. Let's get them out. We know what's needed here. We'll get some food and water in somehow."

Another bomb exploded to the right. A beam crashed down, falling rubble filled the air with dust.

Sam, Rén, and Yán, carrying the babies, ran through streets filled with bodies and rats, trucks of dead men, women, and children, limbs tangled and heads hanging over the edges. Shops and factories were in flames, trees charred, schools and hospitals in ruins.

Sam took the rescued baby to Mary. "I will pay you to look after this boy; just say he's a relative of yours."

"You good man, Sir. Poor baby. I call him Chen Sam. Lucky name."

Rén took the other baby, a girl, to be cared for by his cousin.

* * *

"The Japs have been dropping thirty pound bombs from about three hundred feet," Sam reported to the assistant commissioner. "Here are the photographs. The Chinese need food, clothing, blankets, weapons."

"We can't get weapons in, but we can liaise with the aid agencies and get them emergency access, perhaps. It's estimated that eighty-five per cent of Chapei has been destroyed. Thousands killed, of course. About thirty thousand refugees are trying to get into the Settlements. It's desperate."

"What about international help?"

"The League of Nations thinks the Japs and Chinese should sort it out between themselves. International concern, questions in British Parliament, protests in Hyde Park and all that, but what can they do? Reports say that the Chinese have hardly any troops left in Chapei. Chiang won't help. Still obsessed with communists, and thinks he can get international funds and sympathy."

* * *

Sam, cold and hungry one evening, visited Dmitri Denisov and Raisa. Dmitri chewed the stem of his pipe and offered vodka. "This very nice drink. Good for digestion. Shopkeeper save for me. I hear that a truce will be declared. Japan will claim victory, of course. As usual, Japanese say they are just protecting own interests and people. That's how wars start. They know Chinese can't defend their own country. Divided. When country divided, cannot last."

Sam swayed in his chair. "Give me some more of that vodka."

Raisa shook her head. "Not drink too much. I make nice warm soup and pies."

* * *

Jack Smethers was injured in February, trying to prevent a rush of refugees from breaking down the barricades into the International Settlement.

Sam went to visit him in hospital. "Christ, it's cold out there. The fun seems to be over for the time being, now the rest of the work starts. I'll just take my coat off."

A nurse took it to hang in the corridor. Sam watched her. "Pretty little thing. Nice legs. Lucky you. How are you doing?"

"I'm OK. A bit sore in the shoulder. Broken collarbone. Did you ever see so much strapping? They won't let me out until next week in case of what they call complications. What's going on out there now?"

Sam took out a cigarette. Jack shook his head. "Afraid you can't smoke in here. Matron's a terror."

Sam smiled. "We'll have a few drinks when you're out. Well, there's discussion about what happens to the roads outside the Settlements. The Chinese have set up admin posts out there, but it's agreed that we can go in if there are emergencies. The Japs have set up a military barracks. Senior officers all Japs."

"Seems a bit daft as we're in China."

"I know. And they're all fighting about what the tax system should be. Forget it."

"Never trusted them. Still don't. Christ, what a place. I sometimes wonder why I'm here, but what can you do? No work in the Welsh valleys, except in the pits. I worry about Yana, but she won't leave. How are things with you and Lulu?"

"Can't talk about it. Too terrible."

He looked at the water jug on the table beside Jack's bed and poured two glasses. "I wish it were whisky. Do you know it's filthy under this table?"

Jack laughed. "I dare you to tell Matron. Yana's been to see Lulu. She says she's unhappy. Hasn't heard from her American. Not surprising in the circumstances. He's been in Texas for a month. Why don't you just get Dotchka out?"

"How?"

"Some folks send their kids to a fancy Catholic boarding school in Hong Kong. Good education, they say."

"Dotchka is six next year. It's too young. Anyway, there are good European schools in Shanghai."

"How long will they last? What's her life like here? You two fighting or not seeing her. Big trouble in Shanghai. You never know what will happen next. They say the Settlements can't last forever."

Sam shrugged. "But the Europeans and the Yanks don't believe that. They watched the bombs and fires over Chapei at parties on hotel roof gardens. Lulu took Dotchka to one. They thought it was fun – just like fireworks. I didn't half get mad at her."

"I know. Crazy. Yana's helping with a relief charity for refugees."

"At least that's something. Do you need anything?"

"Don't think so. I just want to get out of here. Too much time to think. It all feels unreal, like trying to swim in a rough sea."

Sam laughed. "Well, don't bloody drown. I'd like to get Dotchka out, yes, and perhaps to HK, but it costs money. I haven't got it."

Jack moved his legs under the sheet. "Christ, I'm getting stiff. You might get a bit of a grant from the force, I think. Mary can stay with Lulu to help out, and that bloody rich Yank should make some contribution to costs if he's serious."

"It doesn't seem right, Dotchka's so young. Lulu will never let me take her back to England. I'll have to think. Bloody mess I've got myself into. Christ I need a fag and a drink."

He leaned back in the chair and rubbed his cheek. "How is Yana?"

"Very upset because she's been told she definitely can't have babies. Something twisted inside. We'll get her looked at again when we're back home but that's not for another two and a half years. Shai might not last that long. And she's not getting any younger."

"I'm sorry about that. She would make a good mother. Not like somebody I could name."

"Sam, forget it. Find somebody else."

"I will. I've joined the tennis club again. Some right lookers there. And the Dramatic Society. I once met a woman there who could fuck like a goat."

"What happened to her?"

"She's dead. Don't ask."

He stood up, shook Jack's left hand, patted the nurse on the bottom, and went to the market to buy a toy for Dotchka and have a whisky at the Café Dauphin.

* * *

He bought a two feet high wooden rocking horse, with orange glass eyes, a red felt saddle, and a brown woollen mane and tail. After three more whiskies with an informer, he strapped the toy across his front over his coat and started the bike.

He opened the door of the apartment and sniffed Lulu's perfume so strongly that he thought she must be in, rather than at one of her tea dances. He went into the sitting room and called her name. No one was there; on the carpet he saw a storybook of *Goldilocks and the Three Bears* and an abacus he had given Dotchka for Christmas. He took off his heavy coat, put the wooden horse next to the book and wrote a note "From Daddy, with love," then tapped the horse's head so that it rocked on its base; the glass eyes flickered in the sunlight and the tail wobbled.

He walked round the apartment. Lulu's underwear was spread across the bed beside a green silk dressing gown. A pair of red, high heeled shoes lay askew on the floor. Sam buried his head in the smells of her body – sweat, vagina, and perfume. He turned and saw, on the bedside table, a photograph, framed in silver, of the man who had been with Lulu at the Countess's funeral, his face square, with prominent cheekbones, dark hair sleek and combed back, parted on the left. He smiled, showing perfect white teeth under thin lips and a thin moustache. He wore an open neck shirt with a spotted cravat folded into the neck. Sam picked up the photograph, signed in thick ink and large letters: "To darling Lulu. All my love, Gus."

Sam flung the photograph across the room. It hit the mirror and both splintered into jagged pieces and spattered glass across the floor. He picked up the man's photograph, took out his knife, looked at the face and slashed across it. He tore the underwear in the bedroom, opened the wardrobe and stabbed at the dresses, furs, and shoes. He picked up the jewellery box and scattered rings, necklaces, and earrings about the room then kicked the red shoes, one by one, under the bed.

He patted Dotchka's bed, sat Dolly on the pillow, and ran from the apartment. He breathed deeply, puffed out a cloud of breath into the frost and started his motorbike to take him back to Wayside Station and the bar.

* * *

Inspector Kenny called him in three days later. "Sam, I've had a letter from your wife. Sorry, but it's a serious complaint."

"What do you mean?"

Kenny handed him the piece of paper. Sam's hand shook and he knew he was turning pale as he looked at the typed page. "She couldn't have written this. It's typed in perfect English. She can't type and her English isn't good enough to write it. Someone, or someone's secretary, has done it for her. I know whose."

28th March 1933

Dear Inspector Kenny,

I wish to bring a complaint against my husband, Sub-Inspector Samuel Shuttleworth. Our daughter and I have not seen the said Samuel Shuttleworth for over a month and he has given us no money on which to live for more than two months. Yesterday, he raided our apartment, damaging my clothes and jewellery.

It is hard for a woman to look after a child and to survive in these circumstances. I appeal to you to remind him of his duties towards his family rather than, as I am reliably informed, spending his wages on women and drink.

Yours faithfully,
Tatiana Shuttleworth.

Sam began to tear the letter. "It's all lies. I pay her most of my salary regularly and pay the rent myself. This is revenge. She is living with a rich American and often leaves the little girl with the amah. I do go round when I can."

"Give me the letter, Sam. Is it true?"

"I wrecked some stuff in the apartment. I was angry."

"And jealous, no doubt. I don't blame you. Why do you let this woman have such power over you? Sit down. Calm down."

Sam dangled his arms between his legs, head bowed.

"This is driving me crazy. She just plays everybody round her little finger. And there's our daughter."

The inspector took the letter from him. "She's Russian, isn't she? Nothing but bloody trouble. I wish you lads would leave these foreign women alone. Jesus Christ. I support you, but incidents like this are not good for your promotion chances. She knows that. I thought you were filing for divorce."

"I wasn't, but I'll think again now."

Kenny spread out the letter. "I'm going to destroy this and ignore her. But just be bloody careful. You're a good officer, Sam."

* * *

Sam thought he might talk to Raisa, but decided against it. Instead, after duty, he went to the Station bar where he asked for a bottle of whisky and sat at an empty table, smoking.

"Friday night, Alan old scholar, have something else to drink," he said to Sub-Inspector Dean who was having a pint of beer at the bar. "I've got the weekend off. How many Russian women do you think I can fuck by Sunday?"

"It depends how much you drink, and how willing they are. Come off it, Sam, what's all this about? Thanks for the whisky."

"How many?"

"I don't know. Two nights? Six, eight?"

"Bet you two dollars for each – woman, I mean, not just the fuck."

"Oh, all right, you silly bugger – you're getting as bad as the Chinks, all this betting."

"See you back here Sunday night at eight."

They met in the bar. Sub-Inspector Dean sat under a light, a glass of beer in his hand. "Christ, Sam, you look done in. Come to collect your winnings?"

Sam leaned on the table. "I'm done in, but you owe me thirty dollars. Call it twenty-five."

"Fifteen women? Where the hell did you go?"

"It was fourteen and a half in fact. Couldn't get the old pecker up with the last one. None of the old tricks worked. Too tired, too drunk."

"I'll pay you tomorrow."

"Never mind, but get me a drink, there's a pal, and one for yourself. Vodka – a good Russian pick me up. Double."

At midnight, Dean dragged Sam back to his room. He lay on the bed, under a spinning ceiling. Dean put him on his side and pulled a blanket over him. "Sorry about your problems, Sam, but no more revenges. It's not doing you any good." Sam was asleep.

29

Cool March breezes gave way to weak April sunshine. Sam telephoned Lulu. "We need to discuss our daughter's education. She'll be six in November."

"I know, I know."

Lulu sat in a tall wicker chair at a mirror in the bedroom of the apartment, brushing her hair with tense sweeps over dark waves. They crackled and floated away from the brush, then settled into strands. A fashion magazine rested on her knees that were covered by a brown silk skirt. Her feet were bare, the nails painted red, and she wore no make-up except for eyeshadow and mascara. A loose camisole drooped across her shoulders and breasts.

Sam looked at the red shoes that lay by the bed, straps open. "I don't know how you walk in these."

"None of your business."

They looked at each other in the mirror, images blurred. He bent to kiss her, but she moved her head away.

He straightened. "I've brought Dotchka an Easter egg and you an enamelled Russian one with a surprise inside."

"I don't like your surprises. Put them on the table. Dotchka back for tea in an hour. She with Mary and that new little relative. She carries him round like Dolly. I hear you have a new girlfriend."

"I suppose one of your Russian bitch friends told you that. Why are you so interested? Well, I'll tell you, apart from the occasional dance, I have no time for women with what's going on out there."

"Why? Cinemas, nightclubs open, tea dances at hotels. Very fine time. Gus and I saw Mae West last week. Mae West and Cary Grant. You wouldn't know. New bands, new music all the time." She began to hum "Stormy Weather."

"No, I don't know about the cinema and new music, though I do get out a bit, you know."

She smiled and began to file her nails.

He put his left hand on the back of the chair. "And it might all change. Remember what happened last year? Well, the Japs have attacked in north China and got through the Great Wall.

"What that to do with me? Sit down and stop looking over my shoulder watching me. Chinese not care. Too poor. They want movies, Chinese stars, gossip, and magazines, scandal."

He sat in the armchair and watched her put on her make-up. "Some of them do, yes, but others are more serious and want the Japs out. Movies are not what life's about and Shanghai is sitting on problems. That's why I want to talk to you about Dotchka."

Lulu smoothed a cream foundation over her cheeks, nose, and forehead. "Dotchka very happy with Mary. She now in a little Church school. She learn good English, sing English songs, count in English, with good accent."

"I'm worried about the standard of education. I'm worried about her safety, and yours, and about her not getting enough attention."

Lulu took out a brush to spread rouge on her cheeks. "How you know? You not here. She get plenty from me and Mary."

"From Mary, you mean, who doesn't speak good English and talks to Dotchka mostly in Chinese. It's not good enough."

"And I speak to her in Russian, you mean? Russian not good enough for you. Russian very fine language."

She stopped putting on make-up and turned to stare at him. He balanced his cap on his knee. "Russian is a beautiful language, but she has to learn to speak, read, and write good English. And you're not here much. Always off with your slick-haired boyfriend or gossiping with your Russian friends. I know some of them, you know. They're a bad influence."

She threw a hand mirror at him, followed by the hairbrush.

He caught the mirror by the handle. He smiled. "Damn good catch that." She threw a powder compact, which hit the chair.

He pushed it to one side with his boot. "Calm down. Like your American, Gus what's-his-name, told *me* to. Bloody cheek. Listen to me. What does this man intend? If you're going to go to America, fine, but Dotchka will stay here and go to boarding school."

"You try to steal daughter from me? You cruel and bad and jealous. Gus want to get married and live in Texas. I too."

"You can't do that until you're not married to me, and suppose I won't give you a divorce?"

"Then I divorce *you*. I know what you do. Tennis club, drama club. You fuck other women – English, French, American – and drink. You look tired, you get fat. I start divorce now and marry Gus in two years."

"Two years is a long bloody time in Shanghai. Dotchka needs more than she's getting. I will put in papers for a divorce if you will agree that she can go to a very good Catholic boarding school in Hong Kong. I can get a small grant and pay the rest. You can visit whenever you want. Your boyfriend has business there. Just think about it. Where is the great Gus now, by the way?"

"He in Texas. Big oil deal. He back in May."

"So who are you flirting with now? Be bloody careful, Lulu. This man has money, good business, good looks – if you like that sort of thing. He won't put up with any nonsense."

"You jealous because you no money, no business, not handsome any more."

"That's not what some think."

He stood, smelled the combined scents of powder and perfume, and looked at her bare shoulders. She pulled a wrap around her. "Stop looking. I think about this. Come back in a week. Now go."

* * *

Lulu agreed that they should send Dotchka to boarding school in Hong Kong. St Monica's Catholic School for Girls agreed to accept her for the term beginning on 20 September.

Sam went to tell Dmitri Denisov and Raisa. The apartment was hot and humid and smelled of sweat, stewing meat, vodka, and tobacco. They listened to his news, coughed, cried, and wiped their faces with cloths.

Raisa sniffed. "I know, I know. Lulu talk with me. I shall miss her. I think of her at birthdays and Christmas if she not here. But I know this best for her. I not want to die, nor do Papa with Dotchka not here."

"No one is going to die. She will write to you, and she will come back sometimes. Lulu will visit and I'll get there when I can. She'll be back some holidays and in the summers and we can perhaps all go on holiday somewhere cooler. The seaside, perhaps. It will be good for you. I will miss her too, but she needs a good education."

Dmitri Denisov wiped his eyes and his forehead with his sleeve. "She better away from this place. It stink. Old Gōng say that. What you do now? Still fighting communists? It all big joke. You done well to get your police and other police to talk to each other, work together. You arrest some important people. But I know what happen."

"What *is* happening, if you know so much?"

"I read newspapers, I listen to radio. I talk to Chinese. Gossip, like you call it, very useful. I know many big boys give up communists to join nationalists. I know about killings – in streets, in hotels, everywhere. He tapped the side of his nose with his pipe and spat out of the window. Raisa waved a newspaper at him. "Papa, don't do that. It's dirty."

Sam patted Raisa's arm and turned to Dmitri Denisov. "Maybe you don't know as much as you think. Yes, there have been a lot of revenge killings. We know who's doing what, but it's complicated."

"You always say it complicated, I always say people confused about who in charge."

"Well, there's that, too. The Municipal Council want to increase taxes. The Japanese want more representation on the Council. They've only got one Japanese deputy commissioner and two assistant commissioners."

"Where Japanese think they live? Tokyo or Shanghai? I read newspapers. I know Madame Sun Yat-sen start National Salvation Movement."

"I can't talk about that, but you should know that there's Russian influence in there."

Dmitri Denisov ignored him. "And Chinese newspapers know plans for assassinations of Chiang gangsters – all fascist. Attack students and professors. Easy targets."

"I can't talk about that either."

"Left and right all same. We seen all this in Russia. Go back and look after Dotchka. That more important. Does she want to go to this school?"

Sam opened the door and turned. "There is no choice. She'll be happier and safer there."

* * *

Dotchka had an early birthday party in the Weiheiwei apartment at the end of August, before she left Shanghai for the beginning of term at St Monica's. Raisa and Dmitri Denisov gave her a book of illustrated Russian stories, Sam a drawing book with pencils, and Lulu a frilled pink dress which Dotchka wore at the party.

Mary made lemonade, sandwiches and cake, and gave Dotchka, from her and Chen, a red paper lantern for luck. Raisa decorated a cake, with marzipan covered in pink icing, and small sugar flowers in blue and yellow. Dotchka blew out the six candles in two breaths. Everyone clapped.

Lulu kissed her. "Did you make a wish? If you did, don't tell anyone what it was or it won't come true."

Dotchka looked at Sam. The family and friends sang "Happy

Birthday." Mary smiled and nodded, tears running down her cheeks. Sam took photographs, his hands unsteady.

"These are to send to your aunties and uncles in England. And you're a lucky girl. You'll have another party at school on your real birthday in November. Now you are nearly six and a big girl, ready to do your lessons."

Dotchka stared at him and blinked her big, blue eyes. Dmitri Denisov and Raisa coughed and blew their noses into serviettes.

Dotchka clutched Dolly round the waist. "I don't want to go." She climbed from her chair and pushed her head into Mary's long, pale blue robe. Mary's tears fell onto Dotchka's hair and she stroked the damp strands with thick fingers. Chen cried.

Sam crouched by her. "Mary will come with us to the dock and will be here when you come home for holidays. And so will Chen. Mummy and Daddy will take you to your new school."

Raisa gave Dotchka a small felt handbag. "To keep your treasures in. Mummy will stay in Hong Kong until Christmas and will see you every Saturday, you know. She will tell us all about you."

Dmitri Denisov put his arms round Dotchka and kissed her cheeks. "Write to your old Grandfather. I might not be here very long."

Dotchka stared at him. "Why? Where are you going?"

Raisa laughed, then cried, and left the room.

30

An early September wind blew across the harbour as Lulu, Sam and Dotchka waited for the Hong Kong ferry. It left an hour late. They sat on deck and watched the coastline, the leaping fish, and the loud seagulls. Sam blew smoke towards them. Dotchka was seasick as soon as the ferry left.

Sam held her hand. "Don't look at the water, Dotchka. It makes the sickness worse. Suck a sweetie and watch the land. Make Dolly wave bye bye to Shanghai."

"Gus will meet us with a car," said Lulu.

"Does he have to? We can get a taxi."

Lulu looked away and shrugged "He very kind. You ungrateful. Dotchka like to go to school in big car?"

She nodded. Sam lit another cigarette.

* * *

Gus waved as they stepped off the ferry three days later. He lifted Lulu and kissed her on the lips. He bent down to look at Dotchka. "Here, a nice posy of freesias to welcome you to Hong Kong."

He grasped Sam's right hand and covered it with the left. "Hello, old fellow. No hard feelings, I hope. I hear you're doing a great job in Shai."

Sam pulled his hand away. "We do our best. It's not easy."

"We'll just get this little lady to school, then have cocktails and dinner at Chez Bruce."

"Thanks, but I can't. I have to meet some police colleagues."

"Gee, that's too bad. Your hotel is all booked. I think you'll like it. Near the harbour. Small but comfortable. Let's go. I'll just signal to the chauffeur."

The school was a solid square of red brick along Causeway Road. Dotchka gripped Sam's arm in the back of the car as they drove up to the wide wooden door. They were greeted by the Mother Superior, and the matron, a nun, both dressed in grey smocks, heavy wooden crosses hanging across their chests.

Sam lifted Dotchka's suitcase from the back of the car before the driver could take it. "Be brave for Daddy,"

"Say goodbye to Mummy and Daddy now," said the Headmistress, looking from Lulu to Gus. "All the paperwork has been done. We just need Mr Shuttleworth's signature on the account."

She waved it towards Gus.

"I'll take that," said Sam. "I'm her father. Inspector Shuttleworth."

Matron patted Dotchka on the head. "We don't think a lot of fuss is good for the little ones, they soon settle in. We'll get her into her uniform straight away."

Dotchka gripped the handle of the leather suitcase with both hands. Dolly was tucked under her right elbow. She blinked, stretched her right hand across her eyes, then looked at her feet where her face was reflected in the patent leather of the shoes. Sam focused on the suitcase and the small hands, the knuckles white and twitching. Matron released the case from Dotchka's grip, took her hand, and walked towards a long, black corridor. Sam stared as they grew smaller. Dotchka turned and waved. He saw Dolly's striped legs turn the corner.

He refused a lift from Gus and took a taxi to his hotel. He was handed a telegram asking him to return to duty in Shanghai immediately due to a bad spate of violence. He ordered a bottle of whisky and booked a ticket for the early morning ferry.

* * *

Inspector Kenny addressed the team meeting. "The communists seem to be less active in cities now, but General Chiang seems determined to pursue them in the countryside. He's assigned troops to cut off supplies."

"What about the Japanese?" asked Sam.

"He still doesn't seem interested in them, and I'll come on to that. The communists have fought through the nationalist blockade in the north and have set off, under Zhou Enlai and Mao Tse-tung, for Western China, heading for Shansi." He indicated the route on a wall map.

"That's a hell of a long way," said an officer. "How will they survive?"

"A lot won't. It's six thousand miles and rough territory. They'll be under attack from the nationalists and they'll starve. That's not our problem. Our focus is on Shanghai."

He pointed to a map on the wall. "See this street, Rue Moliere, number 29. Madame Sun Yat-sen is holed up here. She gets visits from communist supporters. You've heard of this National Salvation Association. This is their base."

A sergeant raised his hand. Kenny pointed to him. "Yes, question over there."

"What are Chiang's Blueshirts up to now?"

"Supporting the Salvation Association. They want to purify China – get rid of laziness, gambling, and sex."

The men laughed and Sam ran his hand through his hair. "That won't work, will it?"

Kenny smiled. "No, but what's happening is more attacks on people they think support the Japs, more boycotts of Jap goods. A lot of trouble. I want a three man guard on that house twenty-four hours a day. Photograph who goes in and out."

* * *

Sam met Jack Smethers for a drink in the bar after duty. Jack looked up from a table. "You look a bit worn out. What'll you have?"

Sam slumped into a chair. "The usual. Had to leave Hong Kong early about this communist shit. Didn't like leaving Dotchka there, but she'll be better off. God, that woman drives me crazy."

Jack offered him a cigarette. A card sketched with the large head and tiny body of a cricketer fell out of the packet. Sam picked it up. "My little brother collects these. Lazy bugger. Only writes when he wants something. Asked me to watch out for cigarette cards. Save them for me, will you?"

"By that woman you mean Lulu. She's always driven you crazy. Listen, my friend, she'll do what she wants."

Sam finished his whisky and ordered two more glasses. "Cunning as a snake. Suits her to be in Hong Kong of course. The fancy man Gus, what a fucking awful name, is there a lot on business. I've agreed to a divorce."

He looked down into his beer. "What the hell happened to Lastochka and Kotchka? All that silly romantic stuff? Now no Lulu, no Dotchka."

"Cheer up, old son, plenty more fish in the sea. Look for one who isn't a bloody shark next time."

Sam nodded and lit a cigarette. Then there was poor old Annabelle. What a mess he'd made of things with women. He'd be more careful. Look for somebody who would be a good wife. But, God, he could see Lulu now on that first time they'd met. Would he ever forget?

Jack interrupted his thoughts and ordered more drinks. "Whisky, I think. Come to us for Christmas. One or two of the girls there will be single or available."

* * *

Christmas cards and a letter from Bertha, arrived in January. They had got a card from Dotchka in Hong Kong and the photographs of her birthday. She wished the little girl hadn't had to go and was sorry things were so bad with him and Lulu.

She and Ben were getting engaged at Christmas and married on Sam's next leave in 1935. Could he be there for October? She wanted him to give her away as Dad wasn't up to it. He had been found wandering in the street twice and went to bed wearing a top hat. Said it kept his brain warm. Billy Wigg was doing well. The baby had been ill, but was better. Nellie's budgie had lost all its feathers again. Happen it was this winter bronchitis.

Sam smiled. It must be hard work for his sisters with Dad like that. He saw him standing in his overalls, backside to the fire, smoking his old pipe. Well, the next trip might be better than the last one – no moaning, complaining, and snootiness. Good riddance. But he wished he could take Dotchka.

* * *

"Look at this, look at this," shouted Dmitri Denisov, waving a newspaper dated 20 February 1934.

Mr Du Yuesheng, esteemed member of the Municipal Council, sets up a new Society for Philanthropy and Social Reform.

"I know," said Sam, "Don't forget all the big opium gangsters want to seem respectable. They have a clubhouse on Bubbling Well Road now. Very fancy."

Dmitri Denisov tapped his pipe on the table. "Chinese newspapers say members of club all from Chinese police, judges, unions. All friends of Chiang. Editors of newspapers in trouble. They call for resistance to Japanese, like Chairman of Municipal Council do. Chiang and Blueshirts not like."

Sam rose to leave. "Well, we know what happens to people who disagree with either the communists or the nationalists."

"They get assassinated like newspapers editors and Chairman of Municipal Council. Now Du take over as well as Opium Suppression Bureau. Gōng know."

* * *

"What a laugh," said Jack Smethers, "the biggest opium boss of all getting that job. And this New Life Movement. All healthy and clean."

"But my father-in-law, I think he's still that until the divorce, tells me his old mate Gōng and the Chinese newspapers say that the Japs are operating the biggest opium scams in the cities."

"The Japs probably want the Chinese drugged up. I suppose you've seen the propaganda?"

"Which in particular?"

"You know, the stuff about the Japanese being a superior race. Everybody else is weak and decadent – Chinese, Indians, and Europeans – so they will all become servants of the Japs. Cheerful, isn't it?"

Sam laughed. "So the Chinese react by setting up this New Life Movement. Hopeless. Why the hell the Chinese factions can't work together, I don't know."

"Nor does anybody, according to reports. One newspaper said they were leaving China wide open to the Japs. At least the Yellow Dwarfs – good name that, don't you think – seem better organised."

"That's true, for sure. Did you hear that Japan and Germany have come out of the League of Nations? People back home are worried about Hitler taking power."

"Don't think that'll come to much. Bloody Krauts."

Sam scratched his chin and lit another cigarette. "Don't you miss Wales sometimes?"

"Only when I'm really fed up. No way back, like I've said before."

"I sometimes wish I were home in Lancs having a pint of light ale in the pub and singing songs."

"Sure, but you've got a leave coming next year, and your sister's wedding. Cheer up. I liked the photos of Dotchka from Hong Kong. Is she having a good time?"

"Hard to say, but Lulu's back next week. I'll let you know. Keep smiling and don't get too decadent."

Jack slapped him on the arm. "That's more likely to be you than me."

31

Lulu arrived in Shanghai from Hong Kong wearing a ring of diamonds and sapphires. She pushed open the door of the apartment and wafted a limp left hand in front of Sam's face.

He stepped back. "You're not divorced yet, you know. You'll have to wait another eighteen months for that."

She threw her coat on a chair. "You just jealous you not buy ring like this."

"You know, you can be such a bitch. I'm not jealous. He's welcome to you. No, put that vase down. Stop throwing things. There'll be nothing left in the apartment. I don't want to talk about rings. I want to talk about Dotchka. How often do you see her?"

"Every Saturday, like I promise."

"Is she happy? Why wasn't she home for Christmas like we agreed? Did she get my parcel? Why have I only had two letters?"

"Stop, stop, too many questions. I say before, I not one of your criminals."

"Well, how is she?"

"She happy. Have nice time at Christmas. Parties, food, presents. She not home for Christmas because weather too bad. She got your present and she like. I have letter to thank you. Here, read. And here are photos."

He opened the pale blue envelope and read:

28th December 1934

Dear Daddy,

Thank you for the lovely doll. I have called her Shirley, you know after Shirley Temple. She is a nice friend for Dolly. I had a very nice Christmas. I went out for tea with Mummy and Uncle Gus on Christmas Eve. There are four other girls staying at school for Christmas and we went to bed early. When we woke up, Santa had been with presents and sweets. I got your dolly and a dress and a bracelet from Mummy and a book of stories from the teachers and a wooden top and a skipping rope from Santa. We had a nice lunch of turkey and Christmas pudding and sang Carols. The teachers are very nice to me and I am doing well in my lessons.

With love from your daughter, Dotchka.

He folded the page. "You know, every letter I get is in a different handwriting which tells me that the letters are written by a teacher or somebody. She couldn't write like this at her age. It's all joined up writing."

"Do you want letters or no? What they say? You get reports from school?"

"The letters are about what she's doing – games, learning to read, doing sums, embroidery, playing with friends. The reports say she is making progress. It doesn't mean a lot."

He looked at the photographs and saw a little girl in school uniform with a school tie and a badge on the blazer. She stared at the camera, unsmiling, her hair longer than when he last saw her, and tied back, her face thinner. He felt tears rising. "She doesn't look very happy."

"She seem happy. She talk well about school. Why you not visit?"

"I will. I'll go this Easter, then bring her back here for a week."

"Then she have to miss some school."

"I don't care. I want to see her."

"They not like she miss school and have interruption. They say that her home."

"Well, it isn't. You know I'm off to England for five months later this year and I won't see her for a long time. There's no need to shake your head, Lulu. No, I'm not thinking she will come with me though I wish she could. My sister's getting married."

"Which one? I thought one marry already. The fat one."

"That's Ivy. She got married a year ago and has a baby. This is Bertha – the one who knitted you the nice cardigan that you never wear, and who gave Dolly to Dotchka."

Lulu laughed. "Does she knit her wedding dress?"

"You are so unkind sometimes. So bloody thoughtless and selfish."

"Calm down."

"Stop sounding like your American cowboy."

"Do you like the ring? Gus gave it me for Christmas. Very expensive. I know where he buy it." She moved her hand to make the stones sparkle.

"What happened to the one *I* gave you?"

"I don't know. Maybe I lose it."

He picked up a cushion and punched it. "Shut up, shut up."

"I tell you, you jealous. You still shooting bandits?"

"It's not a light matter. Ask your father, or Raisa, or your friends. There is a lot of unrest."

"Well, I go back to Hong Kong in March. I only here to see Papa and Raisa. Hong Kong more comfortable than here. This apartment smell of cigarettes and whisky. You bring women here? Friends tell me about you. Galina tell me you try to seduce her."

"Galina? I wouldn't look at her. I'm hardly ever off duty. I stay in barracks mainly, as you know. I work hard."

"So do Gus. But he make money and not get shot at."

"Well, lucky him. Don't stay in the apartment if it's so terrible. Stay at your father's."

"That worse. I stay in hotel. I see you maybe for drink one day."

"I'm off to meet Jack. Why don't you see more of Yana? At least she's steady and sensible."

* * *

Jack Smethers waved to him from across the bar. Sam brushed snow from his coat, stamped his feet, and walked over, taking off his hat and coat. "Lulu's back. Not for long."

Jack ordered two whiskies. "I know. Yana's been in touch. They'll do that Russian tea thing with all those gossips."

"Terrible lot. They spy on me you know and report back to Lulu."

"They like to just catch up on all the scandal. Who's dancing with who, who's flirting, what the film stars are doing, what the gossip in the newspapers says. There are some crazy people about. Some mad Scottish writer and an American woman who keeps a monkey. All in with the Commies. Stirring up more trouble."

Sam nodded. "Ever met any of them?"

"I once had to patrol a lecture somebody gave. Full of students waving their arms and caps. I fell asleep."

Sam laughed. "That's one way of getting a rest. I wouldn't make a habit of spying, though. I hear you're doing some work with the Chinese cops in Chapei."

"Right, working with a couple of our Chinese lads. Mayor of Chapei wants to bring in some reforms – more training, better equipment, fight against corruption. What a hope. It might make a difference if they paid them more."

Sam tapped a cigarette on the table. "Like us. I can hardly keep that apartment going and pay Dotchka's school. Once the divorce comes through, I'm going to get that American to cough up."

"Good luck to you."

"I'm taking a week off in April to go down to Hong Kong and see for myself what's going on. God, I pay enough."

"Roll on Easter, I say. I'm fed up with all this snow and ice."

* * *

Sam booked into the Peninsular Hotel in Hong Kong. He left his suitcase, and went to pick up Dotchka from school.

He trembled as she came towards him. She was tall and thin, her fair hair combed down to her shoulders. She looked sad, but her long face opened and she laughed as she saw him. A front tooth was missing.

He lifted her and placed his face on the back of her neck. She kissed his cheek three times. "Are we going out for cakes?"

He nodded and wiped his tears on the back of her coat before she could notice. He placed her feet on the ground and took her hand.

"What do you like best at school?" he asked Dotchka over tea and cakes at the English Tea Shoppe. She plunged a spoon into a cream bun. "Playing with my friends. We all have dollies and they talk to each other. But they have nearly all gone home for the holidays. My Dolly is very sad."

"Dolly from England, you mean? Does she like the one I gave you for Christmas?"

"Yes, that's her baby. She cries a lot."

"Why is that?"

"Because her mummy is away a lot and doesn't send her presents."

"What about her daddy?"

"She doesn't have a daddy. He is a soldier in England."

"I like your hat, Daddy." He put his grey trilby on her head. "Can I have the feather?"

He pulled the green and blue feather from the band and put it between her fingers. She blew it. The strands shivered. "What kind of a birdie is this?"

"Probably a budgie like Auntie Nellie's. Do you remember?"

She nodded, finished the bun and took a long sip of orange squash. Sam blew the feather.

"Your daddy will go to England for a while soon. I wish you could come with me but it's a long way and you have school. Try to be a good girl and not bite your nails. Look at them, all jagged. You have such pretty hands. Why do you chew your nails like that?"

"I like it. I want to go to England again."

"You will, one day. Are you doing your lessons well? Which ones do you like best?"

"I like sewing and talking. I have made you a handkerchief with drawn thread work round the edges. It will be finished tomorrow."

"What about English and sums? Do you like reading books?"

"I like Milly-Molly-Mandy and stories about girls at school. Sister Philomena reads them to us."

"What do you read yourself?"

She shrugged. "This is a nice cake."

"Do you like games?"

"No, people push me. I am quite good at tennis."

Sam asked for the bill. "Daddy is good at tennis. We can play one day."

She gave him the white handkerchief the day before he left. He looked at the square piece of cloth with the lattice of threads round the border, half the size of the handkerchiefs he used. He would keep it in his drawer.

Dotchka clung to his coat and wailed. "I want to come with you. My friends are all away and they have taken their dollies."

"She will be contented when you have gone," said the Headmistress, "our Good Lady will be kind to her, and we will go straight to prayers. Come, child."

He watched Dotchka's thin legs in their knee-length socks, shuffle down the corridor. She waved until they went into a room. He turned, went outside, and lit a cigarette.

His daughter was lonely and he could do nothing about it.

* * *

Spring arrived on Sam's return to Shanghai. Drenching rain and mist filled the streets. At the end of the afternoon, pale sunlight slit the clouds – a sign of good weather, he thought. He wrote to Lulu.

Dotchka seems sad, and that worries me. She didn't want me to go. The teachers say she likes school and has a lot of friends. They would, wouldn't they? It's all money for them. They say she needs to work harder at her letters and sums and I have told her that I expect her to write to me once a week herself to practise. At least she's speaking English there. She looks thin, though.

Now, I want some information. She says you DON'T visit every Saturday, as you say. It's more like once a month, and that you and the boyfriend just take her out, never to his flat. I think she misses a home. She cried and held on to me when I left. It churned me up a lot, I can tell you. So, I want you to visit more often, now that you are in HK most of the time. And remember that your father and sister are not well and would like to see you.

I think if your American is serious, then he should pay something towards the apartment and to her schooling and towards keeping Raisa and Dmitri Denisov. He's rich enough. As you can see, I am very angry at this situation and want more from you. Remember who pays up all the time.

He read the letter before sending it. He sighed. Why bother? She had made her choice. Nothing to do with him any more. But he still thought of her. Her walk, her clothes, her perfume. Too bad.

* * *

In late June, Dmitri Denisov collapsed in the street, was taken to hospital, and diagnosed with a heart attack caused by chronic TB. Sam telegrammed Lulu to return and to bring Dotchka home early for the summer.

They met Sam at the Central Hospital and watched as Dmitri Denisov wheezed and panted, eyes closed, face pale, and clammy, with a sprinkling of white beard, grey hair long and greasy. A nurse took his temperature and checked the drip attached to his right arm.

Sam watched her. "How is he?"

"He is not good. It was a bad attack and he is very weak. He is lucky to have survived."

Dmitri Denisov stirred and panted, the sheet rose and fell. He scratched at the top edge with long nails, dirty and stained brown.

Lulu sat by the bed, sweat and tears streaking her make-up. Her hair was damp and losing its waves. "It so hot in here. Why not more fans? It hospital."

Sam wafted a newspaper. "It's nearly July. I'm sure they do their best."

Dotchka leaned over to kiss her grandfather on his cheek. "Very prickly. Is grandpapa going to die? I don't want him to die."

"NO," said Dmitri Denisov and lifted his arm to touch her. She stared at the bruise around the base of the tube as it entered his arm.

"This is the first time he has spoken for five days," said the nurse. "It's a good sign."

Lulu called Raisa who was waiting in the corridor, sipping black tea and sobbing.

Sam put his hand on Raisa's shoulder. "Don't get excited, or cry, and disturb him. He is still very ill."

"Drink," said Dmitri Denisov.

Sam tipped water to his lips. "I know this is not what you want, but it's what you're getting. No vodka for a while."

Dmitri Denisov left hospital four days later, with instructions to eat well, drink only water and juice, and report back for check-ups every week for six months.

Sam took Lulu's arm and held it tightly. "Did you get my letter?"

"Why you so angry? Now I not go back for a month. I help nurse Papa. Gus will pay for treatment he say. I take Dotchka back to Hong Kong at the end of August in time for school. Maybe Gus come here a little."

"Well, I just hope things improve. And I'll want to see Dotchka sometimes. Give her a good time."

Lulu shrugged.

* * *

279

In the July heat, Sam took Dotchka to see his office, then to meet Raisa at the Chocolatier Café. After cakes and hot chocolate, Dotchka skipped along the pavement and through the park.

"The dollies like the park. And look at my pretty nails."

Sam held her hand. "Very good. And you will put on some weight eating like you just did. Go back with Auntie Raisa now and I will see you this evening."

He turned into Wayside Road and saw smoke coming from the windows of the Station and three fire engines on the road. He ran past them and up the steps.

Inspector Kenny stood at the door. "Sam, a bomb was thrown into your office. It's completely destroyed except for the desk."

Sam panted. "Was anyone hurt?"

"Two Chinese constables killed. Another bomb went off along the corridor – and one in the administration office that didn't go off."

"Christ. Who did it?"

"We've got one of them – a Chinese communist. He shouted 'Down with Imperialism' when he was caught. We have alerts on all the stations. Don't bring any visitors in again. Too dangerous."

Raisa heard news of the explosion on the radio and telephoned Sam. "I tell Lulu, she very angry."

"Too bad. Not my fault. Why doesn't she look after our daughter more? I'm working."

He knelt on the floor of his office and fingered pieces of glass and rubble.

Lulu telephoned from her hotel and screamed, "I go back to Hong Kong next week. It not safe here. Why you take Dotchka to dangerous place?"

"She wanted to see where Daddy works."

"I go to find her now. She at apartment with Raisa and Mary. At least she safe. She stay with me tonight. Papa much better. We leave."

"I'll come and see you at the hotel, but I have to stay here for a while. People have been killed and injured. We have to tell relatives.

The building is damaged. My office is wrecked. I'll come and see you this evening."

He began to reorganise, coughing in the smoke and the sharp smell of explosives. The windows were shattered, the fan was a heap of twisted metal, its blades crumpled and charred. The bulletin board was split and hung from the grey wall, now blackened and cracked. A pile of reports and pens had been swept from his desk and were scattered round the room. Ink splattered the carpet. The desk drawers, where he kept his father's cufflinks for luck, were intact. A bottle of whisky, half drunk, was in the deep, bottom drawer. He took a mouthful, and sat in his chair, looking at the destruction, then gathered up papers.

Jack Smethers walked in. "I just heard about this. Terrible. Are you all right?

"Yes, but before this went up, I was in here with Dotchka. She wanted to see where Daddy works. Christ. She's back at the apartment. Lulu is going crazy and shouting about going back to HK straight away."

Jack whistled. "Listen, I'm here to see Inspector Kenny, too. I'll wait for you, then we'll go for a drink and some food."

"Better not. I have to go and see the family, especially Dotchka. They're worried, and old man Denisov is still ill. It was terrible, she could have been killed. Two people were."

* * *

Sam went to the hotel and clutched Dotchka. "We'll have tea again tomorrow. Bring Dolly. Go and play in the bedroom now. Mary is making a nice drink for you, and Chen has brought a present."

Lulu hit his chest. He grabbed her wrists. "Don't start. And don't ever talk about this. How do you think *I* feel? You don't care, do you?"

"Too dangerous here. I take Dotchka back to HK."

"But I want to see her before you do that."

"Maybe that not possible."

He kissed Dotchka and slammed the door as he left to visit Raisa and Dmitri Denisov. A constable arrived at the apartment with a telegram from England. Sam tore it open. "It seems that every time I plan to go back to England somebody dies. This time it's my dad."

Dmitri Denisov put down his pipe. "I sorry."

Raisa coughed and cried. "Poor Sam. Too much happen."

Sam sat, his hands on his knees, legs apart. He knew that he was in shock from the day, and this added to it all. He could not cry here, and mustn't start drinking.

He looked up. "It was the best thing for him and for everybody, poor old lad. My sister says he's being buried next to his father and grandfather. At least I'll be there soon."

"I glad you go to England for rest," said Dmitri Denisov. "I much better. Can take little walks soon. Raisa, too. She begin new treatment for TB. Very bad in winter. Now summer coming. It already July."

"You are both looking much better. I shall miss you, but I need a break. Too many gangsters. Too much difficult politics. I'll get a rest on the boat."

Dmitri Denisov tried to push himself out of the chair with his stick, but fell back.

"Nothing good. Japanese want more and more, communists still determined. Chiang still chasing them. You in middle."

Sam handed him a plate of cakes. "Yes, it'll be a bit quieter in England. I feel a bit better now."

Dmitri Denisov stared at him and asked for tea from the samovar.

Sam poured a small amount into a thick glass. "I hope you're not smoking and drinking again. It smells a bit in here."

Dmitri Denisov sniffed. "I smell nothing. Well, I do little drink and smoke now and then – to cheer me up. When Lulu and Dotchka come?"

"I'll bring Dotchka round tomorrow, Lulu will come the day after. They go back to HK soon. Lulu's is very angry about the explosion in my office. Of course, I'm sorry, but there's no need to go on about it."

Raisa smiled. "And she want to get back to Hong Kong. And your travels, Sam?"

Sam looked at the floor. "Well, it's all arranged. I sail for San Francisco on 1 September, spend a few days there with your father's brother, then off to New York and across the wide Atlantic to Liverpool. Hurray."

"Ah, yes, you see Ivan. He do well. Was accountant in San Francisco. You like him."

"Now you know the Weiheiwei apartment is empty, so use it if you want. Mary is still there. She's working for another couple. The little boy's doing well. I'll send a trunk back to England next month and have a small one on the boat with me, nothing fancy this time. I still have a lot to do before I leave in September – make sure all my work is covered. I'll see Dotchka a few times before they go back. Any news of the American?"

"American now buying and selling cars. He have big Hudson for himself, Lulu says. Make lot of money after strike in America, but business now more difficult."

He went to the hotel to take Dotchka out for tea. The hotel receptionist opened his files.

"Sir, Mrs Shuttleworth and Miss Shuttleworth left on the morning ferry to Hong Kong."

"Is there a message for me?"

"No, sorry, sir."

He banged on the door of the Denisov apartment. "Did you know about this? I am very angry."

"We know Lulu want to leave early, but she say she see you first," said Raisa. "Very naughty. She say American come back soon to Hong Kong with big car business, then they come to Shanghai in September."

"That's when I'm away in England, of course. I have a right to see my daughter. Lulu never plays fair. I'm going to get a lawyer onto this."

"What use lawyer? What you expect?" said Dmitri Denisov. "Say hello to Ivan. He like good vodka. You buy some on ship."

32

The *SS Santa Barbara* left Shanghai for San Francisco on the evening of 1 September 1935. Sam stood on deck, smoking and sipping whisky on ice from a large tumbler. The skyline of the Bund withdrew into the haze of the wider river. He went down to the restaurant and sat on the long refectory table where single people ate. On his left was an American sailor, going home on leave, and on the right an Irish car mechanic who had left his job in San Francisco during the great strike, worked in Southern China and was returning to his old job.

"Couldn't stand China. Terrible food, dirty, all those gangsters; cheap booze mind you. No pretty girls."

Sam laughed. "You weren't looking in the right place. Try Shanghai next."

"Two nights there enough for me. Robbed in a bar, lost the rest gambling."

"Nobody gambles with the Chinese. They always win. Let me buy you a drink."

There was a birthday party in the bar, but, after two drinks, Sam went down to his small, single cabin, poured a tumbler of whisky, and wrote to Lulu. His hand trembled as he tried to control the pen. The ink smudged and the paper crinkled. He tore up the letter after a few lines, threw it on the floor and decided to write again the next day.

The churning of the engines and the movement of the ship, combined with whisky, teased him into sleep for eight hours. He woke with a headache, thinking about Lulu and Dotchka, picked up the shreds of letter and flushed them away in the communal bathroom along the corridor, then showered and went upstairs for breakfast. After bacon, eggs, and tea, he sat on deck and watched the grey coils of the waves, and gulls as they hovered and plunged. He lit a cigarette and wrote to Lulu again.

SS Santa Barbara   *2nd September*

My dear Lulu,

Although why I call you that I do not know. I cannot understand your behaviour. It was despicable to go off without seeing me, and worse, to not let me say goodbye to Dotchka. Is this how love makes you behave? If so, it cannot be love. I think AGAIN, it is you being thoughtless and selfish. Do you ever think about anybody else except yourself, Lulu? What do you think this might do to Dotchka? Do you think it is how a good mother behaves? You just seem to act on the spur of the moment with what is best for Lulu, Lulu, Lulu. I shall curse you to the end of my days for the hurt you have caused with your temper and your thoughtlessness. I want to know how my daughter is. I have a right to know.

He crunched up the paper, tossed it into the breeze, and watched the fragments separate – some into the water, some into the air. Let the fish have them. They might appreciate it more than she did. After lunch, he went to the gym, then ran round the deck fifty times.

A woman joined him as he sat on deck. Mrs Dorothy Allen, off to San Francisco for her sister's wedding.

"I've met your wife in Shai. Is she with you?"

"No, it's a long story. I'm going back to England on leave for five months. A good rest, good food, good company. Oh boy, do I need it."

"Things not so good? What a mess Shanghai is in. You must have a tough life there. Tell me about it."

Two hours later, he bought her a gin and tonic and suggested dinner in two days time. Someone had once suggested that he write down words to describe his feelings about work in Shanghai and about Lulu. They said it helped tackle problems. He began. The page about Lulu made him sob and shake… angry, humiliated, jealous, inferior, frustrated. He finished writing, and his anger had, for the time being, calmed. He would do that again.

He remembered the fortune teller in The Great World saying that the lady from a foreign country would make him happy and sad, and that his joy would be his daughter. Well, she was right. He thought of poor old Eddie and wondered what happened to that girl of his.

He wrote more letters to Lulu and more pages about his feelings, but threw them all into the sea. Mrs Dorothy Allen was good company.

* * *

On the morning of 27 September, Dmitri Denisov's brother, Ivan, greeted Sam at the dock in San Francisco. Sam shook his hand and stepped back to look at his face. "My, you could tell you are brothers, but you're a bit healthier than Dmitri Denisov."

"I had the sense to move to San Francisco. Let's get a cab to my apartment on South Street."

Sam looked out of the window. "So this is San Francisco. I've read about it. Hills, traffic, buildings, the wharves. It's grand. I've brought you some good vodka."

"You will have a fine three days. I want to hear about my niece. Dmitri seems unhappy about her behaviour."

Sam laughed. "Tatiana, or should I say Lulu, doesn't understand about behaviour. Any letters for me?"

"One. I think from your daughter. It has a Hong Kong postmark from two weeks ago."

Sam opened the envelope. On the exercise book paper was a drawing of a dog and a cat with writing underneath.

Dear Daddy,

I hope you have a nice time in America. I would like to go there one day. Will you take me? I will bring Dolly and her baby. I send you big kisses and will write to you tomorrow.

Your daughter.

Sam replied the day he left for New York. He knew Lulu would read it so he said what a good time he was having and included drawings of buildings in San Francisco and a sketch of Ivan.

He sailed from New York and arrived in Liverpool on 20 October, and took the train to Warren. Billy Wigg picked him up in his van. "Business is good. Look at this van. Better than what thi' got last time. I'll never forget th' missus's face. Can't wait for thi' to see to see my lass and t'lads."

"It's good to be back. A lot's gone under t'bloody bridge." He thumped Billy's shoulder.

* * *

Sam's large, cedar trunks waited, stuck with labels and customs tickets, in Bertha's tiny vestibule, too heavy to be moved.

Billy offered to help lift them, but Sam said, "Nay, it were good of you to collect me from t'station. Get back to work now. We'll empty these buggers bit by bit. Thanks. See thi' later."

Bertha cried on his shoulder. "It's been a long time and a lot's happened, Sam. I hope tha gets a good rest this time."

"I intend to."

"Ee. Tha' talks right posh now."

Sam opened a trunk. "Don't help me unpack. There are too many compartments. I just want to show you your wedding present to see if you like it. I'll tek stuff up to my room."

Bertha leaned over to watch as he took out suits and shirts, then a layer of silk garments, slippers, carved wooden toys and a plate with the willow pattern.

"These are other presents. There's a couple of wooden horses for Billy Wigg's lads and a plate for him and his missus, slippers for Auntie Nellie – I hope they fit. There's playing cards in Chinese for Derek, and a set for the pub, and cigarette cards for Jimmy. I'm sorry Dad's not here to get a present. I'd have brought him some good baccy."

Bertha sniffed and wiped her eyes. "Dad would have liked that, Sam, but he didn't know *what* he liked at the end."

He patted her arm. "I know. It must have been terrible for you. I feel bad not being here. It were all for t'best. Now we come to the delicate stuff."

He lifted out a package and tore off the brown paper to uncover a white box with Chinese writing and a stamp showing a woman in a long gown, hair pinned back with a buckle and a pin.

"This is the name of the shop, and the other writing says it's finest China."

Bertha put her hands to her cheeks. "Ee. I hardly dare look."

"I'll open one, then you do the rest."

He unravelled green tissue paper, layer by layer and held up a small cup made of thin pottery.

Bertha gasped and held her pinny to her face. "Is this really for me? I've never seen anything like it."

"Hold it. Don't be scared, and look, when you put the base up to the light, what can you see? I'll hold it. Look."

Bertha peered into the cup. "There's the head of a lady with slitty eyes and her hair piled on top of her head held with a comb. How do they do that?"

"The cup is printed with a face and the China's so thin you can see through it. Do you like it? There's saucers to match."

She took the cup and turned it in her plump hands to see a pattern of brown and orange leaves under blue sky, and two women in long black robes with red sashes. "I can hardly get my finger through this handle. I'll never use these. They're so lovely. I'll put them on display in t'glass cabinet for everybody to see. Ben will like them. Let's leave the rest in for now and open them after t' wedding."

"There's a full tea set of six and a little teapot. You've heard of China tea?"

She nodded. "Aye, but I've never tasted any."

"I've brought some. There's a tea set for Ivy too – for her wedding. I was sorry not to be there, but at least Dad was well enough to make it."

"Just about. He didn't know where he were going as they went down t'church aisle. She had to hang on to him. She'll think the china proper grand and keep them away from that babby. He's a real tinker though he's not a year yet. Now then, Sam, I'll put yon kettle on. Ordinary cups, though."

"That's fine. I look forward to a bit of old Lancashire."

"Eee, you can still tell where you come from. You don't talk posh. Sit down in t' parlour. There's a few letters for you. One's from your little girl, and two others look official like."

Dotchka said she was enjoying the holiday in Shanghai, going shopping with Mary and Chen, seeing her friends and having cakes with mummy and Uncle Gus. Jack Smethers wrote that he and Yana were back from their furlough in Scotland. The third was from Inspector Kenny, reporting incidents between Japanese and Chinese gangs on the outer roads.

Bertha came out from the kitchen. "What is it, Sam?"

"Nothing important. Dotchka sends her love."

"Do you hear from… you know?"

"Lulu? Sometimes. She's got another fella. Good luck to him, I say. It's good to be back. Thanks for the tea. Lovely. I'll take you and Ben out for a drink later. Billy will come, too."

"And I expect Maggie will be there. Remember her? Left her husband."

* * *

In the Red Lion pub, Sam ordered a port and lemon for Bertha and a pint of Thwaites Mild for himself and one for Ben, who went off to play darts with a friend from the mill.

Bertha lifted her glass. "I don't know what to say about Lulu, Sam. I wish you'd brought the little girl. It's a bad business. I wish you'd settle down wi' a nice lass."

"It's happened. She's Russian and Russians are unhappy and difficult."

"I'm sure I don't know what you mean. We always made her welcome and I knitted her that nice grey cardigan. Does she wear it?"

"Yes, sometimes. Her sister would like one, too. I don't know if Lulu, Tatiana, will ever know what she wants. I tried to make it work. I'd like to get Dotchka over here some time, but we'll see. I do miss her. I'll write to her every week. Nice, long letters."

He looked towards the dartboard. Ben was poised, the feathered dart ready to spring from between his first finger and thumb. "Ben's a good steady lad. You've done well."

She nodded and leaned back to look around. "He is. Nice and quiet. I'm not used to all this drink. Happen I'll fall over. Here's Billy and his missus."

Maureen hugged Sam, Billy thumped him on the arm. "T' bad penny's back. Everybody knows it." He looked at Bertha. "I'm taking the old bugger fishing on Saturday. Let's see if he can still pull 'em in."

The women laughed. Bertha tapped Billy's arm. "You are a one, Billy Wigg. Never no different."

"I don't know what I'd have done without you picking me up," said Sam, "Let me get you a drink. Isn't he doing well, Maureen? Lovely van. I'll bring your presents round tomorrow. There's a couple of toys for the lads."

Maureen smiled. "You won't recognise them, Sam. Eleven and nine. Big fellows. And right clever."

"So Billy tells me. Well, here's Maggie."

He stood to kiss her on the cheek then held her away from him. "My, Maggie, you're looking well and so dressed up. It's only a pub. What'll you have?"

"Cider, please." She sat next to Bertha who stared at her lipstick and rouge and her hair, dyed blonde under a beret. The dress was tight and low-necked to show the curve of her pink breasts.

"Nay, Maggie. You didn't have to mek a fuss," said Bertha.

Maggie looked up at Sam and smiled. He looked at her breasts. Ben returned from darts.

"Couldn't get me a double five. I'm proper bog ee'yed fro' squintin'."

Sam stood. "Come on. I'll give thee a game."

* * *

Two weeks before the wedding on 10 November, Sam went to visit Auntie Nellie in Camburn. "Poor owd lass," said Bertha, "getting a bit frail but carries on. Must be over eighty now."

"I'll stop overnight then. Give th'owd lass a hand."

He gave her the slippers from China. She turned them over and stroked the silk. "Ee Sam, Is'll never wear these. Too posh. Is'll put 'em on t'sideboard i' mi bedroom."

He sat in a chair underneath the empty birdcage with its frilly bunch of curtain round the bottom. "Why do you keep this, Auntie, unless you're planning on another bird?"

"There'll never be another. Anyway, Hettie down t' road gave me a kitten. One of her cat's litter. She drowned t' rest. You can't have a bird wi' a cat. The bugger jumps up and knocks the cage over as it is. I've called him Reggie."

"Reggie? I were at school with a lad called Reggie."

"Well, it weren't him."

The arms of the chair were greasy, and the table, covered with a yellow oilcloth, leaned over so that his cup slid to one side. The mirror had a layer of dust above it and was spotted black. Sam looked round at the peeling wallpaper. "I'll mend this table for you, and do a bit of decoration afore I go back to China."

"Nay, lad. It's not worth it. I can't see dust any more. I'm getting on a bit."

She was more stooped than when he last saw her, and leaned on a stick. Her unwashed hair was pulled back in a grey bunch, her face pale and tinged with yellow and furrowed like deep scratches.

"Are you all right getting to the wedding, Auntie?"

"Oh, aye. There's a good bus and Jimmy said he'd meet me. Don't let your tea get cold. I wish you'd brought your little lass. I might not be here next time. What happened to that missus, what's her name?"

"It's a long story, Auntie. I'll tell you about it later. I see Hargreaves' pie shop is still open. I'll go and get meat and potato with some peas to warm up. Get t' kettle on."

He slept in the tiny spare room with cardboard boxes and old furniture piled under the windows. There was no shade over the light, the curtains were detaching from their hooks and there was thick fluff under the bed. The mattress lumpy and damp. He slept badly, woke four times, smoked, and thought about Lulu. She could never have fitted in here. He had hoped she would like his home and family. She had been rude and snobbish. He wondered what she was doing now.

"Did you sleep all right?" Nellie asked when he came down for breakfast. "Your Uncle Albert died in that bed when he were staying once. They had a terrible time getting him downstairs. Would you like a boiled egg? Owd Hodson brings me some every week from his chickens. Very nice. And I've got a new loaf and home-made marmalade."

"That will be grand. I'll have a walk before I get back to Warren. See if the old place has changed. I'll come back after the wedding and do a few repairs."

He walked out of the back door, into the alley, and to the end of the lane which led to the pit. He watched the great wheel rotate slowly, heaving on the cable which pulled up the coal and waste. To the right were lifts for the miners' cages which lowered them into blackness for six hours at a time, then returned them to daylight, weary and blackened. His father had been determined that his sons would not be miners. "Too monny accidents. Safer i' t'mill."

He smelled coal dust and steam and felt the grit under his feet as he followed the path between meadows of yellowing grass and wilted dandelions.

The rumblings of the colliery became louder. He listened to the whirring, clicks, and thumps as a lift came to the surface. Ahead of him, he saw a man in a bowler hat standing on the footpath, a pencil in his right hand and a writing pad in the left. He looked up at the slag heap, made strokes with the pencil on the pad, looked up again, put his head to one side to look at the pad and scribbled more. He stopped as Sam came alongside.

"Morning lad. I'm just doodling a bit."

"Pleased to meet you. I'm Sam Shuttleworth." He held out his hand. "What's that you're drawing with? I thought it was a pencil back there."

"It's charcoal. Thicker finish and you can shade it. See?"

The man rubbed the drawing. His hanging jowls and small blue eyes, embedded under thick brows, reminded Sam of one of the lurchers back in the police kennels.

"That's good. But why are you drawing heaps of coal? I thought pictures were supposed to be beautiful."

"It is beautiful. It's beautiful because it has shape. It's real. When I get back, I'll use the sketch to do it in oils."

"Where are you from then?"

"Pendlebury. Not far. I'm a rent collector when I'm not painting or watching Manchester City."

"Burnside Rovers fan myself. What kind of things do you paint apart from coal mines?"

"Mainly streets in Manchester. I watch people, men in cloth caps outside factories, dogs, children in clogs, landscapes sometimes. I paint what I see. Real life things. There's always something interesting if you look."

Sam looked at the drawing again. "Do you sell your pictures?"

"If I'm lucky. The odd five bob here and there. That's not why I do it. What do *you* do?"

"I'm a policeman in Shanghai, live in Warren. Auntie in Camburn. I'm here on long leave visiting her for a couple of days."

"A bit quieter here, I'd say. Do you like China?"

Sam twisted his foot into a patch of shale then stamped on it. "Haven't seen much of it. Only Shanghai. Too busy and travel can be dangerous. But I do like it in a way. I don't like getting shot at, but I like the responsibility and I like getting on. I'm a sub-inspector now."

"Well. That's not bad for a lad from these parts. I haven't gone far from here. Manchester School of Art, holidays on the coast, but not abroad, like you. I hear there's an exhibition in London now of Chinese treasures from Peking. There were pictures of it in the *Manchester Guardian*. I might get down to see it. Have you ever been to Peking?"

"No, I wanted to, but every time I tried there were either bombs on the line, or somebody on a train got kidnapped by bandits."

"Well, don't expect that round here. Tell you what. Have this sketch and take it back to Shanghai to remind you of home. I'll sign it."

He wrote L S Lowry, 1935 in tiny, twisted letters at the bottom of the page, tore it from the pad and handed it to Sam. "You never know, I might become famous." He laughed and his eyes moistened.

Sam took the paper. "Thanks, but isn't it hard to sell or give away something you've made?"

Lowry laughed, his face wobbled and his eyes became smaller in the crinkles of his cheeks and forehead. "If people like what I do, I'm glad for them to have it. You have to let go of things you've created, then they get new life, new energy. No point holding on to things and stifling them. You have to move on. Know what I mean?"

Sam looked at the sky, touched with wisps of cloud, and at the slag heap, dark and ominous, then down at the drawing. "I think so. You've made something live forever. That's something. I'll put this on my office wall. Best be off, nice to meet you and thanks again."

"Bye," said Lowry. "Good luck."

Bertha's wedding was reported, with a photograph, in *The Warren News*. The bride wore a dress in pale turquoise with matching shoes and tiara. She was accompanied by her sister Ivy as Matron of Honour, and her brother Sam, now a sub-inspector with the Shanghai Police.

A special article about Sam appeared on page four.

"Ee, we're getting famous," said Ivy.

Auntie Nellie wore a long cotton dress, bursting with big red flowers, and a wide-brimmed pale straw hat. "I allus wear this for weddings and funerals. Now, Sam, don't let me drink too much stout or I'll be under yon table and who knows what might happen."

Billy Wigg wore a grey striped suit, waistcoat, and a green tie. "I'm not used to dressing fancy. Happier in overalls. Doesn't the missus look grand in that frock? I told her she would suit blue. I see Maggie's well away. How are you getting on with her?"

"Hush. She's all right, nice for weekends, but being at a wedding might give her ideas."

Billy laughed. "Look at yon lads of mine, pushing each other about as usual."

Sam looked at the two boys sitting on stools in a corner, drinking lemonade, eating cake, nudging and poking each other with bony knees.

"They're fine boys," said Sam, "Soon be in long trousers. You're a very lucky man."

"I know, I know. I wish you'd get settled, Sam."

Maggie swayed and spilled cider over her feet. Her hat, with its veil, was tilted over one eye. The blue silk blouse, Sam's present, clung to her breasts, a black skirt with white spots stretched over her hips, and she tottered in high heels. "I heard that. Well, there's one here who wouldn't mind helping him do that."

She kissed Sam's cheek, leaving a blur of red lipstick.

"You've had too much to drink, Maggie," said Sam. "Let's get you home. Billy, we'll fix up some fishing and a few nights with the boys soon."

He wrote to Dotchka with a picture of the wedding and said he would buy her presents soon.

He told her about Auntie Nellie's cat, Ivy's child, Billy Wigg's boys, and the wedding party, and wished she were there to see it all and drink lemonade. Everybody did. He promised to write at Christmas from the boat on the way back.

The Saturday morning after the wedding, Bertha banged on Maggie's door at eight o'clock in the morning. Maggie opened it, pulling on a coat over her nightdress.

"Telegram from China for Sam. T' lad what brought it said they want a reply."

Sam came down the stairs, pulling on his shirt. "What's all this?" He tore open the telegram.

"Christ. The Inspector at my Station has been killed. Shot. Poor old Kenny. No details. The commissioner wants me back straight away to take over. I need to pack and get off. We'll send on the big trunk."

"What about me?" whispered Maggie.

"Listen, love. I'll write to you. I'm not the sort to settle down. It's been grand, but you need to find yourself somebody steady. Come on, Bertha help me pack. I'll just call round and say cheerio to Billy Wigg."

33

On 10 January 1936, a car met Sam at the Shanghai docks and took him, through a snowstorm, to the Municipal Council Headquarters. He walked between marble columns, then along a corridor lined with mahogany panels, and knocked on the door of Chief Commissioner Gerrard's office. A secretary showed him into the outer room and offered him tea before the commissioner came out to meet him and shake hands. Sam stood and saluted.

"Sorry I'm not very smart, sir."

"That doesn't matter, Shuttleworth. Sit down. I know you're straight from the ship. Sorry to call you back. Did you have a good journey?"

"Thank you, sir, very fine. I'm shocked about Inspector Kenny. How did it happen?"

"Shot in the head and chest coming out of Wayside Station after work one evening. Him and two Chinese sergeants Bái and Lóng. You must have worked with them. I've kept the funeral notices for you. Kenny was buried in Bubbling Well. Full honours."

He handed them to Sam who glanced at the headlines. "Who did it?"

"The Chinese blame the communists, or one of the gangs, some blame the Japanese. Unlikely."

"Was there any family? He never spoke of any wife or children, but he didn't say much about his personal life."

"A brother in Dublin. We contacted him of course. Parents dead. No wife. I think, between you and me, he played on the other side. Some of these ex-colonial chaps had their boys, you know. But that's beside the point. Now, the reason I wanted to see you so urgently is that I am promoting you to inspector to take over at Wayside from tomorrow. We'll have a short ceremony there at 8am. I'll make a speech then you can say a word."

Sam sat up and squared his shoulders. "I am very honoured, sir and I will do my best."

"I know, and you're not going to find it easy. Since you left, we've had fifty assassinations across Shai – twelve policemen killed, twenty kidnappings for ransom – a judge, businessmen and so on, thousands of arrests – opium, gambling, prostitution, suspected communist activity – students, bookshops, magazines, you know the stuff."

"I thought that was decreasing."

"It's gone more underground. Chiang's still chasing the communists on their March. Many of them are dying, of course, as we knew they would. Terrible conditions in Western China."

"How is morale in the Force?"

"Not good. Still bribery and corruption going on. The Chinese making the most out of our mistakes, the Japs watching."

"What do you mean, sir, our mistakes?"

"Well, for example, two silly buggers, Sergeants Brown and O'Keiffe, find a beggar in the street, beat him up, and chuck the body into the river."

"I know them. Always been bullies. No respect."

"Exactly, but you know how mud sticks. The newspapers are saying how corrupt the police are, how we hate the Chinese and so on… bloody nightmare."

"It is, but I think I have the confidence of the men and we can start rebuilding. I have a lot of respect for many Chinese officers. They're very brave."

"That's the spirit. And don't expect to stay at Wayside forever. We'll move you to a bigger station next year some time."

"Thank you, sir, I appreciate your confidence."

The same evening, he visited Raisa and Dmitri Denisov. Raisa opened the door. Dmitri Denisov waved from his chair where he shook ash from his pipe.

"You look well again. Fit and strong and suntanned."

"I kept fit on the ship – gym, weights, running, not so much drink except at parties. How are *you* both? You must look after yourselves this winter. I'm back now. I know Lulu's in Hong Kong. I've been promoted to inspector officially from tomorrow."

Dmitri Denisov spat. The stove spluttered. "Other one killed. Like others. Bang, bang."

Sam took a bottle out of his satchel. "Let's be cheerful. Here's some champagne to celebrate. Get the glasses. I'll have a big office, my name on a brass plate on the door, and a driver when I want one."

"Bodyguard better," said Dmitri Denisov, "every day shootings. Two in next street yesterday."

"Papa, Papa," said Raisa, "he know all this. I get glasses, cakes, and pies."

They toasted his success in Russian and in English. "Congratulations, good health and a long life."

Sam put down his glass. "Have *you* heard from Lulu and Dotchka? I've only had two letters from Dotchka. Nothing from Lulu."

"Lulu say she write you at police station about Christmas plans. They want big party."

"I'll get it tomorrow. Look, I've brought presents from England. For you Dmitri Denisov, the brand of tobacco my dad used to like."

Dmitri Denisov took the small yellow and red cardboard box, sniffed it, took out the tobacco stem and drew it under his nose from left to right. "That's real tobacco. I enjoy. Thank you."

"This big package is for you, Raisa."

She laughed and took the floppy brown paper bag.

"I told my sister you liked the cardigan she made for Lulu, so she's made one for you. It's something called cable stitch."

Raisa unwrapped the layers of paper and held the blue wool against her, sniffed it, and stroked the raised swirls in the pattern. "I very like. Your sister knit well. Maybe a little big, but very warm for winter. You thank her."

"I will, and I've brought a little knitting set as a present for Dotchka – wool, needles, and some simple patterns. Maybe Lulu will teach her."

Dmitri Denisov laughed, coughed, and spat out shreds of tobacco. Raisa covered her mouth with her hands and shook. "You joke. Lulu never knit. Some clothes she sew long time ago. I teach Dotchka to knit."

He laughed. "I know, I know. Come on, I'll take you out for a meal round the corner. Then I need to go and see the apartment and have an early night. I'm on duty first thing."

"OK, OK," said Raisa. "Apartment good. Mary look after well."

"How's the little boy doing?"

"He very good, very clever. Only three, but speak already little Russian and English as well as Chinese."

"Good. Let's go and get some pork and noodles."

* * *

Sam arrived at Wayside Station at seven the next morning and paused to look at the steps outside. Frost had begun to melt under the new light. Acting Sub-Inspector Ronald Paterson joined him and shook his hand. "Well done, Sam. We know what's happening today and are very happy. You deserve it. I'll be confirmed sub-inspector when you're made inspector."

Sam drew his foot round the dark stain on the top step. Paterson looked down.

"Yes, that's where poor old Kenny caught it. Damn shame."

"Well, we'll just all have to work together. I know things are difficult. After the promotion ceremony, get everybody together in the meeting room. We'll look at our strategies as a team. I'll talk later to the men who are out on duty."

Paterson took Sam to his new office. Inspector Kenny's desk had been cleared, his picture of Donegal Bay removed, and his files stacked on a shelf.

Sam ran a finger down them. "You can talk me through these later. I'll just go through the post, then I'll join you for the ceremony."

Amongst the official letters was a typed envelope with Lulu's name on the back, another from his sister and one from Billy Wigg. He placed these under a stone paperweight. and opened the one from Lulu.

Inside was an invitation to a party to be given by Gus at the Metropole Hotel. 7.15pm on 15 January. Dress was formal. She had written underneath the print: Back from HK on business for a month. Many important people at party. Dotchka and Mary be here with Chen. We all stay. Very nice hotel.

Yes, he would go. The evening suit he had bought with Annabelle was somewhere in the wardrobe. He would dress up and take presents. And he would see Dotchka.

* * *

He picked up his sister's letter. It reminded him that he had left Warren suddenly, but thought perhaps it was for the best. Maggie was getting far too clingy. His sister said that it was a pity he had had to dash off like that and not say goodbyes properly. Maggie had cried a lot, but had now taken up with a local butcher who made very nice pork sausages. She and Ben had got their dad's house and were doing it up. Jimmy would live with them. He had started work at the paper mill and seemed to like it. Sam's tea set was in the cabinet in the parlour.

34

Sam sat behind his new desk and looked round, deciding how he would arrange his new office. It was light, a large window overlooking the yard with the dog kennels at the back. He heard growling and snuffling, and smiled. That was Hunter, the dog he took out fishing on the river. He would go down later, ruffle the scruff of his neck and take him a bone.

He would put the picture by the man in Camburn on the wall opposite the window and move the desk to face the door. The photograph of himself and Chinese officers on a fishing trip could go next to the window. There he was, holding a large sturgeon by the tail and head – that was just after he was made sergeant. The coolie held a net ready to take the fish. The photograph of him playing Sweeney Todd in last year's dramatic club play could go underneath it. He remembered having a long moustache to twirl. The girl playing Mrs Lovett was a real stunner. Good for a bit of fun, too. Then there was one of him in tennis whites after the team won the cup two years ago. That could go underneath. The lamp Annabelle gave him all those years ago, would be on his desk. It was a bit chipped now after Lulu had thrown it at him twice. He would have a picture of Dotchka just by it. He would put her embroidered handkerchief and his father's cufflinks in the drawer.

After his promotion today, the photograph of him being made

inspector could be hung above the chair behind the desk. He would send a signed copy to Warren. It would probably appear in the local newspaper and they would all be proud of him.

* * *

"Very good speech," said the commissioner after the ceremony. "Uplifting. I like the bit about having your door open and the idea of a suggestions box and regular team meetings. Makes the men feel important."

"I've always said from the beginning, sir, that I would never ask a man to do something I wouldn't do myself."

"That went down well, too. Now I want to have a chat in your office. Some other serious issue you need to know about. It won't take long."

Sam opened a silver cigarette case and offered the commissioner a Senior Service.

"No thanks, I don't, but you smoke if you want to."

Sam lit the cigarette with the silver lighter he had won at a tennis tournament. His initials were engraved on the side. Presented by that Diana woman.

"Now," said the commissioner. "You know there's been something of a financial crisis. What's happened here is that the new Chinese silver dollar is selling well abroad. The Shanghai bankers know it and have been shipping it to England. The Finance Minister has ordered silver stocks to be turned over to the Government – the Bank of China run by the nationalists."

"And the Japanese and the communists are furious."

"To say the least. But I'm just looking ahead. The SMP, I'm sure you know, has been living off its reserves – eighty-one million from the sale of an electric plant in 1929. This financial uncertainty might mean we have to dip into them more, or cut pay, or both. Just warning you."

Sam breathed in the cigarette smoke and blew it out through his nose.

"I didn't realise things were so bad. It's not fair on the men. They'll resent it. Some would have to do a lot of overtime to make up their salaries. Some might leave. God knows where to. But we should be honest with them early on."

"I know. Let's hope it doesn't happen. I'll leave you to settle in and work out your priorities. I'll keep you informed about developments and see you in a couple of days."

Sam took off his new cap, polished the badge with his sleeve and put it on the desk.

He looked at Lulu's letter again. He would have to get his evening suit cleaned for the party. Must look smart.

* * *

Sam arrived at the Metropole Hotel just after 7pm on 15 January. The concierge took his coat and he went to the cloakroom to adjust his bow tie, shape his hair with Brylcreem, and brush down his jacket, before entering the gold and red chamber lit by a chandelier, looped and glistening with drops of cut glass. Lulu kissed him on the cheek. Gus put out both hands, covered Sam's right hand, squeezed it slightly then took his arm. "Come and meet people."

"I'd like to see Dotchka first to give her a present from England. I'll leave *your* presents with Mary."

A Chinese boy in red uniform took Sam in the lift to the third floor and the room Dotchka shared with Mary and Chen. Dotchka flung herself at him. "Daddy, Daddy. Where's my present from England?"

"Welcome home, sir," said Mary. "Look at this big boy. Chen, say hello."

"How do you do?" said the boy.

Sam shook his hand. "He's got nice manners, and my, how he's grown. You're doing well, Mary. I'll bring some more money for his upkeep round tomorrow, but SHH eh? And here's a little present for him and for you."

Mary nodded. Dotchka unwrapped the packet of knitting, ran her fingers along the needles, unwound some wool, and looked at a pattern. "I will make dolly clothes."

Sam patted her head. "You'll have to learn easy things first. Raisa will teach you."

"I also can knit a little," said Mary.

"It's lovely, Daddy, Thank you."

He picked her up and ruffled her hair. "Now, you're here for a month and we'll have some fun. Go to the park, have tea and cakes, cinema and circus."

She put her arms round his neck. He kissed her cheek. "That's my best girl."

He went down to the party, now crowded. Drinks and canapés were served on silver trays and cigarettes handed out from red lacquered boxes with black flowers. He looked across the room and saw Du Yuesheng nodding to two other gangsters he also recognised. He found Gus. "Listen, pal, do you know those men in long gowns over there? Don't look."

"Of course. The small one with yellow teeth is on the Municipal Council. The others work with him."

"They're bloody well-known gangsters."

"Business is business. Come and meet them."

"OK, but say I'm your salesman from New York. I can do an American accent. Call me Dan Sears."

He shook hands with Du Yuesheng, Wang Jingwei, and General Dai Li. Du spoke to him in English. "Very happy to see you, Mr Sears. Here my business card. We meet soon."

Sam looked at the card and the titles, written, in English, underneath the name – Chairman of Municipal Council, Board of Red Cross, President of Fund for Children and Families, Vice-Chairman of Welfare League. "I see you do a lot for charities. I'm afraid I left my cards at the office."

Du Yuesheng smiled and bowed. "I am very interested in your business in the US. Does it make much money?"

"Oh yes, American cars are very popular in China."

Sam began to feel out of his depth and wanted to find Lulu. Du Yuesheng bowed again. "That very good. Maybe we talk more about business. I have many contacts"

Sam looked around. "I'll talk to the company about that and we'll be in touch." They shook hands. Du Yuesheng's skin felt like rough cloth, the nails yellow and sharp.

Sam found Lulu in a group by the door. "I have to go in an hour, but I will telephone you about some trips with Dotchka. I can take some time off over Christmas and New Year. No funny business this time. No running off. I hope you've learned a lesson. I used to curse you, but now I feel nothing."

She stroked his arm. "I not need lesson. I know you very important man now, inspector, but you can't tell me what to do. I part of big business with Gus."

"I need to talk to Gus before you leave for Hong Kong – a man to man. I'll arrange it with him."

She smiled.

* * *

On 20 January 1936, King George V died. Flags were flown at half mast along the Bund and in public buildings – the Union Jack, nationalist flags with the white sun on a red earth and blue sky, and Japanese, with the sun as a hard red disc on a white background.

All police stations held a three minute silence and newspapers covered the death and succession in detail, reporting that the new King, Edward VIII, had waved to the crowds from the balcony of Buckingham Palace with Mrs Wallis Simpson at his side.

"What would YOU do?" said Jack Smethers over a meal with Sam in the Rue Mercier. "Love or duty?"

"Duty might be a bit more reliable. But she's not a looker, is she?"

"She must have some sort of hold on him then."

They spluttered into their beers. Jack wiped his mouth and lit a cigarette.

"Well she spent some time in Shanghai and the East. Maybe she picked up one or two tricks."

"Only one or two? Let me tell you, I once knew a Chinese girl who could do more things with her cunt than a dog can do tricks."

Jack raised his eyebrows. "Tell me more."

"Another time. Your sausages are getting cold."

Jack speared the meat with his fork. "Speaking of sausages, is it true that Chinamen and Japs have small dicks? Is that why they, um – need more attention, shall we say?"

"How the hell should I know?"

They laughed and lit cigarettes.

Jack blew smoke through his nose. "Has Lulu gone back to HK?"

"Next week. I'm seeing her boyfriend tomorrow. Our divorce comes through in March. I want to know what happens then. He should be paying up, rather than me picking up all the bloody bills."

Jack wiped his chin. "Have you stopped trying to make up with her? God, you were smitten."

Sam folded his arms. "Yes, I've given up. No point. She's unreliable and dishonest. OK, I know she's still beautiful, but that doesn't last forever. A bloke I met in England – bloody good at drawing – told me that sometimes you just have to let things go, so I'm trying that. No more girlfriends for a while, though. Too complicated, and I'm going to be very busy. How's Yana?"

"Enjoying work with a Russian charity. They're getting a bit of money from an anonymous donor so things are easier."

"Aren't they worried about who that donor might be? Come on, let's move on to the Bar Eiffel. I'll talk to you about my seeing Mr Gus."

* * *

He met Gus in his office on the sixth floor of a tall building on the Bund. Gus grasped Sam's right hand and placed his left over it. "Great to see you. Some party. Good contacts. Let's sit in the armchairs and I'll order coffee."

A furled American flag stood in one corner, and pictures of skyscrapers and the latest cars surrounded the rosewood desk. Gus picked up the phone to ask for coffee and pastries.

"Now, what can I do for you?"

Sam coughed. "You know our divorce comes through in March. I was wondering what your plans are then?"

"Jeez, you sound like a father. Lulu's not a kid you know. Have a cigar."

"No thanks, but I'll have a cigarette if you don't mind. I am paying for an apartment that's hardly ever used and for our daughter's education with only a tiny police allowance. It seems right that you and Lulu should take some of that on. Especially if you're going to get married."

Gus lit the cigar and chewed a fragment of tobacco. "Listen, we don't plan on marriage until she's visited Texas and she's met my mom. It might not suit her. We'll have to see. And listen, between you and me, business is not so good right now."

He puffed out swirls of sweet, acrid smoke which smelled like the members' room at the tennis club. "It's very complicated here, as you know. You can't trust anybody and the bribes you have to pay don't make things worthwhile. I'm worried about the strikes in France, rumours of civil war in Spain, Herr Hitler and conscription in Germany. People are nervous. We're off back to HK next week. I have things to sort out."

"What about Dotchka?"

"You have a lovely daughter. It's up to you what you do about her education. I'll pay for the apartment if Lulu uses it, and I'll pay Mary for looking after it. How's that?"

"Well, it helps and thanks. Gentleman's agreement?"

"Gentleman's agreement. Sorry I can't be more help. Have a good day."

As Sam left the building, he saw a shadow on the pavement. The shadow became a masked man with a gun who seized Sam round the shoulders and pushed the gun into his neck. Sam heard a click as the gun failed to fire. He swung round, threw the man to the ground, kicked the gun away, and pinned him down. The guard on the building tied the man round the wrists and ankles and whistled for a police car. Sam removed the mask.

"I'm a police officer. Your name?"

The man spat in his face.

Sam wiped the spit and slapped the man across the face. He stood and took a deep breath. His legs shook. He'd been close to death before, but never as close as that. Supposing he had been killed. What would have happened to Dotchka? His family back home would have been in a bad way. Of course, he could be killed any time, but how could he avoid that?

The prisoner was pushed into the police van and sat, cursing, handcuffed to an officer. Sam sat in the front next to the driver. "You're in big trouble – attempted murder of a police officer. Death penalty I hope. Good riddance."

The man spat again.

* * *

Sam's voice shook as he dictated the report. He sat down and phoned Jack Smethers to suggest a drink later. "I need a whisky. Triple."

"Happy New Year," said Jack. "It was almost your last. Christ. Do we know who attacked you?"

"Cantonese gangster, they think. He'll be made to talk and handed over to the Chinese."

Jack put his hand on Sam's shoulder. "And we all know what happens then. Serve him right. I'm glad you're OK. This is happening all the bloody time. Yana's always worried."

35

Police Commissioner Gerrard called a meeting of inspectors from each police station. He stood at the end of the oval table.

"You will know that there are financial problems in the International Settlement. The Council has announced economies. I'm afraid there will be an eight per cent cut in police pay and in allowances. That will not come as a surprise, I think, given how things have gone from bad to worse."

The men murmured to each other, coughed, and stared at him

"Obviously, this is not what I want and certainly not what you want. Shanghai has the most expensive Force for good reason. Things might improve but the SMC has been drawing on its reserves for years."

Sam put up his hand. "Sir, have other measures have been considered?"

"Yes. The raising of taxes has been considered, but the Japanese ratepayers have objected strongly."

"Well, we object strongly to *this*," said the inspector from Central Station.

Gerrard raised his arms. "And so do I, but the Council has had to draw another three and a quarter million from reserves. It's either a cut in pay or job losses."

The inspector spoke again. "We haven't enough men already. They will want to leave. It's bad for morale. I've already heard talk of some wanting to go to Canada or New Zealand. Apart from the pay, it's dangerous work here. I sympathise, but realistically, many can't afford to leave. How could they pay their passages? Would they want to lose pensions? What is there for them anywhere else? We may be able to squeeze out a bit of extra holiday and a small Christmas bonus to sweeten it, but I'm afraid that's about it. I would be grateful if you could pass the message on to the men as best you can."

Sam wondered how he would present this. He imagined the officers' faces when he told them the news. Poor sods. They'd object, ask questions, then go to the bar to complain to each other. No way out and they all knew it.

He put his arms round two of his colleagues. "Let's go for a drink. Let's talk about something different. I hear England's buzzing with the royal scandal."

* * *

Dmitri Denisov waved old English and Russian language newspapers at Sam when he called in February. "I see your king will marry American lady. Why so much interest in kings and queens when the world so depressed? No money, bad weather. I hear big debt on Council of International Settlement. Using reserves. Is this true?"

"It is, and we're having to tighten our belts. I don't want to talk about it. Is Lulu back?"

"I not think so," said Raisa. "She say she go to America for a month. Meet mother of Gus. He say to her business not good and he have to borrow money from bank in Texas."

Sam smiled. "Sounds bad. It seems that everybody's short of cash."

Raisa nodded. "You go Hong Kong?"

"I can't. The men are resentful about pay cuts and some have left. I'm on duty. I'll send Dotchka her presents and try to get there in March."

"She send me something she knit," said Raisa. "Look, bracelet.

Nice stitches. She say she knit Daddy gloves. Maybe she learn fast."
Sam took the bracelet and turned it round his fingers. "She is so clever.
Now listen, I want you both and Jack Smethers – you've met him – and
his wife Yana – she's Russian – to come to the apartment and I'll get
Mary to do dinner for us. We'll have a party."

"What are we celebrating?" said Dmitri Denisov "Look at this
newspaper. Chiang join forces with communists to fight Japs. What
did I say should do? Too late, too late."

* * *

Lulu returned to Shanghai and Sam asked to meet her in the Metropole
Hotel. She arrived in the lounge, wearing a calf-length dress in blue
velvet, a red shawl and red high heeled shoes.

Sam stood to kiss her cheek. "How was America?"

"Very fine. Texas pretty. Very big buildings. Hotels, music. Gus
mother very kind. Kiss me and like me."

They sat, and Sam ordered tea. "When do you go to Hong Kong?"

"I go next week. Take Dotchka nice things from America."

"So when's the wedding?"

She removed the shawl and placed it on the chair. "We discuss.
Maybe April, maybe August. Depend on business."

The waiter poured tea and Sam sipped from the thin porcelain cup.
"When you get married, we need to talk about allowances and who pays
for what. I can't afford everything."

"Everything be fine. Maybe I go back to America."

He put down the cup. "What about Dotchka?"

"She stay in school. She happy. She visit America. If she like, maybe
she stay."

Sam asked for more tea. "I won't have that."

She patted his hand. "Not fight again. Everything be OK. Now,
what happen here? They say your Chiang kidnapped."

"Yes, on visit to Xian. Rescued by a communist."

Lulu laughed. "It sound like American gangster movie. But you now big man."

"Not big enough to earn a fortune. Things are worse. Pay's been cut. It's not good, Lulu. People being killed every day. Don't change the subject. Let's get back to you and Dotchka. What is going to happen?"

She stroked her pearl necklace. "Why you care? I wait see what Gus want. He back in March. Tell me about scandal with king."

"The scandal's over. The new king, George VI, will be crowned in May. Wallis Simpson will marry Edward."

Lulu leaned forwards. "Do you have story from English magazines?"

"No, I've got better things to do."

"You take me dancing one night, Sam? New band at Connaught. Play all new music. Lambeth Walk. Nice English and American music."

Sam called for the bill. "I'm done with that, Lulu. You don't have any hold on me now. I know all your tricks. Anyway, I've got a new girlfriend."

"Who is she?"

"Ah, your spies haven't picked up on that? Pretty girl from tennis club. English. Young." He paid the waiter and stood.

Lulu pulled the wrap round her shoulders. "How young? Why you no tell me?"

"You never reply to letters. I know nothing about what you do. Why should you know what I do? None of your business. I'm going to get my coat. By the way, my sister who knitted you that cardigan has had a baby girl. Called her Elizabeth after my ma."

* * *

The assistant commissioner reported fighting between the Chinese and Japanese at the Marco Polo Bridge just south of Peking in July 1937.

"This is being blown up into a serious affair. The truth is that the Japs found one of their soldiers missing and accused the Chinese of kidnapping him. He was found in a brothel. I know it's funny, but the

Japs are using it as an excuse to move into north China. They've taken over Peking and Tientsin."

"What about Shanghai?" asked Jack Smethers.

"You might have noticed that there are more Jap warships on the Huangpu and that they are evacuating their own civilians. Chiang is now sending in more troops. I will keep you posted."

Newspaper photographs showed the Japanese fleet and its flagship moored in front of the International Settlement.

Sam addressed his colleagues. "Expect trouble. You will have seen all the Jap soldiers on the streets. The Chinese remember what happened in 1932. There will be people trying to get across Garden Bridge and into the International Settlement. The other entrances have been blocked."

In the intense heat of August, men, women and children, with few possessions, tried to cross the bridge carrying babies and old people.

"There are bodies everywhere," officers reported, "and Japanese soldiers are stabbing people and throwing them into the creek, pretty girls being dragged into buildings. We can do nothing."

Sam met a group as they returned from duty. "I know. I was out this morning. It's terrible we're having to deal with all this. I hear the Chinese are going to do some bombing of the Jap ships. It'll be a right mess. Stay clear of the river. It's a job for soldiers now."

Later that morning, Chinese bombers tried to sink the Japanese flagship but failed. They returned in the afternoon and released bombs too early – one landed in front of the Cathay Hotel, another went through the roof of the Palace Hotel next door.

Sam and four officers ran out of the Station when they heard the explosions. They were stopped by ambulance drivers. One called out, "There've been thousands killed or injured and we can't get through to help."

Sam turned to two of his officers. "Get messages back to police stations to clear the streets and help these men get access. You others come with me to see what's happened round the Cathay."

The police and civilians reported seeing bodies blown apart, police on duty killed, cars on fire.

"Sir, another Chinese bomber has dropped two more bombs near the New World on Thibet Street," said a guard. "They say the pilots panicked. Thousands of Chinese and foreigners killed or injured."

Sam and his men pushed their way to the hotel. "The Japs must be laughing all over their faces. Don't let any silly buggers onto the rooftops to watch fighting, like they did in '32. It will be chaos, worse than then."

* * *

He met Jack Smethers in the Wayside Station bar.

Jack was covered in dust. "I think we're all exhausted. And back on duty in two hours. Have a fag and a whisky. I hear the Japs have brought in another two hundred thousand troops. There are attacks from land, sea, and air. Poor bloody Chapei. Apparently Chiang's woken up and ordered his troops in fight the Japs."

"I know. Some are just lads of fourteen or fifteen. They're being dug out of rubble or scraped off the streets. They won't give up. You know what the Chinese are like."

"Don't lose face," they said together.

Sam smiled. "I hardly dare send anyone on duty. Apart from the fighting, there's disease everywhere. Some of my men are catching nasty things even though they're inoculated. The refugee problem is terrible – people living in shops and offices or on the streets. It's so bloody hot. Not enough clean water. Babies being shoved into rubbish bins."

"I know, I've seen black vans picking them up every morning and taking them to be cremated. The consulates say Europeans should get out, but Yana won't leave."

"She could go to HK you know. Lulu's there and thank God Dotchka can stay at the school. The wealthy Chinese are on their way out there, too."

315

Jack pushed his cigarette into the ashtray. "It doesn't seem right to be sitting here smoking and drinking. I just needed a quick break. Let's get back out there."

"And some time, I'd better go and see if Dmitri Denisov and Raisa are all right. He reads the newspapers and gets worried. I've heard a rumour that the Japs are going for Nanking. They say it's to protect their own people."

"Usual stuff. I hope Nanking will hide all the girls and women."

* * *

Sam found Raisa in tears and Dmitri Denisov shouting and punching his chair when he visited them.

Raisa waved a newspaper. "The monsters, to kill all those people in Nanking and to rape all those women. So cruel. So evil."

Sam closed his eyes. "Don't show me any more pictures. All the world knows now and it can't be ignored this time. The Japs have also bombed two gunboats getting refugees out of Nanking."

Dmitri Denisov spat into the stove. "What is going to happen?"

"I don't know but I'm worried about you. Stay indoors. The Japs want control in Shanghai. You must have seen that victory march."

Dmitri Denisov spat again. "And I glad that someone throw grenade and kill four Jap soldiers."

"You must be very careful. The Japanese are on patrol everywhere and the Chinese have to bow to them. If not, they get beaten. Lulu is talking about coming back for Christmas. I've advised her not to. Her friends say there's still dancing and films and parties here. Well, in some places there are, but not many. Businesses have left. Not much money, but more gambling, of course. The dogs are very popular."

"Canidrome doing well, then," said Dmitri Denisov. "People always gamble when they have no money."

* * *

Sam wrote to his sister for Christmas, aware that the letter would possibly never get through. He said he would send a present for the new baby, and was glad she was an Elizabeth. He did not mention the troubles, but said that it would be nice to be in England and thinking about starting a market garden, or in New Zealand raising chickens.

* * *

Dotchka sent him a Christmas card, made at school, with pictures of holly, reindeer, and Santas. Lulu included a note.

Do not send more refugees from Shai to HK. My Russian friend say dirty in rooms with no baths, cockroaches, no furniture, bad food. Gus apartment nice. We have party then he go back to Texas for business. Hope you, Papa and Raisa have nice time. Dotchka on holiday with nice American girl and family at hotel on coast.

Sam showed the note to Jack Smethers when they met for a drink on New Year's Eve.

"I've heard the same. I'm glad Yana didn't go. Anyway, Christmas would have been terrible without her. We enjoyed being with you, old man Denisov and the sister. He's quite a card, isn't he?"

"Yes, but they are both getting weaker. The cold, and lack of good food, is telling on them, and he still drinks far too much."

"I don't blame him. More trouble. What can we do about these bombings of newspaper offices? I've got mates in business who get bombs on their doorsteps. Thankfully most don't go off. People are being sent bullets, fingers, ears, and toes in the post."

"Some of my officers have received them. The newspapers will just close down, or leave, or come under the Japs. One of my tennis partners, a reporter, was shot in his office yesterday. Just injured, fortunately. Watch your back, and your front, I say."

* * *

317

March swept across Shanghai with gales and bouts of snow, then April flooded the streets. Sam was moved to Louza Station with more men under his command.

Dmitri Denisov did not die from TB. He was knocked down by a cyclist on the road outside his apartment on the morning of 7 July 1938, the day that three bombs went off to mark the anniversary of the Marco Polo Bridge incident. They were the last sounds he heard.

He was taken, unconscious, to hospital where Sam joined Raisa. "They say his spine is broken. He will not live long."

Sam patted her hand. "I have telephoned Lulu. She and Dotchka are on their way. Go and get some rest and come back in two hours to take over."

Lulu arrived with Dotchka as Sam was leaving. "You surprised we arrive so quick, but we need to see Papa. Gus get a private plane for us. We go back on ferry when we see what happen. Poor Papa."

She leaned over him and kissed his forehead. Dmitri Denisov lifted his head and shouted something in Russian.

"He say 'Be happy children.'" said Raisa. "Now he go."

Her tears fell on his body as she folded the hands across his chest.

Dmitri Denisov's tobacco and pipe were placed in the coffin which lay open in the little Russian church. Old Gōng placed a small Chinese doll on his stomach. Friends kissed his forehead or touched the stained hands, whilst the priest chanted the Russian funeral service.

"Where has Grandpa gone?" asked Dotchka.

Sam put a hand across her shoulders. "Nobody knows."

Lulu kissed her. "To heaven to be with the angels and watch over us."

* * *

During the heat of August, the streets bustled with rumour and protest. Stories of riots and killings filled the newspapers.

Commissioner Gerrard called a meeting of senior officers.

"The Japanese are intent on gaining political control of the

International Settlement. They have a plot to take over the elections to the Municipal Council. They have rigged voting to increase the number of Japanese on the register before the Council elections in September. Fortunately, we discovered the plot, Europeans will pack the meeting and we expect trouble. The vote to ratify the elections will take place tomorrow at the racecourse as the meeting will be too big for any hall. I have asked Inspector Shuttleworth and fifty men to be on duty and others on standby to control any problems."

Sam placed policemen at each side of a stage as the President declared, on a show of hands, that the motion to maintain European numbers on the Council had passed. The Japanese screamed for a recounting of the vote. Keswick rose to speak.

"As Chairman…"

"Watch out," shouted Sam, "someone's got a gun." The Head of the Japanese Residents' Association had mounted the stage and fired at Keswick, who fell back into his chair. A police officer grabbed the gunman's arm and pinned him down.

Sam waved to the police round the meeting room as chairs and seat covers were thrown at people still on the platform. "Make a line between the crowd and the stands. Call for reinforcements. And hold fast. Five of you, get people out. Mr Keswick can be moved. He's injured, but OK."

* * *

"Here, listen," said Jack Smethers in the bar two days later, "I know you had trouble with the elections last week but here's more trouble. Lulu's boyfriend has been seen in a Shanghai club with a young woman on his arm."

Sam sat. "Bloody hell, get me a drink. Who is she? I thought he was going to marry Lulu soon. The American trip seemed to go well."

"The Russian women spies seem to think she's American and much younger than him, and with a rich daddy. Have you heard from Lulu?"

"Not since April, after I was moved to Louza. Lulu and the

319

boyfriend were in HK, at some hotel by the sea in Laichikok. She wrote to say she would be back in Shai in late autumn."

"Wait until she hears these rumours, she'll be back pronto, then watch for fireworks."

Sam stood to leave. "I'll ask her sister."

* * *

"I hear rumours," said Raisa. "I tell you I not trust American man. I not like his hair and his ties."

"Me neither, or his handshake. Don't trust people who hold both your hands. Not manly."

"He always try to kiss me. That worse than handshake. I think Lulu back soon. Maybe on ferry now."

* * *

Lulu phoned Sam, screaming and sobbing, and asked him to come for a drink at the apartment.

She sat in the armchair, in a red velvet dress, hair drawn back, mascara and eyeshadow smudged. Sam poured a whisky, looked at Lulu, poured another and handed it to her. She waved a piece of cream notepaper. "Read this letter that bad man send me."

Shanghai   *3rd September 1938*

My dear Lulu,

It is very painful for me to write this letter. You have no idea how painful. We had some wonderful times together which I shall never forget. However, I have to tell you that our affair is over and that I return to the US tomorrow.

Sam looked up at Lulu who was dabbing her face with a large white handkerchief.

You see, my business in Hong Kong and Shanghai became very difficult with all the troubles. But I have also to tell you that I met someone else when I was last in Texas. A sweet, old-fashioned girl called Deborah. Her father owns an oil company in Houston and she came to Shanghai with him last month when he was on business – and to see me, of course. She's a bit young, but very mature. Mother likes her and I think you would too. We will be married at Christmas.

Please keep the ring and the other gifts as a token of my esteem.

With all my respects,
Gus

Sam handed back the letter, pulled his lips together and hid his mouth with his hand.

Lulu snatched it. "What he mean, young, mature? How old? He promise me. I plan to go to America, take Dotchka. You smile?"

"No, I'm not smiling, I'm thinking. Are you sure you didn't do anything to drive him away?"

"No, I good girl."

"Now I *am* smiling."

"You my friend or not? Men always think each other right. What about poor women's feelings?"

Sam shrugged. "Well, if he's found someone else, you'll just have to do what you can, leave Hong Kong and come back here."

She threw a cushion at him, then fell back in the chair. "I never like him. You take me dancing tonight? Your birthday soon. We celebrate?"

He laughed. "Same old Lulu. You want your own way. You can't stand to be let down, but you let people down all the time. Anyway, I have a nice new girlfriend from the tennis club. She's English, a secretary at the Consulate, and very beautiful. Just tell me how Dotchka is, then I have to go. And don't come asking for more money than I have to give you."

She sobbed into the cushion.

Dotchka arrived in Shanghai, with two other pupils and a nun, three days before Christmas, on a ferry delayed by storms and fog. Sam and Mary waited at the dock. Dotchka flung herself at Sam and clung with arms and legs. He swung her up to face him and held her against his chest. "You're a big lanky thing. I haven't seen you for such a long time."

Mary kissed her, and tightened the coat. "You too thin. Mary feed you well. Have big Christmas dinner. Many presents."

"Can I play with Chen?" asked Dotchka. Mary nodded. "Yes, yes, he big boy now. Nearly six. Like cards and dominoes and football. Speak good English. Clever boy."

She whispered to Sam, "Mr Gus leave me money for bring up Chen. He say get good education. Mr Gus not all bad."

Sam sat in the back of the car, with Dotchka between him and Mary. Dotchka tried to look outside. "Why does this car have dark windows and thick glass?"

Sam took her hand. "Now, listen, both of you. If you hear anything go bang, you get under the seat. It's probably a firework but do as Daddy says."

"Shanghai change," said Mary. "Once beautiful and peaceful. Soon be home."

"Mummy will meet us there, then Daddy has to go to work. I will see you tomorrow and every day and we'll have a big celebration – Auntie Raisa will come."

"Will I get presents?"

"Yes, from everybody. And things have arrived from England."

"When can we go back to England? Dolly has cousins there."

"I know but we can't go back just yet. Daddy has to work to buy you things."

* * *

Lulu returned to Hong Kong with Dotchka in January. Dotchka clutched Sam's legs and wailed. "Me and Dolly want to stay."

Sam caressed her hair. "But you have school and your friends." He looked at Lulu and whispered, "You mustn't stay; it's too dangerous here. I'll try to get there later this year. I'll see that Raisa is looked after. She must leave the old apartment and move into Weiheiwei. Bad things happen in the street where they are. Mary will look after her."

"Yes, I stay in Hong Kong. I live with Countess cousin. She say she like young person there and I need to do nice things. Go out, not like here any more. Come Dotchka. Hold Dolly. We have good time in Hong Kong."

* * *

Commissioner Gerrard called Sam to his office in April.

"Sit down, Sam. Smoke if you want to. I need to talk to you about a few things."

Sam lit a cigarette and blew smoke towards the ceiling. The commissioner tapped his fingers on the desk. "Firstly, you'll have heard about Detective Superintendent Crighton's assassination yesterday."

Sam nodded. "We are all shocked and sad about that. He was a good officer. What happened?"

"He was off duty, getting off a bus with his wife, and noticed three people holding up a man. Crighton took out his pistol and they fired at him. He wounded one of them and rescued the person being robbed. There was an exchange of fire, Crighton's wife hid in an alley, and he was killed. Terrible story. His wife is with friends now. I'll call on her later."

"It doesn't seem fair to get killed off duty."

"I know. Of course, he'll get the Distinguished Conduct Medal, but one has to ask if a medal and an impressive funeral is worth it, particularly with the drop in salaries and expenses."

"Will his wife get the usual pension?"

"Well, that's gone down too, but she'll get his bonus for bravery. It's a sad day, one of many. How's morale in the Force?"

"Sir, we all respect how you've reshaped this force and set up training programmes. We feel part of a good machine, even with the cut in salaries. But the men are worried about what's happening back home. They know the British Government has said we'll defend Poland if they're invaded, and they get letters about German rearmament and they remember 1914–18. They're not impressed by peace declarations and say that if there is another war they want to go back and join up."

"That's the other thing I want to talk to you about, in confidence at the moment, but it will be public before long. They won't be allowed to leave. Every man is needed here. That's instructions from the British Government."

* * *

Jack Smethers found Sam in his office. "I hear conscription's been introduced in Britain. Is this it, then? If it is, I'm resigning here and going back to join the Welsh Fusiliers."

Sam looked at him and placed a hand on his arm. "Jack, that won't be possible. Don't breathe a word of this yet, but I've been told that we'll all have to stay here. If men resign to go back, there'll be no paid passages, no pensions, no nothing. I'd like to go back too, but we can't. We'll just have to hang in here and do our bloody best to keep some sort of order. We'll see what happens, eh?"

On 3 September 1939 Shanghai radio broadcast Chamberlain's speech announcing that Britain had declared war on Germany, National Service for all men between the ages of eighteen and forty-one was to be introduced, and a war cabinet set up with Winston Churchill as First Lord of the Admiralty.

Sam imagined Jimmy, his eyes like a frightened cow, having to go and fight, and wondered what would happen to the other men in his family and to Billy Wigg.

Lulu phoned from Hong Kong. "You go home join army?"

"Not allowed for one thing. Not enough pay for another. Why do you ask? I suppose it's about the pension."

"You no heart. I worry."

"I'm just as likely to get killed in Shanghai as in Europe. Anyway, the pension is signed over to Dotchka."

"But she not old enough."

"She will be one day. How are you in HK?"

"Very good. Nice people. Nice time."

"Do you have a new boyfriend?"

"Oh, yes, but it secret. He English bank manager. Married but want divorce."

"I'm glad you've gone back to Englishmen. They're more honourable and reliable."

"You still see girlfriend?"

"Oh, yes. She's very understanding and appreciates me. It makes a change."

"You very terrible. That not nice."

He heard a click, then a hum.

* * *

His sister wrote to say that Jimmy would join the Durham Light Infantry, Derek the Lancashire Fusiliers like Billy Wigg, and Ivy's Harold the navy.

A letter from Billy Wigg arrived the next day:

25th September 1939

Not much good at writing, old son. Better up a ladder with a paintbrush. I'm off to be a soldier. Will miss family, but we can't let the Hun get away with it. Father-in-law will take over business, lads will help, but

I've said they have to stop at school. Both got scholarships. Clever, not like their old dad.

Sam re-read the letters. He knew that he, and many of his men, wanted to be back in Britain with friends and family. Sons, brothers, husbands, may have been killed or wounded. What would Billy's wife do without him? How would his own sisters cope with it all?

He put the letters in his drawer and opened a file on a spy ring operating from a department store.

* * *

Sam visited Jack and Yana and took flowers for her birthday. He kissed her and shook Jack's hand. "I do miss Dmitri Denisov, the old bugger, I wonder what he'd have made of this lot."

"I wonder what anybody makes of it. It's bad enough here with Japan bent on getting rid of all opposition, the Chinese flying their flags when they can, and killing off senior Japs. I had to smile at that Jap consul general's dinner party where the cooks poisoned the wine and two died."

"Not really funny, though. Japs very touchy. I hear the British Ambassador in Tokyo, poor sod, has been obliged to back off and accept that Japs are responsible for security where its troops are based and that Britain won't interfere. Yanks not being helpful, I understand."

"Have you noticed how many of our men are saying that collaboration with Jap police is becoming impossible because their soldiers always interfere?"

* * *

Commissioner Gerrard addressed his senior officers at a meeting in November.

"You know that the Chinese police force has grown – more police stations, more outposts, and so on. They've set up their HQ at 92 Jessfield

Road, under Jap control, you will have seen that there are now machine guns outside some of the former villas."

Jack Smethers put up his hand and called out, "And we've seen the sign outside number 92 asking us all to work for *them* at the same rates of pay. What shall we do?"

The men laughed. The commissioner smiled. "I know what you'll do. But I know it's complicated. All leave will have to be cancelled until we can make more sense of this. The recent trouble is making the Chinese Government say we can't keep order in the Settlements and that a change of regime is due."

Sam put up his hand. "Does this mean that the Chinese puppets and the Japanese might negotiate to form a new nationalist government and take over the Settlements? They say they want law and order to protect the Chinese."

"A Jap plot to take over," said Jack Smethers.

The commissioner lowered his head. "Yes, but don't say that too loudly."

"So what are we going to do?" asked an officer.

"Well, this is hush hush for now, but it is likely that a new joint police force will be set up under agreements with Japan, and the Shanghai Municipal Council to restore order."

On 3 January 1940, it was declared that a Western District Police Force should be established with principal officers recommended by the Council. The puppet press called it a step towards an independent China:

Our friendly nation Japan has given indication of a desire to render assistance to China in retrocession of these settlements.

Sam put down his glass on the bar table. "No surprises there, but what the hell does it mean in practice?"

Jack Smethers raised his glass. "It means, my friend, that you might be one of those picked out to be a senior officer in the new Western

Area Shanghai Special Police Force. Good name WASP. You're just the man. All the big guns think you're marvellous."

Sam was called in by the commissioner and chairman of the Shanghai Municipal Council the following day and offered a senior post in the new arrangements, staring at the end of January. He wondered what Dmitri Denisov would have said.

36

A year later, Sam flicked open the calendar for 1941 on his first day back at work after a two day break. He looked out of the window, blurred with frost, and saw a Chinese Constable exercising the lurchers in the yard, calling their names and throwing scraggy bones for them to chase. They jumped, pushed and scrambled, their tongues dangling and flapping, long and pink, and their breath hovering in the frost. Sprinklings of snow scattered, as their long claws scuffed the ground. Sam thought about when he had had time to spend time on the boat, with hampers of food and beer, fishing and hunting, watching the dogs fetching game.

He turned to the files on his desk and read about the latest problems in the Badlands and the new proposals for the Western Shanghai Area Special Police Force, then leafed through the press cuttings. The puppet press called the intention to set up a new nationalist government and return the colonial settlements to China with Japanese help, a step towards independence. The independent press condemned all collaboration with Japan as a trick to enable Japan to take over Shanghai. He shook his head.

An officer brought in the latest police bulletin. The seven new divisions of WASP were listed, with him as Chief Inspector of Division Two. He smiled and cut out the article. Bloody impossible job, he supposed. Dangerous, too. Still, it had to be done. The Japs were intent on taking over China, that was for sure, but meanwhile, he'd have to make the most of it. The men were nervous and jumpy and didn't want to be there, but some order had to be established. Things were too dangerous for the police and civilians. He thought about Dotchka in Hong Kong, and wondered how long that could last. The Japs wouldn't stop at Shanghai.

* * *

The phone rang. It was Lulu sobbing and shouting, "Dotchka very ill. She in hospital and ask for you. Come now. I very frightened."

He stood and reached for his cigarettes. "Look, stop crying, calm down and tell me what is the matter."

"High fever. They do not know why, but she unconscious."

He sat down, his legs shaking. "I'll be there today, somehow."

He put down the phone, and telephoned the commissioner.

"Of course you must go," said Commissioner Gerrard. "Grab some clothes and go straight to the airport. We'll get you to HK in three hours on a Chinese military plane with a good pilot – no bombs on board. Sorry, that was a joke, but you don't feel like laughing. I'm very sorry and I hope things will be all right. Don't worry about work. Telford can be in charge. You don't start the new job officially until the end of January. Telephone me. By the way, some of the French high-ups are getting out whilst they can. More when you get back."

* * *

The plane veered over Hong Kong harbour and the hill, landed, and bumped along the short runway. Sam shook the pilot's hand. "Thanks. I've never flown before, but I've so much on my mind, I couldn't even think about it."

"I hope your daughter be well. There is a car waiting for you."

Sam ran up the steps of the hospital and was directed to Ward 6 on the second floor. Dotchka lay, in a bed in a small room separate from the main ward, attached to a drip. Her blonde straight hair spread across the pillow, a wide frame for her white face and lips. Lulu sat, without make-up, still and pale, and stroked Dotchka's arm. Tears dripped from her chin. Sam took her hand; she squeezed his fingers.

A nurse came to check Dotchka's pulse and temperature.

Sam took her aside. "What do you think this is?"

"It may be malaria, or influenza, or something she picked up at school. We are not sure, that's why she's isolated. It all started with a high temperature and convulsions. We need to keep the temperature down, so you can help by sponging her with cool water."

Sam put his hand on Lulu's shoulder. "You go and get some rest. I know you've been here for hours. I'll stay. All night if necessary."

"I go, but I stay at near hotel. This is phone number. You tell me if any change."

"Of course." He kissed her cheek and patted her shoulder.

He stroked Dotchka's hair and dabbed her face and forehead with a damp cloth.

"Daddy's here. Daddy loves you so much. Please get better."

The nurse returned. "Dr Ying is here now. I'll just open the curtains a little."

A slender woman in a white coat held out her hand. Sam looked at the stethoscope round her neck and realised that this must be the doctor. A young Chinese woman. A white towelling band held back her long dark hair. "Inspector Shuttleworth, I am Dr Lisa Ying."

Sam stood, took her hand and looked at her hair and face. "I'm sorry. I wasn't expecting a woman."

"There *are* women doctors, you know. I am a child specialist."

She smiled. Her mouth was wide, lips soft and lightly tinted with lipstick. Her teeth were small and very white. The skin crinkled round her blue eyes.

He lowered his head. "Sorry."

"That's all right. I have a practice in Victoria Street and work at the school one day a week. I was on duty there when your daughter became ill and thought it best to bring her here. Now, let's have a look."

She turned back the sheet, took the pulses in Dotchka's wrists, felt her neck, untied the loose tunic, and placed a thermometer under her arm. Sam watched as she counted one minute. He thought the accent was American, her voice calm and low. She bent over the bed. He watched the curve of her back and her long fingers, no rings, as she applied the stethoscope.

"Just a slight drop in temperature, but it's still high and her glands are swollen."

"What do you think it is?"

"I don't think it's malaria, and there is no rash, but I'm not ruling out anything at this stage."

"What can be done? Anything? I'm desperate. She is my only child and she means everything to me."

"I know. I will do my best."

She looked at her notes, then at Sam. "Now, with your permission, I would like to try some Chinese medicine – acupuncture and a herbal poultice. I know some Westerners don't trust this, but I have used it to good effect with fevers."

"But you're a real doctor as well?"

She smiled. "I qualified in Canada, then came back here to study the Chinese system and to practise. My father is from Hong Kong, my mother Canadian."

"So that's why…" he began, "Please do as you think best. Anything."

"You were going to say that's why I speak such good English, and you would be right." She looked at his face. "You are as pale as your daughter. I'll ask the nurse to get some tea. Leave me with her for half an hour."

He smoked three cigarettes and sipped a bowl of green tea in the waiting room, then returned, and stood on the left of Dr Ying as she pulled out the thin needles from Dotchka's wrists, ankles, and temple. He watched her quick movements and noticed the blue dress under the white coat, and the slim waist drawn in by a belt. Her hair, falling from under the band, was thick and shiny, with a tinge of auburn in the black. Her blue eyes tightened as she focused on the needles.

"I don't want to be rude," he said, "but you're so young, and…"

"A very good doctor. I'll just pack these needles for sterilisation and apply the poultice to her forehead. I must then deposit the needles and see other patients. I'll be back in an hour. Leave the poultice there."

"Thank you for all you are doing."

"It's my job. I like to cure people. I know you are worried, but you are here, and doing what you can by sitting with your daughter."

"Can I hold her hand?"

"Of course."

She slid the band from her head, shook her hair, and stretched her fingers through it from the temple to her shoulders. He opened the door to let her out, and watched her sway down the corridor, in her low, black shoes, the flecks of hair glinting.

After half an hour, Dotchka's eyelids were still closed but he thought he saw movement under the web of thin veins. She opened her eyes and said "Daddy."

He squeezed her hand. "I'm here. You are in hospital to get better."

He called the nurse who felt Dotchka's pulse and took her temperature.

"The fever has broken," she said, "I am very glad. Dr Ying will be back soon."

When the doctor returned, Sam was wiping tears from his cheeks with the cuffs of his jacket. She smiled. "That's a normal reaction. I'll get you a cloth. I am pleased that she seems to have turned the corner. I'll take off the poultice and get her some water."

"Thank you again. I trusted you from the beginning."

"I see." She smiled again.

Dotchka opened her eyes. "I like Dr Ying."

Dr Ying laughed. "I see she has her daddy's eyes, but she should keep them closed for a while."

"I'll phone her mother. She will want to come and stay for a while."

"You can both stay if you wish."

He looked at her. "I don't think that's a good idea."

Dr Ying glanced at him, took Dotchka's pulses and temperature again and made notes. "As you wish. Your daughter should rest. I will put a night nurse on duty later."

He looked at her hair, her lips, and her slim waist.

"Do you have a long day?"

"Not too bad today. I finish at six, in about an hour and a half, and have no surgery tonight. I have an early one tomorrow, then I will be back here at ten. I expect a big improvement by then."

He stood up as she left. "You're very pretty for a doctor."

"What on earth does that mean?" He thought she had an appealing chuckle. "Supposing I said you're very handsome for a policeman?"

"I would be very flattered. Can I make a phone call? Her mother is at a hotel very close."

Lulu returned, kissed Dotchka's cheek, murmured to her in Russian, and looked at Sam.

"I so glad, so relieve."

Sam picked up his hat. "So am I. The doctor has done well. I'll leave now and come back at seven in the morning. There will be a nurse here tonight."

"I will stay until you come back. I can sleep in the chair and they will give me food."

He patted Lulu's arm, and kissed Dotchka's forehead. "See you tomorrow. Get well for Daddy."

* * *

Sam went to his hotel, had a bath, shaved, and changed into his grey woollen suit, white shirt and tie with the police emblem. He smoothed out the creases in the jacket and looked at himself in the mirror. He patted aftershave lotion on his cheeks. He had forgotten the Brylcreem so he combed back his hair with a pomade bought at the hotel shop. It smelled of cinnamon and he wondered if it was too pungent. He put on his overcoat and trilby and took a taxi to the hospital.

At six, Dr Ying came down the steps, wearing a thick blue coat and high heeled shoes, surgical case and handbag over her left arm. He stepped out from behind a parked car and tilted his trilby. "I wanted to thank you. You saved my daughter's life."

"That's perhaps a bit dramatic, but I'm glad she's better."

"Can I carry your bag? It looks heavy."

"I'm used to it, but yes. Where are you thinking of taking it?"

"I wondered if I might take you out to dinner."

She looked at him, smiled, and turned her head away. He looked at her profile, the curve of her cheek and the tilt of her nose.

"Has anyone ever told you, Dr Ying, what a lovely smile you have?"

She looked at him again.

"And has anyone ever told you, Inspector Shuttleworth, what lovely grey eyes you have?"

"My name's Sam, from Lancashire, England."

"And mine's Lisa, from Toronto, Canada."

"Where would you like to eat?"

"I have a better idea. I need to change anyway, so why don't you come back to my apartment. My amah prepared some food this morning. There will be enough for two, and I'll warm it up. You must be tired from the journey and the worry."

"I'd like that."

"My car's here. Yes, I *do* drive. It's not far to where I live but I sometimes have to travel on calls and between my surgery and the hospital. It's only a little car, a T Ford, but it's enough. Put the case on the back seat. Can you smell cinnamon, Inspector Shuttleworth?"

He smiled and touched his hair.

* * *

She parked outside a modern apartment block near the harbour. They walked up to the second floor. She took out a bunch of keys, selected one, opened a door, and switched on the lights. He looked round the apartment as she pulled the red velour curtains across the window. The furniture, two chairs and a sofa in brown leather, sprinkled with red silk cushions in Chinese prints, were in the centre of the room, the rugs tufted cream wool. The walls were hung with pictures and drawings. A gramophone player, a radio, and a violin case were together on a shelf. Another shelf was packed with books. He saw, through an open door, a table, dining chairs and the corner of a cooker and sink.

She took off her coat and hung it behind the door. "I'll just get changed. What would you like to drink whist you're waiting? Whisky? Gin? Wine?"

"Whisky is fine. Do you have soda?"

"Yes, help yourself from that cabinet over there."

"This is a nice apartment. Warm and cosy."

"Yes, and thank goodness, my amah keeps it tidy and organised."

She went through a door to her bedroom and returned wearing a long dress in green silk, jade earrings, and low, black patent shoes. She wore pink lipstick and he smelled a perfume.

Maybe it was the effect of stress and whisky, but he wanted to talk to her, tell her about himself, know all about her. He wanted to sit next to her and put his arms around her.

"You look nice and smell nice. What's the scent?"

"It's Worth – Je Reviens. It means, in French, I am coming back. I always do. Back to HK. I've had this apartment for five years." She smiled. "I buy the perfume at a drugstore round the corner. I'm glad you like it. I'll just start dinner and set the table."

She came back into the room, poured herself a whisky and sat facing him, legs crossed.

"Cheers. How are you feeling now?"

"Relieved, overwhelmed, relaxed."

"You've had a long day."

He watched the green folds of her skirt shimmer across her knees and ankles. He sipped his drink.

"What are the pictures?"

She pointed around the room. "Those two, the sea and boats, are by a young Chinese painter; the drawings are from Canada, by a

Toronto artist; and the small watercolours are by my mother. She's a very talented artist as well as being a fine doctor, as is my father. They both retire next year. What do your parents do?"

"They are both dead. My mother was at home, my father worked, like all the family, in a paper mill. Not very exciting. It's partly why I left."

"But what made you go to Shanghai?"

"I suppose to escape and for the adventure."

"I'm sure you get too much of that."

He took out a packet of Senior Service and offered her one. "Is it all right to smoke in here?"

She shook her head. "I'd rather you didn't really. It gets into the fabrics, and, you know, many doctors think it's bad for you. There's research on it coming out from Germany. Affects the lungs. Sorry."

He put the cigarettes into his pocket. "Thanks for the warning. Tell me about you."

"Born and educated in Toronto. Father Chinese, mother Canadian. My parents met at a medical conference in the US, married, and went to live in Canada. I used to visit my Chinese grandparents in Hong Kong and always liked it. I have an older sister, a teacher, two years older than me. She married a Canadian and has two children."

"Have you been married?"

"A few near misses, but no."

"Me once. It was not a success. I'm a tiger in the Chinese horoscope. So is she. They say two tigers is not a good combination."

"Well. But you have a lovely daughter."

"The light of my life. I don't want to talk about the marriage. What do you mean by near misses?"

"Three men have wanted to marry me – a French businessman, a Chinese professor of chemistry, and a Canadian, an old friend."

"Why didn't you accept?

"I didn't love them for a start, and I do love my career. Let's go and eat. It's chicken with lemon and garlic. Is that all right?"

"It smells delicious. I should have brought some wine."

"I have plenty. You choose a nice white."

He opened the fridge. "How about this one?"

"A Muscadet. Perfect. You're in charge of pouring. Now, how about you? Married – Russian I believe. Very beautiful."

"We are divorced. Yes, she is beautiful but it was a difficult marriage. I once met a girl who said that love was about wanting to be with someone, and feeling comfortable. I never felt that. Never felt it at all, really. There have been one or two affairs."

He pushed the knife into the chicken. "This is very nice wine and very good chicken. I'm not used to home comforts and wine – I'm a beer and whisky man."

She sipped the wine and smiled. "I see. Have you ever thought of going back to England to find a nice girl?"

He shrugged. "No, although my sister's very keen to pair me off. I like my job, I earn good money. I like Shai in a funny sort of way. I've learned a lot – languages, for one thing. I can speak Shanghaiese, some Mandarin, some Russian, thanks to the wife – ex-wife. Dotchka speaks Russian. Ever been to Shai?"

"Once, briefly, for a conference a few years ago. It looked like hell. What do you like about it?"

"Not much at the moment. It *is* hell and getting worse. It's dangerous, too many people, Japs trying to get control, difficult politics. I like the challenge of the job – my new one is to try to work with all sides to try to get things stable."

"I've read about all the troubles. It must be difficult. No wonder you're tired. But you've done very well. How did you get promoted so quickly?"

"You learn the language, show you can lead, work hard, and take risks."

"That seems like a dangerous way of doing things. Not the usual career path." She laughed again.

He wanted to stroke her face and follow the lines of that smile.

"It's a dangerous place. If you want to get on, you have to join in. Ever been to England?"

"No, but I love English literature, especially poetry. I almost did English at university."

"I don't know much about English literature. Tell me something about it. I'd like to learn. Don't you have to be clever to understand poetry?"

"I wouldn't call it clever. Anyone can appreciate poetry if they let themselves. It's about feeling. Near where you're from, the Lake District, there's Wordsworth. I like him and other romantic poets. I love Keats, Shelley, Byron. I love some of the poets of the First World War. Going back a bit, I love John Donne and Shakespeare. I can lend you a book of English poetry if you like."

"Yes, that would be grand. We almost did a Shakespeare play in the drama group in Shai – *A Midsummer Night's Dream*. Then a lot of the women went back to England during some troubles and we never got round to it. I read it and liked it."

"So the men didn't want to play the women's parts? They did in Shakespeare's time."

"So I've heard. But no."

"So you act. Do you sing as well?"

He leaned back. "A bit. Mainly songs you wouldn't like to hear. This is one of the nicest meals I've had in a long time."

"Good. Dessert is, I'm afraid, the remains of a Christmas pudding someone gave me. But with real custard. My amah knows how to make it. Get some more wine, would you, there's another of the same."

He poured two more glasses. "What do you do to relax, apart from reading?"

"Most evenings, I spend about an hour playing the violin and listening to music. I find that soothes and refreshes me."

"Would you play for me?"

"Only if you'll sing something afterwards. Something suitable. Let's go and sit in the other room. Port?"

He nodded and sat, whilst she took the violin from its case and plucked the strings. "I learned violin and piano from the age of six.

My father gave me this when I graduated from medical school. Shall I just choose two or three of my favourite pieces?"

He nodded. She flicked through a pile of sheets on a shelf. "Here we are. Brahms, Schumann, and Schubert."

He had never heard classical music. Maybe he would have to lie about liking it, and not make a fool of himself.

He looked at her back. Her hair hung loose. He wanted to stroke it and run his hand down to her buttocks. He felt the beginning of an erection and told himself to behave. Perhaps all this was because he wasn't used to wine.

She placed a music folder on a metal stand, tucked the violin under her chin, held it there and tightened the bow. "I'll just play the first couple of movements from this."

He read letters in scrolled black script through the grid of the stand: "Brahms Concerto in D major." He leaned back in the soft leather chair, watched her fingers darting round the strings and closed his eyes. The music vibrated, rose and fell, and he wanted to sleep. He watched her body sway and her head toss, then become still.

She stopped, he applauded. "That was marvellous."

"All right, now two short pieces by Schumann and Schubert, then it's your turn."

During the next pieces, he thought about what he might sing. Perhaps something he had learned in school. They were all decent enough. She came to the end of the Schubert and bowed, the violin and bow held to her stomach. He applauded, and watched as she put them back into the case.

She smiled at him. "Well? Have some more port, and then I look forward to an English song."

"This is a *very* English song. I learned it at school when I was a lad. We had this teacher, Miss Hargreaves, from Scotland. It's called 'Linden Lea.' I won't be as good as you and I'm a bit rusty."

She watched him loosen his tie, cough and sip the port. "What's a lea?"

"A kind of meadow, sometimes with cows." He took a breath, placed his hands by his sides and began:

"Within the woodlands, flow'ry gladed,
By the oak trees mossy moot,
The shining grass blades timber shaded,
Now do quiver under foot;
And birds do whistle overhead
And water's bubbling in its bed
And there, for me, the apple tree
Do lean down low in Linden Lea."

She applauded and called "Encore." He stopped, sipped the port and coughed again.

"There's more of this. Shall I finish it?"

"Oh, yes, please. I love it. You have a very nice voice."

He came to the last lines:

"If I be free to go abroad,
Or take again my homeward road
To where, for me, the apple tree
Do lean down low in Linden Lea."

He sat, placed his hands over his eyes, and took out a handkerchief. She moved over to him, sat on the arm of the chair and placed an arm round his shoulders. He turned and leaned his head towards her.

She put her hand on his neck. "Do you miss England so much?"

"I didn't think I did. I didn't think that song would remind me so much of home. And now war's breaking out, and China has become impossible. I haven't sung it since I was at school."

"Your life must be hectic and difficult, and you've had a shock with Dotchka's illness. Go and get some rest. Maybe I'll see you at the hospital tomorrow?"

They stood, he put his hands on her shoulders, and she moved towards him. He took her face between his hands and explored her mouth with his lips and tongue. She put her arms round him and kissed his face.

He drew back. "Can I see you tomorrow evening?"

"Of course, Inspector Shuttleworth. This time, you can take me out to dinner. But don't wear that cinnamon hair cream."

He laughed and took his coat and hat. "I promise. We'll go dancing as well."

* * *

On his way to the hospital, early next morning, Sam called at a toyshop near the hotel and bought Dotchka a white fluffy toy spaniel and a jigsaw puzzle showing an English cottage garden. She lay in bed, pale, but awake and smiling, and talking to Dolly. Lulu sat, watching her.

He put his hand on Dotchka's head and kissed Lulu's cheek. "Go back to the hotel and sleep. You've been here all night."

"She much better. I go to lunch party, then come back this afternoon. You look better. Not tired. I see you later."

Dotchka held a piece of the puzzle in her fingers. "This is hard, but I will do it today. I feel well, Daddy. I have had a bath. I want to go back to school."

He held her hand and stroked her hair. "We will ask the doctor when you can do that. You'll go with Mummy to the cousin's house, then back to school, if you are well, next week. You will come to Shanghai for Easter with Mummy. That's only two months away. Daddy has to leave on Tuesday in an aeroplane."

"Can I go in an aeroplane again?"

"One day you will. Here is Dr Ying to examine you."

He stood as Lisa came in, and bowed his head. "Good morning Dr Ying. I hope you are well."

She looked at Dotchka's notes. "Very well, thank you, Inspector Shuttleworth. And you?"

"Very well rested, thank you. How about this young lady?"

"No temperature, no rash, no swollen glands. She'll be a little weak for the next few days, so I think she should stay here. Your wife has made arrangements for her to leave when she is ready. I will see her twice a day, to check on progress. My, my, what a pretty dog and a lovely jigsaw picture."

"I can do it all by myself."

Lisa folded the notes and stood looking at her. "Then you are very clever." She smiled at Sam and moved towards the door.

Sam opened it, touched her elbow, and whispered, "I'll be round at seven, with a surprise." She nodded.

Dotchka began the puzzle. "What were you saying to Dr Ying?"

"Just how well you look and how good at jigsaws you are."

37

Lisa opened the door of the apartment. He held out a bunch of lilies and a bottle of champagne. He kissed her cheek, but wanted to hold her to him and kiss her everywhere. Steady, steady, he said to himself. This woman was nothing like those he had met before.

She took them. "Are you trying to impress me, Inspector Shuttleworth?"

"Of course, and you look lovely. The blue dress matches your eyes."

"My mother's eyes. Blue is supposed to dominate. I noticed that your wife has blue eyes, and Dotchka's are sort of hazy grey, like yours. Shall I open the bottle and get the glasses? This is a real treat."

"Ex-wife. My mother had brown eyes and my father a sort of green. Funny, isn't it? I've booked us into Dominic's cabaret for eight. I don't have an evening suit so we can't go anywhere smarter."

"That's fine. Here's to... to what?"

"The future, and whatever it brings."

She raised her glass. "Tell me more about Shanghai."

"Shanghai is Shanghai and I am a policeman. When I go back, I will take over officially as chief inspector under a new arrangement of divisions. A Western Shanghai Area Special Police Force has been set up. We'll be in charge of an area called 'the Badlands' just outside the European Settlements."

"Congratulation on the promotion. Who do you mean by 'we' and 'the Badlands'?"

"A combination of Europeans, Chinese and Japanese. It's to try to crack down on gambling, drugs, and prostitution – a lot of its moved outside the city centre to this area – the Badlands, just like an American cowboy film. We start officially in March with seven branches for crime, foreign affairs and so on. It's a good, but I think an impossible job. Nobody really wants to collaborate. I know that sounds cynical. It is. And some of Shai still parties, dances, goes to the racecourse, although many Europeans are getting out to Manila."

She tilted her glass again. "Well good luck."

"How about you? Do you feel safe here?"

"I worry about the Japanese intentions. They can be so aggressive and ruthless and their Government seems so divided. But I have work to do."

"And you do it very well. Let's go and eat. I'll bet you're a good dancer, too."

Between courses, they danced to a Chinese band, playing a mixture of American and Chinese popular music. Their bodies touched and moved together. He squeezed her hand and held her waist tightly. "Do you like this music?"

"Yes, I sometimes listen to popular music on the radio. I like Bing Crosby, Glenn Miller, and Artie Shaw."

"You surprise me."

"I can only play classical music though."

He requested Bing Crosby's "Only Forever." The bandleader nodded. Lisa placed her hand on his shoulder and moved to lean on him. He placed his cheek on her hair. "Do you think I'll remember, how you looked when you smile? Only forever…"

He held her closer and she put her arms round his neck. "Shall we go back soon? There's a book of poetry I want to give you."

"Let's go now."

She closed the door of the apartment. "Would you like a drink?"

He placed his hands on either side of her head and drew her to him.

She stroked the back of his neck as they kissed and he ran his hands down her body. She pulled back, then grasped his arms, and pulled him towards her. He opened her mouth with his tongue, and stroked her breasts. She loosened his tie and began to unfasten his shirt.

His body tingled, his groin ached, and his cock swelled.

"I want you so much. Can we go into the bedroom?"

She took his hand. "I hope you've got protection with you?"

"Yes, the rubber goods we were always told to carry."

She laughed and removed her dress. He held her shoulders. "Let me take off the rest for you."

She stood naked. Her nipples were tight, the pubic hair a perfect triangle. "You have a lovely body."

"Now my turn." She removed his shirt, stroked his chest and unfastened the belt of his trousers. He helped her open the buttons and slipped his trousers and underpants off. She looked at his erection and stroked the shaft. They lay down together. He wanted this to be slow and gentle, and to watch her enjoyment. He put on the condom.

He raised himself above her, then kissed her deeply. He kissed her nipples, moved down her belly, ran his hand over the pubic hair, and explored her clitoris with his forefinger.

She breathed quickly. He entered and moved slowly, almost withdrawing his shaft as he raised his hips.

She began to move faster, then gasped. He felt sperm rush into the condom. He stayed inside, his cock soft. He caressed her hair and kissed her face and lips. They broke apart and lay facing each other, legs entwined.

He stroked her cheek. "That was marvellous. I feel so close and comfortable with you."

"Me, too. It was wonderful."

He leaned back and touched the curve of her shoulder. "I love you."

"This is a bit sudden. You've only known me for a day."

"It's enough. I know. I feel like a ship that has come into a harbour. Remember I told you about that woman who said love is when you just want to be with somebody. I want to be with you. You know such a lot, you look lovely, you are interesting and very, very nice to make love to."

"Well, that's a start. I have to say, I've never met anyone like you. I'd heard about you before. One of secretaries talked about an attractive father. It was you. They even thought the Mother Superior was in love with you."

"I thought that wasn't allowed."

"I knew you would be waiting outside the hospital. I wanted you to be there."

"And there I was. I want to be with you always. What time do you have to work today?"

"I go to the hospital at eight, then my surgery. Let's sleep until six, then make love again."

"Do we have to wait that long?"

"No, of course not. We can start again as soon as you like. How many condoms do you have?"

"Enough."

* * *

She kissed his chest to wake him at six. "Five times a night seems like a good number."

He smiled. "And each better than the last."

"Why don't you stay here? My amah will shop and do food for us. We can eat here tonight. When do you go back to Shai?"

"I've got a two day extension over the weekend. I leave Tuesday morning. The military plane comes in at 9am."

"I'm very glad. And Dotchka will be out the day after that. I'll bring us fresh juice and toast in bed, then I have to get ready."

He heard her cutting bread and squeezing oranges as he looked round the room. Their clothes were on the floor by the bed. He picked up her underslip and smelled the perfume and her body, then leaned back on the pillow, smiling, his eyes half open.

He pulled on his underpants, went into the bathroom, and flushed away the condoms. He stroked the fluffy white towels and took the stopper from a round blue bottle of perfume. He sniffed it, then rubbed his hand over the soap and sprinkled talcum powder into his palm – "Je Reviens."

She brought a tray into the bedroom. "Do you prefer tea or coffee?"

"Tea. Let me make it. English style. This is a lovely room, like the rest, and like you."

"You are quite a romantic, Inspector Shuttleworth. You don't know where the tea is. I'll be back in a minute. Then I have to have a bath, get dressed and go. I'll give you that book of poetry before I leave. I have a spare key too."

"It's a pity you can't stay. I'll check out of the hotel, then go to the hospital, have a walk round and perhaps have a drink with one of the HK Police inspectors I used to know. Is there anything you need, apart from more champagne?"

"My amah will arrive at 10am. I'll call by where she lives on the way to my surgery and tell her there are two of us tonight. I'll give her time off until Tuesday. She can catch up on the cleaning and shopping after you've gone."

"Both good ideas. I'll leave before she arrives, then I'll come back here this afternoon to chill the champagne and do some reading."

She handed him two keys, one for the front door, one for the apartment. "And here's a copy of *English Love Poems*. Don't spend all your time reading police stuff. Tell me which poems you like best when I get back. I think I've marked the ones *I* like. I won't see you at the hospital. I leave there at nine today to visit other patients."

"What language do you use when you see patients?"

"Mainly English or Cantonese. I treat other nationalities – French, German, Japanese. I can usually get by in those languages. Illness is illness and usually recognisable. Sometimes I use an interpreter for difficult cases, especially if the child is very young and scared."

"You are very clever, as well as beautiful. I'll be waiting for you."

* * *

He returned to the apartment at two in the afternoon, slept for an hour, then walked round. On her desk, in the corner of the bedroom, was a photograph, in a silver frame, of an elderly couple. The man was Chinese, with a round face and big glasses, the woman looked fair, with wavy hair – her parents he supposed. Lisa looked like both of them. Another photograph showed a woman with two children; one had Chinese features, the other European. This must be her sister. He looked at books on a table beside the desk; some were thick medical books in English, two in Chinese. He opened an English one, read about cholera and malaria, then closed it when he came to pictures of rashes and sores.

He poured a glass of vodka, threw the packet of cigarettes into a bin in the kitchen, and settled in an arm chair to read the poems.

He jumped to his feet when she came in. They held each other and kissed. He took her hand and led her to a chair.

"You look a bit tired. Dinner's ready, but relax and I'll get you a drink. Do you want to play your violin first or talk about poetry? I read the whole book, except some where I found the language difficult and I missed you, especially when I was reading some of the poems."

"I missed you, too. I really did. You'll know that Dotchka can leave the hospital soon. It was some sort of influenza. I'll prescribe her a tonic."

"Yes, Dotchka looks well. She says that Dolly is better, too. Her mother will take her to the house they stay at – a sort of cousin related to an old aunt. It's best my ex-wife, doesn't see you and me together, by the way. She can be vindictive."

"What, still?"

"I'm afraid so. Lulu is a strange woman."

"Very stylish, though. Does she have a boyfriend?"

"Probably several. All with plenty of money."

"I see. I'm not surprised. What have you done today?"

"As well as reading poetry, I've listened to your radio and caught up on the war news from Europe. It isn't going well. I knew a couple of lads who were sunk last June on the *Lancastria*, and my brothers are both enlisted. God knows where they are now."

"War is a terrible thing. So many innocent people suffer."

"But it's sometimes necessary. The Germans have bombed Coventry, Liverpool, Manchester, and lots of other places. Our ships have been sunk. A German submarine torpedoed another ship carrying refugees going to Canada, many of them children. We don't want to end up having to speak German."

"And Britain is bombing Germany. All this destruction and death. And so many civilians always killed. I'm sorry. It must be difficult being away from your family and not knowing what is happening. They must worry about you, too."

"They do. I haven't heard from my sister for months. They'd like me to be back home. If I were, though, I'd be fighting in France. Let's talk about the poetry."

"Which ones do you like best? Read some to me."

"Well, I liked a lot. It was surprising. But I did like Byron and Keats, like you said, and the war poems. So terrible that they died at such a young age. The First World War was hell according to some of my dad's mates."

"All war is hell. But you know, Rupert Brooke died from an infected mosquito bite, not in battle."

"What a terrible way to go when you're expecting to die a hero, or not expecting to die at all."

"I suppose every way's a bad way to go, especially for those left."

"Then there's two more in particular. Firstly, listen to this by John Cornford. It's called after a town in Spain, Huesca."

"Ah, I know, written to his girlfriend. He was killed in the Spanish Civil War when he was only twenty-one. Read."

He opened the book and found the poem.

"I am afraid to lose you,
I am afraid of my fear...

Think so kindly, dear, that I
Sense you at my side.
And if bad luck should lay my strength
Into the shallow grave,
Remember all the good you can;
Don't forget my love.'"

They sat in silence. Sam looked at the floor and coughed. "How can anyone write like that?"

"Some people just do. And you read very well. Lots of emotion. I bet you were a good actor."

He nodded. "Now the next one is sad, too, and I will always remember it. It's about parting. 'Sweetest love, I do not go...'"

She interrupted. "'For weariness of thee...' One of my favourites. John Donne. Beautiful poetry. Very sensual and that poem always makes me cry." She took out a handkerchief.

He saw the tears on her cheeks and held her. "It makes me cry, too, especially now that I've met you. I couldn't bear to lose you."

"Nor I you. But we can enjoy the times we have together. Come back as soon as you can."

He kissed her. "I will come back at Easter. Dotchka and Lulu will come to Shanghai then, and I will come back with them, and stay for a week. If the ferries are delayed, due to weather or pirate nonsense, then I will fly on my own. I have friends in the military."

"Can we talk on the phone? We can perhaps get through on our official phone lines – the domestic one is unreliable."

"And I will write to you every day."

"That may be a problem. The post often doesn't arrive because it's stolen, or confiscated, or lost. Don't write."

"I'll write in my head then. Maybe I'll try some poetry. Let's eat and plan the weekend."

* * *

On Tuesday morning, he drew back the curtains in Lisa's apartment. A thin mist was coming in with the dawn. She lay against him on the sofa as he waited for the taxi to take him to the airport. He kissed her fingers and stroked her hair.

"Don't see me off. If you cried, my love, I would cry. Thank you again for being so good with Dotchka. And thank you for being here for me. I will get back as soon as I can."

He kissed her face and neck. She touched his cheeks and forehead. "Stay safe. Take the book of poetry. Keep it."

"You know, I'll remember everything about you – your looks, your walk, your smell, your touch. I haven't got a photograph of you."

"And I've got none – at least nothing good – to give you."

She held the lapels of his coat. "Let's get some photographs taken together next time."

"We will. And I am going to bring you something very special when I come back. I'll read a poem a day and think about you. Sweetest love…"

"I told you, you were a romantic, Inspector Shuttleworth."

38

He arrived back at his office to find, on his desk, a telegram from his sister, saying that brother Jimmy had been sent to North Africa. Derek had been badly wounded at Arras and evacuated to a hospital in Southampton. She had no addresses.

He thought of his sisters, in cold, damp Lancashire, with all their brothers in uniform out of England. He dictated a telegram back to say he would write and to keep smiling and chin up.

"It might never get there, sir," said the secretary.

Sam lit a cigarette, inhaled once, and put it in the ashtray. "Just do your best."

He prepared for a day of meetings about the transfer of responsibilities to the Western Shanghai Area Police Force, and was officially sworn is as chief inspector of Division Two.

"I am going to set up systems at 57A Great Western Road," he said to two new British sergeants. "Mr Pan is there already as new commissioner. Why are you smiling?"

"Sir, Mr Pan was involved in infiltrating the police last year."

"I know. But then was then and now is now. There are two good deputy commissioners, both Brits. We will have to do the best we can. Crime is likely to get worse in the Badlands because the villains are being chased out of the Settlements. We have to organise against that and cooperate with whoever we need to. Just think law and order."

"Crime's getting worse, Sir, more armed robberies – jewellery, fur coats off people's backs, anything. Kidnappings, hold-ups every bloody day."

Sam tapped his pencil on the desk and turned to point out a map on the wall. "Our first priority is to crack down on the gambling. That's the source of a lot of trouble. You know where it is happening – in a lot of those big old houses where the Brits used to live along Avenue Haigh and Edinburgh Road, for example. You know the Japanese gangsters operate mainly under one of the sections in the Japanese army and that the Chinese operate from 76 Jessfield Road. We have infiltrated both those sites." He drew circles round areas on the map.

"So we're talking about the high end of gambling?" asked a sergeant.

"We'll raid them at unexpected times. There's bound to be opium involved too. Keep your eyes open and your guns ready. And watch your backs."

He told Lisa, on a phone line which buzzed, crackled, and cut out regularly that WASP was gaining control and that he was happy with the situation.

"I miss you," she said. "I want you to be safe. I love you."

He shook the telephone and hit it with his hand. The crackling stopped for a minute. "I will see you in April and *I love you.* Always remember that. I am reading the poems and thinking about you every day. Don't cry."

He invited Jack Smethers for a beer near the police centre on Jessfield Road. "I have a secret to tell you."

"Only one?"

"When I was in HK I met the woman I want to marry."

"Is that all? Who is she? It's a bit sudden. Have a fag."

Sam took one, tapped it on the table, and gave it back. "No thanks. I'm trying to stop."

"Are you stopping drinking, too? Who is this woman?"

"I'll have a beer. She's wonderful. A half Chinese, half Canadian doctor called Lisa Ying. She cured Dotchka. We are in love. I'm going back after Easter – taking Dotchka back to school and asking to marry me."

"Marry? It's a bit far to HK. I've never known you have a long distance affair."

"This isn't an affair. It's serious. Oh, bugger it. Give me a fag."

"Well, old son, good luck to you. You've got problems trying to work with all sides – nationalists agitating from Chongqing to pick out Jap targets. Japs killing at random. It's what I've always said, they're out to take over Shai and don't care how they do it. Collaboration my arse."

"I have to try to work with everybody, including the Japs, and, by the way, they do have some good police officers – steady, honest, and committed to fighting crime. But everybody's in line for attack, from judges to factory workers. The Chinese don't like us working with the Japs and the Japs don't like us working with the Chinese. I've had a couple of men killed. Who did it? No idea – nationalists, Japs, they're still dead. This is what I want to talk to you about."

"This sounds serious. Are you getting out?"

"You know I can't do that, but supposing something happened to me? I am going to give you Lisa's address and phone number. Hide this bit of paper, but you know what to do. And give her stuff of mine that you can get your hands on."

"Now, don't go into a panic. OK I know you never do panic, but you're in love. What about the lady? I thought the Japs were power crazy in HK too? Well, you never know. The Yanks might step in – but fat chance, I'd say."

"I know and I'm worried about Dotchka and worried about Lisa. I might have to get them both out to somewhere safe."

"Where would they go? Too late for England. Poor buggers over there, in those air raids. I wish I were there for a crack at the Hun."

"I know how you feel about being stuck here, and you're not the only one. I don't know where they might go. Then, there's Lulu."

"What's she up to? Yana hasn't heard anything about her for ages. She was with some English bloke at one time."

"You know Lulu. She'll look after herself. To be fair, she'll always take care of Dotchka, too."

Jack finished his beer, and lit another cigarette. "You know the Chinese newspapers are now being run by the Brits and the Yanks. I've got one or two mates in the business. Useful contacts. I'll pass on any news."

* * *

In March 1941, the Mayor of Shanghai declared all gambling dens in the Badlands closed.

"It's a joke," said one of Sam's sergeants. "Of course, they'll stay open."

Sam rubbed his chin. "I know, there's an understanding that they will pay protection fees to Japanese charities.

"So what the hell are we supposed to do?"

"Keep our heads, don't trust anybody and negotiate. I'm delaying my leave to have some high level meetings about all this. I won't go to Hong Kong until we get some agreements. But my daughter's here and I do have to get her back to school. Her mother can't leave because her sister's ill."

* * *

They were delayed by bad weather and pirate raids on the shipping route. It was not until late April that they were given clearance to travel.

At the dock, Sam bought a newspaper with photographs on the front page of the heavy air raid on London.

Dotchka stared at the pictures. "Is that Shanghai?"

He folded the newspaper. "No, it's England, but your aunties are safe."

"I don't want to go back to Hong Kong. Dolly doesn't want to go either. Why is Mummy staying here?"

"Because Mummy has to look after Auntie Raisa. You will be all right in Hong Kong. I'll come back for you in July when school has finished, then we'll see. Don't cry. Dr Ying has said she will see you sometimes."

"I like Dr Ying. I think she likes you, too, Daddy, but school is not nice. A lot of my friends have left, and it's a long way. Will we see pirates?"

"No, but there will be other children on the boat. You can play dolls, and hide and seek and things, and we'll play cards. I'll teach you some new games."

"For money?"

"No, that would be gambling and Daddy doesn't like gambling."

Dotchka scratched at a heat rash. "It's hot. Dolly has too many clothes on. She didn't like being sick on the boat."

"Nor did other people. Take some of her clothes off for now and we'll buy her a summer outfit later. We have to go and see your teachers."

Sister Veronica patted Dotchka on the head and shook hands with Sam. "Thank God and our Holy Mother for your safe arrival. I'm afraid some pupils have left due to fears about travel and the Japanese threat. We cannot continue if the situation gets worse."

"I'm sorry to hear that, but let us just see. Hong Kong is British territory."

"Ah, yes, but poor Britain has problems at home. I know that. I worry. Let me take the little one to her dormitory now. I will pray for you and your family. How are they?"

He took her aside to whisper, "I don't rightly know, but Dotchka's Aunt Raisa is very ill in Shanghai."

"I will pray for her also."

He hugged Dotchka. "Don't cry. I'll see you at the weekend, that's only four days away. I'll bring you a nice present, and we'll go shopping. You can choose some clothes for Dolly."

He took a taxi to Lisa's apartment, changed into a lighter suit with an open neck shirt, and went to wait outside the hospital until she finished work at six.

He watched her walk down the steps. Her green full skirt was belted into a white blouse and swayed as she moved. She saw him, waved, and strode towards him. She gave him her bag. "Don't hold me or kiss me until we're back home. I'll drive as fast as I can, with all these Japanese roadblocks about."

They ran up the stairs and into the apartment. He took off her light coat, kissed her neck, and stroked her breasts.

She pushed herself into his erection and kissed him. "I've missed you so much. Let's go straight into the bedroom. We'll eat later."

* * *

At seven, she made tea, toast, and poached eggs. "Get up, darling, you must be starving and I have to go to work soon. I've got you some English marmalade."

"I certainly am starving with all that exercise." He pulled on his underpants. "That's grand. Wonderful smell. What time do you finish today?"

"I have a meeting at the hospital until after six. I'll get back myself. Just relax here. Turn on the fans if you like. My amah says she'll cook an English meal for tonight. I don't know what she means by that, you'll have to instruct her."

"We'll have roast beef, Yorkshire pudding, and apple turnover with custard."

"Sounds good. I see you're not smoking."

"Only one now and then. Hurry back. I've brought you a present."

* * *

He poured champagne and handed her a glass. She watched the bubbles. "So what's the present?"

He laughed. "You sound like Dotchka. I'll go and get it. It's in my pocket. Don't drink yet."

"All right. I'll just check the beef. Everything else is ready. I'm afraid this Yorkshire pudding looks very strange."

He sat next to her on the sofa. His hand shook as he handed her a small square box with a ribbon round it. She tilted back the lid and stared at the ring – a cluster of diamonds and rubies.

She blinked back tears. "It's lovely. Will you put it on my finger?"

He thought that he had never been so happy.

"Of course. Will you marry me, Dr Ying? As soon as possible?"

"I will, Inspector Shuttleworth."

He kissed her on both cheeks, jumped from the sofa, and punched the air with his fists.

"Chief Inspector now. Don't you forget." He laughed as he pushed the ring along her finger. "When? May's a nice time for a wedding. Here's to us. Now you can drink."

"It will take a few days for a licence, but we could apply tomorrow and we need two witnesses. I can arrange that."

"I'm flying back on the sixth, with an American diplomat who wants protection. Let's start planning. We'll buy the wedding ring today."

"Two of my registrars will be witnesses. What about Dotchka?"

"I don't want her to know yet. She'll talk and I want it kept quiet. I don't want her mother to find out. She's one of Shanghai's biggest gossips."

"By the way, my Chinese horoscope is snake – quite compatible with the tiger, I believe."

They were married at the town hall on 2 May and they drove to a hotel down the coast for a night. They sat in the bar, breathed in the smell of the sea and watched gulls swooping through the dusk.

"I wish we could live like this," he said, "in peace, just the two of us."

"Maybe we can, one day."

He held her hand and twisted the rings on her left hand. "I've been thinking. We both have British passports. You have your parents in

Canada. How about if I resigned next year and we went there? I could work in the police, you could practise."

"But will you ever resign? I know you now. You like excitement."

"There's too much excitement at the moment. I've got cynical about the trouble ever ending. The Japs will take over. Then what? I want to be with you."

"What about England? What about Dotchka?"

"If it's all right with you, I would ask for custody of Dotchka. Her mother might oppose that, of course. England is falling to pieces. Who knows who will win the war. I don't see us settling down there. But Canada… I could even start a farm."

"But now you have to go back to Shanghai and chase criminals, not cows and chickens."

"I'll be back in July. I am coming to collect Dotchka. She can't come back to school here in the autumn if things carry on like they are. The Mother Superior's worried that the school might have to close. But we'll face that then. I like your ring, Mrs Shuttleworth."

"Dr Ying. Doctors keep their professional names."

* * *

Sam returned to Shanghai to find Raisa in hospital and not expected to live for more than a few days.

Lulu sat by the bed, holding Raisa's hand. "She want to see you. I be so lonely without her. Maybe I get married again."

"Who to?"

"Nice American colonel. His wife just die."

"Good luck to you."

Raisa lay still and pale, breathing with difficulty. "I go to find Papa, Sam. You good man. Are you happy?"

He placed flowers on her bed. "Yes, at last, I am."

"Give love to Dotchka. I want her be happy."

She coughed again and stopped breathing.

His tears fell onto her hands. He wished she could have met Lisa and him together and seen their happiness.

"I will telephone the school. Dotchka will be very sad. She has always loved her Aunt Raisa."

He turned to Lulu as they left. "Raisa was one of the nicest women I ever met. So kind and caring. She was a good friend to me."

"You mean not like me?"

"I didn't say that. I just wish that you could be really happy and not always looking for the next best thing."

Lulu adjusted her hat and walked away.

Raisa's body was taken to a chapel of rest in the hospital. A Russian icon was placed in the coffin. She was buried next to her father.

* * *

Sam met Jack Smethers in the American bar after the funeral. "She was a lovely woman, Raisa. They had a bloody hard life. I don't really blame Lulu for trying to do better. It's just that she caused so much chaos around herself."

"She certainly did. Always will. How was HK and the lady?"

"We got married. Here's a photograph. You can keep it but don't tell anybody. I don't want this to get back to Lulu. That's Lisa. Lovely, isn't she?"

"Very. Will she be OK in HK? I hear they're evacuating people."

"It's like here. The women don't want to go. Nobody believes the Japanese will take over."

Jack took out a pack of cigarettes and flipped one towards Sam. "Oh, no, still not smoking?"

Sam shook his head. "Not much. I'll have one now. What's the latest?"

"The US marines have left Shai for other duties in the Pacific. I'm pessimistic. The newspaper office in Bubbling Well Road has been blown up; a train on the Shanghai – Nanjing track was bombed yesterday; Japanese Military Police have been attacked; the Japanese have erected barbed wire barriers around Shanghai; and bridges are closed. It's as bad as that."

"What's the news from your newspaper pals?"

"One's badly injured. They say so much for the Shanghai Council and the Japs working together. All they can agree on is rounding up communists. Christ, I do wish I were fighting in Europe."

"You think it's more friendly there? There's been bombing in Scotland and Liverpool, Parliament has been damaged by bombs and the Bismarck sank the Hood in the Atlantic. All but three dead. Pride of the navy, they called it."

"I know, it's a fucking mess, but listen, at least I'd know what I was fighting for. Do you know, some people here can't wait for the Japs to take over? They're fed up with this chaos."

"So am I, but I have to maintain morale in the WASP, and try to get all sides to work together to keep some sort of order."

"Always the optimist. Compromise won't work in the long run. When are you going back to HK?"

"Middle of July. I'm bringing Dotchka back here for good. The school will have to close. She can live with Lulu in the apartment and I'll get a private teacher."

In June, he telephoned Lisa to say that he had won a cup, a medal, and a pay rise for apprehending the assassins of a Japanese Police chief.

"There I was off duty in downtown Shai when I heard shots. An old Jap colleague I always got on well with – a police commissioner, a good man, reasonable, fair officer – was shot getting into his car. I grabbed a motorbike and ordered two Chinese constables to come with me. We caught the buggers a mile along Haig Road. Sadly, the Jap commissioner died. I'll bring you a snap of me getting the award. This line's terrible. I love you. I miss you. Don't cry. See you soon, Mrs Shuttleworth. Sorry, Dr Ying."

"I love you, too and I fear for you. It seems that all sides will think you are the enemy."

"You just get used to this sort of violence. It happens every day."

* * *

He saw her as he came down the gangplank at the end of July. It was already hot and humid at nine in the morning. She wore a cream, short-sleeved dress, and sandals, and a sun hat.

He took off his sunglasses, removed her hat, and pressed his face against her hair. "You look thinner."

She smiled. "I'm worried about the way things are going here. We have Japanese guards on the hospital and have to show passes. There are roadblocks and people are being arrested for nothing."

"Let's go and eat somewhere. Food on the ferry was awful."

He held her hand and kissed the rings on her finger. "Do you want to leave for Manila?"

She shook her head. "I am a doctor. I have work to do. I hear about China. All the killing and death. All the refugees dying on the streets. I don't know how you stand it? How can you *ever* get used to it? Manila has problems, too. I hate it. I cure people. I save lives. I must do that. I worry about you in Shanghai, and I know I cannot join you. I wish I could."

"No. I couldn't take you back there, but I do intend to resign next April. I'm getting old and cynical."

She laughed. "Don't say that. I hope all will be well by next April. Maybe Britain will win the war, maybe America will join in and we will all be rescued."

"I think we should still go to Canada. Have you seen Dotchka?"

"She is fine. I have taken her for tea once or twice. She wants you to take her back to Shanghai. She misses you and her mother. I take my wedding ring off when I see her, by the way."

He laughed. "I'll go and talk to the Mother Superior today. She knows Dotchka is leaving. I'll leave the nuns a donation. They might need it. It's Friday so Dotchka can have her last weekend with them. I'll see her a lot next week and organise her packing."

"I must go to my surgery now, then to the hospital. Let's go somewhere really nice tonight. Let's dance."

"And I will recite some poetry to you and you can play the violin.

I hope you've got time off, and food in, because we're going to stay in bed all weekend."

She nodded. "That would be nice."

* * *

When she came home, he gave her a parcel wrapped in newspaper. "Another present. I've brought something to show you a bit of where I come from. It's a drawing of a coal pit done by a funny chap I met on a walk. I think he's becoming quite well known. One of the newspapers said he had an exhibition in London."

She unwrapped the Lowry drawing. "Thank you. I like it very much. It's very well done, very realistic. I wish my mother could see it, and one day she will. I'll hang it on the wall here next to her work. Is your family all right?"

"Very little news. Letters aren't getting through. I only see newspapers. Oh, one from my sister *did* get through. My older brother is back in Warren – shot to pieces and a bit crazy. Shouts and screams and points his finger at people like he's shooting. She is glad the other is in a Prisoner of War camp – says he'll be safer there. I've written to him, but doubt he'll get it. It makes me sad."

He imagined a battlefield, men lying shot and maimed. Blood everywhere; now his brother's mind had gone. He looked out of the window. Lisa put her hand on his wrist.

"I am very sorry about your brothers, and I wish you wouldn't do crazy things when you're off duty and unarmed."

"I won't. I'll slow down. Oh, and here's the newspaper cutting from when I got the award and the cup for bravery."

"You look very handsome and smiling. I will put it in my desk."

* * *

Dotchka cried as she said goodbye to her teachers. The Mother

Superior gave her a crucifix on a chain. "God bless you, my child. I hope that you will be safe and well."

Sam took Dotchka's hand. "Thank you, Reverend Mother. I hope you will be, too. What will happen if the school closes?"

"We will go back to the Convent and live our lives in peace there, worshipping and praising God and the Blessed Lady. Thank you for your generous donation."

He asked Lisa not to see them off. "Dotchka would get suspicious. Let's say goodbye tonight. I will telephone as soon as we reach Shai and I will be back in November. Before if I can. Just look after yourself. Phone me."

38

Sam lived in a room in barracks near his office. On the small dressing table he placed two photographs – one of Dotchka in school uniform and one of Lisa the day they were married. He kissed them both every day and kept small photographs of them in his wallet.

On his office walls were photographs of himself at tennis tournaments or fishing, and one of the ceremony where he was honoured for capturing the Japanese officers' killers. In the drawer, he kept the book of poetry and his father's cufflinks. He read some poetry every day and tried to write poems to Lisa and Dotchka, but crunched up the papers and tossed them in the bin.

Lisa phoned him at his office on his birthday in September. "I have a birthday present which I will keep for you, and I have another present which will arrive much later. I am pregnant. We are going to have a baby. Can you hear me?"

"I hear you. I hear you. That's wonderful, wonderful. Are you all right? When will it arrive? What will we call it?"

"I'm fine, very healthy, the baby is due in March. Things are even more chaotic here. The Japanese are taking over banks and offices and putting up more barbed wire. The Governor General protests but he can do nothing."

"I will be there next month to see how you are, and to say hello to the baby. I think it's a boy."

"How can you tell? Well, if it is a boy, one of his names will be Sam."

He needed a cigarette and a drink. A baby with Lisa. They would be so happy as a family in Canada. Get some peace. Live normally. Dotchka would like a baby brother.

* * *

He invited an American journalist friend of Jack Smethers to dinner. "What's the story on Hong Kong, Lester?"

"I'll tell you what I think, and what is predicted. Japan will take over the whole of the Pacific. Hong Kong is a prize target. They will take over by Christmas and intern anyone with a European passport. You know what the Japs are like. No mercy. Why?"

Sam arranged a meeting with the police commissioner. "I know this is unusual and nobody knows, but I married a Canadian citizen in Hong Kong at Easter. She is expecting a baby and I want to get her out to Canada. I would like permission to go there as soon as possible for a few days and I would appreciate confidentiality, sir. I can leave Jessfield Road Station in good hands. Things are as quiet as they ever will be, at the moment. I know my responsibilities, but this is urgent."

The commissioner tapped his desk, paused, looked round the room, then at Sam.

"Highly unusual, but I agree, and I know you are due a lot of leave. Get her out. Make the arrangements for her before you go. The travel company near the docks is still operating. There are Hong Kong planes to Manila and Pan Am flies from there to San Francisco. It will cost you. Take out a loan from your superannuation if you need it. Get back as soon as you can. Use our military contacts for flying to and from HK."

* * *

He booked flights with Hong Kong Air and Pan Am and left Shanghai in the early morning mist of 20 October. He visited the Hong Kong police and arrived at Lisa's apartment in the evening. She was waiting for him, dressed in a long silk robe which cascaded in pleats from above her waist. He held her breasts then put his hand on her belly and kissed her.

"It's wonderful to see you. Nothing showing there yet. I think some movement. I haven't been sick, just a little tired, but that is passing. It usually does by three months. Have a glass of wine. I'm not drinking."

He sat and watched her. "You look well. More beautiful than ever."

"The pregnancy bloom."

"Lisa, my love, come and sit next to me. I need to talk to you."

"You sound very serious. Have you resigned?"

He held both her hands and interlaced their fingers. "No, and you will not like what I have to say, but it is for the best."

"You look so sad and worried. What has happened?"

"Lisa, we know that the Japanese are moving in on China and on Hong Kong. I've talked to journalists who know what is likely to happen. They get information from the consulates. The Japs will probably take over by Christmas. I want you out of here. I have air tickets to get you to Manila, then to San Francisco, the day after tomorrow."

She pulled away from him, stood with her back to him, and then turned.

"I can't do that. I won't go. I have work to do. I have you in Shanghai. I won't go back to Canada without you."

"Listen, sit down. You must go. You may be raped, you may be killed, you will lose your apartment and all you have. Our baby will not be safe. You will not be allowed to practise. The Japs will not care that you are a doctor. You must know this."

She leaned on him and sobbed into his chest. He stroked her hair and back. She looked up.

"I do know, but I cannot leave. What about you? What about my patients and colleagues? What about my things here?"

"You must not tell anyone. I will stay and say you have had to go to Canada suddenly. I will find a reason. Your amah will still look after the apartment. Pay her for a year. Leave all your belongings except a few things you can pack easily. Your colleagues can cover for you. I am sorry, but I only care about you and our baby. I will join you next year. Be brave."

She sat with the back of her head against the brown leather sofa, her face wet. He wiped the tears and kissed her on the mouth. "I will take you to the airport. You must phone your parents from your office and ask them to meet you in San Francisco to take you home to Toronto. I will join you when I can. Do you understand?"

She stared at him. "How do you know it is so dangerous here?"

"There are secret papers between the British Consulate, and the Swiss, the French, and the Americans. Journalist friends have told me this. A takeover of Hong Kong is inevitable. I know the Europeans don't believe it and still carry on with their social life. They should have left."

She sighed. "As we were advised to last year. People made excuses to stay. But I know that you are right. I have heard rumours too. I will make arrangements."

"Now, you must eat and rest."

"I want you to make love to me."

"Is that all right when you are pregnant?"

"Of course. You can't dislodge a healthy foetus by exercise or making love. I *am* a doctor you know." She smiled. "There is a nice pork stew with rice. And I have a birthday present for you. Sorry it's late."

She gave him a gold tie pin, engraved with their initials, and a silver framed picture of them cutting their wedding cake.

* * *

She returned from her office the following afternoon, carrying papers and files.

"I have phoned my father from the surgery. The line was bad, as usual, but he understands the situation and sends you his thanks and good wishes. He looks forward to meeting you. I have begun to sort out my records and will leave instructions. I feel very bad."

She wrote down her parents' address and phone number in Toronto, then the names and addresses of her amah and colleagues he should contact.

"I will play for you once more this evening and you can read some more poetry. I will cry and will not sleep."

"Let's make the music and poetry cheerful. And I'll sing you some funny, naughty Lancashire songs."

The taxi picked them up at 6am. Lisa took her passport, two sets of clothes, photographs of her and Sam, her violin, the picture of the Camburn pit and her jewellery.

The airstrip was hazy in the early light. Two planes throbbed on the runway outside the waiting room where a few people sat smoking. Manila was called. Sam held her and whispered into her hair "Sweetest love, I do not go from weariness of thee…"

"Don't. This is a terrible moment. I can't bear it."

"Go. I know when you will arrive in Toronto and I will telephone you. It's a long journey. Look after yourself and our son."

She turned and waved from the steps of the plane. He waved until the plane took off, went back to her apartment, drank half a bottle of whisky, and slept until the evening. He was numb. He thought of her on the plane, crying and wanting him. But he was right to get her out. And he would get to her and their baby as soon as he could.

He touched everything in the apartment, sniffed her clothes, took one of her mother's paintings, a scarf, the remains of a bottle of "Je Reviens" and left for a hotel.

* * *

He returned to Shanghai the following morning and found Jack Smethers. "I have got Lisa out to Canada. I've written down her parents' address and phone number. You know what to do if the worst happens. Look in my office drawer. There's stuff there I want her to have. This tie pin she gave me will be in there, too."

Jack looked at the paper. "Toronto. At least she'll be safe."

"And I'll join her there next year, all being well. Don't tell a soul."

Jack folded the paper and placed it in his wallet.

"Any other bugger except us in uniform can go to Australia. If they're white, of course. We'll have to stick it out. Marines gone. Businesses panicking, and trying to get assets out."

39

Sam was on night duty on 8 December 1941 when a call came from Central Station to say that Japanese troops had crossed Garden Bridge and were setting up military emplacements along the Bund. Almost immediately, news came in that Japanese forces had attacked the American base at Pearl Harbor. Sergeants who were not on duty came into Sam's office to listen to the radio. They were interrupted by loud cannon fire and machine guns. The Japanese warship *Idzumo* had sunk *HMS Petrel* on the Huangpu River.

A sergeant ran in. "Sir, our Japanese officers have left to join the military commanders at the Town Hall. It's been taken over."

Sam stood, put on his hat and strapped on his gun. "We'll leave a skeleton service here, take the jeeps, and get to Central Station to see what we can do," said Sam.

"The Japanese are marching through town, waving flags, and chanting," said the police commissioner at Central Station. "They're seizing buildings, including prisons, power plants, and hospitals. The planes you can hear are the Japs distributing leaflets in many languages saying that war has been declared. The Chairman of the Council is coming to address us at nine tomorrow. He's meeting the Japanese command tonight."

The Chairman came into the meeting room, and leaned on the

desk, his fingers spread and trembling. He looked towards the back wall. "The Japanese say that Europeans are not in danger, but they are placing guards at all consulates, clubs, newspaper offices, the council buildings, and hotels. The whole place is full of armoured cars and tanks. Japanese gunboats have arrived. They were very well prepared. Hong Kong is under threat."

Sam thought of Lisa's escape. He would tell her about Hong Kong when he phoned her parents' house later, even though he knew she would be upset. What would happen to Dotchka's school, and the hospital?

"If you have families here, go home and wait. Otherwise, go back to your stations. You all have green armbands to get you through. See what happens. You will find the streets covered in ash. Industries and banks started burning documents early this morning. If you can burn any papers, do."

Sam was driven to the apartment in Weiheiwei Road. He passed billboards proclaiming that Japan had declared war on Britain and the United States. Troops banged on the car, gesturing and shouting.

Lulu met him. "What is going on?" She sat on the bed, with Dotchka, who played with necklaces, winding them round her wrists. He threw his coat over a chair. "There is a war. Japan has taken over. Here is an emergency edition of *The Shanghai Times*. The foreign concessions have been taken in Shanghai, Tientsin, and Peking. Travel and meetings have been banned."

Lulu put her arms round Dotchka. "What about *us*?"

"You must stay here. No shopping. No parties. No phones. The Japanese say you will be safe, but I'm not sure about that. Hong Kong is also under attack. The Japanese have bombed the airport."

Dotchka wailed. "What about my school? What about the Sisters? What about Dr Ying?"

Sam looked through the window. "I think they will all have got to safety. It's difficult to get accurate reports. There are no phone connections and very little news coming out except official bulletins."

He went to find Jack Smethers who had gone home to check on Yana. "Can you come outside for a fag for a minute?"

They stood in the damp, cold stairwell, breathing out smoke. Jack patted Sam's shoulder. "It's as well you got her out. How is she? I hear that the Governor General in Hong Kong will be forced to hand over to the Japs soon, but that the Hong Kong secret societies might kill all the Europeans first. It must be hell down there. Chinese nationalists still taking potshots at the Japs, looting, murder, nurses raped."

"How do you know all this?"

"Some of it's just rumour, but a cousin of Yana's has set up an amateur radio receiver. He gets news from all over the region."

"Don't believe everything you hear. Lisa is well. The baby is due at the beginning of April, just before spring arrives in Canada. God, I wish I was there for Christmas."

"Come to us if you can, although I expect you'll be on duty. The Badlands can't get worse, though, can they?"

"I think they might. I'm so weary. I just want to be in Canada. I'll be on duty over Christmas. The rest of the time, I'll sleep.

* * *

In January, he wrote to Lisa, giving her news of the situation, telling her that he loved her and wanted to be with her, and that she must look after herself and the baby.

He put the letter into his desk drawer, next to her scarf, perfume, book of poems, tie pin, and his father's cufflinks. He would see if he could persuade someone to get it on a ship or a plane to North America when things were a bit calmer.

* * *

Just before midnight on 15 January, a call came through to Sam's office reporting an affray near an opium den in Jessfield Road. All his inspectors and sergeants, except one, were on duty. He decided to investigate it himself and instructed four armed constables to meet him at the door of the Station.

He stubbed out his cigarette, pulled on a bulletproof vest, jacket, heavy overcoat, boots, and his inspector's peaked cap. He breathed on his sleeve and polished the badge. He put his pistol, loaded and cocked, into the holster and pulled on one leather glove, leaving his right hand free. He pulled out his desk drawer and looked at its contents. He thought of reading to Lisa. He put her scarf, smelling of her, next to his face, and touched the letter he had written. He opened his office door and rubbed the brass nameplate.

Downstairs, he beckoned the officers.

"All set? Let's go. On foot, down towards Kong Kajong alley."

Their boots crunched the sprinkling of snow on the pavement. Dimmed lights from buildings lit up the frost and clouds of their breath. Two cyclists passed them, wobbling and skidding on the road.

The cyclists stopped, turned to face Sam and his men, and began shooting. Six masked men rushed from a building, firing pistols. "It's a trap," shouted Sam as he watched a constable fall. He shot both cyclists and turned to fire towards the building.

He felt the cold steel of a gun on the back of his neck and knew that he could not be lucky again. As his skull shattered and light burst through his head, he saw Lisa, holding a little boy; they were smiling. He saw Dotchka's face shimmering, and hoped that she would be safe and happy.

Road barricades were set up round the Badlands as he, and two constables, were carried back to the Station.

* * *

Reports of his funeral appeared in the press three days later. The manner in which he died was never mentioned. Alongside the report, and the long list of mourners, was a picture of the cortège, his coffin draped with a Union Jack. He was buried at Bubbling Well Cemetery, with full honours. The Church of England minister spoke of his devotion to duty, bravery, and ability to command. Senior British, French, and Japanese officials gave tributes.

There were flowers from a hundred individuals and organisations, including the Big Three gangsters, all of whom attended, in mourning dress. The central wreath on the coffin was labelled "From Lulu, Dotchka, and Alan."

Jack Smethers, in tears, searched Sam's office and his room in barracks. In the coffin he placed the book of English Love Poems, Lisa's scarf and perfume, photographs of Sam and Lisa and one of Dotchka. In the office drawer, he found Sam's letter to Lisa, the gold tie pin, Sam's father's cufflinks. He unscrewed the brass nameplate from the door. He put them, with the photographs from the walls, in a bag to send to Lisa.

Jack persuaded the Japanese command to allow him, under supervision, one phone call to Canada and permission to send the bag of Sam's effects with the diplomatic courier.

"I was expecting this. I dreaded it," said Lisa. "You are very kind to telephone. Thank you. I can be brave, as he was. I will always treasure what you send, and I will think about him every day and tell our son about his brave father."

EPILOGUE

Sam's sister, Bertha, received a telegram from the Shanghai Municipal Council three weeks after his death. She sat on the stairs, clutched her small daughter, sobbed into her flowered pinny, then went to tell her sister and Billy Wigg's wife.

Lisa had a son on 2 April 1942, the year of the horse. He had his father's nose, chin, and eyes. She called him Huan Sam Ying. Her father leaned over the baby. "I know Huan means joy and satisfaction, and the horse is talented, adventurous, and popular." Lisa smiled.

In 1943, Lulu and Dotchka and the other Europeans in China, were interned by the Japanese. They were allowed to take one personal item with them to Yangchow camp, north of Shanghai. Dotchka took Dolly, Lulu her red high heeled shoes. She left furniture and ceramics with Russian friends and collected them on release. The Japanese took over the apartment. Bertha tried to trace Dotchka and Lulu through the Red Cross, but failed. She thought they may be dead. Ivy said maybe they didn't want to be found.

Jack Smethers was sent to Bridge House, the Japanese torture centre, accused of spying. He was beaten, deprived of light and found, by rescuers, barking like a dog. He died of his injuries. Yana went to relatives in America.

After the camp was liberated in 1945, Lulu met an American

Colonel who asked her to marry him. She and Dotchka left Shanghai for San Francisco in 1947. She married in Virginia and, six months later, began divorce proceedings, on the grounds of the Colonel's infidelity.

* * *

Bubbling Well Cemetery was destroyed and redeveloped in 1951. It is now a peaceful park amidst the throb of Shanghai's traffic. The original avenue of plane trees goes though the centre, past a lake of nodding water birds. A weeping willow dabbles the surface. An old man plays a reed flute in a craggy grotto.

The music lilts over the burial ground of those who chased hope and opportunity in a distant country, and who, like Sam Shuttleworth, died, caught in its complex patterns. The gravestones are gone, smashed in 1951, used for other buildings and replaced by grass. Men and women move in graceful t'ai chi formations and play chess on flat rocks. The bronze sculpture of a burly rhinoceros eyes the ground where bodies have disintegrated.

Beyond the border of the park, the gold topped Jing'an temple of peace and tranquillity glints through the frayed edges of sycamore branches.

Acknowledgements

I am indebted to the authors of the many books I read whilst researching this novel. Their reflections on Shanghai in a tumultuous period are graphic and painful.

Many people have supported and encouraged me in the writing. I am particularly grateful to: Les Massey for his patience and for his practical help in reading and commenting on the progress of the book; Ben Massey for his painstaking research and checking; the pre- readers – Hazel Slavin, Anna Ford and Mike Shaw for their incisive comments and their positive criticisms.

Those who have been particularly helpful with the research include: Vivian Murray for sharing family history; Greg Leck for his scholarly work on internment camps and what led up to them; Tess Johnston for her devotion to Shanghai and for her recording the fascination of old Shanghai in wonderful books; Peter Hibbard for contributing his first- hand knowledge of Shanghai; Henry Hong who guided me round Shanghai with skill and expertise.

Staff at the newspaper and police archives in Shanghai and Washington were patient and helpful.

I would also like to express my appreciation to those who have contributed to the production of this book – the late Rebecca Swift, Yen Ooi, Kate Ahl, Lucy Llewellyn, Melanie Marshall, Robert Harries, and Catrion Robb. I have benefited from their professional advice and it has been a pleasure to work with them. The final work, with any errors, is mine.

AUTHOR NOTES

The novel was inspired by the life of my uncle who was a policeman in Shanghai between 1924 and 1942. He married a White Russian and they had a daughter. He visited his family in Lancashire twice during this period. This much is true. These slender facts, which I learned as a child, finally encouraged me to write what is a work of fiction. I know little about my uncle's life in Shanghai except from anecdotes, photographs and a few letters.

I have therefore created a story based on research into historical events in Shanghai whilst my uncle was there. The action unfolds to a backdrop of the appalling violence which led to the destruction of Western dominated Shanghai and the shift of power to the Japanese. Some of the minor characters existed and some names are retained. The action and dialogue associated with the characters in the book come from what I imagined their lives to have been.

SELECTED BIBLIOGRAPHY

Abkhazi, Peggy, *Enemy Subject: Life in a Japanese Internment Camp 1943-45*, Alan Sutton Publishing Ltd, 1981 (1995 UK)

Arnold, Doris (Missy), *Missy's China*, Old China Hand Press, Hong Kong, 2008

Ballard, J.G., *Empire of the Sun*, Victor Gollancz, 1984

Bickers, Robert, *Empire Made Me: An Englishman Adrift in Shanghai*, Penguin Books, 2004

Buck, Pearl, *The Good Earth*, Methuen and Co., 1931

Caldwell, Bo, *The Distant Land of My Father*, William Heinemann, 2002

Collar, Hugh, *Captive in Shanghai: A Story of Internment in World War 2*, Open University Press China, 1991

Cuthbertson, Ken, *Nobody Said Not to Go, The Life and Loves of Emily Hahn*, Faber and Faber, 1998

Djordjevic, Nenad, *Old Shanghai Clubs & Associations: A Directory of the Rich Life of Foreigners in Shanghai from the 1840's to the 1950's*, Earnshaw Books, 2008

Dong, Stella, *Shanghai: The Rise and Fall of a Decadent City*, Harper Collins, 2001

Earnshaw, Graham, *Tales of Old Shanghai*, Earnshaw Books, 2012

Elder, Chris (ed.), *China's Treaty Ports*, Oxford University Press, 1999

Erh, Deke and Johnston, Tess, *Shanghai Art Deco*, Old China hand Press, Hong Kong, 2006

Fairbank, John K. (ed.), *The Cambridge History of China, Volume 12, Part 1, Republican China 1912–1949*, Cambridge University Press, 1983

French, Paul, *Carl Crow – A Tough Old China Hand, The Life, Times and Adventures of an American in Shanghai*, Hong Kong University Press, 2006

French, Paul, *Through the Looking Glass: China's Foreign Journalists from Opium Wars to Mao*, Hong Kong University Press, 2009

French, Paul, *The Old Shanghai A–Z* , Hong Kong University Press, 2010

Harmsen, Peter, *Shanghai 1937*, Casemate Publishers, 2013

Heung Shing, Liu and Smith, Karen, *Shanghai: A History in Photographs 1842–Today*, Penguin Books, 2010

Hibbard, Peter, *The Bund Shanghai: China Faces West*, Odyssey Illustrated Guides, 2007

Hibbard, Peter (Foreword), *All About Shanghai and Environs. The 1934–35 Standard Guide Book*, China Economic Review Publishing for Earnshaw Books, 2008

John K. Fairbank (ed.), *Cambridge History of China, Volume 12, Part 1, Republican China 1912–1949*, Cambridge University Press, 1983

John K Fairbank and Albert Feuerwerker (eds), *Cambridge History of China, Volume 13, Part 2, 1912–1949*, Cambridge University Press, 1986

Johnston, Tess and Erh Deke, *Frenchtown Shanghai*, Old China Hand Press, Hong Kong, 2000

Karns, Maurine and Patterson, Pat, *Shanghai: High Lights, Low Lights, Tael Lights*, Earnshaw Books, 1936 (Reprinted 2009)

Krasna, Reina, *The Last Glorious Summer, 1939*, Old China Hand Press, Hong Kong, 2001

Laing, Ellen Johnston, *Selling Happiness: Calendar Posters and Visual Culture in Early 20th Century Shanghai*, University of Hawaii Press, 2004

Leck, Greg, *Captives of Empire: The Japanese Internment of Allied Civilians in China 1941–1945*, Shandy Press, 2006

Ling, Pan, *In Search of Old Shanghai*, Joint Publishing Co. (Hong Kong), 1982

Lu, Hanchao, *Beyond the Neon Lights: Everyday Shanghai in the Early 20th Century*, University of California Press, 2004 (Paperback)

Mitta, Rana, *China's War With Japan, 1937–1945*, Penguin Books, 2013

Oakes, Vanya, *White Man's Folly*, The Riverside Press, Cambs, MA, 1943

Pan, Lynn, *Old Shanghai: Gangsters in Paradise*, Marshall Cavendish, 1984

Pan, Lynn, *Shanghai: A Century of Photographs 1843–1949*, Peace Book Co., Ltd, 2009

Peh T'I Wei, Betty, *Old Shanghai*, Open University Press China, 1993

Peters, E.W., *Shanghai Policeman*, Earnshaw Books, 1937

Sanbrook, John, *In My Father's Time: A Biography*, Vantage Press (New York), 2008

Sergeant, Harriet, *Shanghai*, Crown Publisher, Inc., NY, 1990

Von Sternberg, Josef, *Fun in a Chinese Laundry*, Columbus Books Ltd., 1987

Wakeman Jr, Frederic, *Policing Shanghai 1927–1937*, University of California Press, 1996

Wakeman Jr, Frederic, *The Shanghai Badlands: Wartime Terrorism and Urban Crime 1937–41*, Cambridge University Press, 1996

Wasserstein, Bernard, *Secret War in Shanghai*, Profile Books, (London) 1998

Willens, Liliane, *Stateless in Shanghai*, Earnshaw Books, 2011

Wood, Frances, *No Dogs and Not Many Chinese*, John Murray (Publishers) Ltd, 1998

4107191686 BRG

484416 3090
267441 3061

69132479R00231

Made in the USA
Middletown, DE
04 April 2018